ORR: Murder Genetically Engineered

By Lynn Marron

A Grace Farrington DNA Mystery

Book and Cover Design and Artwork By Lynn Marron and Leonard J. Bloom, Jr.

Published by Kear Press
Stratford, CT

LIBRARY OF CONGRESS: 2017937672

ISBN:978-1-942888-15-4

e-book ISBN: 978-1-942888-16-1

To contact the author go to:

lynn@lynnmarron.com

This volume is dedicated

Louise and Ed Gernat

for their help to a

struggling, unpublished writer.

Prologue

Peru 1911

Beneath the high blue peaks, it was a crowded market day in the dirt square before the gray stone Cathedral. Professor Hiram Bingham had to halt as a string of dirty white, heavily loaded llamas crossed before him. The man leading them wore a gray wool poncho, and Bingham saw women, some in bare feet, some in boots, most, in short, calf-length skirts, carrying heavy baskets before the squatting Catholic church.

As he scanned the crowd the professor didn't see that senora with the blue peasant blouse decorated with the blackened silver ornament. A first, when Bingham had seen it, he thought it was just another Pecos or Doubloon, or some other foreign coin that the woman had pierced and then sewn on her blousey tunic.

But its trapezoidal shape, with its wide border of five engraved lines, stayed in his mind. He remembered it, and her, when he saw that shape again. An old scholar had invited him for cocoa at his palatial hacienda. As the Spaniard proudly showed a fellow scholar his treasures, there on the page, Bingham saw it: a short bottom, wide top, like the strange stone doors of the Inca, outlined with five lines, now drawn here in the yellowed, seventeenth-century manuscript. This had been copied from rare, no longer surviving parchments by a Friar Estaban, who traveled through Peru after Francisco Pizarro's conquistadores and their bastardly cultural subjugation.

A shape that was symbolic of the missing city of Vilcabamba, last redoubt of the Inca. Now the professor looked harder about the market square, finally finding the old woman stewing guinea pig meat in a ceramic pot, in a fire set on the square's stone pavement. She stirred a pot that was probably ancient before she was born, a priceless relic of the past, blackening from the fire...he looked closer at the wood. Splintered boards, with intriguing pre-Columbian carvings on them.

Looking at him suspiciously the old woman stretched out a skinny hand and fed the piece of wood he'd been looking at to the licking flames. The wind shifted, and white smoke choked Bingham's throat. "Senora, I wish to buy your wood." He held out sols.

She looked suspiciously at him. "Pro favor," he awkwardly tried again pointing to the wood.

She looked at his offering. The senora signaled with three fingers–indicating his money would only buy three boards.

The professor looked fast through the pile. Looking for those with the oldest markings. Finally, he selected three of the largest. Picking them up, he pushed the sols towards her. Under the woman's hostile glare, he retreated. Bingham looked about the market finally spotting Damesco and noted his guide had filled a huge basket of potatoes for camp. Potatoes that he had never seen before reaching Peru, small red, bluish, and a strange pale, long split one, perhaps some of this could be the '*Food for the Gods*' fed to the Lord Inca?

To his guide, Bingham indicated the old woman and the wood in his arms. "The wood she feeds the fire with has markings of your ancients."

Damesco showed no interest. "Lots of wood, many old marks. The senora must cook her food."

The professor must make him understand. "When those markings are gone, their meanings will be lost."

The guide just shrugged. "All who could read them are now dead."

That attitude angered the Bingham. "These things of your ancestors, they should be in a museum for your people."

"You told the Allande that, and what did he say?"

That confrontation with the local government had left a bitter taste in Bingham's mouth. "He said that '*before the Spanish, the Indeos idolaters were savages, incapable of great, enduring art.*' He was wrong!" As they walked nearer the massive edifice that was the Cathedral Basilica of the Virgin, the Professor adjusted his wire frame glasses then pointed to a gray rock foundation explaining, "This Cathedral is built on an Incan Temple, massive rocks, thirty tons or more. That one with seven ground sides, each block edge fitting so perfectly, I can't side my knife blade between them. A people who build like this make their Spanish conquerors look like barbarians..." Bingham took his calloused hands and rubbed them against the granite, smoothed to a rough polish, then worn with the water and neglect of centuries. Looking at it the professor said sadly, "How can a civilization reach such great heights, then be forgotten? It's achievements completely swept away."

The professor looked back at the boards in his hands. So far he had found no one who could translate these markings for him. He remembered the chronicles blasphemously speaking of all the writings that were burned before the people in the squares. He looked up to the high, blue mountain peaks about them. A forbidding land. There must be something the Conquistadores hadn't reached. Looted. Destroyed. He thought out loud, "Isn't there anything from the ancient ones that are still untouched?"

Damesco sounded bitter. "The temples were stripped of their gold and silver. Even the cloths woven by the sun's maidens were carried away."

Was there unspoken reproach in his guide's eyes, like Bingham, was part of the looters? "It doesn't have to be gold– the tools, the picture writings, even the food bowls of your ancients should be treasured."

"The Catholic fathers said all were the works of the Devil and must be burnt."

Sadly, the professor looked about him. "If I could have just seen one city before it was looted."

Damesco looked at him shrewdly. "There is one."

"Vilcabamba, the legendary last redoubt of the last Inca, it's not a myth?" asked Bingham eagerly.

"No, this is not Vilcabamba, that was destroyed, this is a city only inhabited by ghosts."

Bingham was getting excited. "This other city, why

did not the Spanish find it?"

Damesco smiled showing wide white teeth. "They did not know where to look."

The professor stuffed the wood into the rucksack he carried, as excitement flooded him. "An untouched city, with artifacts of daily living...of nobles' tables, pheasants' huts. Tombs of royalty. Could you lead me to this?"

"It is far away and would take many men and more llamas to carry supplies. Who pays for this, senor?"

A hard-line pressed in the professor's lips. Funds. Always a problem. He had exhausted his present grant, but for an untouched city. "The University that I represent might pay for an expedition..."

"Why do they do this?" asked his guide shrewdly.

"To find works of great art to put in a museum for all to see and marvel at the achievements of your ancestors."

"They will build a museum here? For peasants?" scoffed Damesco.

"The museum will be built in my country."

Damesco smiled, showing his teeth again. "Si, they will only pay for something taken away."

The professor looked back to the old woman, feeding her people's heritage to the fire. "Is it better to let it all go up in smoke?"

Central Square of Cuzco 1915

"Senor Bingham, the bearers carry the last crates down. Now you leave us?" asked Damesco.

"I must go home," answered the professor.

"Many of my men ask if others will come to...." The guide was trying to think of the English word.

"To hire you?" Bingham finished. "I can't promise, but when my people see the displays of the great works of your ancestors more probably will come here to study the Ghost City you led me to."

A small, well-dressed man walked to them, and the professor looked at him. Dark skin, black hair, some Indian blood, but not local, dressed up with a bowler hat and a yellow brocade waistcoat.

"Senor Bingham?" This visitor spoke English with a slight Spanish accent.

"Yes, sir."

The man held out his card. Bingham glanced down at it. '*Jose Cartagena, Esq. Procurer of Rare Artifacts and Stupendous Oddities.*' The professor nodded, as he looked down at the man.

The gentleman drew himself up to his full 5'3" height, "Senor, you have hundreds of crates of fine treasures."

"Probably not those you would be interested in. My crates are filled with incense burners, wooden platters, stone knives." Bingham turned to a still open crate, and reaching down, took out a ceramic jar. From inside the jar, he dipped out something gnarled, black streaked, and globular. "Bulbs and a blue maize kernels, buried in a noble's tomb. Perhaps the '*Food for the God*' that increased the Lord Inca's lifespan that the records speak of?"

Cartagena looked unimpressed. "I am a collector for the Great Showman's museum. You may have heard of his wondrous presentations in New York City? George Washington's 114-year-old Negro nurse? The Fiji mermaid..."

"I thought he was dead?"

"The showman? Yes, but in his will he desired a museum be built as his legacy."

Bingham took out his pipe and tamped some tobacco in. "A museum in New York?"

"No, in the city of Connecticut."

"Connecticut is a State," the professor corrected.

Confused, Cartagena started again. "Bridgeport, is that also a state?"

"No, a city in Connecticut. You are hunting far afield my friend."

Cartagena looked at the stacks of crates. "Your magnificent discoveries have piqued the interest of the insatiable public. Your University Museum will have many artifacts, but public always wants more…"

Looking at him tiredly Bingham said, "You seek gold and mummies?"

"The public doesn't wish to see the makings of tortillas, it wishes to see something extraordinary!"

Trying not to sound too superior the professor said, "My collections are bound for the University's Natural History Museum in New Haven, for educational purposes only."

The little man didn't seem to take offense. "Our progenitor understood that entertainment brings in the crowds, but what they leave with is an enlarging of their horizons. If you have something worthy, I can offer one hundred American?"

Bingham tamped down the tobacco into his pipe's bowl. "I have nothing that I wish to sell."

The little man stopped, seeming to judge whether he should try to sweeten his offer, then decided against it. "But you do have those who talk with you. Perhaps they have mentioned something not worthy of your great institution but of interest to my patrons? I am authorized to pay a finder's fee."

Taking time to light his pipe mix, Bingham evaluated the eager man. "Am I interested in a bribe…" The Cartagena quickly raised his hand in denial, but before he could speak, the professor continued. "No, thank you, sir, but in the interest of not seeing priceless heritages lost, I might be able to put you on to something."

"Gracious, Senior." The man smiled widely.

Bingham looked over the square. "The local Cathedral is built with stonework from the Incan temples, like the ancient stones, previous friars have incorporated the peoples' beliefs into their church.

"This current man, Father Sebastian, seems to want to sweep with a new broom. He was disposing of a number of relics." The professor walked to the pile of crates and tapped his pipe against a small, wooden box. "This is the contents of a church reliquary, the mummified arm of a local 'saint.' A 'saint' that for centuries was carried before the people so they could worship him in this open square. The early friars took this relic into the church to be venerated until the people could be trained to accept something more worthy. Now the priest feels it can be disposed of, and he has allowed us to add it to our collection.

"Unfortunately, he kept the long, custom crafted reliquary itself." Bingham looked back to the cathedral. "Shame. Beautiful box, eighteenth-century beveled glass, forty-two inches long, twelve inches high, custom fitted to the arm with a frame of figured silver leaves, fruited with embellishments of emerald and crystal cabochons. Pity I couldn't get it, I offered the highest price I could go, an excellent example of high Colonial craftsmanship."

"The arm it held?"

"Mummified fingers to shoulder. From the beaten gold arm band it appears to be pre-Columbian. Of course, it's of little academic interest, because there is no way to even know if it is a native or a later Spanish addition. But, yes, you are right, the flash of gold and dried human skin does bring the curious into the museum." Cartagena had sense enough to just wait, as Bingham savored the blue smoke of his pipe before continuing, "This priest is also cleaning out the crypts beneath the altar. He's unsealing tombs that the locals hold sacred, tombs that they still lay flower offerings and burn candles before. The good father is distressed about this, he intends to make the contents disappear so that the pagan ways can truly be forgotten."

"And this Father Sebastian, he will accept payment?" Frowning Bingham looked to the cathedral. "I'd be careful about that. Perhaps you could start with the suggestion of a donation to the church for a new communion plate or whatever. But you must hurry, to the side of the church they're laying wood for a bonfire. Father Sebastian intends to cleanse the House of God from the sinful practices of the ancients very soon."

"Gracias, Senor." The man bowed and hurried back toward the village. His work done, Bingham planned to just sit and smoke for a while, but when he looked about, the men had stopped piling up the crates, and they were clumped together whispering among themselves.

Annoyed he walked over to Damasco. "Is there a problem?"

"Si, the workers stop."

"Why?" The professor asked impatiently at this latest delay.

"There is this man, the Villacamu, he is a high priest of the old religion from the mountain people."

"He wants a payment of sols?" The professor asked.

"No, senor."

"But he is stopping the workers?"

"He is angry."

"Because?

"He says the spirits of our ancestors are disturbed now that you take their poss... Po..Poss..."

"Possessions? "

"He says it not yours to take. It belongs to the ancestors whose spirits watch over us."

The professor had been through this before. "Can you explain to him that we take these things to honor his ancients? To teach others of the magnificent achievements of your people."

"I do this," said Damesco without much confidence.

Not pleased, but knowing he had to, Bingham said, "Talk with the old man. See if he will take sols to rest his spirits."

Damesco talked respectfully to the forbidding old man, then he walked to the workers, and talking more with great gestures, and finally, he came back. "For double sols, they will pack, but if you take what is here, the Villacamu places a curse on your people and your descendants. A curse on you!"

Yes. Cursed again, Bingham just smiled, as he tightened his teeth on this pipe and watched the blue smoke rise upwards to the white tipped peaks. Finally, he said, "Tell them to continue packing."

Chapter 1

New Haven Airport, Present Day

Shifting her laptop case's shoulder strap and her leather handbag on to her right shoulder, Grace grabbed for her suitcase just as it was passing on the airport carousel. Then she realized the taped cardboard box holding her Guru award and paperwork was before it. As it glided away, she dropped the suitcase and chased after the box. A considerate man noticed her struggling and pulled the box off for her.

"Thank, you," Grace said sounding tired. Usually, on her lecture travels, she could just easily carry everything, but today she had to grab a cart and load up. Then she'd have to find a taxi.

Only outside, a very tall woman in a long, deep-purple skirt sprinkled with silver stars was waving to her. "Grace!" It was Freya, always looking and sounding like she could sing lead Valkyrie in a Wagnerian opera, "Over here!"

In her early forties, Grace Farrington was a slender 5' 8", with short black curls with touches of early frost making her a total mismatch with her golden-haired, solidly built, 6'1" friend. Freya towered over her reaching for the cart. Feeling happy to see a friend Grace still admonished, "You shouldn't have closed your store to pick me up."

"Didn't. I got Lilith in–so if there's a run on Buddhist incense or crystal balls, Haunts of Wôden is covered. My van's over there." They started walking. "You shouldn't have gone to Seattle alone to get that Guru award! I wish I could have gone with you," her friend said regretfully.

"Waste of time and money. I flew to Denver, then Seattle, shook hands with a bunch of people, signed papers for the annuity, wore my gold, Chinese blouse, ate a really good steak at the banquet, got up, accepted the award, and flew back the next morning. That was it."

Easily hefting the heavy box and Grace's laptop from

the cart Freya said regretfully,

"But you should've had a supporter there clapping."

"They clapped." Freya still looked unhappy, so Grace added, "Adam talked about coming as President of Oyster River Research, but the Institute would've had to pay his expenses. I didn't want that." They were walking to Freya's van. Grace wished she had thought to put on something warmer than her light wool suit jacket. New England in early November was a bit cooler than Seattle.

"David Gardiner? He could've afforded his own, first-class fare? His own jet!"

"He's still busy in Greece, financing that shopping mall he's building," said Grace wanting off that topic.

"What about that idiot, Kurt? He claims to be a scientist. He could have gone...wearing Klu Klux Klan robes, with his leather biker gang-jacket on top."

"Dr. Kurt MacKay is a very good marine biologist, even if he rides on motorcycles and likes to shock people. I didn't need him or anyone else to collect a big block of mahogany and poured resin, that I have no idea of what to do with."

"You're going to display it in your laboratory."

"If I need a doorstop."

Freya did a fast glare at her. "It's time you set up a display of all your awards. Inger and I are going to help you, and we're leaving room for the big one!"

Her Nobel? Grace had gotten tired of holding her breath for that one. They loaded Grace's laptop bag, suitcase and Guru award box into the back of Freya's beat-up van between the boxes of geology books, semi-precious gems, and power wands she was always selling at rock and mineral shows. Freya pointed out, "That Guru award means a yearly check, right?"

"That'll help me keep on my three assistants. Maybe even make Inger full time."

"Can you stop teaching the postgrads?"

"No," Grace said regretfully. "That still brings in the other half of Bobby's salary."

"Well the MacAlpin Guru award is considered a precursor to winning the Nobel prize, isn't it? That's more money and prestige."

Grace twisted her lips tightly. "As we say in New England, 'aaup.'"

"You'll get it!" As she drove, Freya was picking up I-95 South, listening to Grace's description of the Seattle's green food market. After Freya drove through Stamford and turned off on to the back roads, they headed for the small harbor town of Oyster River.

"I can play hooky so we can get lunch?" Freya asked hopefully.

"Not today, I'm sorry. I owe you a fancy restaurant for this pickup, but Adam Greenfield's called some special meeting at the Roost that I promised to make."

"For your award?"

"No, they've already done that. This is something to do with a contract for Dr. Huang Wong."

"That kid wonder? Now 'Head of Research?'" said Freya with contempt.

"In title only," Grace corrected.

"Wong's trying to outshine you."

"The boy wonder is now into his late thirties, with no new discoveries, but it looks like Huang's landed some big research contract, with a guy named Jensen..."

"Axel Jensen?" said Freya sounding impressed.

"You've heard of him?"

"The billionaire who donated millions to the Green movement? Oh, yes. He's been married seven times! And he's only our age." As she waited for a green light, Freya shot Grace a calculating look. "Mr. Jensen is currently divorced, and he's rumored to be attracted to super intelligent women."

They passed farms and houses, and just before the harbor, Freya turned on to the main road. To their left was the State Fish Hatchery, to the right, the peninsula owned by Oyster River Research--which to Grace's surprise--was now swarming with people, some standing in the middle of the road.

Grace looked saying, "What's this?"

"Maybe they're here celebrating your winning the Guru award?" Freya suggested.

"Not likely. That crowd looks like college students and seniors citizens picketing. This is great, I need to freshen up and be at the Roost in twenty-five minutes, and we can't even get through the protesters. What's on the placards?"

Slowing Freya pulled into the private road, but couldn't get in any farther with the picketers doing a tight circular march across it.

Grace looked over at the Captain's Roost--the mustard yellow, marron trimmed, 1840s sea captain mansion, that housed Oyster River's largest meeting hall–it looked closed. There were two private security officers watching at the front entrance, now one was walking toward them.

She looked back at the demonstrators. They carried placards with: "STOP G.E.!" "FRANKENFOOD'S A HORROR! KEEP PESTICIDES OUT OF OUR CANOLA! And a three-foot high cartoon of a baby's bottle, with a skull and crossbones across it.

Grace said softly, "If you just roll forward very slowly–maybe they'll get out of the way?"

Freya was looking to the side. A tall, thin woman, wearing a straw sun hat was moving through the pickers, seeming to be directing things. "Astrid?" said a puzzled Freya. "She's usually up at the State Capitol demonstrating with C.U.R.S."

"Curs?"

"Creatures' Universal Rights Save–it's an animal

protection group. Is ORR doing any vivisectioning of dogs?"

"No!"

"Wonder why we're out? I didn't get a notice."

"You're a member?" Grace looked at her.

"Not really a member—well, I send in a donation when I can. ASTRID!" Freya waved to a woman in her straw hat. "Grace, roll down your window." With those angry looking demonstrators, Grace really didn't want to roll down the only barrier between them, but she did. That tall, tough-looking woman dressed in a shirt of tie-dyed cotton that hung under her pea jacket came over to Grace's side.

Leaning down to look out the window Freya asked again, "Astrid? Why are we out?"

"Is this the renowned Dr. Farrington with you?" Astrid asked coldly.

"My **friend**, Grace, yes," Freya emphasized friend in almost a militant fashion.

"Dr. Farrington," Astrid looked straight at her as she demanded an answer. "Are you supporting Humanity's Harvest goals?" It was asked in a tone that reminded Grace of *'have you stopped beating your wife*?'

Grace looked in puzzlement to Freya. "Humanity...?"

"Humanity's Harvest," Freya supplied. "That's the name of Axel Jensen's company that I couldn't remember. It's a worldwide conglomerate, started as a heritage seed crop production and went into fertilizers and pesticides. Now it's into pharmaceuticals and a lot of other things, like..."

Astrid cut Freya off grimly as she said, "Genetic engineering!" She pronounced it as if it was synonymous with *'bubonic plague.'* "Dr. Farrington, do you support G.E.?"

Oh, God, all Grace wanted to support was getting to her condo and climbing into a warm shower. Which she wouldn't have time for with this nonsense. Behind them, two other cars had turned off the road and were blocked. Probably more people coming for Adam's meeting. Grace chose her words carefully. "I am not currently working on genetic manipulation of seed stocks."

"Will you state in writing that you will **never** support G.E.?" Astrid demanded.

"No!" Grace replied. "I'm not stating anything!"

A young, earnest-looking woman pressed close to the car. "She doesn't know what it is. What they're doing to the planet!" The girl pushed several multi-colored brochures at Grace. "Read this."

Grace found herself taking the brochures, but saying quietly. "Freya, can we go?"

Most of the picketers had moved back from in front of the car, as the two green-uniformed security guards moved in, saying firmly, "You may picket, but you must stay on the sides of the road! You may not obstruct traffic!"

Freya was only looking at Astrid. "Why are you picketing Oyster River Research?"

Grace cut in trying to focus Astrid's answer, "If you're against animal cruelty, why are you picketing basic research in genetic manipulation?"

Astrid looked at her pityingly. "Homo sapiens are earth's creatures. We are all inter-dependent in the great web of life. They're using genetic engineering to produce rbGH. A cow cruelly injected with rbGH produces milk tainted with higher levels of IFG-1, that winds up in baby formulas."

Grace challenged her. "RbGH is a natural, growth hormone already found in the cow. The milk produced is just increased and has been tested as safe."

Astrid's voice lowered, "To increase production, those cows had to be fed increased protein! They used recycled dead animals–including other cows."

"A mistake," Grace admitted. "I believe that's been stopped."

"After mad cow was spread! The cruel increase in

milk production resulted in a higher infection rate of the cow's udders.   You think cow puss in baby's milk is progress? Do you think local, non-rbGH using dairies being driven out of the market by cheap milk is good long-term policy?"

"The public has a choice..." Grace started only to be cut off.

"Not if your conglomerate friends legislate to make it against the law to label G.E. Frankenfood!"

The picketers were between her and the harbor, but Grace could see down to the ORR dock. Kurt MacKay, standing 5'9"--or if you counted sheer chutzpah--more like 6'10" was marching up the hill, carrying a clam rake as if it were a club. Oh, shit, she didn't need Kurt defending her to the point of blood-shed!

"I've got a meeting to attend, Freya." Grace looked at her friend. The two security guys were trying to herd the last picketers lingering in front of her car, but obviously being experienced at this, other placard carriers quickly slipped behind their backs, so her friend couldn't move the car.

Freya looked at Astrid and said firmly, "I will talk to Grace."

Without saying a word, Astrid gave a small nod of her head, stepped back, and the C.U.R.S. people pulled away from the car, clearing the path.

Seeing Grace and the other cars released, Kurt had stopped at the little-unmanned guard booth at the top of the docks. God, Grace hoped he stayed there. Tired she leaned back in her seat and found herself dripping with nervous perspiration. "Your friends are seriously over the line."

"They're very passionate about what they do," said Freya, defensively.

"They can't be allowed to disturb Oyster River's research."

Freya headed toward the two-story, brick building on

the right, overlooking the harbor, that housed Grace's condominium. "I'd don't know where the police are. Maybe I should call Mac?"

"No! Don't call the police, I don't want your son wading in. Adam Greenfield has probably given orders for ORR's security to try to stay hands off. Adam's usual courageous policy, *'if you look away–the problem will just disappear.'*"

Her friend was frowning. "Grace, maybe you should listen to them. Astrid may overreact at times, but her facts are usually right."

"I've got to get to Adam's meeting." To be displayed like a stuffed turkey.

"Are you taking your award to show?"

"No!"

"Do you want me to drop the box off at your lab?" Freya asked.

"That would be great." Freya just pulled in at the curb, and Grace grabbed her suitcase, handbag, and laptop from the back and hurried up the stairs. Her second-floor apartment was owned by Oyster River Research. It was part of her contract, and very convenient for a woman who worked all hours. Before the door, she saw a white envelope on the floor. Message from Adam? Maybe they called off their meeting due to raining protestors? Grace ripped it open fast and read, **'Farington! Don't do G.E.! It's wrong for the planet! Not good to do it for $$$s'.** Totally juvenile and they spelled her name wrong! But how did they know where she lived? Annoyed Grace unlocked her door and tossed the note into the wastebasket inside.

Already running late, she refreshed without showering and headed down. With a new patron being roped in, she would have to be on display as an extraordinary example of one of Oyster River Research's leading scientists. God, she hated this but helping Dr. Huang Wong and ORR get grants was necessary to keep her own work going. Science was her life, science was also her business.

In the lobby, from the Jamison's apartment, she could hear crying. One of the twins was not happy about his brother being fed first, how did Sara do it? Three babies in diapers crammed into a two bedroom apartment? Her husband, Bobby, was one of Grace's assistants and still working on his dissertation. Of course, when he got his doctorate how could they find a larger, affordable apartment in this shoreline of millionaire's estates.

Outside, Grace passed her old Champagne Gold Subaru Forester, should she take time now to start it up to keep the battery charged? Later. Nice cool day, more Spring-like than Connecticut in November. She started walking up the peninsula's road, past the 1950's glass and beige brick Administration building, and the first suite of labs--one she would always call Eric Larsen's–that was now Dr. Huang Wong's. Past the two-story building that housed classrooms and her own laboratory 5. She so wanted to just go in and get back to work. How much time would this miserable meeting waste today?

Ahead she could hear more chanting–demonstrators still there. But off the road, she saw Freya's beat up, blue van still parked. Scanning the crowd, Grace didn't see her tall friend standing above the demonstrators. To the left Grace could see the sunlight sparkling on the Harbor and ORR docks, with the *Big 'Un*, Kurt's diesel lobster trawler, and the *Lovely Lady*, the permanently docked 36' Cabo Rico Cutter sailboat he lived on. Grace missed the harbor while she was away. Maybe even missed Kurt a bit.

The hillside was rising to the main road. There perched the mustard yellow and maroon trimmed 'Captain's Roost.' Freya ran her extended '*Hauntings of Oyster River*' ghost tours by here. She claimed the ghost of Jersillda Smith had been seen, watching from the widow's walk. It was there,

Jersillda saw her husband drown, as a freak June northeastern wrecked his whaling ship in the Harbor. That 1890's Italianesque captain's house had become the nucleus for the Oyster River Research facility. ORR started as a rich man's summer project to cure cancer, but later, under Steward Brewster's leadership, it evolved into a premier research facility with an out of proportion roster of Nobel laureates.

Instead of walking around the front, Grace headed for the back wing that had been added to house a large, commercial type kitchen. She hurried up the wooden back stairs and pulled on the door. To her surprise, it was locked. When this building was in use, the back door was always left open!

Chapter 2

Damn! She was already late. Now she would have to run around the side of the building and go in the front entrance. Wanting to avoid the demonstrators, she turned right. Past the Victorian livery barn, now a storage shed for ORR Landscaping and some of Kurt's stuff, including his motorcycles. One of those bikes usually worked, while the others were always projects in progress.

As she rounded the Italianesque front tower, Grace could hear the loud chanting of multiple people in unison, **"POISON THE FOOD! POISON THE EARTH! YOU'LL DIE TOO!"**

Nervously Grace looked down toward the harbor. The demonstrators were still there, but they were now off the road. And she could see a Town of Oyster River police car parked. Looking down the hill, Grace also saw a 6' 5" cop standing tall, Mac Dell looking very much like a male version of his golden-haired, Viking mother, Freya.

Seeing Mac made Grace feel a little safer, as she climbed the wide wooden steps to the grand, double-doored entrance to the tower. No knocking, she just pulled it open. The entry hall was a masterpiece of the ships carpenters' art. Set in the floor was an eight-foot wide marine compass rose, inlaid in ebony, maple, rosewood, and oak. Surrounding it was an oak floor with a maple and ebony band of stars and moons alternating at the edges. From the back, a wooden, curving staircase soaring upwards, looking like it just grew there a la Jack's beanstalk.

Now, a jarring note in the nineteenth-century perfection: an armed, uniformed, private security guard stood at attention beside a cheap fold-up card table where Gail-- ORR's secretary--was now sitting. The blonde, blue eyed, self-proclaimed, 'polish doll' was a temporary employee, but Gail had been working for ORR for years; Grace had to speak to Adam again about getting her permanent status. Gail gave Grace a big smile. "Congratulations! Now we've got an official Guru!"

"Still have lunch with me?" Grace joked.

Gail laughed back. "Of course, but we're going to have to move into the cafeteria. It's been too cold for the picnic tables. First snow forecasted for Tuesday."

Grace was walking past, when the guard said in a stern voice, "One moment, mam."

Surprised, Grace stopped and looked at Gail, who was rising, with a paper name tag in her hands. "They want you to wear a badge. Everyone. Even Adam, I'm so sorry."

Grace spend a good part of her working life doing government classified research, so the formality of a sticky paper badge really didn't bother her. "That's fine." She took it from Gail and pressed it to her suit jacket, hoping this one wouldn't leave a glue stain again.

Ever upbeat Gail smiled at her, saying, "This means we're totally safe unless the demonstrators spend twenty bucks at Staples and pick up another box of these badges."

The uniformed guard did not appear amused but did move to open one of the double parlor doors for Grace. Past the short hall with the cloakroom on one side, the main building's story and a half downstairs had been gutted and reconfigured into one large meeting hall. Now it smelled of roast beef, that made her mouth water. This event would apparently offer more than the usual domestic white wine, dry cheese, and crackers. She tried looking around, but Grace couldn't see much. The heavy black velvet curtains had been drawn across the original, tall windows, that overlooked the hillside and harbor. The curtains muffled the demonstrators' chanting but also darkened the room for the film being projected.

The lowered, twelve-foot wide screen played a commercial-quality video showing abundant windblown wheat fields. Then close-ups of a weathered farmer type, pouring wheat grain into the hands of a tall, strikingly handsome man. Grace focused on him, sandy blond hair, rugged features, goatee beard, and an aura of strength. Both of the men were studying the seed yield intently, as a baritone voice narrated, *"Field production has tripled. Even in drought conditions! Genetic engineered resistance to pesticides has allowed earlier, heavier spraying, that controls the weeds and actually decreases pesticide use."*

As her eyes adjusted to the low light Grace could make out thirty or so folding chairs that had been set up theater style. She could pick out Adam, Huang, and Fritz with several of the Board of Directors up front, and to her surprise, there seemed to have a larger turnout than usual. She took one of the few open seats at the end of the row, next to Kurt, whispering, "Where's Bobby?"

"Guarding the dock. While I'm stuck here, I don't want to those protesting, animal worshiping num-nuts outside trashing me boats!"

"Mac's there now," Grace whispered back.

Lowering his head, Kurt leaned closer to her, saying, "Not for long. Our valiant leader has told the police to go away, so *'we won't have trouble.'*" The film finished, and she blinked when the lights came back on. Now, Grace could see most of the audience consisted of a number of men and women in business suits that she didn't recognize. Probably from Humanity's Harvest, but this wasn't to be a press party, it was just a contract signing.

Two red jacketed bartenders manned the built-in bar near the kitchen, stocked with a much wider range of bottles rather than the usual white and red wine. And at the side of the hall, an abundant buffet had been set out, obviously lavishly financed by this company. Into the microphone, Dr. Huang was waxing long about his efforts to bring science to the cutting edge. Grace looked at the others on the podium who sat listening, ORR's President, Adam Greenfield stood 6' 1", and the sandy-haired handsome man next to him looked a bit taller, maybe 6" 4". She recognized the man from the film, blond, with his longish, waved hair and a neatly trimmed goatee. He was wearing a dun-colored safari type jacket, which matched the tanned face and wind-blown image. Possibly a little bored, his green eyes lazily scanned the room, while the shorter Huang Wong prattled on into the microphone. Others shifted impatiently until finally Huang shut up and released the crowd for the bar and buffet on the linen-draped tables set about the room's edge. A still talking Huang stayed with Adam and the other man. As Grace watched the handsome hunk looked in her direction and said something to Adam, and the President of ORR interrupted Huang, calling out, "Dr. Farrington."

As per her usual dog-and-pony act, Grace forced a smile and walked over to be introduced to the latest possible big bucks patron. As she joined them, Adam was smoothly saying, "Dr. Farrington is just back from receiving the MacAlpin Guru award in Seattle. Grace, this is Axel Jensen, founder, and C.E.O. of Humanity's Harvest."

Axel had a warm smile and warmer hand. "Congratulations, Dr. Farrington. The Guru award, that's quite a lifetime achievement, especially for a woman as youthful as yourself."

Oh, the man's deep baritone voice had charm. What did he want?

But Axel was introducing the twentyish, dark complected man next to him. "This is Ekkeko Vascelo, my vice president of botanical research in South America." The short, thinner man had a Spanish name, but his features looked more Indian blooded. "Ekkeko hails from Peru, has a Ph.D. in Plant chemistry, and will be our liaison with you, on Humanity's Harvest project with Oyster River."

Say what? Grace corrected, "He'll be working with

Dr. Wong."

Ekkeko looked to Axel, who frowned and asked, "As well as yourself?"

Grace said, "No."

Axel glanced at the Peruvian man then very deliberately said, "Humanity's Harvest contracted with all of Oyster River. Dr. Wong assured me that you would be the senior consultant on the project." Grace looked from an embarrassed Adam to the foolishly squirming Huang, who loudly declared, "They make a contract with me! To study genetic engineering of my superior algae!"

Axel Jensen didn't look happy as he turned to Adam. "Actually, we'd thought we were forming a partnership with the entire Oyster River Research team?"

From Adam's flushing, Grace intuited that he knew a misrepresentation had taken place, but their president explained gamely, "Of course, Grace is very helpful to all her fellow researchers. She hasn't been in the loop, with her Seattle trip."

"What loop?" Grace asked.

Looking less friendly, Axel explained, "The arrangements for Humanity's Harvest funding of genetic engineering studies with Oyster River Research."

Adam was coloring deeply, as he looked at Jensen. "Actually, all our researchers work independently. They chose their own research topics and go after their own grants. Oyster River provides laboratories, some funding, and a place for high powered minds to gather and grow." Then Adam turned to Grace, "But Humanity's Harvest is offering generous terms for cooperation on their projects.."

Huang cut in, "She not working with my algae!"

Grace would agree to that, but apparently, Ekkeko didn't. "Dr. Huang instructed us to make out the contracts in his name only, but we were under the impression that Dr. Farrington and the rest of the Oyster River team were with us? That our grant money was being split between all of you."

"No split money!" Huang yelled, sounding a bit shrill.

Grace added firmly, "And I'm not able to take on any on new projects at this time."

Even Kurt immediately got back to the pressing matter at hand. "Outside Huang, none us have seen any of yer money."

"That certainly was our mistake." Axel's smile was grim. "I didn't expect that Dr. Farrington would be on the algae project. In my conversations with Dr. Huang, he mentioned that since Dr. Farrington was already unlocking the secrets of the genetic code, that she might be interested in working on some basic research into South American plant origins?"

They looked to Huang, who just smiled blandly. "She study everything."

Feeling tired, Grace looked up at Axel. "I study what is–using genetic splicing and manipulation to reveal the basics. I don't see myself as playing God to improve DNA coding. And, no–I'm sorry--but I don't think I will be looking into commercial applications at this time."

Axel listened to that, then quietly stated, "In Africa-- every day--it is estimated that over one hundred thousand people die of starvation."

Kurt said pointedly, "Not because this world can't grow the food to feed them. We do. But due to financial means, natural disasters, or outright genocidal political practices, they die."

"The world population is growing exponentially. Do you think our present food level production will feed these people in twenty years?" challenged Axel.

"No...we don't," said Grace looking at a man who seemed to be honestly worried about the future of the planet. "But there isn't much anyone can do about that."

"No, mam, there is! I can. And I am," Axel said simply. " Dr. Wong's algae is a start. But we're going to need more than that. Actually, Dr. Farrington..."

"Please, Grace."

His smile warmed again showing rather cute dimples. "Grace, Humanity's Harvest is quite willing to pay for the expertise it requires..."

She shook her head. "It's not the money. It's the fact that my research schedule is completely full at this time."

"Would you be willing to at least discuss perhaps future projects, over..." he grandly indicated the buffet. "Our sumptuous feast?"

Appreciating he was lightening the situation, Grace smiled. "That would be a good idea." As they walked to the tables, they left Kurt glaring at Huang. Usually, the very best of ORR's receptions got cold cut sandwiches of ham or chicken salad. For the official announcement of Grace's Guru award, Adam had sprung for a wine bar, while Sara Jamison and Freya baked trays of sausages ziti, wine chicken, and cupcakes.

Now the round tables that had been set up in the huge room had real, fresh red carnation centerpieces. The tables were set with pale yellow, stiff linen tablecloths, and real, gold-rimmed china. The white-jacketed serving staff sliced pink roast beef and ham, while waitresses circulated with trays of shrimp, cheese, and warm hors-d'oeuvres.

As they walked to the table together, Axel politely passed Grace a plate. His aftershave lotion had a sage-like aroma, and she had to admit this man had manners. Charm. His just being beside her seemed to put her in an agreeable mood. Grace found herself enjoying the moment, and she certainly was hungry. She took some salad, pink roast beef, shrimp, and got some butter garlic roasted potatoes from the chafing dishes. Inevitably she found herself joining Axel at one of those round tables, as his Peruvian assistant sat down on his other side. Ekkeko, the slightly built man had taken only rice and vegetable dishes, and sitting down he gave Grace another of those cold, dark-eyed glares.

Since Grace really looked quite unremarkable, most people who didn't know what she's done in the scientific field didn't pay her any attention. Of the ones that did know what Dr. Farrington had pioneered, Grace had uneasily gotten used to fawning deference. Despite his dominating attitude, Axel Jensen appeared to respect her, but not hold her in awe. On the other hand, Ekkeko stared at her coldly, with a look that gave her the feeling of hostility, but as the meal progressed, Grace realized that Ekkeko seemed to have that look for everyone around him.

Kurt Mackay just walked over and sat down on Grace's other side, commenting to Axel, "Nice spread."

Axel held out his hand, "We haven't been introduced?"

"Dr. Kurt MacKay. Marine studies." He gave a slight smile as if enjoying a private joke. "I can assume Huang and Adam forgot to mention me."

Axel brushed past that comment. "Actually, I brought your name up to Adam, I had already learned quite a bit about your studies of ocean currents, and shellfish diseases. I was particularly impressed with your work on the local lobster die-offs."

Kurt looked pleasantly surprised. "Haven't had time to write that it up, meself."

"Word gets around," Axel returned.

After eating a bit, Kurt decided to get down to business. "Hear you guys are planning to put out a line of pesticides for oyster parasites?"

"Actually Humanity's Harvest was thinking more in terms of a developing a super bivalve mollusk, resistant to parasites, pollution, and temperature change." Axel glanced at Ekkeko, who appeared embarrassed. "I allowed the negotiations with your facility to be conducted by my staff. They seemed to have wrongly assumed that our contract was with all of Oyster River's researchers. It appears if I want Grace and yourself, I'll have to renegotiate personally."

"Aaup." Kurt stabbed a fork in the lobster Newburg. "Separate contracts for myself...and Dr. Farrington."

Grace added, "And Bobby and Dr. Fritz Wilshuen."

"Bobby?" Axel asked.

"Robert S. Jamison, Jr.," Grace explained. "He hasn't got his doctorate yet, but Bobby's a talented worker in the field of marine genetic research. Those classes I'm listed as 'Senior Lecturer,' those are really his work. He's very good, and Bobby's just starting to look for grants of his own for a projected study on how DNA controls jellyfish metabolism."

Kurt cut her off her Bobby promo. "Do our friends demonstrating outside come with all your deals?"

Axel turned to Grace. "I'm very sorry for their intrusion. These people are anti-G.E., anti-all scientific progress basically. They want everybody to eat '*locally sourced food supplies only,*' good luck with that if you live in New York City."

"Have you tried reasoning with them?" Grace asked.

"Oh, yes." Axel smiled bitterly. "Here. In Missouri. In France. In Peru."

"The same people are demonstrating in Peru?" she asked in surprise.

"Different groups, but pretty much the same ideas. They all hold rock bound beliefs of purity, harmony, oneness with the Universe. They see all of us being content to live at subsistence levels for the good of Gaia. They seem to be able to successfully ignore reality, and continue to demand that everyone agree with them, but their fantasy world has never existed. Can never exist. Still, they just demonstrate and lay down in front of the train of progress."

Ekkeko   pointed out disapprovingly, "Your ORR President sent the police away, that was not wise."

Axel looked over in Adam's direction. "Great." As he glanced back at Grace, he looked genuinely concerned. "That's Adam's choice, of course. Humanity's Harvest has a strong in-house security division, who are used to dealing with these people. I've offered them to Oyster River..."

"But Adam is afraid of escalating things, so he shows a weak-womanish posture and things escalate," Kurt finished with contempt.

Axel seemed to want to change the topic. "For over a hundred years Oyster River Research has been dedicated to improving the health and longevity of the world's population through basic research. Humanity's Harvest is attempting to do the same thing by increasing and enhancing the food supply."

Kurt looked at him hard, "Hasn't genetic engineering been more focused on increasing profits, with things like tougher skins on tomatoes, so they can be machine harvested? Producing tomatoes that are machine practical, but wind up tasteless?"

"Farmers and Humanity's Harvest have to make a profit to continue in business, Dr. MacKay," said Axel obviously taking Kurt's measure. "You don't work for free do you?"

Chapter 3

Kurt smiled. "You're right, I don't. But let's keep the focus on genetic engineering. Hear tell you're working on salmons engineered with massive growth genes?"

"Not our project, but I'm familiar with it," Axel acknowledged. "To modify Atlantic Salmon they added a grown hormone regulator from Chinook Salmon, and a promoter from ocean pout..."

"Promoter?" Kurt asked.

Grace stopped eating to explain. "For transcription to take place an enzyme that synthesizes RNA must attach to the DNA near the gene, for that a promoter is needed." She glanced over at the buffet tables wondering if she should get up and get more of that delicious citrus shrimp.

But Axel was continuing, "Those genetically spliced fish put on weight three times faster. Introducing these fish commercially will increase salmon production sevenfold, which increases the world's protein production, and eventually will bring the prices down for the consumers."

Kurt didn't sound so impressed. "They want to breed these super beasts in pens in the open ocean. Some of those fish are going to escape. What happens when they mate with the wild population?"

"You're talking about the '*Trojan Gene Effect* ,'" Axel acknowledged.

"Aaup. All the ladyfish are gonna be attracted to mate with your bigger, faster, super boys. But those super fishes have a high rate of premature mortality, which will be passed on to their offspring. I've read estimates that say if only sixty G.E. fish enter a salmon population of 60,000, the super salmon will outbreed the wild fish, and the whole shebang would gone in forty generations."

Grace tried to lighten the conversation, "Maybe the lady salmons will prefer the shorter, traditional male fishes?"

Axel ignored that, and tersely commented to Kurt, "You're talking unproven theories, untested predictions. How about another forecast, in 2012 the world's population exceeded seven billion, by 2020 we're predicted to reach eight billion. That's a billion more hungry people on this planet, where today--according to the U.N.--malnutrition is the key factor in the death of 2.6 million children a year."

Kurt loved a good verbal sparring match. "The U.N.'s 'research' is oriented to sending more money to that black hole, the all mighty U.N. This world is currently producing more than enough food to feed the entire population on the planet–but transportation, poverty, and outright governmental genocidal practices are not allowing that food to get to starving people. Raising food prices to cover your expensive gene engineering projects isn't going to help that much either."

Not seeming to like the conversation's drift Ekkeko spoke up, "Axel, we have that meeting with Global on Long Island?"

Axel looked at his watch. "Yeah, it'll take forty minutes just to get my seaplane in the air. Ekkeko, you come with me, have the limos take the rest back to New York."

Kurt said in an admiring tone, "You've got that white and red restored two engine on floats moored over near the point?"

"Yes, she's a restored 1954 Beech 18. One of the last four remaining in operation. Best way to avoid the commuter traffic. Listen," Axel looked from Kurt to Grace. "I would like to continue this conversation at a better time. I have scheduled a series of Oyster River Laboratory tours with my employees, Dr. Huang said it would be all right. Grace, I had expected that your lab would be on the tour, is that incorrect?"

She hated time-wasting interruptions, but she owed Oyster River Research a lot. "Please arrange times with my assistant, Inger. No one will be allowed in my clean room, and it would be less interfering to my work if they could come in groups."

"Your wishes will be respected," Axel said.

And maybe Grace could get something out of this intrusion. "These will be upper management?" she asked.

Axel nodded. "Yes, my team worldwide."

"Maybe I could take samples..." Grace said, not even realizing she was speaking out loud.

"Samples?" Axel asked.

Kurt smiled wickedly. "Grace likes to get to know people on the genetic level. Sort of like a border collie in the park, running over to sniff at the anus glands of a golden retriever."

Grace's cheeks grew hot. "Thank you, Dr. Mackay, for that lovely image!" Classic Kurt. "Actually, I'm doing some studies concerning genes connected with leadership traits."

"Excellent match!" pronounced Axel. "Your visitors will all be senior management from my headquarters in New York City or visiting International vice presidents. They can give blood..."

"Not necessary, it will only be a painless mouth swab," Grace reassured him, getting really excited about that DNA. "It would help if they were willing to fill out one of my standard profiles, either the short or long form."

"How many pages is the long?" Axel asked.

Again Grace had to realize her research is not the top of everyone's agenda. "The long is thirty-pages, that's asking a bit too much, but even filling out the short three-page profile would be helpful."

"They will fill out your long form," stated Axel firmly. "Have your assistant e-mail it to me at my headquarters in New York. The forms will be filled out in advance before they arrive in your laboratory."   Then with that oh, so promising smile, that handsome hunk, and his assistant were gone. Grace absently reached up and patted her curled hair. Damn, she shouldn't have canceled her hair cut, she needed it. Maybe she could get an appointment tomorrow?

Kurt looked around the room. "Lady, we've got to find out what Huang committed us to, and how much he got paid." Most of the others had left, and now the caterers were cleaning up. By the kitchen wing, Adam looked like he was trying to get away from Huang, but Grace and Kurt ambushed them.

She started, "What exactly did Oyster River contract with Humanity's Harvest?"

Adam shifted uneasily. "Prices on the greenhouses renovations were way overrunning their original cost estimates. Axel Jensen has promised to pay off the whole thing..."

Kurt noted Adam's evasion. "What else did Oyster River promise Jensen?"

Huang interrupted him, "Contract is all mine! Humanity's Harvest do deal with me–me alone!"

Grace wanted to know more about that deal, but their discussion was suddenly ended by the sound of shattering glass.

"**What the hell?!**" Kurt headed to his right and the first window. The others followed as Kurt pulled the heavy velvet curtain back. He was looking through a broken pane of a nine over nine window. Looking out to the grass and harbor below it was easy to see that the Oyster River's police car was gone, and so were the private security party guards. The demonstrators were quietly holding up placards to the Main Road, and now looking their way.

Kurt turned to Adam. "Where's the cops?"

Adam was picking up a fist-sized rock from the floor. "I told Mac to go. We didn't want a problem."

"We have a problem!" Kurt looked down to the dock

area. "Where're your rent-a-cops?'

"My instructions to ORR security were to stay inside the Administration building, and keep this a peaceful demonstration."

"Your peaceful demonstrators just broke a window!" Kurt bellowed.

"We didn't see them do it," said Adam.

Grace looked up, "We have security cameras."

"For night only,"   Adam said, again looking uncomfortable. "We have to pay for monitoring, so we only turn them on at night."

Kurt was still staring out the window, "Oh, shit!"

Grace followed Kurt's gaze to a clump of picketers. "What is it?"

"It's not a 'what,' it's a 'who.' An old friend of ours, Joshua Jeffers."

Oh, double shit Grace thought to herself. Looking down she could see the solid body of a flaming-red-haired man. When she was trying to get Kurt out of jail for the murder of an ORR Board member, Grace had gone to the Jeffers brothers' gas station and bait shop. Trying to break Josh's alibi, when she thinking that he might have been the killer, and committed his murder on Kurt's boat for revenge.

He hadn't, but Grace had the feeling the only reason the hot-tempered, threatening Josh hadn't physically assaulted her was the intervention of his more responsible identical twin, Greg. "I thought Josh hated the catch restrictions that killed his fishing business, why is he partnering with a rabid environmentalist group?"

"Call the cops now!" said Kurt to Adam.

Their fearless leader only replied, "I run a construction company. Being president here is only a volunteer position!"

"But you're in charge!" Kurt demanded.

"Oyster River is a prestigious research facility–we don't want television film of defenseless animal rights picketers being dragged off by the Gestapo!"

A furious Kurt glared at Adam. "Acting like a chicken trying to duck your head and hide, only attracts the guy with a hatchet!"

Not wanting to get into an endless argument, Grace abandoned them. Leaving the Roost by the back kitchen wing, Grace saw Freya's van gone. Shame. She would have liked to ask her friend more questions about C.U.R.S., but Freya would have to get back to her new age store in the village.

Catching up with her, Kurt insisted on walking with Grace back to her laboratory. "You call me when you leave at night, I don't want you walking alone with these crazies about."

Grace raised an eyebrow. "You'll have your cell phone charged? That'll be something new."

"Yeah, if my trawler's out, I won't even have cell coverage." He looked genuinely worried. "Listen, you leave the lab, you are to call security to escort you!" he ordered sternly.

"Why? You think I can't deal with a bunch of yahoos hollering at me? C'mon."

"Grace, don't underestimate them," he said quietly. "In the Northwest, they've crippled loggers. They've set fire to labs..."

"These people are only here to publicize their cause and get T-V time and newspaper photos. They're an inconvenience, not a serious threat!"

"One of those guys out there is Josh Jeffers!"

That did stop Grace. "Prime recruiting member for your Klan friends."

"Klan wouldn't take him–Josh's too much of a loose cannon. They don't want to get shot at their own meetings!"

She looked at the protestors. "Josh hates anyone responsible for restricting the catch limits that ruined his fishing business, why would he partner with rabid environmentalists who want to end all hunting and fishing?"

"Sharks smell blood, they swim over."

Chapter 4

Grace's lab was in a two-story wooden building, built back in the 1920's. Two generously sized labs on the lower floor. Two above with classrooms. She walked down the ceramic titled central corridor, and into her zone of safety. God, it was good to be back home

Her white painted front room was huge, with tables for computer stations and two walls of specimen tanks. Only an antique elegantly crafted maple specimen cabinet looked out place. She'd set the Dr. Floyd collection cabinet in the front by the windows that overlooked the road before the Harbor. Seeing her enter, taller, blonde Inger stood up from her desk and hurried over to greet Grace. "Congratulations on the Guru award!"

"Thank you." The Grace looked around back and remembered. "But I left that box in Freya's van..."

"She dropped it off. We've got your award–I peeked. It's beautiful!" Inger lifted the heavy box up to her desk. "Freya said she couldn't stay, but before she left, she was going to talk to those demonstrators."

A worried Grace asked, "Have they been giving you problems?"

Inger shrugged, not looking happy. "Every time I drive in, they walk in front to slow me down, and they just keep stuffing pamphlets in my windshield wipers."

"Adam's going to have to do something about this."

Looking like she hated to bring it up, Inger said, "There's another problem. In the clean room–your main freezer unit is making noises, and I've had to set the temperature lower for it to remain level."

That is a major problem! In the Airlock room, Grace switched off the UV lights in the Clean room, and then she and Inger suited up with lab jumpsuits, disposable boot covers, gloves, face masks and plastic screened helmets before headed in the clean room. Inside another large room, bright overhead lights lit lab benches and white ceramic tiled floors and walls. On the left side of the room, stood her replicators, and her sequencers, set between were the workstations which held computer screens, keyboards, cabinets above, and endless blue plastic trays for holding hundreds of tiny pointed ended vials. To the right, Grace headed to the long steel bank of refrigeration and freezer unit doors. The largest, central one was now making a worrisome grinding sound. Grace turned to Inger. "Call that repair guy, what's his name?" Where would she have his card?

"Jim Jessup," Inger supplied, her voice muffled by the masking. "He's looked at it and says it's failing, but he can't say when it will go. He says this equipment is more advanced than the refrigeration units he usually deals with. With the requirement that your units do not have a defroster, it's not an item you can just go and grab off the shelf at Home Depot. If he can get the parts, Jim said he might be able to rebuild the compressor, but that will mean shutting down the unit for him to work on. He's checking on replacement parts now, but he thinks this model is over ten years old." More like fifteen Grace thought as Inger continued, "Jim advises you to replace before it completely fails."

At times like this David Gardiner's Greek Island, with its brand new laboratory really called to her. Well, buying a new freezer would probably take the rest of this year's Guru award money, but she'd have to replace the unit. "How long have we got?"

"Jim can't say."

"Great." Grace wanted to kick something.

"I've moved everything I've had room for into the other units, but..." Inger started.

"Aaup." Grace better start hunting a new unit. Back at her desk, she began pulling up laboratory freezer units on the Internet. Ones with no defrost...built in battery back up...some of these had glass doors, all had hefty prices. Her phone was ringing, yet another distraction, allowing herself to sound annoyed she answered shortly, "Laboratory 5."

"Grace, Dr. Farrington?" asked a deep baritone voice.

She waited, choosing not to answer until the caller identified himself.

After a moment, the voice said, "This is Axel Jensen."

Okay, a patron of ORR. "Axel, this is Grace, I'm sorry, it's been one of those days."

"I'd had mentioned talking with you about a possible research commitment for Humanity's Harvest?"

No, she didn't have the time for this, but looking at these screens a new laboratory refrigerator unit the same size as Grace was losing, without the fancy extras like glass doors, was going to set her back twenty thousand. "When will you be at ORR again?"

"I was thinking of flying into your harbor about eleven tomorrow. If you could recommend an excellent restaurant, Humanity's Harvest would be pleased to treat you to a gourmet lunch, so that we can talk..."

While they talked, she was bringing up her unread e-mails, 1095 of them. Most would be requests from students told to write someone important. And now he wanted lunch--that would take how long? "Actually, with the Seattle trip, I'm a bit behind." But she didn't want to turn him down, he might still be a source of grant money, and it would be so nice to spend some time with a handsome man like him. "We have a small cafeteria in the Administration building. It's certainly not gourmet, but the sandwiches and salad platters are decent. They usually have one hot entree."

"Sounds delicious," he laughed.

"Meet you at the cafeteria at 12:00?" she suggested.

"Who's walking with you from your lab?" he asked.

"Walking with me? Why should anyone walk me?" Grace remembered. "The demonstrators? Hopefully, they'll be gone?"

"Don't count on it. Push Adam to accept my security people."

The next day she got through nearly her whole e-mail backlog before Inger pointed out Grace had a luncheon appointment in five minutes. She hurried out of her lab coat and slipped on her black suit jacket, just wishing she had time to go home and maybe shower and dress up a little more than this plain pants suit. Even knowing he wasn't interested in her as a woman, Axel Jensen had a powerful effect on a female, and Grace intended to fully enjoy her lunch break with him.

Grabbing a car coat, she hurried outside, two buildings down from her lab was a large, two-story 1960's glass and beige brick building that now housed ORR Administration. Inside was an airy, glass-windowed entry hall, with Gail's desk in the center. To the right was the walled glass library, with groups of students in there now. Behind Gail's desk, was a corridor with storage rooms and at the end, Adam's office. And to her left was a small, but now fairly decent cafeteria rechristened the 'Oyster Café.'

With a smile to Gail, Grace hurried into the cafeteria and got the first shock. Ahead, before the openings for the food lines was a short wall, now adorned with a life-sized photograph of herself printed up as a poster and framed with gold trim. Adam must have ordered it. Probable Gail's idea and footwork.

Grace inwardly cringed. The photo portrayed a smiling, grey-haired man handing Grace that blocky MacAlpin award. Oh, God. She hadn't even been smiling back? What had she been doing? Sitting in the banquet room, thinking about the alleles of an octopus' eye so when she was called up Grace had been annoyed to be disturbed. It showed on her face. She looked so distant, so awkward, so thin and forty. God, she hated that picture! Grace'd wait a week and then that poster was going to disappear!

She looked around the room. Some students were eating at round tables for four or six. In the corner a hand raised. It was Axel, with that assistant, whatever his name was? Grace nodded, then ducked into the steel railed food line, glancing over glass shelves with saran wrapped sandwiches and salads. A small grill had burgers and one other hot entree a day. Today it was Swedish meatballs with mashed red potatoes, and the soup smelled like chicken. Not too hungry, Grace picked up a roast beef sandwich, chocolate chip cookies, and a cup with a lemon tea bag. When she got to the register Axel's assistant was there to pay, his name was? The grey-haired lady cashier gushed at seeing her, "Oh, Grace, you got an award! I'm so glad."

"Thank you," said Grace, appreciating once again how ORR was like her family. After getting hot water for her tea, she carried her tray over to Axel.

Smiling warmly at her, Axel politely rose up, as she approached, to pull out her chair.

The assistant had a mango salad, which he was unhappily picking at, while Axel had the Swedish meatballs. "Small selection, but not bad," he said.

Grace explained, "When the last contract came up, Adam switched the cafeteria to the local caterers at the Cheese Shop. They kept most of the employees but upgraded the menu. It's much better now." But feeling a little devilish, she went for a bit of lab humor. "Just don't ever eat any of the entrees that have a student with a clipboard standing by."

Axel's green eyes looked puzzled, then he understood. "Yes, Dr. Wong has told me he plans to try out the viability of his algae in several dishes." Theatrically, he suspiciously poked his fork at the parsley flakes on his meatballs.

"How is the algae project coming?" she asked

Axel didn't look too happy. "I'm told it's fine, but Ekkeko and I were over at the greenhouses, most of the tanks are empty and dry. Those others are only partially filled, the building is cold, and the whole northeast greenhouse floor is under half an inch of water."

That was embarrassing, Grace didn't like Huang and his bully ways, but she also didn't like ORR appearing as anything less than professional to a patron.

Ekkeko was still looking nervously at his mango salad, as Kurt MacKay joined them uninvited, placing his plate of Swedish meatballs down beside Grace.

She looked at him. "The demonstrators still by the dock?"

"Oh, yeah," Kurt said gruffly, starting to eat his meatballs.

"Is Adam going to do anything about it?" she asked.

Axel was observing quietly, as Kurt spoke stiffly, "As for Adam's *'they'll get tired and go away,'* whal, they're setting up tents before the docks."

That shocked Grace. "They're actually moving in on private property? Near your boats?"

"Aaup."

"What's Adam doing about it?" she said.

"*'Watching the situation carefully,'*" a furious Kurt quoted.

Grace felt that was so wrong.

Axel shook his head. "I'm sorry that Oyster River's relationship with Humanity's Harvest has caused you all such a problem."

Kurt growled, "Ya can't give in! Then that crew will be dictating when we can be allowed to pee."

Grace wondered if Axel would resent Kurt joining them, but he seemed to be speaking to the both of them. "You know, when we spoke with Huang, I was under the impression that I was contracting with all of the scientists as Oyster River," Axel stopped.

"Most of us aren't doing genetic engineering," Kurt pointed out.

Axel turned those penetrating eyes on Kurt. "Actually, my company is researching a great deal more than just G.E. Humanity's Harvest started by doing research into configurations of the heritage plants and animals that already existed, so we are very interested in your marine research. By discovering and cataloging what exists we're trying to increase the range of agriculture access to promising food sources. To feed this planet, it's a race against time, with promising marginal species going extinct every day.'

Grace put down her fork. "I saw an interesting paper on your company's attempts at backcrossing corn, to get closer to the original ancestral maize DNA configuration?"

Axel nodded. "Right now corn is incapable of successfully seeding itself in the wild. Without man's intervention, it would just cease to exist."

"Because of centuries of selective breeding of my people," Ekkeko said primly.

"A form of manual gene manipulation," Axel said for Kurt's benefit.

Grace wondered idly, "Do you think the original stock exists anymore?"

Axel looked at her, with those deep green eyes. "Professor Hiram Bingham thought so."

"Yer talking the first quarter of the twentieth century?" Kurt asked.

"Professor Bingham?" Grace asked.

Ekkeko spoke with a touch of disdain, "In the early 1900s, Professor Bingham studied the culture, history, agriculture of Peru. He was fascinated by the pre-Colombian period. He set out to find El Dorado, the lost City of Gold.

He claimed he wished to *'preserve the cultures of our ancients,'* he did this by robbing tombs and digging up pots, then shipping them all to the university he served."

Axel interrupted. "Bingham wasn't an archeologist, the field wasn't too advanced in those days. He was an anthropologist, in Peru to study the cultures present and past. He learned the language and documented the customs. The professor took the time to sketch the exact details of marked wood and fantastically wrought, massive rock foundations. He questioned dancers, tasted the traditional foods, and wrote it all down in his invaluable journals."

"While his stolen booty was shipped to Connecticut, without proper recompense," Ekkeko replied.

Kurt smiled, "So you don't have a problem with being violated, yer just unhappy because yer guys weren't paid enough?"

Ekkeko glared at Kurt. "Those artifacts were stolen!"

"That so? I heard Professor Bingham did buy them from the local landowners and government," Kurt stated as a hard fact. "Also he did pay Peruvians to crate them."

"Like the English did with Elgin marbles," Ekkeko said bitterly. "Got some corrupt officials to sign off on phony papers, sawed off the marble masterpieces, removing a nation's treasure from the Greek Parthenon to adorn the British Museum."

Grace wished Kurt would shut up, and gave him a look, but he was wading in deep. "The Government at that time was using the magnificent ruin of the Parthenon as a fort and munitions dump. One lit match---those exquisite sculptures and the whole temple would've have been a cloud of marble dust."

Ekkeko ignored that. "The Greeks quite rightly demand their marbles back."

"To put out in acid rain?" Kurt countered. "In Greece, some of the early statues were burnt down to produce lime for building materials. Or would you put the Elgin marbles inside a Greek museum for tourist cash? Maybe the English could just send them a cut of British museum's entrance gate?"

Ekkeko looked with contempt at him. "Oh, it is better for the iconic bust of Nefertiti to reside in Berlin because an archaeologist managed to find it, then talked dishonest officials into letting him remove it from Egypt?"

Grace saw that fighting glint in his eyes that Kurt got when he had a true believer to battle with. "Yes, the Egyptians have always respected their heritage. Let's see. They stripped the Great Pyramid of its limestone cladding for their mansions. Sold the bodies of their sacred dead to the Europeans, to be ground into mummy powder, or burned in fireboxes of steam trains."

A true believer Ekkeko wasn't listening as he sat rigidly. "Treasures looted from Egypt should be returned! The International community demands it!   They wish them to be preserved in Egypt, as a guardian of its world heritage."

"Keep it safe in one country? In the center of the Mideast? Sounds safe to me. Israel got nukes. Iran's got nukes. Even if Egypt wasn't supporting the Palestinians sending them missiles, anything in that area is subject to possible being black-glassed. Actually, for any countries historical treasures, perhaps being dispersed is the best hope of their future survival?"

Ekkeko just glared him, he was not a grand battler that Kurt enjoyed. On a night, with the whiskey was flowing, Grace had seen Kurt and Deadeye, lay bets on the Alpine bar, then one hotly argue amnesty for illegals, while the other opposed. At every ten minutes by the bar clock, they'd stop, switch sides, and got at it again, with the other patrons being the judge of the debaters' expertise. Kurt usually won.

Axel had been quietly enjoying the byplay. "Professor Bingham's diaries are a heritage in themselves.   He often mentions searching for the *'food of the Sun God.'*   It was some special ground meal that was eaten only by the Inca, himself, and his close family, that *'endowed them with vitality and longevity.'*   I believe Professor Bingham searched for and perhaps even obtained samples of seed and pods that still exist in storage up in the University Museum in New Haven. The current curator has logged a number of them that I believe could yield DNA if an expert could do the testing..." Axel looked at Grace.

Kurt roughly calculated, "Those artifacts are what six, seven-hundred-years-old?"

Axel shrugged, "They've taken wheat seeds from a five-thousand-year-old Egyptian tomb, stuck in soil, watered it, and watched as it successfully sprouted."   He looked directly at Grace.   "Dr. Farrington, if you'd accept, Humanity's Harvest would be willing to generously fund a day's expedition. Only a day out of your schedule, unless you find something promising to culture?"

Another time waster. Grace merely said, "You don't need me.   A good doctorate candidate could easily survey everything and bring back the necessary samples to be cultured in my lab.   Bobby Jamison instructs most of the advanced genetics classes at Oyster River. He'd be an excellent choice."

Axel studied her quietly.   Grace had the feeling that it was just the two of them at the table, and the man's innate sexual magnetism was undeniable.   He was speaking quietly, "Humanity's Harvest is not really interested in funding an assistant.   I've long believed that paying for the best is a sensible investment in the long term. I'm relying on the fact that you'll have the knowledge and instincts to find what others overlook."

Her immediate reaction was to still refuse, but her main refrigeration unit was failing, and Axel's company might pay two to maybe five thousand toward a replacement for what might only be a day's work lost. But before she could make up her mind, Kurt waded in, "Grace and I are currently working on a dual marine study that's finishing so she might be available. But having the best doesn't come cheap."

With a brief glance at Ekkeko, Axel asked. "How much are we talking?"

A little annoyed at being left out of negotiating on her own services, Grace started to open her mouth, but Kurt cut her off. "We'll have to get back to you on that. After you give us a proposal on just what you want to be done, and what Humanity's Harvest expects to get out of it." He stood up, "All right, gentlemen. It's been pleasant, but Grace and I have to get working on that other co-project." He looked at her. "We got to talk about our moldy lobsters."

Chapter 5

Wanting to tell Kurt to go to hell, she just politely smiled at Axel, picked up her finished tray and left with Kurt. Outside it was overcast and the air smelled of clean sea salt, with the tide running high.   Some of the last yellow leaves were blowing over the grass, as the Harbor started to whip up white caps. Kurt was staring over by the docks. Studying the few C.U.R.S. picketers still valiantly marching in a circle in view of the road. "Jes women. That's good."

Ignoring the dig at the helplessness of her sex, Grace pulled her jacket tighter. "I don't appreciate you taking over my negotiations."

"Grace, DNA you're great at, financial negotiations you stink," he stated, as they walked against the cold wind to her lab.

She had to admit he was right. "Okay. I put half a day into Axel's work. Extract and try to replicate up to twenty samples to see if we could get anything, and do a general findings report, advising whether I think it's worth continuing any investigation. No breakdowns of the DNA, unless he wants to talk a full grant. For that, I want five thousand, I've got to replace my main refrigeration unit in my clean room."

Kurt shook his head in disgust. "That's why you have me negotiating. You'll go collect samples in New Haven. Do a preliminary survey of what the University Museum has to offer. For that, you'll want..." He looked at her. "How much will the new freezer unit cost?"

"Looks like twenty thousand and up."

"I'll have a look at that freezer. Did Jessup see it?"

"He's going to try to rebuild it..."

He frowned. "But it's old, and you can't take a chance losing your specimens. Okay, you need twenty thousand? We'll have an understanding with Jensen, that you'll go up for a day, but may have to extend the time and payment if the collection warrants it.   When you're done, you will do a verbal report to Humanity's Harvest on whether you think it might be worth attempting an extraction of DNA—and, Lady, you'd better find something that looks promising! For that, Mr. Jensen will pay travel expenses, replace you refrigeration unit with a new high-end model, and get me a new fridge for me boat."

"A refrigerator for the boat you live in, off of my work?" she asked sharply.

"Whal, I'll keep champagne in it, so when ya come over to spend a night with me, you'll have something to drink."

"He's not going to pay for that," she said.

"Then I'll have a counter-proposal for five thousand to get Bobby up there." But Kurt looked from the top of her head to her legs. "Course the way he was looking at you, he'll pay full rate."

"Oh?" Grace said. "And what if, up in New Haven, I find something that looks intriguing and looks like its DNA hasn't been sequenced before?"

"At that time, you don't talk to him, ya come tell me and let me do the renegotiating. Might be able to get him to pay for you, Bobby's full salary, and an overhaul of me lobster trawler's engine."

"Pollution wise, the E.P.A. would appreciate that," she said drily.

"What I need now is the price of a new unit for your clean room—pick high end."

She had doubts. "That'll be more than twenty thousand for one day's work, that might find nothing. He won't pay that."

"He wants the best—Humanity's Harvest will pay for it! Pick a bigger one than before, with all the bells and whistles. You can fit it in the lab."

"Kurt..." she started to argue.

"Trust me. When a guy pays more for the party boat, he thinks the fishin' is so much better."

At that Grace just gave in. "Sounds like my freezer unit is failing fast...can you go back to speak with Axel now?"

He shook his head. "Bad bargaining. Let him come to me–he will. Mr. Jensen don't let the boil cool too long, and I read him as wanting his work done now."

"When will you two gentlemen tell me what I shall be doing?" she asked with poisonous sweetness.

Kurt chuckled. "Today's Friday.   Weekend, the museum will have too many families and kids running around under yer feet, and it's probably closed Monday. Keep all of this coming Tuesday's schedule free."

Grace expected Kurt to come in and go over the lobster-blue-mold-skin regenerator study with her. Instead, he just seemed satisfied to see that she got safely to her lab. At the door, he stopped before her. "I'm taking me boat over to Little Neck this evening. Bobby's gonna be teaching your postgraduate class, then he'll come over and put his hours in working in your lab. He's gonna be waiting to walk you back to your condo."

"No, he's got a wife and family and dinner to get home to at 5:30."

"He'll wait until you leave!" Kurt said with dead finality.

She was beginning to resent this. "I'm not going to be tied in marching home on somebody else's schedule."

"Grace, these environmental loonies are taking over the peninsula. You go home with Bobby, or call ya the cops and ask Mac to escort ya home."

"Oyster River has private security."

"Who has been ordered to stand down! Grace, Mac told me some wackos in that picketers group have served time for setting laboratory animals free and setting fire to labs they were in! And Josh Jeffers is having a great time dancing with those Curs people. I went over and talked to his brother, but Greg can't rein Josh in. The fools are telling our explosive tempered boy that us scientists are poisoning the oceans, killing off the salmon, and tuna for the sheer fun of it."

"He can't believe that?" she said.

"A feller like Josh don't spend too much time fishing for reality."

This escorting business was not going to continue, but Grace didn't feel like fighting it now. "I'll go home with Bobby--tonight."

"And you won't come back alone until you go out on yer balcony and see my lobster trawler's back in the dock?"

"For today." And today only!

He moved forward to give her kiss. Annoyed at his nannying behavior she turned her face away, so Kurt just kissed her cheek, then smiling he left.

Grace looked about. Axel and Ekkeko had walked out of the Administration building and were walking to Axel's car. Did Axel see Kurt kiss her? What would he think of her relationship with Kurt? Hell, more importantly, what did she think of her relationship with Kurt?

Chapter 6

Monday, Axel Jensen dropped by her lab, no doubt making sure that this time his second-hand negotiations had actually landed him Grace. "Dr. Mackay is doing some seaweed tests for me as part of the arrangements, and I've brought this contract for you."

Grace looked at it. Typed and double-spaced it was only three-quarters of a page, obviously not written by lawyers. It stated one collection trip, with possible extension for a follow up at the discretion of both parties. Also cleared stated a generous maximum value for her new refrigeration unit. And the price of a 'specimen cooling unit' for Kurt's boat. Yhep, Kurt had vetted this. Grace noted that Axel had signed and dated it on the single line at the bottom, but there was no line for her signature. Just a handshake deal. He was signing on fully, and leaving her to honor it or not.

Those light jade eyes watched her. "If that's acceptable, tell my assistant Ekkeko the make and model of your refrigeration unit, and he'll expedite the order."

"I hadn't really picked out the exact unit, the price may be..." she started.

"I understand that you need it soon. If the price is a few thousand more, submit the estimate to Ekkeko, he'll order it immediately. If I have a problem–and I won't--I'll get back to you."

"But I haven't done your collecting yet."

Axel ignored that. "We have a mutual understanding in good faith–that's enough for Humanity's Harvest."

Grace shook her head. "You must have some interesting budgetary meetings with your Board of Directors."

He gave her a Cheshire cat smile. "I founded Humanity Harvest, and I still have a majority of the stock–for all practical purposes I am the entire Board. Now, you'll need a limo driver and what personnel will you require? I'd love to go up myself and watch you work, but unfortunately tomorrow, I'll be handing out the awards at a swim meet."

"Swim meet?"

"Yeah, years ago my neighbor sponsored me, and I made the Olympics. Had the record--for a time--in Freestyle." He smiled modestly. "Too bad it's so cold here in November."

"Come back in June," she offered. "We've got a great beach at the point."

He studied her intently. "That's a date. Now, back to this Tuesday, Kurt tells me that your assistant Bobby is teaching all day and that your other two employees are off, and he's got a previous commitment." Axel was thoughtfully continuing, "that's a big job..."

Grace corrected him. "I won't need an assistant or a limo."

Axel looked pleased. "I've notified my contacts at the University. They said to go to the ticket desk and say Dr. Roberts is expecting you." Axel handed her an index card with Robert's name and telephone numbers carefully printed. "He has been instructed to give you any assistance you'll need. Do you want me to arrange for Ekkeko to go up with you?"

Actually, having someone as anti-University museum as Ekkeko sounded like a really bad idea. "I rather just go by myself, I've been doing specimen collection for years." Oh, God, why had she said that? It made her sound so old.

* * *

She had to pass some chanting picketers on the way out of Oyster River Research, but ten A.M. Tuesday, Grace was driving up the ramp of I-95 to head up for New Haven. The interstate followed the shoreline. Lord, she remembered as a child, when except for the church steeples, the highest buildings in Stamford were three-stories high. Then it was an old seaport town of mostly shabby, but friendly grey-wood housing, and brick mill buildings. Now, with all the punched-metal appearing skyscrapers it looked like a little New York. When Stamford had asked the citizenry to provide a city motto, Kurt had submitted, "Stamford--Victim of Corporate Rape." The town fathers hadn't used it.

At the New Haven harbor--below the raised interstate--Grace saw the masts of the *Amistad* moored along the dock. A replica of an 1839 slaver, right down the road from a nine-story high, rotating experimental wind turbine in a public park. Another Connecticut seaport, with factories and warehouses for goods, now replaced by hotels, colleges, and corporate headquarters. She pulled off the ramp, then started passing the red brick and wooden gingerbread trimmed houses, that displayed a certain faded elegance under their layers of paint. She drove back streets lined with bodegas and Polish butchers, and then Federalist brick buildings. For over three hundred years, the University had been taking over more and more of the city; this was called gentrification by the Rotary, but the old time residents referred to the school's spread as metastasization.

It was tough to find a parking spot on narrow streets, but soon Grace was hauling out her three foot high, sample case with its collection equipment; thank God, they'd come up with the idea of adding wheels to these things. The University's Museum of Natural History's original building was a towered, red brick Gothic manse built in 1924. Grace went through an arched entrance in the tower and walked to the ticket desk. "My name is Grace Farrington. I believe," she looked down at the index card in her hand, "a Dr. Helmut Roberts is expecting me."

The woman on the desk made a phone call, as Grace stepped aside, to allow a mother to purchase a bunch of tickets for a dinosaur themed birthday party. Shortly she was facing a tall man, in a tan, new looking business suit. For a brief second, she thought it was Axel Jensen coming to greet her. Both had wavy sandy-hair that reached the top of their shirt collars, and Axel may have been a shade taller, maybe not, but they both had the same easy athletic build. Well, Axel wore a goatee, instead of the full beard that this younger man had, but still, there was a remarkable resemblance.

Helmut was eagerly holding out a hand to shake. "Dr. Farrington, I've heard so much about your work, your Popcorn Gene theory, and your Farrington's Fusions! You've made a tremendous impact on the field of genetics, I was expecting a much older woman."

A small woman had followed him. She looked like she might have stepped out of the display cases, a living Incan Maiden of the Sun. Beautiful skin with high cheeks, caramel brown eyes, and long, lustrous black hair. Now the hair was tied up the back with a large, butterfly-shaped barrette, and she wore a sage green pants suit. She seemed to be waiting impatiently to be introduced.

But it took a while before the gushing Helmut seemed to remember her, slightly flushing he said, "This is Inez. She works here." Inez looked in askance to him, making him quickly continue. "She hasn't gotten her Ph.D. yet, but we're working on it. Inez is an expert in ancient textiles, the preservation, repair, dating, and construction...she spins her own thread for repair. Works any looms. Dyes her own colors, from original formulas, one of the recipes needs my urine."

Now Inez looked embarrassed but seemed to be willing him to say something more. Looking at her, he knew it, but Helmut obviously just didn't know what it was she wanted. Discreetly, she raised up her graceful hands, pointing a slender index finger toward the plain gold band on her left hand. Helmut finished with a flourish. "Yeah, and we're legal! As of last month, we're married." He reached down and hugged her. "Hell, we've lived together for years, since before I went back to college, but with the baby coming..."

Grace noticed Inez's slight baby bump that she'd missed before. Inez colored, partly with embarrassment, and partly with joy at his touch. "Maybe Dr. Farrington would rather talk in your office then out here in the open lobby?"

Actually, Grace would have just preferred to get her sampling started and finished up as soon as possible, but for the best cooperation, and good basic relations one had to go through the rituals of politeness. Helmut's office was on the second floor, cramped with books, exhibit signs, and all sorts of boxes and crates in front of, behind and on shelves over his desk. For her visit, three chairs had been cleared and a pot heated in the coffee machine set on a table, also loaded with books and a human femur.

Immediately Inez asked, "Dr. Farrington, would you wish some coffee?"

"Call me Grace, please." She said, struggling to get her collection case inside. Grace didn't like coffee, but to be polite, she accepted a styrofoam cup of dark, very bitter coffee, which she tried to weaken a bit with four packets of sugar and some powder white stuff, that lightened the color but unappetizingly floated in clumps on top.

"My wife..." Helmut said it, then looked to Inez, both still seeming to marvel at their new status. "Inez made you some cookies."

Inez passed Grace a paper plate, then held out a glass platter of round cookies. She pointed to the first sandwich saying, "Alfajores. These are caramel. The dark with powder sugar are chocolate. And these are anise, with brown sugar syrup."

To be polite, Grace took one of each. The coffee was excretable, but the cookies were delicious, spicy, sweet with butter and chocolate. "These are delicious, thank you."

While Helmut took a phone call about setting up a new showing, Grace studied the cubical. Behind what was his desk, she saw several photographs. Mostly of a smiling, blond Helmut before his beard. A picture of him, young and skinny, hugging a long-haired beauty, that must be a younger Inez. A picture of Helmut in boy scout uniform, in a special flag decorated frame. When he got off the phone, she asked, "You're an Eagle Scout?"

The happiness fled from Helmut's face, making him appear much older, and sadder. "That's not me. That's my older brother, Hendrick. Hennie was a true good scout, in every sense of the words. When I dropped out of college in my last year to bum around South America, he quit a great paying job just to come and keep an eye on me." Helmut took a bracing sip of his coffee, and then said flatly, "I killed him."

A horrified Inez looked at Grace, quickly correcting, "He really didn't."

Grace could see that. Easily.

Helmut put his coffee cup down and stared at the photograph of his brother. "In South America, we were bumming from job to job. Get a little money, move on to another country. Started in Mexico and worked our way down to Peru. Cuzco, that's where I met Inez." He looked at her, and the pain in his face softened a bit. "We'd have been okay, but I met this guy. Another American, with great ambitions. Also out of college, but he was down there to get money, any way possible. " His eyes seemed to darken, with memories of the past. "Well, I wanted to marry Inez, take her back home, and go back to college. Dutch--I never knew his real name–he was into making big bucks. Said he'd cut me in on the deal, all I had to do was just drive a truck across the border a few times..." Helmut looked ashamed. "I didn't ask what was in the truck. My brother insisted on going with me, only that last time we didn't know the authorities had caught Dutch. To save himself, he turned us in. Guys with guns stopped the truck, we were surrendering, but they shot Hennie. My brother bled to death in my arms, still trying to shield me."

"You didn't kill him–it was Dutch! He betrayed you both!" said a bitter Inez angrily.

Helmut spoke almost as if he was lost in his own personal hell again. "The joke was the truck had already been unloaded. Hennie was dead, I was wounded, but they didn't find any contraband, but I was still coming up for trial, then Inez's uncle got me out on bail or bribed someone. He gave us both tickets to the U.S., and we fled. Hennie's still buried down there."

Inez reached for his hand. "He lived a good life. Your brother will always be young."

Coming out of it, Helmut shook his head. "I don't know what made me get off on that, I haven't spoken about Hennie for years. I am sorry."

If Freya were there she would have hugged him, and said something healing, but Grace wasn't Freya, so they sat there in awkward silence. Then Grace more clumsily started, "I understand that Humanity's Harvest has obtained permission for me to sample the Professor Bingham collection."

Helmut was back to himself. "Yes, we'd better hurry before we have to return it."

"You're returning...?" Grace started.

"Initially, Peru demanded four thousand artifacts back. Ones that Professor Bingham rescued from dumps and fires. Even though by our laws and theirs, those artifacts were transported as a legal transaction over a hundred years ago, the University's P.C. segment bullied our gutless Administration who caved, and we agreed to return four thousand artifacts."

Inez agreed. "They did."

As her husband continued drily, "And Peru thanked us by demanding another forty thousand."

"Do you have that?" Grace asked.

The curator smiled wickedly. "In the basement, we have the Professor Bingham's collection of native seeds. We intend to take out all those hundreds of packets, and then count each and every seed as an 'artifact.'" He laughed and looked at Inez who smiled with love for her husband. "Course even now, I can't ever go back to Cuzco."

Inez disagreed, "That is foolish. They have forgotten, you are older, and you've grown a full beard."

Helmut colored a bit. "The beard is to make me look more distinguished for career advancement. Dr. Farrington, would you like to see the Incan display, before we check the storerooms?"

Finally. Grace nodded. "It's Grace, and that would be interesting."

He indicated his cramped office. "You can leave your collection case here, for now, I'll come back for it if you need it."

The second floor Grace found was dedicated to Incan culture. Grain grinding bowls, murals, skulls, and remnants of iridescent-green parrot feather capes. Amazed at the workmanship, Grace walked down the high, curved ceiling halls, looking at glass cases that exhibited finely woven textiles, with black stylized llamas marching across the hem. At the end, she could peer inside at an elaborate diorama. It had light cinnamon colored plastered walls, with life-sized figures of an Incan noble in a flat fronted gold crown and armbands. An Inca himself? Kneeling on the floor was a model of an Inca maiden using a backstrap loom to weave intricate patterns into the woolen cloth. Another female figure also knelt to grind corn with a stone roll on a granite slab. Standing outside, looking through the glass, Grace marveled at a lost world reconstructed. "Those seeds in the baskets? From the tombs?" she asked.

Helmut looked. "Don't think so. Been here for years. They're probably real–probably soaked in rat poison, to keep away the building's rodents. I think we can safely say that's all re-creation. But we do have some actual grain samples in storage." He turned, pointing out another bank of glass cases. "But I think those vessels contain original residues from burial offerings. Would you like to sample them?"

She walked over and peered in the hollowed stone vessels. "Yes, can you get my sample case, please."

Helmut hurried off. Inez stayed with Grace, unlocking the display, to give her a better look. When he returned with her case, Grace slipped on her disposable mask, gloves and hair cap and handed the same to them. Examining each of the offering vessels, she noted out of the six, five of them seemed to have residue that she could get samples from. Inez read the descriptions off the museum signs for Grace to write down on her the control sheet as she slipped preprinted, numbered labels on her collection vials.

When they were done, Helmut closed up the case by struggling with the old, heavy glass lid, as he explained, "In the 1920's they built this section of the museum just to house the Incan collection. Professor Bingham collected everything he could, wanting artifacts that furthered the understanding of the indigenous culture, of all the South American civilizations. This particular exhibit hall is aimed for pure education, but the professor knew what brings in the crowds."

Helmut walked towards a glass case, jutting out from the wall, built chest high. Only three feet wide, maybe two foot tall, it was suspended from the wall. As Grace got closer, she could see a varnished wood frame, with antique, beveled glass insets. Inside was a ghoulishly fascinating object.

Chapter 7

A human's mummified arm, from fingers to the shoulder. No Egyptian style bandages wrapping on it, just taut gray-blueish skin, looking a bit like an overcooked turkey leg. Probably naturally freeze-dried in the mountain ranges. There was a heavy, polished, gem-studded, golden bracelet encircling the upper arm. The upper shoulder part was propped up a bit, its raw end covered with the faded maroon velvet that lined the box, and at the other end, the hand and fingers curved away, but Grace could see nails still attached. "Is this real?"

"Oh, yes. We always get some flack from the politically correct crowd, for exhibiting human remains, but it's been in that case since the late 1920's. I think 'Arnie' here is probably the most viewed exhibit in the museum. Big with the kids."

"How did you get it?" asked Grace.

"It's supposed to be the arm of a high noble lord from Peru. Possibly a close relative of the Inca, or an Inca himself. That's corroborated by the care taken in preparing the body for mummification and the jeweled solid gold bracelet on the arm. Note the clear, highly colored emerald carbuncles. Large stones. Obviously owned by an individual of extreme wealth, high in their society."

She bent closer to view the arm. "Man or woman? It seems to be small boned?"

"But probably male, judging from his status in the society. It is small boned, but the Incas were a very compact race."

Grace looked at the arm's end, covered by a fold of the dusty velvet the arm rested on. "DNA could determine the sex, but how did it get here?"

"When the conquistadores superimposed their religion on the native population, they either destroyed the native religious artifacts or incorporated them into the Catholic

Church. This was an arm–perhaps a whole mummy--that in pre-Colombian times was venerated as part of Incan ancestor worship. To maintain contact between the living and the realm of gods at crisis times, these mummified remains were brought out to the village square, where they could be dressed, 'fed,' and worshiped properly. Propitiating the spirits of the powerful lords for the people's protection."

"But just an arm?"

"We don't know what happened to the rest of the body, but existing documentation states, that in times of hardship, this arm was displayed to calm the populace. Just as the Catholic Cathedrals were built over the foundations of Incan temples, the arm apparently was taken into the church as a 'saint's' relic, to be worshiped by further generations of the faithful.

"But in the early 1900's, the Catholic fathers apparently felt their hold over the people was strong enough that they could purge the more outrageous pagan elements. At that time, Professor Bingham managed to purchase a number of the pre-Colombian religious artifacts. Apparently, he just saved this arm from the purifying flames."

Grace looked at all that remained of what once might have been a ruler of thousands, even worshiped as a god after his death. She wanted to know more of this personage, without thinking of consequences she said, "I'd like to try to get a sample from that arm."

"Sample?" Helmut sounded surprised. "Why?"

"If I could get culturalable DNA, we could confirm the sex. We might discover eye and hair color, uncover tendencies to hereditary diseases, perhaps even pinpoint a member of the royal Incan bloodline. It could be a fascinating look at a vanished civilization."

Helmut didn't sound too thrilled with the idea. "What would that entail? Would you just scrape a little bit of the skin off?"

"No. The exterior probably would have been contaminated by skin cells from dozens of hands over all these centuries." She bent down and opened the equipment case. "I assume there is still a bone inside that arm?"

Helmut just stared at the case. "Probably...I don't think they would've taken it out."

From her collecting case, she took out her smallest drill. "If I could find a small hole–and insert the drill in, about this diameter," she held her fingers less than an eighth of an inch apart. "reaching the bone and boring out a small core."

Inez was eagerly pushing. "If she did it from underneath, nobody would ever see it."

Grace could see the curator was embarrassingly torn. Yes, he wanted the information she might be able to develop for him, but damaging a prize exhibit went against his guardianship of the museum's treasures. Even Grace had to admit her endless curiosity did carry her away sometimes. So she gave him an out, "But you have to get permission from your superiors. Pass on in my request, and perhaps sometime, when I'm up here again, we can do a sampling." She let it politely trail off, returned her drill, and started walking to see the rest of the South American collection.

They walked back along the cases, seeing remnants of green parrot fans, and ceramic bowls of dried up, dark gray bulbs, hand-woven baskets holding corn cobs, and fantastic, intricate gold work. Incan. Moche. Aztec obsidian sacrificial blades. Now Helmut eagerly offered to open any of the cases and take out anything she wished to handle and sample. Then they started into the back, storage areas of the museum. Behind the exhibits, up narrow, circular stairs to attic bays, he hauled up her bulky collection case. Grace saw Professor Bingham's photo albums of Peruvians in native costumes and close up prints of their amazing stonework.

There were drawers of pinned, shiny-bright blue

butterflies, and sections of various vines wrapped into thick rope cables. It seemed the professor wanted to preserve everything and anything. Then Helmut carried her collection case down the tower stairs to a green-metal, old-fashioned scrolled iron cage elevator, that creaked and clacked its way to the basement. There was more custom built cabinets for Bingham's collections after collections. One whole five food high cabinet, with narrow shelves, protected wool fibers–llama, alpaca, vicuña. "Vicuña?" Grace asked.

Helmut explained, "A rarer, smaller, more endangered version of a llama-like an animal, probably distantly related to the camel. The vicuña's extremely soft wool is highly prized. It may be the ancestor of the alpacas." Grace pulled on another set of disposable gloves again, to take multiple fiber samples from a selection of all animals fibers in the drawers. Inez was helping her now, by writing down the origin descriptions that related to the number placed on the sample's clear plastic envelope.   At first, Grace rechecked her work, but it was obvious that Inez's hand lettering was perfectly legible, and that the woman was as meticulous as Inger about keeping the numbered order faultlessly correct.

They were collecting a lot, but Grace was well aware that Axel was looking for more than just an ancient nutritional source. She didn't really see a basic DNA that could be manipulated for the benefit of mankind.   What she was getting was small, dried kernels of blue maize and chili seeds. She took two or three blackened potato samples, but they seemed too far gone for any viable sampling. Moisture over time usually killed DNA. And heat didn't do it much good either. This room held drawers of grass seeds in small, tan paper envelopes, and Grace was beginning to recognize Professor Bingham's concise notations in his well-rounded copperplate handwriting.

God, Professor Bingham must have written up

hundreds of samples at day! So strange. The man had been dead for almost a century, but he was now communicating directly with her, almost as if he was standing at her shoulder, eagerly watching to see what she would discover, wanted to further unwrap the next set of secrets in the collection he had so lovingly preserved.

But as the hours grew longer, Grace had to admit none of these samples were labeled '*Royal Food.*' No shriveled potato or rock like bulb looked like an unrecognized miracle plant that Axel Jensen wanted, one that increased the life force and vital years of the noble Inca.

Still, Grace was sent here to collect samples and that she would do, setting about raising yet another choking cloud of dust on yet another cabinet full of trays. She pulled on another pair of latex gloves and started to put self-adhesive numbered labels on tiny glass vials, calling out the two alpha six-digit number, as Inez carefully lettered the items origin on the corresponding control sheet.

Helmut offered to treat her to lunch at a nearby restaurant, but Grace put him off, she didn't want to stop her work. She willingly would have skipped lunch to get done with this sooner, but at two Inez went out and brought back cokes, spicy fried chicken, and flaky biscuits in red striped boxes, refusing to take any payment from Grace. The three of them ate perched on packing crates in the dusty basement. Actually, with honey butter, the food tasted quite good. Soon Grace could return to work with renewed hopefulness she might find a super seed. And as Grace started back down the rows of specimen cabinets, she could hear Inez whispering to Helmut. His wife seemed to be working on him for Grace to sample that mummy's arm.

The museum was officially closed two hours before Grace could strip off her hair cap, mask, and endless pairs of disposable gloves as she packed away the last of her samples. Tired, with a slight headache from the gritty dust, she was more than ready to head back home, fairly certain that Axel was getting nothing of practical interest for his considerable investment, and that thought depressed her. She had completed the letter of her contract, beyond it, but she would have liked to have brought him some small discovery, or just something that might at least looked promising. And Grace wished she could have gotten a sample from that mummified arm.

But Inez wasn't giving up so easily. "Hellie, it is for science. It will give the museum more knowledge of one of our most valuable exhibits. It could make the arm even more treasured."

Grace shouldn't have gotten this started. "But we don't have permission. Another time." The young curator's face finally slipped from reluctance to acceptance. "Actually, the Chancellor has given you complete access to anything you want from the collection. He's a fan of your work, Dr.–Grace... And of course, Humanity's Harvest is giving us a substantial grant to re-organize and digitalize the collection."

With growing excitement, Grace followed him upstairs to the small windowed display bay, that stuck out from the wall, almost floating. There was no door hinge she could see. "Is there access from the rear?"

"No–that's a solid masonry wall," said Helmut, studying it from all angles.

"How do you get into the case?" Grace asked.

Helmut seemed reluctant to take the next step, but Inez was pushing, "She'd only be taking a small piece. A tiny hole. She could do from the end, covered by cloth–or maybe where the bracelet covers the arm?"

Grace waited. She really wanted this–but she wouldn't push it.

Inez continued. "Dr. Farrington's work is famous. Just think of what secrets she might be able to unlock for us!"

"Well..." Helmut still seemed reluctant.

"Dr. Madayo said to give her full cooperation," Inez reminded him.

"Yes, but..."

"We could learn so much from the artifact," Inez pleaded. "That is what Professor Bingham wished when he kept it from being burned."

"Yes," Helmut agreed, getting down on the floor, looking up underneath the case. "Grace, do you have a slot screwdriver in that collection case?"

She did. Grace pulled on another set of disposable gloves and mask, while he was carefully unscrewing the base of the display. But to their disappointment, without the screws, the base still stayed attached. Helmut had to thump it firmly until it broke free, and the three of them gently lowered it to the floor. It came with a musty smell of age as Grace gently pulled back the velvet covering the shoulder end. Here the skin had been ripped away, leaving a dried, fiber-like muscle and the edge of the bone. Could this have been a battle wound? If she made her insertion here, she wouldn't be cutting the outer skin. The arm was heavier than it looked, even accounting for that solid gold armband with the large emeralds. Through her latex gloves, it felt smooth and solid, but the dried skin powdered a bit when touched or was that dust of the centuries? There must be solid, untouched bone inside.

She, Helmut and Inez discussed possible entries, then finally agreed on an appropriate site in the arm's muscle bundle at the chopped shoulder end. Grace readied a coring rod, screwing in an extender section. With Helmut and Inez looking like worried parents, Grace started with a long, sharp awl to make the initial cut, then firmly pushed in the drill point, praying she hit bone on the first insertion. She drove in the point, getting a stiff resistance, probably dried, rotted muscle fiber. No bone. Grace twisted, pushing harder.

Then she hit something solid. Taking her rubber hammer, she lightly tapped the rod's end. And using quite a bit of her strength Grace pressed down on that rod until she felt something give. Trying desperately not to drive right through the narrow bone, she rotated the drill slowly, trying for as much material as she could get. From the look of conflict on Helmut's face, Grace didn't dare go for a second insertion. God, she hoped she'd gotten something.

She was packing up her collection case again, as Helmut and Inez waited. "I'm sorry to keep you here so late."

"When can you tell us anything on the arm?" Inez asked eagerly.

Grace smiled. "I'm sorry, but if we have anything, it'll be weeks before it's cultured and on the computers. But I'll send you a copy of anything that develops as soon as I can."

Helmut politely offered to carry her heavy case out to her car. When they reached the lobby, Inez looked expectantly at Helmut, as if urging him to say something more, but he just unlocked the museum entrance. Finally, Inez gave up and hesitantly started, "Helmut's always been interested in the Oyster River Facility. We go down that way sometimes...maybe we could see your laboratory?"

That was it, Grace certainly owed them, so she immediately said, "Of course. Let me know when, and I'll give you a tour."

"That would be wonderful." Inez smiled brightly, looking at her husband, who also seemed to be happy, but reluctant to say anything else, so the wife started again. "When could we do that?"

Grace thought about it. "Actually, this Thursday, Oyster River has a reception for the public announcement of Dr. Huang Wong's contract with Humanity's Harvest. It will be at the Roost, that's the big Italianate Mansard roofed villa on the peninsula's entrance, starting at 7:00 p.m."

Not looking happy, Helmut turned to Inez. "Then you can't go. You have a class."

"You will go alone," she stated firmly.

"Not without you..." he started.

But Inez looked to Grace. "Since it is Humanity's Harvest's grant, will Senor Axel Jensen be there?

"I can't promise that, but I think so," confirmed Grace.

That overcame Helmut's reticence, but he sounding worried as he asked, "Do I need a tuxedo?"

Inez quickly cut in, "We can rent one."

Grace laughed. "It's not that formal.   Most of the men there will be coming from work, in business suits or sports coats. It's just a formal announcement of the grant. Hopefully, press people, a few deadly dull speeches, then a wine bar and some hors-d'oeuvres."

"At an important reception, all the big donors will be there won't they?" Inez's eyes were shining as she looked proudly at her husband. "It'll be important for your career." Then she looked at Grace and blushed.   "I'm sorry, I shouldn't have said that..."

Grace only smiled. "Networking with people is the only reason for attending one of these boring 'parties.' And if Helmut's comes, I can introduce him to the scientists at ORR, and maybe some of our directors and donors, but you've got to know, I'm just terrible with faces and names."

Inez smiled at her husband. "Hellie, you will be mingling with important people! Making connections...our baby will have a well-connected father!"

Even Helmut smiled at that.

Chapter 8

The sky over the harbor was black with sharp stars, as she drove into Oyster River, but the protestors were still out there. Seemed to be fewer marchers than before, and they were staying on the grass. But their camping tents by the docks were gone, and Grace realized why when she passed Ben and his parked police car. Maybe picketers shouldn't have been thrown out, they were really harmless Grace thought, then she heard yelling, and saw a raised fist shaking at her and the angry face of Josh Jeffers. "STOP POISONING MY FOOD!"

Grace drove a quarter of a block and parked in front of her lab. One of the protestors, a fortyish woman, had run after her, and as Grace was walking in, the woman crossed into the street screaming at her, "NO MORE GENETICALLY ENGINEERED FOOD!"

Angry Grace realized this was her lab, her home, she shouldn't be scudding away in fear. She turned and spoke louder than she had intended, "If you don't want it–don't buy it!"

The woman was getting uncomfortably close, she had lowered her voice, but not her intensity. "You've made deals with politicians on the take! Genetically modified plants aren't marked! In some places, by law, organic farmers are not even allowed to put 'non-genetically modified' on the label!"

"That's changing I think, but that's an issue to talk with your legislators, not scientists!" Grace didn't know what further to say but didn't have to. Ben, in his patrolman's uniform, was marching up to the protestor. "This is private property, mam. You are allowed to picket at the entrance! Anywhere else and you are going to jail." The woman backed off.

Deciding not to be scared off, Grace walked back to

her car and hauled out her heavy collection case before heading inside. The lab door was unlocked, and she stopped. That lab should be locked. That did make her a little nervous. Nick was in Albany for a family wedding, and right now Inger should be in her Latin class. Should Grace retreat and call ORR security?

More waste of time! Grace opened the door and marched in with her collection case.

A male Her height. Sitting facing the other direction. Solid build. Dark hair, light skin. Making himself at home in her lab. Hearing her, Bobby turned around. He was sitting on one of the desks reading a thriller and obviously waiting for her.

"It's eight-thirty," Grace said tiredly, "why aren't you home for dinner?"

"Thought I'd wait and walk with you."

"I plan to work," she said stubbornly.

Bobby's face turned down, but he was game. "Yeah, I wanted to review some of your slides for the class you'll be lecturing next week."   He reached over and took the collection case from her, to carry into the Air Lock suiting up room.

"You're a poor liar. Kurt stuck you here to walk me home?"

At the insult, he just gave a lopsided grin. "Actually, it was my own idea. Well, with a little pushing from Sara, you know it's getting dark really early."

Grace looked at him and thought about that crazy woman outside. It had been a long day, and he was probably as tired and hungry as she was. "Okay. Just let me suit up and refrigerate these samples, and then I'll walk home with you. I can do my e-mails from my apartment, but this is not going to be an everyday thing! I see that the picketers' tents are gone, that's progress."

Bobby shook his head, sounding really angry. "Nope.

Adam's been negotiating. The protestors have had to move their tents to the woods area at the end of the Point. And since the bushes around here had begun to smell a bit gamy, our courageous Mr. Commander-in-charge has rented two port-a-johns for their convenience."

"Oh, God." Grace had just about had it.

Like the New England weather, Bobby went from dark stormy to a warm sunshine almost instantly. "Want me to suit up and stash the samples, while you set the assignment logs up for Inger and Nick?"

"Thanks, Bobby, that would be great. Then we'll head home, I promise."

With the collection case in tow, he headed off to suit up. Even through the first layer of air pressure controlled doors, she could hear him working inside. Giving her a few precious minutes to complete her logs.

"Dr. Farrington?" a male voice spoke.

Definitely, on edge, Grace looked up in alarm. Had the protestors breached her lab walls? When David Gardiner had wanted to install a buzz-open security door for her, she should have said yes. But looking up, she relaxed recognizing the tall, blond figure of Axel Jensen, in a dark blue business suit.

Then she stiffened again. This man was not Axel, he had the same wavy, sandy hair, he stood over six foot. He could've been Axel's younger brother, but this man didn't have the van dyke beard, he was clean shaven. Although he carried himself with the same proud, almost arrogant walk, he was a little thinner, less muscular. Younger perhaps. This was the second time she had mistaken a man for Axel Jensen today, Grace must have Axel imprinted on her brain. She'd better calm down and focus!

This man had something in his hand, but Grace was relieved to see it was only a standard, black leather briefcase.

"You are?" A nervous Grace asked a trifle too frostily.

"Daniel Novinski, a lawyer." He gave her a bright smile. "Quite harmless, honest."

"With Curs?"

He hesitated, then chose his terms precisely, "More currently 'associated' with them, then counsel of." Daniel delineated further, "C.U.R.S.'s main thrust is in animal rights protection, while my core focus is the food chain and opposing dangerous alterations. I'm the founder and executive director of 'The International Food Web Center Foundation.' We monitor the technology that is altering the food chain."

"Monitor?"

"Study. Understand. Explain it in non-technical terms to the public that's been drafted as unpaid, unconsenting guinea pigs."

"What if those advancements are beneficial?"

"My foundation does try to promote best practices–in sanitation, in food chain delivery, and in nutritional enhancement."

"Yet you're demonstrating with Curs?"

"My foundation also politically opposes unwise or dangerous additives at the grassroots level." He stopped. "May I come over, so we don't have to raise our voices? It's okay..." Daniel reassured her. "I haven't thrown blood on anyone today yet."

"You approve of those tactics?" Grace asked tartly.

"Actually, no." He could have just walked over, but he was politely waiting at about ten feet from her.

Grace gave in. "Please." She indicated one of the two chairs in front of her desk for her visitors. Like Axel, this tall blond man had that charming manner that made you want to smile along with him. Now he said, "I've spoken up to Astrid quite a bit about her tactics. Unfortunately, to mold public opinion, there is a definite need for publicity, but sometimes the 'acting out' manages to obscure the importance of the message." Daniel finished, as he sat down before her.

She didn't reach out to shake his hand, but he just ignored that, giving her a comfortable, easy smile, with wide, even white teeth as he continued. "Those people outside, with the chants and placards. The ones shivering in tents out on the point, they may be a little over the top, but they feel very passionately about something that's nearly out of their control. Give them credit, they're peaceably demonstrating to save their–and your--world."

"Ever bother to research and understand what you're opposing first ?" Grace asked.

"Actually, I have. I've written several books on Genetic Engineering. The first, *Grow Your Own* was on sustainable agriculture. I did one on the Green Movement, *Sustainable*. Another on the dangers of giving control over the world's food reserves to people only interested in profit, *Mass Marketers–Hogging The Food Chain*." He opened a black leather briefcase and took out a 'coffee table' oversized book and placed it on her desk. The full-color cover showed an adorable baby, drinking milk from a bottle, but the bottle had a skull and crossbones on it. In huge red letters, the book was titled "*Genetic Engineering---What They Won't Tell You!*' This is a--very popularized–view of G.E. I would like you to read it."

She didn't take it, asking coolly. "You think I'm unaware of the science of genetic engineering?"

He flushed, but then laughed easily. "No, actually I know you're credited with pioneering many of the DNA processing techniques that make genetic engineering possible." He leaned back a little, studying her. "But I was wondering if you are as well versed in the nutritional and political ramifications of a movement that could revolutionize the way we feed ourselves."

"You're against that?"

"With few exceptions, most revolutions leave the

common people worse off than they were before."

She looked down at her desk, "I'll glance over your book. How will I get it back to you?"

"It's been signed to you. It's yours." He started to rise.

"How long do your friends plan to stay out picketing?"

Still, utterly charming, the Greek god looking, man, just shrugged, "I'm not included in the strategy planning--by my choice. Thank you for your time, Dr. Farrington. Hopefully, we can talk again."

He was starting to walk to the door when Grace heard the police sirens.

Chapter 9

Grace rushed outside without her jacket, with Daniel hurrying ahead. Deep in the clean room, Bobby probably couldn't hear the sirens. The night's dense blackness was formidable, so a little scary, and Grace found herself wrapping her goose bumping arms around her chest as the cold hit. Daniel left her behind, taking long-legged strides heading toward the small group of protestors under the big security spotlight on ORR's dock. That dock was further illuminated by the white and blue light bars atop three police cars.

Also in those headlamps were about ten, maybe twenty motorcycles; getting closer Grace could recognize the helmets and leather jackets. This was a mixed bunch of biker clubs and biker gangs. Young, skinhead Turks, and gray beards, all drinking buddies of Kurt from the Alpine Bar and Grill. Now Curs demonstrators and bikers were shouting at each other. Josh Jeffers was menacingly waving a placard nailed to a solid looking 2"x 2" in front of the mountain of motorcyclist that was Kurt's friend, Wayne. A biker near Wayne was wearing a Prussian officer's helmet, with its spear pointed top. Kurt MacKay, three worried looking security guards, and two cops seemed to be the only thing standing between the warring parties. This was just what ORR needed, no, the press hadn't shown up to the party yet! But as Grace stood across the road, watching and shivering from the cold, Bobby, still in disposal cap, gloves, and booties joined her saying, "What the hell's going on?"

Definitely what an erupting fight did not need was Bobby Jamison's flash temper, so Grace quickly said, "Did you finish refrigerating the samples?"

"Yeah. But the compressor in the main unit sounds terrible."

"There's a new unit on order." She had to get Bobby out of there. "Let's close up the lab, and go home, Sara will be waiting." Bobby took one last look at the mass of angry picketers and anti-demonstrators and then moved off with her. Being a father of three had really settled him down a lot. She was successfully getting Bobby away when Grace heard an excited voice coming up beside her.

"What this?" Waving his arms, Dr. Huang Wong looked about. "This wrong! No fights–my research facility!"

For a brief moment, Grace wanted to throw Huang to Wayne and the boys, then her better nature reasserted itself. "Nothing is happening. Let's just leave and let the cops take care of it."

Huang spoke in an agitated voice, "Where Adam? First yellers! Now bike gangers! This not right!"

Grace decided to try and distract him. "Are the greenhouses are finished?"

"Yes, all finished!" He pronounced and then promptly contradicted himself. "Still need fix floor. Tanks leak! No good here!"

"But your tanks are operating? Is your F_1 generation growing?" Grace asked.

"Why you ask?" he said suspiciously. "This my project! You don't nose in!"

Actually, the newly rebuilt greenhouses were to be used by all scientists at Oyster River, on a rotating need basis, but Grace just commented, "It's been my experience that new technical equipment, especially plumbed works, often need adjusting before they function optimally."

"No, mine must work!" Huang pointed at picketers-police-bikers. "Now! You make trashy people go away!"

Saying that he stomped off, and as Bobby finished locking up her lab, more police were arriving. Yes, for Grace, it seemed a great time to just go home and forget all of this! Back in her condo, she was deciding between a frozen dinner or a box of deluxe cheese and macaroni when she heard a knock on her door. Grace had an irrational jolt of fear–would a placard carrying extremist be knocking at her door? Another hate letter writer? Or maybe a furious member of the biker gangs? Normally Grace never even bothered to lock the door of her condo, now she reluctantly walked to it.

At the door, Grace hesitated for a second, then called out as sternly as she could, "Who is there?"

"Jack the Raper." Came the laconic reply from the other side. Then he pulled the door open. A man. Not too tall, worn leather biker jacket, and bike helmet in hand, Kurt MacKay.

"Damn it–you scared me!" she said.

"This door unlocked? With you getting threatening letters?" he looked stern.

How did he know about the letters? Grace found herself flushing. "Well, the door never needs to be...how did you know about the letters?"

"Got one meself on me boat. You report yours?"

"No."

"Grace, you got to take these fools seriously! They put sugar in gas tanks. They burn down labs!"

He still glared at her as he threw his helmet on her daybed couch. "The entry lock to the lobby downstairs is broken."

"I know, Sara kept locking her self out, with one kid still inside the hall, so it got broken, and we decided not to have fixed."

He looked at her grimly. "Great."

"What happened with the great Picketers vs. Biker showdown?"

"Nothing, but I was surprised to see Mother Farrington jes walking away?"

"Figured you could handle it."

"I was little outnumbered," he pointed out.

She wasn't impressed. "What did the Texas Rangers always say '*one riot, one ranger.*'

Kurt grinned wickedly at that. "Aaup."

Grace walked back to her kitchen nook. "I'm tired. Tired of picketers, tired of worrying about grants, and organizational politics. Huang was out there thinking I want to steal his slimy algae, so since I didn't hear anyone getting shot, I figured you guys could work things out on your own."

"We did," he said mildly.

She pulled out a pot to heat water for the macaroni, he'd probably be staying. "Why did you get a bunch of outlaw bikers involved?"

"Pictures of the picketers were marching across the screen on the Alpine bar's television, so the guys showed up–uninvited–to give a show of force to support me. Wayne says he's been worried about you being alone when me boat is out."

"Oh, no..." It was a kind thought, but she didn't need the gentle giant's guarding.

"I give the word, and he could be persuaded to sit in your lab, or stake out your condo entrance, and protect yer against a mad attack by the pamphlet wavers."

"No! Absolutely not." Grace started opening the box of macaroni and threw the foil cheese packet in the water to heat up. "Is this going to be in the papers?"

"Whal, only one reporter showed up as things were winding down. That foxy looking, red-headed Samantha Carson."

"Sam? Oh..."

"Probably won't get published. She couldn't get a cameraman here in time, and with it darkening, she couldn't get any decent pictures on her cell phone. So, if we're lucky, some house will have had a gas leak, blow up the entire neighborhood, and take over the front page from the Battle of Oyster River Research."

"You want dinner?" she asked.

"Macaroni, naw, let's go out. Taking the bike over to

the Alpine, we can have chili, while I buy a few rounds to thank the guys for showing up." Getting behind her Kurt put his arms around her waist. "Got an extra helmet on the bike." He nuzzled ear. "Coming with me?"

Actually, that did have its appeal, but although Grace didn't really want to be alone, she also didn't want to face a smoky bar full of loud motorcyclists. "No, thank you."

He turned to pick up his helmet and leave.

Grace realized she didn't want that. They both were usually comfortably leading solitary lives, but tonight she didn't want to be alone. "Do you really have to go?" Grace asked softly and reading her tone, his quiet, dark eyes turned back to her, as she continued. "You know when I was nearly killed, we decided we had to make time for each other. Maybe not tonight, but soon..."

Putting the helmet back down again, Kurt leaned up against her, taking his hands and running them up her arms. "Now let me think this over.   You and I could get comfortable, eat something, then I could take yer blouse off, run my calloused fingers up and down, feeling some softness, or I could go to the Alpine. There I could run my hands along Wayne's hairy muscles." Kurt gave a small leering smile. "This may be a hard choice, I may have to think about it for awhile, you may have to tell me what yer truly offering if I stay," he said closing his big hands on her shoulders, kissing her slowly.

They left his helmet sitting on top of the bookcase by the door.

* * *

The next day in her lab Grace checked the samples from New Haven. Some of them were developing well, but nothing that she felt Humanity's Harvest would consider a possible miracle plant, still she would really love to see what she would get out of those burial vessel residues.   And that intriguing mummy's arm. Would she owe Axel a refund if they found nothing? Better speak to Kurt about that, what had he negotiated for her?

But she wound up speaking to Axel first. That afternoon, taking off aviation sunglasses, that totally magnetic man was standing before her desk. "Grace, have you heard about your new refrigeration unit? Ekkeko tells me it should be installed by the end of the week."

Yes, under Kurt's prodding Grace had picked out the highest end to start the bargaining and Axel apparently signed off on a sub-zero unit with no defrosting, full battery back up, remote temperature monitoring control online, and even glass doors. That it was coming in, while her old unit was just hanging on meant Humanity's Harvest got a lot faster service than she'd ever managed. "Thank you, it's marvelous. I just wish I could be more hopeful about the New Haven samples for you. I'm continuing to process sixty or so that look like undocumented species, but I really don't think any of them will be what you are looking for. I'm very sorry, I think I owe you some money back...."

"No, you certainly do not. Grace, it's alright, the importance is we looked." Sitting on her desk Axel didn't look that disappointed, and Grace found herself concentrating on the magnificent thigh line of his in those now tight pants, as he continued talking. "We'll have to extend your contract, we were only paying for twenty samples being worked up, I'll talk with Kurt. Do you think it would be worth another trip to New Haven?"

She shook her head. "Not unless we had a better idea of what we're looking for. The—what was his name? The curator is going to look through some of the unopened cases, and let me know if he thinks he has anything different for me to sample." Grace stood up, stretching stiffly from her hours in front of the computer as she joined him.

"What did you think of the curator?" Axel asked.

That guy had hauled that heavy collection case up and

down those spiral tower steps, he had been so accommodating, so eager to be of service, Grace should give him a glowing report. "Very helpful, knowledgeable, Dr....uh...uh...Harry...Henry..."

Embarrassed Grace stumbled over his name, and Axel supplied it. "Helmet Roberts."

"Yes. Helmet. He seems to be a very thorough young man, with a great interest in the Bingham collection and South American botany. He and his wife made themselves so very useful as assistants. If you speak to their director, please mention that her name was...." With all her supposed genius, Grace always had such trouble identifying people.

"Inez," Axel supplied chuckling. "My third wife, the inventor, had an IQ they couldn't even measure, and she could never remember names either."

Grace nodded and continued, "I believe Helmut will be attending the public announcement of Humanity Harvest's contract with Huang at ORR. I'd like you to meet him. "

Axel nodded, but he was already thinking of his research. "But probably the best venue for getting what I want would be to do research in the South American highlands. Actually, I've planned an expedition in February, which I would like to employ your services for a couple of months."

"Too much time off," she demurred, going back to the protection and professionalism of her desk.

"How about taking even more time off? After our expedition to Peru, I've chartered an icebreaker, and I'm taking a private party to Antarctica just to look around." His dancing green eyes stared deeply into hers. "Do you ever travel just for pleasure, Grace?"

She gave that a thought. "I've always wanted to see Antarctica, a place with probably almost no DNA."

"Come with me."

What was this handsome man offering? Grace

couldn't think of a delicate way to phrase it, so she just blurted out, "What would the sleeping arrangements be?"

Sitting on her desk, he leaned in closer. "That's entirely up to you. There are seven luxury staterooms for my guests. But there is also an opening for you in the master stateroom in the bow, but you'd have to share the king sized bed with me."

Grace found herself blushing like a teenager. "I've been planned to do it that sometimes–Antarctica that is."

"I've got the boat."

Thinking of Freya endlessly dreaming a traveling someday, Grace asked, "What if I wanted to bring a guest with me to share a stateroom?"

He pulled a long face, "I'd be disappointed, but you're still welcome with a guest, and he could share your stateroom."

She didn't bother to correct him, it was an offer hard to refuse. So who was being invited? Dr. Grace Farrington? Or Grace, the woman? Or both? All Grace knew was she wanted to say yes but had to think about this. And she wanted the conversation to get off the personal question, back to waters she was comfortable with, "What do you really expect to find on your Peru trip?"

He stopped to think of that. "With the goal of engineering a hardy, drought-resistant maize line for its maximum nutritional value, I want to find a wild legacy plant, maybe even find the 'food of the Inca God' that could be spliced into its domesticated cousins?"

Grace thought about that. "Actually I've been reading about more success with adding domestic characteristics to the hardier wild varieties."

"That's what I want to know. Tell me, Grace, for inserting genes in an embryonic state, to you prefer bacteria insertion or gene gun?"

"I have problems with both. Especially with the

antibiotic markers needed and the imperfect delivery. I'm much happier with the CRISPR method using RNA to guide a gene-editing platform to a particular place within a genome."

"That does?" He looked fascinated.

"Cuts out a section if you wish, and could insert a replacement sequence."

"My scientists have mentioned CRISPR." Those sea-green eyes studied her carefully. "But do you have something better in mind?"

Grace found herself cowardly staring down at her desk. Yes. She had been thinking of something better for a number of years, a better way to splice and insert alleles, but it hadn't quite jelled to the point she wanted to formulate a test. And, as Grace unfortunately, learned early in her career, that sharing of her thoughts prematurely could leave her open to having her discoveries pirated. "My ideas on delivery vectors are not ready prime time yet."

"But you are working on something?" His instant concentration and the speed that he went from a silly flirtatiousness conversation to a focused, intensive business application unsettled her. "Of course you can, with your Farrington's fusions. Humanity's Harvest stands ready to fund your research in that area."

She raised her hand, to halt the onsault of his intensity. "What I do would be pure research, something that most corporations are not willing to support anymore. I couldn't promise to develop an application that would be useful to you."

"I wouldn't expect you to. My own people would be tasked with continuing your research, and perhaps find practical applications, but your track record in DNA pioneering is unequaled. Remember, I'm not in business only to make money–that helps–but I'm also trying to make this world a better place. You come up with a better vector for genetic engineering, Humanity's Harvest would see it will be treated as 'open source,' with anybody free to use it."

"But..." She started to shake her head.

"Just tell me how much you need to work on it? A grant will be arranged.   No pay back.   No need for justification on how you spend it."

What he was offering was generous support for her science, and on the personal side, that more intriguing trip was still on the table. She glanced at the clock. "Would you like to join me for lunch in the cafeteria? We could talk further."

Axel looked at his sports Rolex, then shook his head. Looking back into her eyes, he said, "I'd love to–but I've spent more time with Dr. Huang here than I'd planned. I've got to be off." He stopped and looked at her. "You know–I always plan to spend some time talking with you, about us. Something besides genetic engineering or my corporate problems. But I'll be back for the reception tonight. Think about my offer.   Both of them.   We'll talk again."

Then he was gone, and although she usually regretted the time any socializing costs her, with him gone, her laboratory actually felt a bit empty.

Chapter 10

That evening, Grace dressed in a simple black cocktail dress, with a pearl and jade necklace for the public announcement of Huang's grant. God, it was getting dark so fast now, and the wind off the Harbor had a wet chill that pierced her jacket. As she walked to the reception, Grace didn't see the demonstrators' tents under the street light by the dock. Maybe they'd given up and left?

There were two police cruisers parked up by the entrance. Adam must be paying for their overtime. One would be directing traffic from the main road. The other? She figured the back kitchen wing of the Roost would be locked up, so Grace stayed on the road until she rounded the front of the building. There, under the building's decorative lighting, she found the demonstrators. Under a patrolman's watchful eye, they stood behind four information tables. The first held stacks of pamphlets and brochures on animal cruelty, the horrors of Genetic Engineering, and mankind caused Global Warming.

Glaring at her from above pictures of maimed dogs and starving horses was that friend of Freya's. Alice? Anna? The demonstrators were silent, probably that was the deal Adam had made to allow the tables here. Just to be polite Grace glanced over the tables as she passed, the next had stacks of books for sale. She recognized the lawyer's anti-genetic engineering one and a few more of his food chain books, but no tall lawyer. Actually, she wished Daniel was here. A lawyer's careful and reasoned voice would keep things calm with the other demonstrators. But Grace was relieved not to see Josh Jeffers. That was one good thing this night.

The last table by the steps was very artistically arranged. A blue tablecloth had been spread with an old fishing net. Inserted in it were dried starfish, shells, small plastic fish, and a red spear gun. Tucked under a spear shaft were two pamphlets. One contrasting beautiful, freely swimming salmon near a school of tightly packed 'farmed fish.' The other brochure showed a child weeding rows of corn, with his grandfather for 'sustainable agriculture.' So much time and such care lavished to stop change, it depressed Grace feeling that these people were rather like children kneeling on a beach, trying to keep rebuilding a dam to stop the incoming tide from washing away their sand castle.

Still, she just smiled tightly at the eager activists, even picked up the salmon brochure, knowing that she was just putting off going inside. Finally, Grace decided she had to get it over with, and she climbed up the wooden steps to yet another social ordeal. Always hating receptions, hating any large groups of people, and she dreaded being publicly displayed. At the door, police uniformed Mac Dell was standing to the left. Alongside, looking up at him and talking in an animated fashion was that reporter, Samantha Carson. Grace would have to give her a quote for her newspaper.

Grace should say something about Oyster River Research and Dr. Huang being a good match with the altruistic goals of Humanity's Harvest? That sounded pompous. Grace wished she'd thought of something better, but when she got to the door, the reporter was still focused on Mac, so Grace was relieved to just slip inside, unquoted.

In the tower, there was also a private guard on duty in the foyer, but no table with name badges or security lists. Apparently, anyone nervy enough to walk past the police could just go in. Within the doorway, Grace handed her jacket over to the hat check person, then had to start forward. At the entrance, Grace hesitated again, she hated going in there alone, but Freya, Gail, and Inger couldn't make it. Kurt would already be inside and have a ring of males guffawing to his off-color stories. All she could see around her were strangers, some seeing her, then nudging the person next to them. Grace just wanted to retreat, but she had her duty to ORR.

A full crowd in the cadaverous hall, with the buzz of a multitude of private conversations, with well-dressed groups, clumped around each other like bacteria in a petri dish. Mostly Axel's people and the press. Grace walked to the bar, pleasantly surprised to see it was again 'complementary,' courtesy of Humanity's Harvest. Its choices had been upgraded from white or red to mixed drinks with some really great labels, Black DuBennet, and for Kurt, no doubt, a keg with Samuel Adams on tap. Grace was delighted to see Bailey's Irish Cream among the selections, she liked that sort of chocolate malt with a kick, and she ordered one from the second, red-jacketed bartender. "No ice, please." He poured her a large one. It was a great drink for a cold night, real Dutch courage, but so strong, she could only have one, this Roman circus was business after all.

Feeling self-conscious, she moved away from the bar to the center of the room, letting people walk past her. Grace braced herself when she saw Rachel Greenfield steering a well-heeled patron her way, but they just walked past her. With a strange feeling of novel discovery, Grace sipped her smooth drink and realized she was not being shown off tonight! Huang's was in the spotlight. At first, it was a little disconcerting, but then as Grace sipped more of her sweet, chocolate cream like brandy, she realized she was very comfortable with that.

Ruckus laughter. Grace looked to the side of the bar where Kurt was holding court with several of the male directors. Again, she scanned across the huge hall. Where was Axel? And what was she going to tell him about Antarctica? She scanned shifting islands of people conversing, and Grace saw the flash of a scarlet satin cocktail dress, Sara Jamison. Dressed really a bit too fancy for this gathering, but Sara didn't get much of a chance to go out. It would do her good to get away diapers and shine a little. And she was. Sara looked years younger, standing prettily posed before Axel Jensen. Axel leaned down and said something softly to her, and Sara preened. Grace looked across the hall. Holding a glass, Bobby Jamison was over by the bar, listening to Kurt but glancing balefully at his wife and Axel. Bobby's jealousy was legendary, Grace was sure Sara's banter with Axel was totally innocent, but Grace should go over and try to quiet the waters–but she didn't want to.

Another tall, sandy-haired man coming over. That lawyer–what was his name? Coming over to her. To cover while she desperately tried to remember his name, Grace sipped at her drink. This guy had a tom collins in his hand, asking, "Grace, did you have time to read my book?"

Oh, God, who was he? Mentally she pictured the cover of his book–she couldn't do names or faces, but she could almost always recall exactly what she had seen. Now she remembered a fuzzy green background. Baby sucking bottle. At bottom, the byline in red script reading 'Daniel Novinski.' That was his name! "Daniel, I've been looking at it, when I have a chance."

"And?" he asked with an author's pride wanting a favorable critique on his child.

"You've certainly done your research, and you've made some important points," Grace acknowledged.

He kept pushing, "That you will be acting upon with maybe a Dr. Farrington quote for our bulletin?"

"Not at this time," she said wanting to get away. Axel's assistant was walking over to obviously join them, he was such a pain she could remember his name. Grace introduced Daniel to Ekkeko. "Ekkeko, this is Daniel Novinski. He's an author and an activist into food protection. Ekkeko..." Damn, she forgot his last name! "...is in charge of the Humanity's Harvest genetic engineering projects in South America."

"Peru mostly." Ekkeko added proudly, "We're trying to develop drought-resistant crops that can flourish at high altitudes."

"Can't this be done by cross-breeding?" Daniel started quietly. "Without going through the known dangers of G.E.?"

"Perhaps, if we had hundreds, maybe thousands of years," Ekkeko acknowledged. "But my people starve now, so we engineer."

Daniel gave him a big smile. "Having a great salary blots out your obligations to your fellow mankind?"

With smoldering eyes, Ekkeko took another drink of a glass nearly empty. Grace suspected it wasn't his first, when Axel's assistant said with a slight slur, "You're a scientist who is an expert on G. E.?"

"I'm a lawyer, who has taken the time to study the matter."

"So you presume to inform those of us who do understand the science?" said Ekkeko with a contemptuous tone.

Daniel wasn't intimated. "Your field is genetics?"

"Botany," said Ekkeko. "How do you justify working for people stopping science?"

"Rather like how you justify working for a corporation that is using your native country as a test tube?"

"And in your rich, well-fed country, it must be easy for you to decide how others should go about forgetting their hunger?"

Fortunately, Ekkeko's drink was drained, so he walked away, which is what Grace just wanted to do, but with Daniel talking to her that wouldn't have been polite.

"But surely, Grace, a trained scientist such as yourself can see the danger of releasing genetically modified salmon into the sea's wild populations?"

"At the moment, they're not doing that." Grace

looked to see if anyone was coming to rescue her from this conversation.

The lawyer had stopped talking, looking over her shoulder, seeming to have lost interest in her tepid answers. Grace turned to see Axel–no it wasn't Axel–it was another, younger man. Full sandy beard instead of Axel's neat Van Dyke. "He took me up on my offer," she said.

The lawyer looked at her, "What?"

"That man coming in. He's the curator of the South American collection at New Haven University's Natural History Museum." What is his name? Oh, God–Henry...? Something like that.

Daniel downed the dregs of his white wine. "What's he doing here?"

She was surprised at his unfriendly tone. "The same as the rest of us. Trying to make career connections."

The lawyer looked at his empty glass. "Which is what I should be doing–after I get myself a refill. Would you like another, whatever that is?"

The brandy was already making Grace feel a little looser than she should be. "No, thank you."

Daniel walked away, as the curator approached, smiling now to have seen Grace. The man made a beeline to her, probably the only person he knew here, a lifeline in a sea of threatening people, Grace could readily sympathize with that feeling.

"I took you up on your invitation—Helmut Roberts..." He slowed, seeming to lose his confidence mid-sentence. "The curator from..."

"New Haven," Grace could thankfully supply. "I'm so glad you could make it. Is your wife with you?"

His confident smile flashed back. "No, Inez has a class she had to teach."

Grace nodded. "Perhaps some other time she can come down when I can give you both a tour of my lab."

Taking Helmut in tow Grace introduced him to Adam and several of the Board of Directors.

Meeting Oyster River's big buck sponsors, Helmut's initial excitement came back, but as he looked around, he saw Huang Wong in his midnight-blue tuxedo. Helmut frowned and looked down at his tan sports jacket. "You said they wouldn't be so formal."

"You look fine." Grace pointed around the room. "Dr. Mackay's in that cream fisherman's knit sweater–that's certainly casual enough." She looked further. "Axel Jensen is over there by the bar, he has a sports jacket on like you do." Grace didn't point out that by its cut and fit Axel's casual beige jacket showed its several thousand dollars worths of tailoring.

"That's Jensen?" Helmut spoke the name worshipfully, "God–he owns whole countries! I figured he'd look older."

"You haven't met him?" Grace asked. "I understood that Humanity's Harvest had given extensive grants to the University and your Museum?"

Helmut flushed a bit. "That's arranged at higher levels than us peons."

Grace understood. "Let's go over there, and I'll introduce you." She started to walk, but Helmut was just standing there with a deer in the headlights look. She walked back and asked, "You okay?"

"You know, Inez wanted me to come here...to meet people. Advance my career, but–he's a billionaire. What could I say to him?"

Grace just hoped her smile was reassuring enough. "Axel's a very approachable man, and he has a great interest in your South American collection–especially the seeds and bulbs. C'mon. I told him how helpful you were, and I've been telling him about that mummy's arm. Maybe you could give him a little more background."

They started walking across the hall. Axel stood talking with Fritz, and some men Grace recognized as top management in Humanity's Harvest, but as usual, she didn't remember their names.

Helmut was talking behind her. "How did that DNA you extracted work out?"

"The seeds?"

"All of it, the seeds, the mummy's arm sample–did you get anything?"

This required the standard explanation, "Culturing freshly swabbed DNA takes about a day to three days minimum. Culturing something as old as your mummy's arm is going to take a lot, lot longer, if we can even get anything."

They were walking towards the bar. Ekkeko, having to refill his glass again, moved to them. "Dr. Farrington, will you be on the dias tonight?" The man had a way of asking a polite question in a normal tone and making it sound like he was mocking her.

"No," she said politely, smelling the whiskey heavy on his breath. "Ekkeko, I'd like you to meet Helmut Roberts. He's a curator at the Natural History Museum up in New Haven."

Helmut looked eager to meet him and reached out his hand to shake, but the Peruvian didn't return the friendly overture, asking coldly. "Curator to the University of Greedy Acquisition?"

"I beg your pardon?" Helmut looked at Grace.

But Ekkeko was continuing. "Your revel in the Professor's grand theft! You hoard the treasures of Peru!"

"Do you mean Professor Bingham's legacy collection?" asked Helmut finally seeming to understand and not liking it.

"His loot!" sneered Ekkeko. "His enduring legacy of cultural colonization!"

Helmut was flushing again. "The University

authorities have agreed to return..."

"A token amount. Do you think that is fair?" demanded Ekkeko.

The museum curator looked down at the angry little man. "No, sir, I don't. I personally think all those artifacts where acquired quite legally and should remain exactly were they have been for nearly a hundred years."

"The United Nation's court will force you..." Ekkeko started.

Helmut cut him off. "Sir, you know what, the U.N. hasn't taken over the United States just yet."

As the men raised their voices, people were looking in their direction, and Grace wanted to end this. "Actually, those artifacts were delivered to Connecticut before any of us were born."

"And they were legally removed!" Helmut began...

"By cultural thieves!"   returned Ekkeko loudly, sopping the overfilled whiskey glass in his hands, so some of it spilled on the floor.

Because this was going so badly, Grace's head was starting to pound. "Look..." she started, but was cut off by Axel's voice behind her, "Grace, it's wonderful to see you again."

She looked at the tall man. "Axel, excuse me, I'd like to introduce you..." Grace carefully added, "a good friend of mine, Dr. Helmut Roberts, curator of the University's Natural History Museum in New Haven. Helmut, this is Axel Jensen C.E.O. of Humanity's Harvest."

Ekkeko leaned forward, "Dr. Roberts makes his living displaying the sacred to the gawking public."

Axel smiled, but his eyes were glittering dangerously, as he ignored his assistant and reached out to shake Helmut's hand. "Dr. Roberts, your Chancellor spoke quite highly of your research. He expects great things of you. I'm glad to meet you."

From the smell of his breath and his dulled reactions, Ekkeko may have had a bit too much of the free drinks. "Roberts is obstructing the return of artifacts belonging to Peru. The courts should stop this!"

Axel turned on his subordinate. "Well, actually, a transaction that's nearly hundred years old is not really actionable in court, although the University might wish to err on the side of goodwill."

Even with angry eyes, Ekkeko had sense enough to back down from his boss. He walked away.

After he left, Helmut was honest, "There's a lot of people that feel like him."

"And a lot who don't," Axel said. "As it happens I'm am one of them." He looked around. "You know, Helmut, I'd like you to meet Thomas over there. He's one of my employees, who is now trying to set up a website database useful to natural history curators such as yourself. He could use your input." Looking flattered Helmut walked away with Axel.

Shortly after, Adam Greenfield got up and as President of Oyster River Research made a brief speech of introduction, turning it over to Axel, who also kept it brief. Then Huang got up and started rambling on about his grant. His algae. His early successes. His schooling in China. As Grace stood there listening, she was stifling a yawn and nursing a growing, splitting headache.

Kurt had offered to escort her home, but the moment Huang finally stepped down, Grace was headed to the exit, alone. Grabbing her jacket and going out the front entrance, she passed the informational tables outside. Apparently, the picketers weren't breaking down and were now covering their tables with plastic sheeting, which had beaded with glinting water droplets from the Harbor's damp fog. Another weak-kneed deal of Adam's must be allowing them to stay sitting at their tables tomorrow. Would this idiocy ever end?

Chapter 11

At dawn, Grace was pulling on her running shoes. Yesterday Bobby had asked to go with her, too as he said, '*Discuss her upcoming student lecture, the first one for this new class.*' But she figured it was Bobby's way to keep her from running alone. Actually, Grace liked the idea as she walked downstairs and back to the Jamisons' door. With winter getting closer, Sara already had put up a wreath she had handcrafted out of holly and dried orange slices. Lord, it wasn't even Thanksgiving yet. Bypassing the doorbell, Grace knocked lightly, it was early, and there were eight apartments in this building, four on this first floor, no use waking everybody up.

Carrying one of the sleeping twins, red-haired Sara opened the door, saying softly "C'mon. Bob's still getting dressed." Grace went inside, walking through the toy-strewn living room to the dining set up before the French Doors. The downstairs two bedroom condo was roughly the layout of her own. Roomy for an individual, crowded for a family of five, the parents now slept on a pullout couch in the living room. As Bobby came out, he moved as if to kiss his wife, but Sara turned her face away. Obviously, they'd had another of their fiery spats.

Outside Grace and Bobby started to run. His sudden need to run with her every morning might have been orders from Kurt, to guard her from the savage protestors. Now, as they headed up towards the main road, they passed two forlorn, elderly women, wrapped in blankets on top of their coats, sitting beside the three lone tables of pamphlets, under plastic held down by rocks.

They did only two miles, then Grace and Bobby stopped for traffic, as Bobby seemed to be stretching a sore calf he said, "Could we head back?"

"Sure." Back at their condo building, she asked, "How

long did you stay at the reception last night?"

"Too long," his voice sounded bitter.

That set off silent alarms in Grace's mind. "What happened?"

"That hunk of bull meat was coming on to Sara."

"Who?"

"Mr. Humanity's Ripoff in his phony Jungle Jim jacket."

"Axel Jensen?"

"Yeah. My wife really lapped up his attention," he said resentfully.

Grace could guess what that meant. "Did you take a swing at him?"

"No." He evaded her eyes.

"What did you do to Oyster River's latest big bucks patron?" She asked sternly.

Like a guilty kid, he stuck his hands in the pockets of his sweatshirt. "Sara was all blushes and smiles every time he got near, and he kept hovering over her. Asking if she'd like a drink–hell, I can get my own wife a drink!"

"Especially with a free bar paid for by Humanity's Harvest," Grace reminded him.

"So he's a billionaire–why should Sara be smirking like a nubile teenager?"

"Axel has that effect on every woman within thirty feet. And it's not just his money, or those custom fit clothes, or his seaplane." She started to say it's his 'innate sexual magnetism,' but switched it to, "He's a handsome man who enjoys flirting a little. No harm was meant."

"Yeah? Well, I told him he could play Sir Galahad with somebody else's wife!"

Oh, God. "And he said?"

"Mr. Billion-bucks just laughed it off, then Sara walked out."

"Did you go home her?"

"No! We paid the babysitter until one a.m., I wasn't gonna just leave!"

"So you stayed and did what?"

"Talked with Kurt. Drank a little," he said that aggressively. "When the party broke up, I must have walked down by the boats. Don't remember climbing on board Kurt's Lobster Trawler. Well, hell, I woke before dawn with a bad back, from sleeping on the bench under the gunwales. Then I figured the condo's much mine as it is hers, so I went home," he finished defiantly.

Would he ever grow up? "Bob, Sara is stuck all day in a tiny apartment, diapering three crying babies. It's harmless for her to get dressed up for one night, and enjoy a handsome man's attention. You know it was innocent!"

"She was glowing..."

"Every woman glows around Axel! I glow around Axel. He knows it! He plays it."

"Sara's my wife," he said a bit bitterly.

"Who loves you deeply." Although sometimes Grace wondered why. "She came with you, and she would have been leaving with you if you hadn't acted like a jealous idiot!"

"Yeah," he reluctantly admitted. "I just see her with him–he's got so much....Look, I got some paperwork back at the condo. I want you to switch your Monday's lecture from transcription to epigenetics. This group doesn't seem to need the basics. I've got printouts of the new slides at home." She followed him, as he stopped to unlock his front door. With the protestors about, it seemed the Jamisons were now locking up too. Grace hated the need for that.

As he opened the door, Sara hurried over still carrying one of the twins, "Honey," she looked in the direction of their four-year-old daughter standing at the sliding glass doors. Sara was obviously trying to sound okay, but she said, "Ginjer was looking outside. She saw something in the water."

"A whale!" Ginjer said. "With clothes on!" she

giggled.

Bobby and Sara made eye contact. Then Grace followed him inside, as he strode through the living room with its playpen and teddy bears, to the dining area before the east wall that was mostly floor to ceiling glass. The patio door slid open on to a bluish flagstoned terrace half overhung by Grace's balcony upstairs. Bobby spoke, trying to keep it casual, "Honey, it's cold outside, pull these curtains closed after I go out."

Grace followed him closely, feeling the wet sea wind on her face. Upstairs her condo had a balcony, while the Jamisons had the patio with a table and their bar-be-que. When Ginjer started crawling, Bob had built a makeshift, chicken wire fence around the patio to keep her from the grass that leads down to the narrow strip of beach. Bobby jumped over the chicken wire in one leap, and Grace followed, slower. Down the grass hillside was a retaining wall with a three-foot drop off to seaweed clumped sand. At high tide the water would reach the wall, now the tide was just beginning to come in, as waves washed over big reddish boulders.

Reaching the big rocked beach, Bobby was pulling off his running shoes and socks.

At first, Grace didn't see anything, then, as he started wading into the low waves, she saw a dark, dun-colored flash, bobbing among the boulders in the green water. Only closing the door, Sara still followed them outside, stopping at the fence, carrying the baby. Bobby looked back and yelled, "Call 911! Tell 'em it's a floater." Trying to walk barefoot on what was slippery, seaweedy rocks, Bobby had made his way to the sodden mass. Bending over he reached down and picked up an arm. Bobby felt the hand, then looking sick he dropped it back into the water.

Now wading in herself Grace could see it was a man in a tan colored jacket floating face down. His long, blond hair streaming in the translucent seaweed. "Is he?" she asked.

"Long dead."   Looking around, Bobbie saw a driftwood branch stuck in the rocks. He reached down and pulled it out.

Unconsciously, Grace was walking forward. Cold, wetness steeped into the shoes she hadn't taken off and up her pant legs. She looked down. An incoming wave washed frigid water over her calves and Bobby commanded, "No, stay there!"   He was using the branch to keep the man from floating away.

Grace backed up to the damp sand. "Shouldn't we pull him out?"

He looked around at a distance to the sea wall. "Wait till the police get here."

She just stared in horrified fascination. "It's Axel Jensen, he's won swimming awards.   If he fell in, he shouldn't have drowned."

Bobby shook his head. "Would've been hard trying to swim with that sticking out of your back."

Grace looked where he pointed and saw the red painted spear shaft. Not only was Axel Jensen dead, but he had been murdered!

Chapter 12

With sirens blaring two patrol cars arrived, one just after the other. In his navy blue police jacket, Mac Dell came around the condo side first. Sara had taken the baby inside and closed the curtains in front of the patio doors. A shivering Bobby had gotten on to the rocks, out of the freezing water, but he stayed by the body, only touching it with the driftwood branch, to keep it from floating away.

Now the incoming tidal water with small waves lapped on the small strip of beach before the rock retainer wall.

Mac looked at her asking, "Grace?"

"There's a man. Floating. I think's Axel Jensen."

He looked surprised. "The rich guy Ma's been talking about? The one with the seaplane?"

"Axel was here, representing Humanity's Harvest for Dr. Wong's reception last night."

"'Oyster River kills a billionaire,' that'll be great for the news!" Mac said bitterly. "Go inside, Grace. We'll take care of it."

Bobby looked to the beach, which was rapidly disappearing as the tide came in. "Gotta move him, or he's gonna float out, but it's a murder scene."

Mac nodded grimly, "Don't turn him over, we'll carry him just as he is."

Grace watched as Mac reached the end of the grass, pulled off his shoes and socks, then turned up his pants legs before wading into the waves. The water was up to Mac's knees still wetting his trousers. He took an arm, and Bobby took the other and they both starting to drag Axel's body in. Not being able to stand it any longer, Grace walked away. And kept walking, it seemed to help a bit.

She went inside the Admin building. Gail was in early at her desk getting the new catalogs ready for the printer. She looked, up, "Grace..."

"Axel Jensen is dead." Oh, God, why couldn't she say it any better?

"I know, Sara called me. I've already called Adam. He's ordered all classes canceled. He'd like all senior staff to go to an emergency meeting at the Roost.

Grace headed out on the sidewalk, towards the Roost, but decided she wouldn't go there. Several demonstrators were on the waterside of the road. They were looking down at the cluster of police cars, and they were worriedly looking at her as she had to walk past them. Grace said nothing, and they apparently didn't dare ask.

She headed past the narrow guard booth, then down the slant of the ramp to the docks where Kurt's lobster trawler the 'Big 'Un' was tied up. Since that boat was in, she just passed it and walked to the end of the dock where a sleek thirty-six footer Cabo Rico Cutter was permanently tied up. Even with its damaged bow, Kurt made that into his '*home sea home.*'

Gace walked on his decks with leather soled shoes, she should have boat sneakers, but in a daze, she just knocked with her knuckles on his hatch entrance.

A male voice boomed from below. "Go away!"

Grace just pulled the hatch open and started down.

Kurt was sitting down there in his main cabin. He was wearing a red flannel shirt as he two-finger typed his Harbor temperatures into his computer. Across the cabin, on the narrow kitchen counter, Grace saw the remains of take-out Chinese and two wine glasses in the sink. There was bright red lipstick on the rim of one. Still, according to their rather loose arraignment, he could have outside friendships, as could she. Since he was, maybe she should invite someone one to her place, but she'd certainly lost her chance with Axel.

Kurt looked up, concerned, "You're not in yer lab working. What's the matter?"

"Axel Jensen's dead."

"What?!"

"Ginjer saw a man floating face down in the Harbor. The police are over there now."

"He drowned?" Kurt sat looking at her in disbelief.

"Was Axel drunk last night?" Grace asked.

Kurt thought about it. "He was drinking, but not more than the rest of us–damn well-stocked bar. Well, if Jensen fell in and drowned himself, we won't be getting that bar again." He didn't sound happy.

"He was murdered."

Kurt looked shocked. "The Curs people shot him?"

"It wasn't a gun–it looks like a scuba spear."

Kurt automatically looked forward towards his bedroom cabin in the bow. He got up and left her alone. Feeling worn out, Grace sat down on the built bench on the side of his table, it was a long time until he came back.

"Whal, all mine are there."

"Can you prove that?"

"Hell, no, Scuba guns don't have registration numbers, like handguns. And you can't do any ballistics tests on a spear shaft."

"Does Bobby have a spear gun?"

The look on his face gave her the positive answer. She continued. "He had a fight with Axel last night."

"No fight!" Kurt looked away. "He just spoke a bit sharply—over nothing! That's Bobby. If he killed people for paying a compliment to Sara, we'd all be dead."

"But Sara went home without him. I understand he stayed and kept drinking, then he wound up sleeping on your lobster trawler, blotto. If the police fingerprinted your spear guns?"

"That's what I was doing in the bedroom. Cops gonna find the cleanest wiped scuba gear they have ever seen."

Grace started to get up, "Adam's called a meeting at the Roost to talk."

"Has he cleaned out the demonstrators?" Kurt asked grimly.

She shook her head and rose to go up to the Roost.

He put a hand on her arm. "First, Grace, we gotta talk! Honey, I'm leaving on the December 15th."

Leaving? She suddenly remembered, what she had been trying to forget. "Yes, you're doing that Science Channel project–you'll be on a ship, following the Gulf current." Her voice trailed off, sounding as lost as she felt.

"I told ya I can take yer aboard as my assistant again. You'll have yer own cabin, seems like a good idea, with a murderer stalking back here.

She wasn't dropping her work to spend two months stranded on a scientifically outfitted steamer. "We've been over this. No."

"Then I'm staying here!" he said, going into stubborn mode.

"Give up your chance of being on TV? Last time you were on the program you got a fistful of study grants."

"I'm not leaving you alone with a killer loose here..."

"**No!**"   Grace said even more firmly then she intended. "That is the heart of our agreement. Our personal relationship can never cut into the work we've chosen to do!" More than any supposed danger, she hated not having him around for the Christmas holidays—still, as she held her research goal sacred, she had to respect his. "No, you're going! And by yourself!"

He stopped and studied the firmness in her face. "And you're as stubborn as meself." He came over, briefly kissed her, then pulled his leather jacket on, reaching down under the dining room table, pulling out a drawer that she hadn't even know was there. Taking out a semi-automatic pistol. "You're licensed to carry, aren't ya, Grace?"

"No–I never got around to..."

He looked pained. "Fill out yer paperwork! After the meeting, this Ruger's is going in yer bed-stand! If you have to use, claim that it was mine, waiting for my return."

A loaded gun with little Ginjer toddling around? Still seeing that spear gun shaft sticking out of Axel's back, Grace didn't feel like arguing, because there was a murderer who was also around, but, "With the baby downstairs..."

He demonstrated for her. "You'll take the magazine out and check for one still in the chamber, take that out and slip it back in the magazine." He slapped it back in again. "Now you do it."

She did.

He watched carefully, then said, "Keep the gun in your endstand drawer and the magazine under your pillow beside yer–kid Ginjer's age can't load it. Aim like you are pointed your finger. Remember, Jensen sure didn't have time to call 911."

When they climbed up the dock, the same two elderly demonstrators were still there, now joined by four strong looking male teenagers. All silently watching them as Grace and Kurt walked to the Roost. Grace found herself uneasily thinking that last night, in the darkness, one of them could have easily shot Axel in the back.

In the Roost kitchen, Fritz was spooning coffee into the urn. A rotund, white-mustached man of the old school, Professor Fritz Wilshuen had his usual welcoming smile, but the place had the atmosphere of a funeral. In the main hall, Kurt was setting out folding chairs, while Grace made hot water for their tea in the kitchen. She should have gotten breakfast. Grace looked for some cookies or crackers, but there was nothing in the cabinets, it was going to be a long day. Soon they were sitting in the center of the cold room, warming their hands, drinking from steaming styrofoam cups when Dr. Huang Wong walked in, "Why you bother me?"

Huang demanded.

Kurt stated, "That contract you got with its anti-genetic engineering demonstrators just got Axel Jensen murdered."

"He dead? Axel dead? " Huang repeated. "What happens my contract? Only got first money! Axel runs company–he dead. Company dead! No money for me?"

Changed into his teaching clothes a strained looking Bobby came in and sat down. "Nice of somebody to tell me my classes were canceled."

"I'm sorry," Grace said, then turned saying quietly to him, "The police are probably going to be checking for spear guns."

Bobby shot her a fast look. "Mine is in the basement storage. Sara's afraid to have it around the kids."

But Kurt added. "People know you, and I own them, and you were seen after you left the reception last night when you went on my boat to sleep." He looked to Grace. "Do we have any idea when Axel was murdered?"

Bobby's eyes widen slightly. Apparently, he just realized he might be needing an alibi.

Dressed in fleece lined jacket and work jeans the volunteer president of ORR was walking in. Adam looked about and said, "Good. You're all here." He was followed closely by the lawyer, Daniel Novinski.

Seeing Daniel Kurt started, "Sir, this a private meeting!"

"About the demonstrators–which why I am here," replied Daniel. "I understand there's been an accident?"

Kurt glared at him. "There's been a murder. Your friends apparently couldn't stop Axel Jensen, so they killed him."

Daniel immediately went on the defensive. "You have proof of those charges, Dr. MacKay? Because if you don't, you are open to a libel suit."

Adam looked sick, "Axel Jensen was a billionaire–with influential friends in Washington, all over the world! The publicity for Oyster River will be devastating!"

Grace winced, saying, "It's not like we deliberately killed him."

Becoming the chief inquisitor, Adam turned on Grace. "Did you see who did it?"

"No."

He looked to Bobby, "You're sure it is a murder? Maybe it was just an accident. Axel fell off the dock, hit his head, and drowned?"

A disbelieving Bobby looked at Adam. "Then he stabbed himself through the back with a spear gun shaft."

"Damn!" Adam looked down at the floor.

"It's the demonstrators you allowed to stay!" Kurt thundered.

"Or our homegrown nut case, Jeffers!" Adam shot back.

"Not Josh," Kurt said firmly. "Not from a distance. Not in the back. And besides Jensen's death, I've been getting threatening letters. "

Adam appeared to pale. "Anonymous? Mailed? One printed line on white paper?"

"Aaup." Kurt closed his mouth tightly. "You too?"

The president of ORR looked sicker. "Huang got two, I've gotten one. I gave mine to the police, and Axel Jensen had also gotten at least two. Warning him to stop his genetic engineering or else."

"Why didn't anybody say anything?" Grace asked. "I got one."

"You turn it in?" demanded Kurt.

"To the police?" she asked. "No, it seemed like a bad joke, I threw it out."

Adam looked grim. "Axel's threatened his life. He thought they were a joke too, but his private security people are analyzing them. All standard envelopes, paper and probably cranked out on an eighty dollar printer, everything stocked and commonly sold at any big bucks office supply store. No fingerprints. No way to trace 'em."

"We should have been swabbing them for DNA." Grace looked at Adam. "I got one delivered to my condo address, the first day I got back from Seattle. How did they know where I lived?"

"They looked at the label on your mailbox, checked the phone book," said Kurt laconically. "Why the hell didn't Axel have his security with him last night?"

Adam shook his head. "He didn't seem to think the letters were anything more than a juvenile attempt to scare us..."

"Well, somebody certainly proved they were serious!" Kurt finished for him.

"All right, the demonstrators are gone!" Adam pronounced.

Daniel immediately objected, "You can't. They're on public land!"

"No, they aren't," Grace started. "This whole peninsula is privately owned by the Oyster River Research foundation since 1896!"

"Was totally private...." the lawyer continued. "Several years ago your president turned over the road and end of the point to the town as a wildlife preserve."

Kurt, Grace, Huang, and Fritz looked to Adam. He reluctantly explained, "It was done so that the town would pay for the snow plowing in the winter, and for a large tax deduction for ORR."

"Great," said Kurt. "After a murder, the Town Fathers of Oyster River are going to have their police clean out your demonstrator city." He looked at Daniel. "I suggest you tell your friends to start striking their tents."

"You try to evict my clients, and I'll see you in court!" said Daniel directly to Adam.

Hearing someone coming in from the back entrance Grace turned. Would it be that reporter, Sam? She suddenly took in her breath. Seeing the shocked expression on her face, the others turned to look too.

There stood Axel Jensen. Tall, sandy-haired wearing a blue business suit with his usual charming, masculine smile, looking very much alive.

They all just stared at him.

Drawing closer to the table Axel said, "I like to make an entrance and be noticed, but, guys, this is a bit much?"

It was Daniel, whose lawyer instincts kicked in first. "C.U.R.S has been accused of murdering you!"

"Yeah, I heard that at the Admin building. Like Mark Twain once said, *'the reports of my demise are vastly exaggerated.'*"

Adam looked sternly to Bobby saying, "Is this some kind of a joke?"

A pale Bobby was still staring at Axel. "There was a guy floating face down! Dead. Very dead."

"Well, who the hell is he?" asked Kurt.

Grace pictured the drowned man. They'd only see his back jacket, that long blond hair rippling in the water. And the seawater soddened jacket that had once been a light tan, suddenly Grace knew who the victim was. And it was her fault that he was dead!

Chapter 13

Adam was turning to her. "Grace. Can you identify the body with a DNA sample?"

Grace ignored the question, as she hurriedly got up to leave. It was Kurt who answered behind her. "Not unless she has an identified sample to compare with. Hell, figuring out the victim's identity is the cops' job." Kurt glared at Adam. "Now that somebody's dead, when are you going to clean out these Curs people?"

"There is no proof that any of the picketers had anything to do with this!" Daniel shot back heatedly.

Everyone was staring at Adam. The president took a handkerchief out and wiped sweat from his forehead. "We don't know if C.U.R.S. bears any responsibility. We don't even know who the victim is! So we don't know why he was killed or by who."

A puzzled Axel had walked over to them. "Why did anyone think it was me?"

Grace had pulled on her jacket and left the others to explain it to him. Feeling like a robot as she walked through the back kitchen as she could hear Kurt's furious words, "So you aren't doing anything until we're all killed!"

Going outside, the cold hit her. Her shoes were still uncomfortably wet from the sea water–water that must have had the murdered man's blood in it.

Taking long strides she quickly passed her lab, then breaking into a lope, Grace passed the other buildings on the left side, finally running across the street to her condo building. Here the land widened a bit, and with several police cars parked on the grass, rotating blue and red lights flashed against the building walls. Now a large red ambulance was parked there, and a black stretch station wagon, with 'Medical Examiner' lettered on the side.

It be easier to go inside, knock on the Jamison's door,

and have Sara let her out the back patio entrance. Instead, Grace threaded her way around the Medical Examiner's vehicle, walking near the seawall. The cold air was making it hard for her to breath, making her take short, shallow breaths, that didn't give her enough air. Grace rounded around the side of the building, with its boxwood shrubby lovingly tended by Sara. There was a tricycle parked on the patio.

Coming out in the backyard, she stopped again. Steeling herself.   It was a busy scene with a man in plain clothes photographing what was left of the beach, as the foaming tide washed in. Two uniformed cops were hauling a heavy, black, six foot plus body bag up on the grass. Grace didn't recognize anyone there, then she saw a group of policemen with a tall, sandy-haired man in blue uniform jacket.

"Mac." She meant to just call out loudly, but cold air and stress had made her sound like a frog croaking, but he turned, looking concerned he moved towards her, trying to block her view of the body bag.

"Grace, maybe you should go back inside."

"I want to see him," she said tightly.

Mac looked at an older man, also in uniform. "Why?" That other man asked.

"I have to see his face!" she repeated.

"Grace,..." Mac started frowning, but she cut him off again.

"I must see him!"

The two policemen exchanged looks, then another man, in plain clothes joined them. He apparently had been listening, and he nodded to Mac. Her old friend's son came over, and put his hand under her elbow, as he walked Grace to the bag.   The body bag was twisted at an awkward angle. Grace realized it must be because of the shaft still sticking out of his back.

Another officer was kneeling beside the body bag, and

Mac said, "Unzip the face."

The other officer looked at Grace, then slowly unzipped the bag. Grace smelled salt water and gasoline, and she felt nauseous, sagging as she leaned a little against Mac. When this was over, she would go back upstairs to her apartment and barf.

She could see the face now. Bluish-white skin. Long, dripping blond hair. Brown eyes wide open as if in permanent surprise. Then, not Axel's goatee, but the same sandy-colored full beard on his face. Grace had invited him so he could advance his career, and now it was over. "I think I know him. It's not Axel Jensen," she said haltingly. "This is the curator up at the University's Natural History Museum in New Haven. His name is Dr. Harvey, Harry Rollins...oh," She stopped, then it all blurted out. "You know I'm bad with names—but he was here, at the reception last night! I invited him. His wife is pregnant." Grace couldn't stop her voice from breaking. "You can't tell her!"

At Mac's nod, the other officer reached down and zipped the bag up again. "It is Helmut Roberts," Mac said. "When he didn't come up home last night, his wife called the New Haven police. It was too soon to put out a missing person's bulletin, but they sent down a request, and we checked the parking lot. His car is still here. We've also sent up a photo of our floater up to them, somebody in New Haven put two and two together. His wife has already identified the picture."

Grace still found herself babbling. "He looks like Axel. They both have sandy hair and beards. They both wore tan jackets. They both were at the reception. The demonstrators–well, it might not be them--but they might have thought they were killing Axel."

Putting his arm around her shoulders, Mac was turning her away from the body, saying gently, "Leave it to the detectives. That's their job. I'll walk you back to your condo, c'mon."

Grace found herself moving without willing it. "Helmut's never been here before. He'd have had no enemies. I invited him here, just for the reception. He wanted to make contacts. Advance his career. He was so happy and proud to be here. I killed him!"

With concern, Mac said, "Because you invited him to a reception? Grace, No! It's not your fault."

"You want to know when I last saw him. I...Helmut had been hanging around me for confidence, then I introduced him to Axel, and they walked off to meet other people. Afterward, Helmut probably looked for me, but all I cared about was my aching head, and getting out of that too hot room. I left him alone, to die."

As Grace stood there, someone was picking her up way along the thin ribbon of beach left. A woman. Tall and slender. A flash of long, scarlet hair. That newswoman was walking towards them, with the cold waves rolling in. Probably her shoes were soaked too.

Grace looked down at her.   "That reporter, Sondra—how did she know?"

"Sam.   Samantha Carson.   She's got a radio and monitors the police bands."

"That's legal?"

"Unfortunately yes," he said sounding annoyed.

"I don't want to talk to her," Grace said looking down.

"Then we'll just go back to your condo.   If you keep walking, Samantha will leave you alone.   I wish Ma were here for you, but Freya won't be back from her mineral show in Ohio until Sunday evening."

Grace's condo looked out over this water where Helmut had died. Grace couldn't bear to look out at that water. "I don't want to go upstairs."

Kurt had come up behind them. "When yer detectives want to talk with Gracie, she'll be in her lab. Working. She'll feel better there."

Lowering her head, Grace nodded and moved to him. "It was that curator from New Haven." Kurt put his arm around her, and they started walking up the hillside. Mac had walked to the seawall and was giving Sam a hand up. The reporter watched them go past but didn't pepper Grace with any questions.

When they walked around the building, up to the road, Grace stopped and scanned about. At the entrance, with lowered placards, the now quieted picketers were looking over to the police cars, probably still wondering was happening, but they were holding their ground. Like a robot, she followed Kurt to her lab. 'Why was the curator killed?" Grace didn't even realize she was speaking out loud.

Inside Grace's foyer, Kurt answered, "Poor bastard was killed caused he looked like Axel Jensen."

"He was a kid, only here to advance his career. His wife's having a baby." Grace started to tear up as she walked toward her desk.

"Want me to go get us some tea from the cafeteria?" She didn't answer, he tried again, "Whiskey from me boat?"

Grace stretched out in her chair and got some tissues for her nose, it seemed to release some of the tightness. "There's a coffee maker in the corner for water. Tea's in the cabinet, but I don't want anything. In fact, if you don't mind, I'd prefer you get back to your work and leave me to mine." Understanding Kurt left.

Deliberately trying to shut everything out, she immersed herself in reviewing several manuscripts that had been submitted to genetics journals. She typed in her critiques, then tried to settle on the architecture of her own experiments going forward. But she couldn't. Restless, Grace took an early lunch. Gail was still making desperately needed changes to the course catalogs, so Grace ate alone, really not eating, just moving stuff around her tuna salad platter.

After lunch Grace decided to brave the demonstrators. Near the road, the picketers still had a table, spread with animal welfare brochures. Was the one who killed Helmut with them now? Grace took a deep, calming breath, and then walked past a line of four picketers circling. The grass sloped down to a small guard booth at the top of Oyster River's dock. The small shack, with its boat oars and motorboat keys, was now neatly pad-locked, with a shiny new hasp screwed on. On the door a hand-scrawled note was taped, '*If you need a boat see Dock Master Kurt MacKay or Bobby Jamison.*" At the top of the dock ramp, there was a larger hand-printed sign in red, anti-rust marine paint, '**NO TRESPASSING! THAT MEANS YOU!!**' hanging between two posts was a heavy chain stretched across the dock at nearly a meter high. It wouldn't stop anyone. She just stepped over it.

Her leather heels echoed on the plastic wood boards, with the tide coming in the ramp angle down was less steep. She passed the rowboats and no frills motorboats the students were allowed to take out for their personal research or a picnic.

Kurt's lobster trawler the Big Un was tied up and unmanned, so she continued to the end of the dock to The Lovely Lady, now Kurt's year-round home. Grace climbed aboard and knocked on the hatchway top. And answering shout came down from below, "This gun's loaded! Don't make my day!"

"Kurt?" she asked.

Steps below and the hatch doors were unbolted from inside and swung open. Seeing her, he looked up and smiled. "Pretty lady."

Then climbing up, he looked over to the hillside demonstrators. "So we're still under siege–despite Adam's big words! Can't throw them out until he's consulted ORR's attorney."

Shaking his head, Kurt headed back down, and she

followed him saying, "That chain with a sign hanging off it isn't going to stop anyone."

"If the damn fools cross it, then the police charge is trespass and maybe breaking and entering." Down the ladder into his tidy cabin, Grace could smell garlicky chili.

"Want some?" he asked.

"Just had lunch," she said.

He gave her a leer. "I wasn't talking about the chili, but you could have a bowl of that too."

She shook her head. Really didn't feel like joking or eating or even moving. Feeling numb Grace slid into the near side bench of his built-in dining table. He moved to the other side, putting his bowl down next to his laptop. "Eating in the office today. Gotta get this finished before my trip, and then I gotta pack."

She kept forgetting about his trip, his leaving made her feel even lower. "Need help?"

"Men aboard a ship with other men? Ain't packing much. Ain't even packing a razor."

Shaking her head in disapproval Grace said, "You have to look decent on camera! And wear that white wind jacket, and trim your beard, you shouldn't be looking like a wild man."

He didn't look up, just typed some on his laptop, then he finished a few spoonfuls of meaty chili, leaving her alone, to soak up comfort in his warm little world. Finally, he asked, "Find anything worth studying in New Haven?"

"Nothing Humanity's Harvest is going to want to pay for."

Kurt gave a tight smile. "Too bad. That Jensen guy's an easy bite."

She thought about the body in the water. "I wish Huang had never gotten Oyster River into this."

"Why? Because some yahoos are demonstrating? Adam's right, nights are getting colder. They ain't gonna be sleeping in those tents when it snows, and Adam's already having those porta johns pulled out and having all the buildings with bathrooms locked up at 7 p.m."

"You think that's gonna stop them?"

"Actually, the bushes are beginning to stink real bad." He studied her with the dark eyes. "But why are you so against genetic engineering, you used to think it was gonna save the world?"

"Still do. If it is used prudently, " Grace said.

"But?"

"Well, they're still commercially inserting the genes with antibiotic resistance as a marker."

"Antibiotics resistant?"

"They use it to test the gene insertion. Testing the G.E.ed cells with antibiotics. If the cells survive, then know your new material got in."

"But doesn't using heavy duty antibiotics on cells breed resistance..." he sounded doubtful.

She agreed. "To life-saving antibiotics. To make those inserted genes function unlike natural genes, they are engineered to be 'on' all the time. Another possible problem."

"But you've played with this stuff before. I know you refuse to talk about it, but I've followed that Coast Guard cutter that's been taken you to Crab Apple Island. Course, I could only follow so far, that being restricted waters." Stubbornly she said nothing, so he continued. "We both know what kind of research the Government does there–something that could wipe out millions if spread on land. What are ya doing? Working on our stockpile or figuring which country is preparing biological weapons against us?"

The fact he kept harping on something she was not a liberty to talk about annoyed her. "And this is important to you?"

"The stuff ya are working on at a restricted military facility is a lot more dangerous than any oversized salmons and herbicide-resistant canola."

"But worked on it in sterile conditions, on a guarded and restricted island, buffered by large distances of seawater, that's a lot different situation then planting albumin producing flax in an open field."

"Albumin?" He looked startled. "They get human blood protein from a plant?"

"Yes–and if the flax is planted in an open field, those albumin gene splices will almost certainly cross-pollinate with any other flax in the area."

He frowned. "And, the U.S. government tends to let the big guys police themselves..."

"The USDA and FDA rule that if a food is accepted as safe, like peas, only anything adding an allergen gene needs to be tested, but they have inserted a safe bean gene into a safe pea plant and wound up with a food that causes an allergic reaction in humans. Which was unexpected, because when that same gene expressed in its original bean plant, it didn't cause allergic reactions." Grace stopped, mulling over that interesting nugget of information, then she continued, "It's also finally being recognized that genes that are ingested as food, can jump into a digesting organism's cells. Our homo sapiens ancestors might not have mated with Neanderthals, they may have just eaten them. And if alien genes are incorporated into an organism's chromosomes, those genes could be inheritable. "

He seemed to be ahead of her. "Hell, these digested, inserted genes, will they turn on and start to function?"

"Sometimes, perhaps, but those digested and inserted genes are a very, very rare occurrence. Still, it's interesting to wonder what roles they may have played in evolution."

"So if I eat pork ribs, I could become a literal chauvinistic pig?" he asked.

"That's assuming you weren't one already," she said smiling sweetly.

He narrowed his eyes. "So Dr. Farrington is going to come out and say she'd like all genetic engineering outlawed?"

What would she say? "That's not my call. Grace Farrington says she wants to be left alone, to do the work she's trained for."

"That's what we all want, but if you live in this world, sometimes you've got to take a stand."

Despite his outside crust of his sneering, argumentative attitude, Kurt had a hidden stream of kindness, a wide one that shouldn't surprise her. He'd gotten Grace off the death of Helmut, focusing on the comfort of the center of her life–her work. Shaking off the paralyzing hold of depression, she could function now. "I've work to do, and you have to go pull in your lobster traps and test your salinity, you'll be traveling soon."

"Don't want to leave you alone," he said quietly.

"I'll be fine!" She slid out and started toward the hatch.

He continued, "After work, I'll pick you up–I'm staying at your place tonight."

"My place?"

He smiled wickedly, "Aaup. I'm afraid to be alone, need a teddy bear to hug to keep me safe tonight."

"I don't need a bodyguard." She glared at him.

"Not even with a murderer on the peninsula?"

Wrapping up thoughts vectors and alleles, that fact had been driven from her mind. "Do you think he's still here?" Grace asked.

"I don't even know if 'he' is a 'she.' That hatch nosed Astrid looks like she could wield Carrie Nation's ax. And I do know that random robbers usually don't hold their victims up with a spear gun unless they're robbing you underwater at two fathoms."

"Kurt..."

He stood up and walked to her, looked straight into her eyes. "You don't want me to be with you tonight?"

She thought about that dark walk from her lab to her condo, about the black night, and the even blacker water outside her balcony where Helmut's body had bobbed. "I'll wait for you in my lab at 5:30–we can have a frozen stir-fry at my condo. And, yes, I would like to be with you tonight." Sadly, with him traveling, Grace realized that it might be their last night together for some time to come.

"I'll walk with you now," he offered standing up.

"No, I'll be fine," she said feeling strong.

Kurt kissed Grace lightly, then she climbed up to the bright sunlight on the deck.

Being alone and getting back to work, that's what she wanted, but contrary as ever, Grace felt empty and totally alone as she walked off the ramp on to the grass. The demonstrators were still there, talking among themselves. How long were they staying? Grace briskly walked passed them toward her lab. She gave a glance back once and saw Kurt standing there at the top of the dock. Watching to see Grace made it to her laboratory safely.

Chapter 14

Inside Inger was sitting at her desk, opening the laboratory mail and sorting it in piles. At her own desk again, Grace tried to open her endless scroll of e-mails, also sorted into directories by Inger, but Grace just kept picturing the sodden tan jacket, the drifting blond hair floating in the frigid water. That spear shaft sticking out of his back bobbing gently like a ship's mast on the incoming waves.

Desperate to get something done Grace closed out the mail, then pulled up her spreadsheet program. Early in her career to help her work out thorny DNA problems, Grace had started focusing her thinking using spreadsheets. Even formulating a title aided in defining the question to be worked out, and the results from her spreadsheet helped her to form hypotheses that could be tested.   Pro and Con columns allowed her to study all aspects of the questions, and assign percentages of what she considered the answer to be. Those numbers were highly subjective–only to be used focusing her thinking on the problem and working out her 'To Do' lists.

Usually, the more she worked with the sheet, Grace was able to modify her questions, narrow her parameters, giving her a structure to focus her efforts–and finally get her answers in her 'Farrington fusions.'

She started typing in the *Murderer of Helmut Roberts*. Under that, she set up seven columns: Suspect; Motive; Means; Pro; Con; Total; and To Do. Under the Suspect column, she started making rows: Unknown diver. Motive: None, accident 0%. Means: Spear gunshot gone wrong 12%. Pro: Could have panicked, run 10%. Con: Why be diving or carrying a spear gun at night in winter? -10. Total 12%.

Next row, Suspect: Enemy of Helmut's from New Haven; Motive: Job-related? Love triangle? 30%; Means: Unlikely to haul down a spear gun -5%. Be recognized -5%. Pro: Wanted to kill away from his area 10%. Con: Strange to follow Helmut down -10%

Total: a weak 20%.

Suspect: Picketers. Their Motives: None for killing Helmut. Mistook him for Axel? 10%. Means: Spear gun on the table. 20%. Pro: Wanted Axel stopped 15%; Con: Outside marching, but non-violent -15%. Total: 30%.

Also on site were the ORR Personnel: Didn't know Helmut/no reason to kill Axel, but Means: Kurt & Bob own spear guns 10%. Pro: In area 10%. Con: No motive? -15%. A weak total of 5%.

And finally Ekkeko Vascelo. His Motive: Angry words over Prof. Bingham legacy 15%. Means: Enraged, Strong 11%; Pro: Alcohol fueling a hot temper 10%. Con: Wouldn't kill a man over relics? -30. Total 6 %.

The highest percentage at 30% was the Picketers? Didn't seem probable to Grace, but 'To Do' would be to observe the activists. Of course, random violence was also possible, but a robber or attacker with a spear gun? As far as she knew, Helmut knew only herself when he got to Oyster River that day of the reception. It's hard to come up with sufficient motivation for murder when you really don't know the victim. But if she changed her sheet, to a different premise, to *Who Killed Helmut Thinking He Was Axel Jensen*?

Top of the list was the Picketers. Motive: Stop G.E. 30%. Means: They had a spear gun; were outside 20%. Pro: They are passionate about case & ignored 20%. Con: Security was watching them -20%. A high total of 50%, for her 'To Do' she would have to break down the picketers into individual suspects.

Next two rows, enemies from Axel's business and personal life. Well, the man was running a conglomerate, and he had seven ex-wives, he has to have someone mad at him. Still, he would have recognized them at the reception, or maybe he did, so Grace gave those rows a 20% and 30%.

Now Huang Wong. Relations with Axel were not going well and he was there, but Grace didn't think he had the backbone for cold-blooded murder, Huang came out as a weak 5%.

Ekkeko Vascelo, This was different, he had a grudge against Helmut and Axel seemed angry about his drunkenness. Ekkeko was near the protesters' spear gun, but killing his boss to avoid a reprimand? Total 6%.

And since it was Axel as the victim Grace added two rows. One for Daniel Novinski and one for Astrid. Both were near the spear gun, passionate about their causes. But killing Axel didn't fit with Daniel's calm lawyer temperament, and Freya swore Astrid was non-violent. Still Grace typed them in at 20% and 25% respectively. But there was one more suspect to consider, Josh Jeffers. Motive always unclear with a volatile person like him, did he have a spear gun? He and his brother ran a bait shop selling fishing equipment, and he was on the grounds. But attacking in the dark, from behind with no witnesses was not Josh's style. She put him down at 20%.

The anti-G.E. picketers collectively were coming out the highest, and she knew nothing about most of them. That was a 'To Do' list item, talk with Freya and try to learn something about these people. They wouldn't have had anything against the museum curator, but some other crazy than Josh might have gone after Axel Jensen to oppose Humanity's Harvest's genetic engineering.

Discouraged Grace closed the spreadsheet program and looked up. Inger was sitting there, staring fixedly at a letter in hand. "Are you okay?" Grace asked.

Inger didn't answer, so Grace got up and walked over to her. In an unsteady voice, Inger said, "I got one."

"One what?"

Grace took the letter from her hand reading: 'Inger, you are helping them destroy the world. You will be punished too.' Fury shot through Grace, the threatening letters to her didn't matter, but to go after someone just because she just worked for Grace! "Call Security–no, call the Police! 911."

"It's not an emergency." Inger started.

"The hell it isn't! Call!" If she had been Freya, she would have gathered Inger up in a protective hug, but Grace couldn't do that. Instead, she thought about it, it was going to destroy her schedules but, "You need a vacation. You are going to take two weeks. It'll be paid."

"That's not budgeted," Inger objected.

"It will have to be!"

"Who will do your work here?"

"Nick and Bobby will have to come in extra." And Grace would have to keep after Nick!

Inger looked down at the mail before her. "No. You can fire me, but I staying here!"

Grace sighed. "We'll try to pull off some DNA from that letter, but I assume the writer would have been careful."

Police showed up in the person of a detective, who took the letter, interviewed Inger and left. ORR security also showed, upset that Grace hadn't gone through them, and Gail called Adam who also agreed Inger should take some time off, but Inger was not moving. "Grace, I'm not leaving you alone."

Chapter 15

Coming back from dinner to her laboratory, Grace entered the lobby, and then had to unlock the right door to her lab. What a waste of time. She expected Inger to be out of sight working on the Clean room, but instead, Inger was sitting at her desk near Grace's doing what? Her assistant should be sequencing now.

Grace looked across the room. Two figures standing and waiting uncomfortably. A tough, straight-backed Astrid and a worried looking Freya. Spotted her, Astrid strode over. "Dr. Farrington."

"Can I help you?" Grace forced a polite smile.

"You're helping Humanity's Harvest poison the earth we live on!" Astrid's voice was harsh and brooked no argument.

She was moving uncomfortably close, but with Freya and Inger nearby, Grace felt in control. "If you any have solid proof of that, I suggest you call the police," returned Grace mildly.

Seeming not to have even heard her, Astrid stridently continued to accuse, "You're working for Axel Jensen!"

Grace almost said 'no,' then remembered by collecting samples for him in New Haven that she actually was, followed quickly by a third thought. "It's none of your business who I'm working for."

Watching them, Inger was picking up the phone, probably to call ORR security—a possible confrontation Grace did not want. She raised a hand to Inger while giving a brief shake of her head. Reluctantly Inger put down the phone.

Freya moved closer to Astrid. "Grace is listening to you. That's what you said you wanted. You wanted to explain that C.U.R.S. had nothing to do with that murder."

"She knows none of us killed that young man!"

Astrid sounded outraged at the very thought. "We don't even know who he was."

Grace looked at her. "I don't know who killed Helmut. The police think he might have been mistaken for Axel Jensen, and he was killed because of that."

"Not by us!" The protestor stated, looking frightened, while Freya was unconsciously nodded her head in agreement, Astrid turned to pleading, "But Jensen's genetic research is wrong! It's unnecessary! They genetically engineer growth hormones for cows to create more milk. They're dumping unused milk to keep the price up, they don't need to add adulterated milk!"

Grace so wanted to end this. "That sounds like a commercial or political problem, not a scientific one."

Astrid didn't want to end it. "One of your commercial companies inserted a single Brazil nut gene into a genetically engineered soybean crop. The *New England Journal of Medicine* reported that independent testers found allergic reactions in people allergic to Brazil nuts. Genetically engineering one gene caused this! The powers-that-be say soy is a safe food, that it doesn't need to be tested, and your conglomerates fought to have their crops not 'labeled' G.E. But what about people, who know they're allergic to Brazil nuts, how are they going to know that one of the myriad of products made with soybeans might give them a possibly fatal reaction?"

"Grace, is that true?" Freya asked.

Unfortunately, it was, so Grace admitted, "Yes. If you oppose this, then you have to work with your government to require regulations, correct labeling, and long-term testing."

"No!" said Astrid. "We just have to stop genetic engineering all together!"

"By sending anonymous threatening letters to me and my staff?"

Freya looked terrified. "You were threatened?"

"And Inger," Grace said.

Freya looked to Inger, "Astrid isn't doing this–I know it!"

Inger looked back to Freya, saying without as much conviction, "I know..."

Grace hesitated, gathered her words, before speaking slowly to all of them, "History has shown us that when we have an important advance in technology, it gets used, whether the masses wish it or not. There are problems with genetic engineering, but the science is still in its crudest infancy. For all the fearful horrors of manipulation at the genetic level, there are definite possibilities of increasing harvests, of producing masses of affordable medications, the ability to repair genetic defects in utero, or even increasing mankind's healthy longevity. This is something, that whether we should or should not do it, it will be attempted."

Astrid just glared at her.

"We have to leave now." Freya was trying to push her friend to leave, but Astrid started furiously, "Genetic Engineering—what else have they done so far? Produced tropical fish that glow in the dark!"

"The addition of genes for glowing does not seem to have altered the fish in any other way," Grace said tiredly.

"But why would they do it?" Astrid countered.

Freya answered that. "People like them. They are willing to pay for them."

A furious Astrid spat out, "A fellow creature on this earth should not be a plaything! A sentient being should not be used as a tank decoration!"

"I surprised you would allow fish tanks at all," Grace commented mildly, wanting to get this over with as she and Freya kind of herded Astrid to the door.

"I wouldn't!" Astrid agreed. "But manufacturing playthings by manipulating DNA is a bastardization! Your genetic engineering starts with hormones to increase maple trees' sap runs—and ends with in utero monestrous operations to produce perfect, blond, blue-eyed, male, genius babies!"

Grace had to defend her work. "Using DNA to check if a child has a tendency for hemophilia or cystic fibrosis is not really genetic manipulation. It's not making super babies, it's only advanced intrauterine testing, and perhaps, in the future, instead of aborting a fetus doomed to chronic suffering, we will be able to correct the problems in utero with genetic engineering."

Astrid didn't look impressed. "And what if that baby is going to be gay, and his parents don't want that?"

Not wanted to argue this Grace pointed out, "Again you are talking about guidelines and decisions that should be made legislatively, not by someone working in a genetics lab." They'd reached the door, Grace opened it.

She hoped the woman would just leave, but Astrid was just getting started. "To clone that first Afghan puppy named Snuppy, they created and destroyed 1095 embryos."

Grace should know better than to argue with a fanatic, but, "They didn't 'destroy' them, the embryos were not viable, either because of genetic problems, or a failure in the techniques being pioneered. The scientists originally trying to produce test tube babies had years and years of unsuccessful attempts, until the correct, complex techniques were developed, and the miracle child, Louise Brown, was born. Since then an estimated five million in-vitro children have been born to what would otherwise have been infertile couples. That may not fit your definition 'natural,' but it brings happiness to a lot of families."

"It's not Gaia's way!" pronounced Astrid, finally turning to leave.

Although she chooses not to comment further, Grace knew of a great many more genetic engineering horrors. Still, there was something to be said about the truth of the old Irish proverb '*life is an island of dangers, surrounded by a sea of instant death.*'

Freya said to Astrid, "I join you at the roadside." When the picketer was gone, Freya turned to Grace. "Are you still going to work for those Humanity's Harvest people?"

"Just a few days ago you thought Axel Jensen was a most eligible bachelor in Oyster River, and that I should be out hunting him?"

"I thought **he** should be hunting you! I still do." Freya stopped and thought about it. "But if Astrid's right, if his genetic engineering destroys family farms, creates mutations, and stillborns..."

"Natural breeding practices produces all those horrors and lots more."

"But if you don't know the outcome of manipulating life forms..." argued Freya.

"The reason you experiment is to find out what you don't know."

"Some of the C.U.R.S. people are more fanatic than Astrid, what if they hurt you or Inger? Grace, what are you going to do?"

If anything happened to Inger because of her, Grace would never forgive herself, but being honest she could only say, "I'm going to read my e-mails and continue with my research."

Freya sounded greatly concerned. "C.U.R.S. may not allow you to do that."

Grace looked up at her old friend, "They'd better not try to stop me."

Chapter 16

The next day Grace determined nothing would disturb her work, she wouldn't allow it. Couldn't. Then a stricken-looking Inger was bringing over an envelope. Her assistant had been opening up the day's pile of mail with latex gloves on. Seeing the scared look on her face, Grace pulled on a pair of gloves from her desk, putting them on before she took the white number 10 business envelope. It looked strange, then she realized why, no logo, no return address, just stamp and computer printed label: Dr. Grace Farrington, Lab 5 at Oyster River Research's address. Strangely afraid, she opened the envelope with a scalpel–being as careful as she could not to touch it more than necessary. A single, folded sheet of white paper that Grace had to unfold was printed with, **'You were warned! You seek to destroy the earth! You will be killed too!'**

Feeling sick Grace put it down on the desk, trying to get control. Whoever it was, knows where she worked, where she lived, where Inger worked, and the threats were escalating. "Call the police–no call ORR Security, then call that town detective, whatever his name was." While Inger did that, Grace attempted to get a DNA sample off the paper and envelope. Probably it would be like before–nothing, but at least this anonymous threatener had learned how to spell her name correctly! She pulled up her murder spreadsheets. Grace skipped the Helmut sheet, if G.E. was the motive, then the intended victim must have been Axel Jensen. And by her venomous stance against his company and himself personally, Astrid seemed to have gained a lot more weight – 50 % as the possible murderer.

ORR Security came first and stood by as the police detective asked his same inane questions. Since the day's work was already interrupted, and Inger seemed really upset, Grace told her assistant to go home early. Deciding she could do her thinking better away from the lab, Grace grabbed her laptop, jacket, and closed up. Outside, the harbor looked like polished gun metal, with clouds that had come in low and dark, resembling the underside of a fleece blanket. Walking she felt a sting of on her cheek–sleet? Could be. Here in Connecticut it actually warmed up a bit before it snowed.

In the Cafeteria, Grace set her laptop on a table for four, glad to be able to eat her salmon alone with her questions over her murder sheets. That didn't last long, because when she looked up, a tall figure was standing there. Axel changed his mind? No, Daniel Novinski, C.U.R.S.' friendly lawyer. The cafeteria was supposed to be off-limits for the picketers, but Daniel obviously ignored this. He stood holding an egg salad on his tray. "Did you have time to read any of my book?"

"Some," she admitted. Actually, last night after Kurt had fallen asleep she'd been restless and read the whole thing. Although one hundred and fifty pages, his book relied on loads of emotion wringing photographs, lots of highlighted text boxes, and endless graphic tables. Not a long or deep read at all.

"Has it changed your mind about genetic engineering?" he asked, almost too eagerly, still standing.

"Not really."

That seemed to put him off track. "Then you don't accept my arguments?"

"They're a little one-sided," Grace said mildly.

"One-sided?" Daniel looked deflated.

Not being that way herself, Grace had to sometimes stop, realizing when she pointed out a problem with their work how badly some people took it as if you were personally attacking them. Grace reviewed the text in her mind, trying to be careful about how she phrased things.

He was looking down at the chair beside her. "May I join you?"

She didn't want him to, but politeness dictated. "Yes."

He quickly sat, looking unhappy. "Can you give me an example from the book?"

"You state that the nutritional value of a genetically engineered tomato was not equal to the nutrition provided by a 'natural' tomato."

"That's a verifiable fact!" His voice was rising. Students are other tables were looking over.   "I provided documentation in the appendix!" he continued sounding more lawyerly.

She nodded in acknowledgment. "I read the citations at the back of the book. Not having done the work myself, I will grant that the laboratory who did the testing is known to be thorough and accurate, but your argument is a Straw Man. That particular strain of tomato was genetically engineered with a tougher skin for the ability to survive mechanical harvesting undamaged.   "I'll give you that it is nutritionally inferior," she continued, "but that's not saying that a tomato or any other food source that is deliberately G.E.'d for enhanced nutritional value, wouldn't be equal or superior to existing food stocks."

"Do you think a profit-oriented concern like Humanity's Harvest is going to be G.E.ing for nutrition? Or even flavor? They're going to produce something that's economically advantageous for themselves. Something cheap to harvest, with a long shelf life, and a deceptively wholesome appearance.   Since I wrote that book, an independent laboratory studied a G.E. soy called 'Round Up Ready' that showed a decline of up to 14 percent of phy..ess..." He started to stumble over the term that she knew well.

"Phytoestrogens. Plant-based estrogens, whose effects we don't fully understand as of yet," Grace completed.

"You know this–but you're not opposed to genetic engineering being controlled by for-profit corporations?"

"Traditionally, businessmen who ignore the needs of

their customers don't stay in business long.   That's the correction of the marketplace."

"That used to be true...before a conglomerate could strangle an entire worldwide market," Daniel retorted.

"That hasn't quite happened yet."

"Hasn't it? It's hard to start a political movement, to convince people that the newspapers they're reading, the TV news they're watching is controlled by monied interests, who have a financial stake in overlooking safety concerns?"

Grace was trying to understand him. Did he believe it all or was it just a platform for his ambition? "So you connect yourself with people who scream at passing cars? That's your idea of productive discourse?"

"Oyster River Research and yourself have sterling reputations. Aren't you afraid that connecting yourself to a controversial entity like Humanity's Harvest could destroy that?"

"In other words, if you can't reason with Axel Jensen or his company, you can arrange protests to stop anyone from working with him?" she asked. "That isn't going to work here."

He flushed angrily. "Actually, I'm not here to demonstrate. Astrid's an old friend, and I'm here to see that her C.U.R.S. people stay out of trouble, or at least stay out of any legal predicaments." Daniel stopped and nervously ran his fingers through his sandy hair. "Look, we keep getting off on the wrong foot. Can't we start again?   Please?"

She quieted, finally saying, "Of course."

He stuck a fork full in his egg salad and said, "Dr. Farrington, how did you find Oyster River? For such a small place, it's turned out an amazing number of Nobel winners?"

"After I attended one of his lectures, Eric Larsen started unofficially mentoring me. Years later he persuaded Oyster River to give me a position as his teaching assistant."

She had no intention of discussing her disgrace at the time

with him.

"Larsen. Didn't he earn the Nobel in Physiology?"

"Yes."

"That will be the category you'll be winning in?" Daniel asked.

Grace wanted to push past that. "Eric had a brilliant, one in a million mind. He was magnificent as a scientist and as a human being."

"He died suddenly in his fifties, didn't he? Quite a loss."

"Yes, I teach his classes now, well my assistant, Bobby Jamison, does most of the work. But we'll never be as good as Eric was–he had an almost subliminal way of connecting with the students. Of illuminating their ideas, of drawing out the best in each one." They ate in silence for a moment, then it was Grace's turn to ask, "What about yourself? Why did you start the Center for Food Sourcing?"

"Because I feel that safe food is of paramount importance." She studied him, as he continued sounding satisfied with himself. "Well, it's even more than that, I've always felt I was born to do something in this world. Something that would last."

"Well, you've done that," Grace acknowledged. "You've become a lawyer, so you can defend people, and you've written books on topics that are obviously important to you."

Daniel shook his head, gazing past her. "No, something way more than all of that. I became a lawyer because that was my best chance to make a difference because I wanted to make changes in this the world."

"Judicial activist?"

"Yes, I'm not ashamed of it! Today that is a career path. Who makes the most decisions in your life, the Supreme Court. Yes, legislators make the laws, but it's the Justices that interpret them, determine how they will be enforced. The High Court constantly is making permanent changes in the way we all live."

Grace could well understand working toward high goals. "Then you plan to be a Supreme Court Justice?"

He colored again. "Might happen. A progressive President could appoint a well know activist lawyer." Daniel spoke proudly, "Actually, in representing my center I've presented four cases before the high court."

"Win any?"

"Won one, lost two. The other is still pending. We might win. But win or lose, I think my arguments were sound and may have changed some people's views," he ended proudly.

She nodded. "It's good to have goals. And you seem to be working successfully towards yours."

"Right now, I'm busy alerting people as to what is happening with their food chain. And sometimes, legally, going after those that would damage it with civil suits, that hold them accountable for their harmful actions against all of us."

"Were there lawyers in your family?"

That stopped him. "Family? Well, it was just my Mom. It was hard for her, and she died when I was seventeen."

"But you went to college and law school?"

"With no money? Yeah, I took a bit longer than most. At first, I bummed around in San Francisco. Did drugs. Worked in a Head Shop, for a big-time Chinese drug dealer. That looked like a lucrative career path, until I opened up the store one morning, and found him in the back room, filleted."

"That would be discouraging," Grace said.

"That afternoon, I signed on with the Merchant Marine. Traveled a lot. Saw Tokyo, China, Australia, Amsterdam, Africa..."

"South America?" she asked.

Her interruption kind of threw him out of his happy revery. "Not much in the Pacific area...but working those boats was good money," he finished.

"Union job for a young man, without college, I should think so."

"Got certified as a hardhat diver."

"Why?"

"While I was working a cable laying tender, frying in the hot sun as I chipped paint off the bulkheads, and I see this guy sunning himself on the deck. I asked him what's his job? Turns out I could get certified as a diver, so I worked a lot less for more money."

"Scary job?"

"A little, but fun. I brought aboriginal carvings for pennies back in Australia, and I sold them for big bucks in San Francisco. From that money, I bought an electronic game set up and rented it out to the other guys when we were at sea, and they were bored."

"Very enterprising," Grace had to admit.

"Saved enough to put me through college, and after I corralled every scholarship, I could apply for I finished up in Harvard law school."

"Sounds like you and Axel Jensen would have quite a bit in common."

Daniel stopped reaching for the last of his salad. "Except Axel's goal in life is to make money, mine is to save people." He leaned forward towards her, again she was struck by the intensity of his blue eyes. "Dr. Farrington–Grace–my foundation would love to have you as a director?"

"Are you really interested in my research opinions? Or just my name on your website?"

"Whatever I can get." He gave a boyish smile that had a touch of Peter Pan in it. "It'll be minimal work unless you're interested in doing more. Just a quote or two a year for our bulletins." He switched into heavy duty persuasion mode. "You know many of the people that vote on awards are progressives–people who want to make changes for a better world. Having your name on our Foundation might help realize your own goals."

"Sign up with you and win a Nobel?" Grace asked tartly. "Joining your foundation would be putting my scientific reputation on the line." He said nothing, so she continued, "If I were interested in working for your cause, I'd have to fully delve into it. And I'm sorry–I don't have time enough to complete the work I already have."

He leaned closer to her. "But think of the advantages, for just attending a meeting or two a year, or maybe even just reading and commenting on our publications, you would get a tax deduction for the contribution of your time, and we would value your time highly." As Grace started to say 'no' again, Daniel continued, "and, more importantly, by joining my International Food Web Center Foundation you would have a chance to keep pesticides of babies' formulas," he glanced at her plate commenting, "and peanut genes out of your salmon specials."

Finished eating they were both setting up their trays to return them, but as he spoke Grace found herself mentally visualizing those C.U.R.S. tables. Seeing his books and Astrid's pamphlets, and suddenly she remembered the last table near the entrance to the reception hall. That fisherman's net, artfully decorated with dried starfish, shells, and a spear gun. "The night that Helmut died, one of those information tables at the Roost entrance had a red spear gun on it?"

"Possibly," said Daniel in a noncommittal manner.

"That might have been the murder weapon."

Daniel looked away from her. His lawyerly advocate instincts obviously warring with not wishing to protect a murderer. Finally, he said, "I don't think that could be provable."

"Where is it?"

Finally, he met her eyes. "It's missing. It got back to the tent camp on the point that night. The spear gun was seen in a box, just within the doorway of a tent, but now it's missing."

"Do the police know that?" Grace questioned.

"I advised Astrid to tell them." But he slipped into all advocate again, "That doesn't mean that particular spear gun was the murder weapon."

"Do you know who decorated that table?"

"Yes, Holly Morris, a sweet kid. But the spear gun didn't belong to her, she just borrowed the gun, netting, and seashells from someone else."

"Who else?" she asked.

"A local fisherman, who has been hanging around with the protestors." Grace figured she knew the name, even before Daniel said it,   "Some guy named Josh Jeffers."

Then with that endlessly successful smile, Daniel left her.

Chapter 17

The next morning, with the sky still a sprinkle of phosphorescent stars Kurt got out of her bed and kissed her forehead. Deliciously half asleep, Grace heard him moving in her kitchen. Soon she savored the smell of bacon frying, as sputtering eggs hit a hot pan. She showered, and when Grace came out, he was taking out the toast. He'd already set the table before her wall of glass doors that overlooked the balcony, with its unobstructed view of the ruffled waved harbor.

As they sat down, he said, "Okay. I got a look at Huang's contract with Humanity's Harvest."

"How'd you do that?" she asked digging into her egg.

"Adam has a copy of the contract filed in the Admin building."

That didn't sound right to Grace. "It wasn't locked up?"

"Whal, not locked up too well," he admitted.

"Kurt!"

"It's pretty obvious, when Axel Jensen signed that fat contract, he was under the impression that both you and I were on it–under Herr Huang's direction."

That last 'direction' bit rankled. "Was I mentioned by name?"

"No–only 'Huang's Team' was written–sounds like he dictated the whole thing. But from that definite anger behind Axel's eyes, and Adam Greenfield's embarrassment when you told them you weren't involved, there must have been a lot of verbal promises of your services, as one of Huang's obedient team members."

"Shit."

"Hey, I think I was included in that mix," he said proudly. Looked out at the harbor they both could see a distant white dot with the bright red body strip, where Axel

Jensen's Beech 18 bobbed at anchor. "That seaplane is big bucks, maybe it's time we made our own deal."

"We have my go-to-New Haven-Inca sampling study?"

"That got your new refrigerator unit, but I think we can do a lot better than that."

"In what time? Axel wants me to spend two months sampling in Peru. That's not happening. We both have a full schedule of studies funded."

"Think long term. Axel Jensen and Humanity's Harvest could be the new funding force behind Oyster River Research."

She thought about it. Him funding them would keep Axel around. "Maybe one of your lobster or oyster studies?"

"Axel hot for genetic engineering. What do they call that processing?"

"Recombinant DNA technology." She chewed a bit, Kurt always made such great breakfasts. "How do you get the bacon so crisp?"

"Forget the bacon.   How do they insert an alien gene into a cell?"

"There are several methods, all of them have drawbacks. Originally in the most commonly used procedure, you used an enzyme to isolate the desired gene, that can be turned on..."

He gave her the usual leer. "The little fella can be aroused?"

She primly ignored that. "The default for a packaged gene is 'off' because every cell in your body carries copies of all your genes, so you don't want 'liver enzymes' being produced by your skin cells."

Even joking Kurt seemed to be really trying to understand, as he asked, "So first you've got to isolate an unpackaged gene that you want to put in?"

"Then you've got to insert it in your organism's cells. If you were working with plants, originally the most commonly used method was to piggyback on a bacterium vector. Agrobacterium..."

"Agro-what?"

"A soil bacterium, that causes gall growths in plants. It readily penetrates cells–we don't fully know yet how–when the package inside, hopefully, your target gene gets incorporated in your cells chromosomes. Then the modification should be inheritable."

Always quick to understand Kurt asked, "So what's wrong with that?"

"A few things. The inserted genes are always 'on,' and we have no control over where in the chromosome that gene inserts. And to test whether it worked or not, they usually include a gene for resistance to antibiotics."

"Why?"

"If you subject the newly created cell mix to antibiotics, you know all the surviving cells have antibiotic resistance and presumably the rest of your gene insertion package."

"But over the long term, you'll decrease the effectiveness of antibiotics?"

"Unfortunately, yes."

"Any other methods?"

"You can shoot your plants with a gene gun. Microscopic particles of metals, such as gold, will shoot your snipped gene into the plant nucleus by brute force."

He had started finishing his eggs but listening carefully. "Sounds safer."

"But a lot less reliable. And when you get into animal cells and gene therapy on humans, the problems compound. Now with the CRISPR..."

"Chris what?"

"CRISPR stands for Clustered Regularly Interspaced

Short Palindromic Repeats."

"That does?"

"It's a method working with a lot more advanced techniques using RNA guides to locate and snip out gene sequences."

"Snip out?" he asked.

"During replication cells need a way to edit and repair broken or incorrect DNA. Scientists found naturally occurring endonuclease that chemically cut out bacteria or foreign DNA from the cells. We now utilize this to allow removal of a specific sequence and sometimes replacement of a specified string that becomes naturally integrated into the host genome."

"Works good?"

"Like you taking shears to cut out rotten squares of a fishing net and reweaving them with a stronger line of the same material. CRISPR facilitates cutting out the targeted and controlled replacing of sequences with modifying genes from the same species, so this isn't being classified or treated as 'Genetic Engineering.' With the CRISPR you permanent modify the genes, but you can bypass some of the more egregious red-tape and labeling now surrounding G.E. "

"Is that a good thing? Or are yer against genetic engineering?" he asked studying her carefully.

Getting up, Grace started picking up the dirty plates. "I see genetic engineering as the future hope of medicine, of extending human life, but there's an awful lot of work to be done before it's dependable enough, much less safe, for routine work in higher order animals. And if G.E. is used irresponsibly now, governments may legislate uninformed laws to stop all of it, which is exactly what has been done in some countries. Now, sir, it's been lovely, but I've got to get back to my laboratory."

She started to walk to grab her handbag and jacket. Behind her, Kurt put out a hand, running it along her arm.

His warm breath was on her back. His lips pressing her neck as he murmured, "Hey, lady, this seaman is getting ready to ship out for two months. Ya got to hurry that much?"

Well, maybe she didn't have to hurry that much. Grace smiled as she turned back, snuggling into his arms.

*   *   *

Later, his lobster trawler was out on the harbor dipping for salty samples and pulling up his lobster traps. With him gone, she still felt a warm afterglow leaving her too energized to just go to her lab, so Grace pulled on her running shoes then drove to the Village of Oyster River, diagonally across the Harbor. After her run, she stopped at the Firehouse Deli and picked up a cherry danish and today's copy of *The Sound Times*.

The headlines she expected: 'Murder at Oyster River Facility.' The article was bylined, 'Samantha Carson,' that copper-haired reporter, the woman dating Mac. Yes, murders do bring lurid publicity, but did it always have to be that reporter digging around? There were pictures of Helmut Roberts, standing proudly in his museum. Sam must have gotten them from Inez. How could the woman cold-bloodedly interview a new, grieving widow? The story had a rehash of former Oyster River murders--that Grace had played a part in–fortunately not mentioned her by name.

But sadly she concluded that Sam-the-Reporter was just going after Mac-the-Cop to further her journalistic reach. Grace thought of dropping by Freya's to just vent, but Freya always read the local paper and would be coming to the same conclusion, so her friend would be in a poisonous mood. Grace decided just to get back to the safe, peace of her lab.

Or she would have if about twenty police cars and vans weren't blocking the entrance to Oyster River Research.

She had to park across the road, in the fish hatchery's parking lot and then walk over. The protestors were linking hands and chanting, as private security were evicting them in full view of two television van crews and the police. Canvas and boxes--remains of their tent city from the point--were being dumped off trucks and piled up by the road. The picketers were chanting. Crying. And, of course, seeing a flash of new penny hair, Grace saw that reporter Sam was scribbling away in her notepad.

And there was a lot to cover as Grace stood back on the hillside by the Roost. People milling about, ORR security, the local police, state police, protestors, and journalists. Grace heard outraged hollering, as police in black riot gear were hauling a struggling Josh Jeffers off. Naturally that reporter, Sam, squatted before them, photographing it all.

Protestors continued to chant, "KEEP FOOD FREE!" As Astrid followed the cops dragging Josh, she was screaming "GESTAPO!" Grace recognized one of the town police dragging the struggling Josh as the stocky Ben. Standing between him and the crowd was the tall, uniformed figure of Mac. He turned his focus to the screaming Astrid, not touching her, but firmly blocking her way with his body. Behind him a young woman demonstrator raised a placard over her head, swinging its heavy wood stick handle to hit Mac's head.

Chapter 18

Literally dropping her camera, Sam screamed, "Mac!" As she bolted forward.

He twisted to look at Sam, as the demonstrator swing the placard stick at his head, but Sam had sprinted forward, grabbing the back of the 2" x 2", pulling the picketer off balance, so the placard just painfully glanced off Mac's shoulder as Grace ran over to help.

The woman picketer furiously tried to kick and hit Sam with her stick, cutting her cheek, and kicking her shin. Sam twisted, using her elbow to throw the woman off balance. Then did a jumping side kick to knock her down. Mac was over the demonstrator, with his handcuffs. Hauling the woman to a standing position, as more police were running to aid them.

Astrid was there, screaming, "You have no right to arrest her!"

"Armed assault on an officer and a civilian? I think we do, mam!" said Mac, as he had finished cuffing the cursing demonstrator. Mac turned her over to two cops that Grace didn't recognize, who dragged the screaming demonstrator and her placard away. Then he walked over to Samantha, who had picked up her camera and was examining it for damage. He looked down at her and softly said, "Nice side kick."

"I'm going for my black belt," Sam said proudly.

"Got my third-degree black belt while I was in the Marines," acknowledged Mac. "By the way, I'm a big boy–I don't need saving."

"She had you from behind," said a concerned Sam.

"But as a trained cop, I can handle all 120 pounds of her."

Sam pointed towards the road, where a mobile t-v crew was set up. "You want to be filmed as the monster bully beating up a poor, defenseless little girl picketer?"

He looked over at the cameras and sighed, "Can't say 'girl.' It's not politically correct." There was a trickle of blood on her cheek. Mac reached up to gently wipe it with his fingers, and to give them privacy Grace walked away.

"Whal, bout time something was done." Kurt's voice came from behind Grace.

"They arrested Josh," Grace said with mixed feelings. Joshua Jeffers was a nut, but Grace didn't think he'd killed Helmut.

"Josh? He didn't kill that museum guy. They won't be able to hold him long. He'll be back. Blaming us." Kurt was looking over the crowd, grimly. "When I'm gone, you got to keep my revolver with you."

"Even without yours, I have got my grandfather's rifles and a shotgun in the condo."

He shook his head. "Too awkward at close range. Yer can't stuff a rifle your purse."

"I don't have a carry permit, and I hear they take forever to get," she said.

He kept scanning the crowd, looking deeply concerned. "Grace, you gotta get one! Think about protecting Inger."

She shrugged, Grace should have done this before. "To get fingerprinted and checked out will take months."

Mac was coming over to them, and Kurt called him over. "I'm getting Grace to sign up for a Carry permit. She's getting those anonymous threatening letters, but she'll still need fingerprints, a safety class..."

Mac nodded. "I can get her fingerprinted today and arrange for an NRA Safety Instructor for a free private class, he owes me a couple." He looked to Grace. "When you get the papers filled out give them to me, and maybe I can expedite the F.B.I. clearance."

"I don't have the time for safety classes," protested

Grace.

"Yer making time!" Kurt's mouth was set hard, and the steel eyes that glared at her were harder.

Actually, visualizing that red metal shaft sticking out of Helmet's floating body, getting a carry permit did seem like a good idea to Grace. Mac was looking toward Astrid, figuring out what the protestors would be doing next. A cadre of about four female pickers stood around Astrid, valiantly holding their signs, waiting to be arrested, while other picketers tried to salvage what they could of their tent city.

A blue Durango pickup pulled past the police cars. Shiny. Driving up fast and parking near them. A red-headed, stocky built man climbed out and hurried over. For a second Grace tensed up, then realized it wasn't Josh Jeffers; it was his twin brother, Greg, coming to try and straighten things out.

Astrid looked at him, but Greg hurried over to Mac, Kurt, and Grace.

"Do you know where Josh is?" A worried Greg asked as he glanced at the cops.

"He was taken in," said Mac reluctantly.

Greg closed his eyes in pain. "Fighting cops?"

"Yeah, but I don't think that'll be charged. They had a warrant for him, they want to question him in Dr. Helmut Robert's murder investigation, and some threatening letters folks have been getting."

"Letters?" Greg asked in surprise. "You think my brother sits down to write letters?"

Kurt added a warning, "Greg, the cops are probably gonna search yer house, Josh's boat, and yer bait shop."

"Why? Josh didn't kill that guy," Greg shot back, but he looked scared.

"Mr. Jeffers?" Daniel Novinski and Astrid were joining them.

"They had no right to arrest your brother!" Astrid

started.

Greg didn't look too happy to see her. "Well, that's not going to help him much, is it?"

"Excuse me, sir, I'm Daniel Novinski." He reached out to shake Greg's hand. "A friend of Josh's. A lawyer."

Greg didn't shake his hand. "Lawyer?" Greg looked at Kurt. "My brother's gonna need that?"

Kurt nodded.

Greg turned to Daniel said with a tinge of contempt. "You're with Curs?"

"Not actually as a lawyer. I'm here as a food web activist, but I am licensed to practice in Connecticut, New York and the District of Columbia."

"Criminal law?"

"Not usually. My specialty is food chain related civil suits. But I have helped arrested demonstrators before, and right now with a murder charge involved, I think your brother should have someone with him, protecting his basic rights."

"Keeping his big mouth shut be more like it!" said Greg, looking to Kurt and Grace. "Our regular lawyer is having a hip replacement."

So Daniel said, "With your permission, I could defend your brother, pro bono until your guy is up again?"

Greg Jeffers looked from the picketers to the police piling boxes of broken tents on the grass. "You're hired. Meet ya at the police station."

With a nod to Kurt, a slumping shouldered Gregg Jeffers walked back to his truck.

Kurt turned to Mac. "When I'm gone, you keep after Gracie about that carry permit! And Josh didn't kill that guy."

Mac looked down at her. "Aaup." Then Mac headed off to help with the protestors' boxes.

Daniel Novinski hadn't left yet. In fact, he seemed to be wanting her attention. "Grace?"

"What do you want?" Kurt asked in an unfriendly manner.

"I just wanted to talk to Grace for a moment," the lawyer said, then Daniel fell silent. Kurt didn't move. Daniel tried again, "Privately, if you don't mind."

Kurt stuck his jaw out. Grace knew that gesture of stubbornness, but she raised her hand slightly, calling him off. "I'm going to walk Daniel to his car."

Reluctantly, Kurt stayed put, just glaring as they walked away.

When they were at some distance, Daniel said, "I have to go to the police station to see if I can get Josh released."

"Is that a good idea?" she asked.

Daniel just gave a twisted smile. "A lawyer's job is not to judge, it is to see his client gets his full rights."

More private ORR security guards were carrying protestors' tents, and garbage from the Point. Dumping them before the last picketers.

"That looks like my tent," Daniel tartly commented.

"You want to go get it?" Grace asked.

"Nope. I got it second hand. The last few nights I actually was showering at a room I rented at the Shoreline Motel. Moving in there will be a lot more comfortable than sleeping here."

"If you were renting a room why did you camp out?"

"To be near the C.U.R.S. people, in case–well, in case this happens. Astrid and I wanted everything kept legal, and I needed to see your security people didn't cross any line." He looked over the growing mound of clothes, mashed cardboard, and cooking pots. "It should've stayed a peaceful protest."

"But it didn't. Helmut was killed."

He looked as the demonstrators were salvaging what

they could. Astrid just glared at security, daring the cops to arrest them. "That wasn't our people."

"You know this for a fact?" That would mean Daniel knew who the killer was.

He smiled ruefully. "No, but I know most of the demonstrators involved. It's kinda hard to kill someone with a cardboard peace symbol."

Remembering that woman using her 2" by 2" wooden handled placard to swing at a policeman, Grace didn't have his confidence. They had walked to a bright red Prius, and Daniel took out his key lock and clicked it open.

"You wanted to talk to me?" Grace reminded.

Daniel seemed to look about first, to see if anyone else was in hearing range, then not looking in her direction while he opened his car door, he very quietly said, "You seem to know that policeman personally? The tall one?"

"Mac? He's the son of my friend, Freya. He was only three foot tall when I first moved here."

"Look." He stopped, pressing his lips together, like he was in a battle with himself, then when he spoke it rushed out, "I heard something." He looked directly at her. "Nothing I could testify to!" Daniel stopped, then started again. "Last night. At the C.U.R.S. tent camp at the point. Well, the last time I tried that porta-john somebody had threw up in it, so I just stepped off the trail into the woods, and was in the bushes when I heard these guys."

"Guys?"

"Two men. Well, two deep voices in the shadows, almost whispering. One guy was explaining to the other how to set up a cell phone, so it can be used as a timer to detonate."

Coldness flooded Grace. "Detonate what?"

"They didn't say, but I assume it was a bomb."

"Do you know who...?"

"No. They moved out, I stayed in place, hey--I've got

no desire to face off with two possible mass killers, okay?"

"Do you think the Curs people would...?"

"Some of these people believe that by stopping genetic engineering they're saving the world. Hell, they've given up their jobs, their family time to come here, and sleep out in the cold and march in public, with other people calling them crazy..."

"But a bomb—it kills anyone around it—guilty or not. What about the innocent students here? Bobby's kids?"

"Maybe they were just talking?" Daniel shrugged his shoulders, but she felt that even he didn't believe that. "Maybe they knew I was there and it was a joke on me?"

"Maybe it wasn't!"

"Grace, it's not my call!"

"Maybe you could have reined in some of your people before Helmut got a spear shaft in his back."

"Look," Daniel said slipping into his car and starting the engine. "From my standpoint, there were a bunch of innocent people in that camp that shouldn't have their reputations smeared with being labeled potential bombers since I can't identify anybody! If you want to pass what I said on to your friend, go ahead. But if it gets back to me—we didn't have this conversation." He closed the door and was pulling out as she stood there helplessly watching him leave.

Grace looked back towards the water. Several Curs people were crying or begging to be allowed to stay, as security herded them off the property. From a distance Kurt was watching her, as Grace hurried back to the dock were Mac and that girl, Sam, were talking. Both seemed reluctant to turn their attention to Grace.

"Mac, I've got to speak with you." Grace looked at Sam. "If you don't mind this is not for publication."

Sam looked in askance to Mac, but at his nod, she moved away, going back into the crowd finding a crying

C.U.R.S. woman to interview. Grace waited until Sam was busy with that and then turned to Mac. "A witness, well, he says he can't identify the persons involved."

"Our careful lawyer friend, who just had a talk with you?" Mac supplied sarcastically.

She ignored that. "Last night, it was dark, he was off the trail in the woods. He didn't want to use the porta-john. He heard two deep voices-- probably guys--talking. One was telling the other how to use a cell phone as a detonator for some sort of bomb."

"Shit." Mac looked around at the demonstrators. Most older women, but some young males and two older men.

Kurt was walking over to them as Grace looked at Mac saying, "Maybe the police could check for explosives? Do you have explosive detecting equipment?"

"The Village of Oyster River does not have an airport," the cop said sourly.

"Well, can you borrow a dynamite sniffing dog? Check out those tents in the boxes?"

"We don't have a warrant–but they're being evicted off private property–so we're already looking for anything that might be a weapon. Did they mention a target? A time frame?" Mac asked.

"No," said Grace. "Getting information on a bomb detonator--that sounds like Josh Jeffers."

Kurt's voice came from her side. "No, it don't! Josh is all smash and hit! Patiently building a weapon isn't his style. And the Jeffers boys grew up working in their father's gas station. Mechanics don't need some guy to tell them how to make a detonator."

"Could Josh be teaching someone else?" Grace asked.

Kurt seemed to mull that over. "Don't see him using a pricy dingus like a cell phone to blow anything up. Cheaper to buy a used alarm clock at Goodwill."

Grace looked about it.   None of those serious

protestors looked like they would give the police trouble, much less kill people, but someone had killed Helmut. "You need some sort of explosive to make a bomb. It's illegal to possess explosives. Nobody here could get any, right?"

Mac nodded. "Of course they couldn't, unless they had five hundred dollars, and could drive over to Rye to pick up a bunch of M 80's."

Kurt looked up at him, "Actually, I know guys in Connecticut that could set yer up with real plastic explosive C4 for a lot cheaper."

"You can buy explosives around here?" Grace asked.

With his best stern cop frown, Mac was glaring at Kurt. "Not if we catch you." Kurt just gave a lopsided grin, and Mac shook his head in disgust, then he turned back to Grace. "I'll pass your friend's knowledge to the detectives. They won't be happy about anonymous tips–let me know if you hear of anything more specific." His worried eyes swept the crowd again. "Grace, with them leaving threats at your condo, maybe you should be living off this peninsula. Move in with ma for a bit?"

"I thought your house rules didn't allow stay overs?" she asked.

"You're family," stated Mac firmly. "And even if Ma's arguing with you over this stuff, the door will always be open. You know that."

Kurt chimed in, "Grace, you should go stay with Freya, especially if I'm gone."

"I'll be fine here," Grace said. Mac walked off in the direction of his patrol car and the waiting scarlet headed reporter, as Bobby ran up to Kurt. "Two Curs ran over by our boats!"

"Shit!" Kurt said, heading off to defend his crafts.

Grace had enough of this, she needed to just forget it all, and get some work done. Going back to her lab she had a few hours of working in her Clean room, but finally, when she walked back into her main lab, a tall, handsome man awaited her. He was with Inger, but all Grace really saw were those square shoulders in his khaki safari jacket. She found herself being excited that Axel Jensen was casually standing there asking, "More problems from the protestors? I'm so sorry, this should not be happening."

Pulling off her disposable haircap, Grace smiled tiredly. "They're clearing out the demonstrators' tent city, so maybe they'll just go away."

The line of his mouth just tightened, then he said, "I doubt that."

Inger had a sudden need to disappear into the Airlock to check supplies, and the obviousness of that made Grace flush a bit in embarrassment. Standing beside this man always seemed to jumble her thoughts so, but she had to stay on course. "You shouldn't be worried about us, the man murdered was your height, had your hair color, a beard not a goatee, but he was wearing a tan jacket. You do realize that the murderer must have thought he was killing you?"

Axel's smile was ironic. "I figured that out the first five minutes. Of course, the police were by to ask if I have any enemies."

"Do you?"

"Lovable me?" He laughed, with a touch of bitterness. "Enemies?   Just because I've done hostile corporate takeovers?   There are rebels against regimes I have to do business with?   My girlfriend's ex-boyfriends?   People, who think my money should be theirs?   Yes, there are a few people who aren't enchanted with me, but," he looked out the windows, toward the calm harbor and said, "not here, that I can think of."

She followed his gaze out her laboratory windows. Both knew that to the right, across the main road on the state property of the fish hatchery three, maybe four, protestors still faithfully circled with their placards. "There's a whole lot of those dedicated, anti-genetic engineering activists."

His lips twisted wryly. "People, who in their own way feel they're doing the right thing to save this world. I may disagree with them, but I'm not afraid of them."

Although the muscular shape of Josh Jeffers was under arrest, Grace didn't share his confidence and wanted to change the conversation.   "How is your project with Dr. Huang coming along?"

Axel's face hardened. "Not too well. Apparently, Huang and the rest of you don't spend much time communicating?"

"As I have stated, the scientists at Oyster River work independently."

"Wish I'd know that before I'd signed the contract with Oyster River." His mouth spread in a tight line, then he glanced at her and smiled ruefully. "Totally the fault of my organization. Ekkeko should have vetted that contract thoroughly, checking with you and the others–then there would have been no misunderstandings. " She didn't wish to displease him, but Grace had no intention of being included on Huang's 'team,' still Axel was continuing, "Huang said that you had done extensive research into genes that expressed only under certain conditions, but my researchers can't find anything you've published on that. Was that another slight exaggeration of his?"

"No. I haven't published my work, but at a Beijing conference years ago I did speak about my studies in that area. It's been a lifelong interest, that started in grade school when I first read about Barbara McCormick's work." As much as Grace disliked Dr. Huang Wong, Oyster River's reputation was something they should all guard, so she asked, "What do you specifically want to get out of Huang's algae?"

Axel stopped to think about that. "He's promised quite a bit. Algae that would have a short growing span be edible and highly nutritious. A single food source that could have definite, changeable flavors, according to the temperature that the algae was cultured at." He looked to Grace with those deep green eyes. "Do you think that's genetically possible?"

Grace also gave it some serious thought, before saying, "Yes, I do. In theory, there are many cases of genes that express under different conditions–temperature is often one of them. The sex of alligators is determined by the temperature that their eggs are subjected to in the nest. External manipulation of genes to express different flavor phenotypes in a food source is an interesting concept." He stayed quiet as Grace stared at the side wall, running various scenarios through her mind as she considered the penetrance of the algae alleles controlling the plant's taste. "It's theoretically possible, but your choices of favor genes for splicing with your algae may be a very difficult reach. Why aren't you working with more complex biological forms with an increased flavor palette, like say the herbal families?"

Axel seemed totally focused on what to him was of vital importance. "The one cell form of algae lends itself to culturing large amounts of nourishment for a closed population of humans. In a famine situation, tank trucks could be brought in to rapidly produce enough food to be life-sustaining–a sort of modern manna. With his genetically engineered algae, Huang promises an abundant, tasty, renewable, recyclable food source for space travelers."

Since the space program began algae as a possible food source had been studied, so Grace had to admire Huang for taking it in a new direction. "It's certainly an ambitious undertaking," she admitted.

"He promises a moon shot with his project, but unfortunately, Humanity's Harvest isn't interested in paying for only a few concept papers..."

Grace cut in. "Huang just started the project, he should only be in his first generation..."   Axel looked disgusted. "He can't even get his growing tanks working! The only yield Humanity's Harvest is going to get out of this project is a bounty of bad public relations."

Grace pictured those threatening letters, and Helmut's body. "Are you canceling? My assistant, Inger, has gotten a threatening letter too."

He looked so frustrated. "I'd like to station some of my security guards in your lab, we..."

"Not necessary," she said firmly. "Security patrols regularly, and Kurt has got Bobby walking me home at night." As charming as Axel was, Grace felt they'd wasted enough time on this. "Now, I'm sure you've got work to do."

Not taking the hind, he just sat down casually on the edge of her desk. "Actually, I was thinking of taking you out to dinner–to talk. The city has some fine restaurants, and it's time to eat. If you like Pakistani, there's Nirvana?"

Driving to New York and back? During the commute? That would take hours, but Grace realized she did want to spend some time with this charismatic man, and she was getting hungry. "How about something locally?"

Axel said disparagingly, "New England cooking? Boiled potatoes and dried codfish?"

Grace laughed. "And hard tack biscuits. Yes. New England is not exactly known for its haute cuisine, but we have some hardy, creamy clam chowders. And, if you can find it, order a real lobster pot, with oysters, and corn-on-the-cob, steamed in seaweed. Try that with Samuel Adams hard cider and cheddar-apple pie." Grace deepened her twang, "It's Yankee grub at its best."

In his careless, languid voice, Axel asked, "Where could we get something like that tonight?"

She had to think about that. "Actually, just across the harbor, at the Captain's Mansion. I don't know if they'll have a full clambake, but they're known for their clam chowder, raw oysters, fried stuffed shrimp, steamed Captain's platters, and crocks of molasses baked beans."

"Sounds delicious. Will you join me?" he asked.

"To talk about research?"

"And to defend the honor of Connecticut's cuisine? And maybe, just learn a little bit more about each other?"

She smiled. "Fine." Actually, she would like to hear what he had to say.

"What time should I pick you up to?" Those deep looks again, actually this man could really make Grace forget her research priorities–at least for a little time.

"Give me an hour to run an errand and change. Six thirty at my condo?"

"Sounds good to me," he said.

Chapter 19

Grace headed over to what she would always call Eric's lab. When she had her work stolen, and her scientific reputation shredded, Nobel prize-winning scientist Eric Larsen had reached out and--as she learned years later--forced Oyster River to give her a teaching position. Grace hated teaching, but the position came with her own time in a shared lab, and Eric's encouragement and backing enabled her to start getting her own grants.

The four-story beige brick building built in the 1980s contained several laboratories–the largest, Eric's took up the whole first floor. As she walked inside, Grace realized it had been redecorated. Once the blue tiled floor lobby had been hung with Eric's poster-sized microscopic glimpses of cell division; now there were now photographs of Dr. Huang Wong: a twenty-two-year-old Huang at Tiananmen Square accepting some award from a business-suited, Chinese man. Hu Jintao himself? More pictures of Huang at this or that dinner receiving an award. Huang conducting a water sampling on a Chinese fishing boat; and Huang Wong in a lab coat at ORR, studiously peering into a tray of vials.

There were more posters inside Eric's–no, Huang's--lab. With a touch of acid, Grace noted they were all a lot younger versions of Huang, nothing recent. The real version of Dr. Huang Wong looked worse for wear. He seemed to have been living in the lab, his white coat was stained and wrinkled–unusual for the normal perfectly turned out scientist. There was darkness under his eyes, even a jumply tic in one eye. As they talked, he seemed to be nervously, compulsively moving about. "You come here–why?"

"I was wondered how the Humanity's Harvest research was going?" Grace started.

He didn't look friendly. "This interest you–why?"

"Because I work and live in Oyster River Research,

and I want to see any project it's involved in as a success."

Huang drew himself up straight as he said loudly, "It goes well! All my projects go well!"

"That's good." Now maybe Grace could get another questioned answered. "You saw Axel and Helmut at your reception?"

"Who Helmut?" An uninterested Huang was looking back to his computer screen.

"Dr. Helmut Roberts. The museum curator from New Haven. The man who was killed."

"So bad–newspapers write all of him!" Huang looked up in outrage. "Not write about my important grant!"

"Do you remember seeing Helmut at the reception?"

"Yes. Bearded man. Shakes my hand. Axel introduces him to me."

Even Huang could remember who he was introduced to thought Grace bitterly. "Do you remember when he left?"

"I stay till end. Think he there. Hang around Axel."

This was going nowhere. "Was Ekkeko still there? Bobby Jamison?"

"Maybe. It my reception, Grace, I busy." Then he asked in a worried fashion. "Jensen, he wishes to hire you?"

"Axel seemed to have been under the impression that the contract he signed with you also hired me and the rest of the ORR's staff." She answered in an annoyed fashion.

He brushed it off, walking to one of the tables. "He no understand. Contract with me–only!"

"I spoke with Axel today, he said your tanks aren't working?"

Huang slammed his hand down on the table. "Greenhouse not working! Roof leaks! Piping leaks! Water all over! Algae can't grow–grows on the floor!"

Okay, that could be fixed. "If it's not functioning, the builder has to fix it," Grace said calmly.

"Corrupt builder does not return telephone call!"

"Tell Gail in Administration. She'll call, or she'll get Adam on it. In the meantime, you have to get your tubs producing a first generation." Grace thought quickly. "We'll get Kurt to work on this, and we'll have to do it before he leaves."

"MacKay? What he know plumbing?" Huang spoke contemptuously.

"Kurt lives on a boat. If he doesn't keep things shipshape and handles leaks, his home sinks."

Huang stood there, overweening male pride warring with desperation for a study going down the drain. His need for keeping Axel's grant money won out, as Huang said sharply, "Kurt look at it. See if he do anything."

Well, that was as close to a 'thank you' as she was going to get. Now she'd have to go tell Kurt she'd volunteered his services again. Great. Walking to the dock Grace noted the demonstrators were gone. She felt a little sorry for them, they meant well, but Grace still had to step over that stupid chain across the upper dock. Hurrying down the ramp, she saw Bobby at the helm of the lobster trawler, as Kurt was casting off the stern line.

"Kurt!" she called out over the diesels.

"Jes casting off," he said walking to the next roping. "Gotta take samples, if you can't wait, turn to your vibrator."

He was in one of **those** moods. "Kurt–I need your help!"

"For what?" He asked as he bent to cast off the bowline.

"The greenhouses. The new tanks are leaking, so Huang can't get his first generation started."

Stepping closer to the boat, Kurt looked at her with total disinterest. "And we should care why?"

She took a deep, bracing breath. "I promised you'd take a look at it."

He glared at her. "Grace, I've told you before–stop

volunteering me!"

"Can't you just look at it? Tell me what needs to be done?" Grace pleaded.

Shaking his head, Kurt was climbing aboard his boat. "I got to finish two months worth of work before I leave! I'm still packing! If it were your project, you know I'd do it in a minute, but for Huang, no way!"

Bobby was holding the lobster trawler near the dock, but Grace was forced to yell over the engines, "Look, if you're trying to rope in Axel and his company's money for your own studies, Oyster River's has got to look good! If Huang can't even keep water in his tanks, we'll all look like incompetent fools!"

At least he could see the reasoning, but Kurt looked tired as he yelled back, "Let's talk about this when I get back. Gonna be a short run, want dinner at the Neptune?"

"Previous engagement. Tomorrow?" She asked, then added, "You'll just look at the tanks for me, please?"

Unhappy, he nodded, then signaled Bobby, who shifted the powerful diesel engines into gear, spitting salty water on her as they pulled out. Grace had to hurry back to her condo to get dressed. With Kurt and her non-exclusive dating arrangements, Grace should have just told him she was going out with Axel tonight, but somehow she just didn't.

It was dark outside when Axel came to her door. She planned to just go out, but he came in and settled down on her couch. They both sat and talked for awhile, about places they'd visited. She gave lectures and moved on, so Grace marveled how he always seemed to stop time in each, and burrow a bit into the local culture. Finally, they headed down to his black Cadillac Escalade. Because it was her fanciest, Grace had worn a light evening jacket trimmed with black beads. Fortunately, the night had warmed up to about forty-two degrees.

Leaving ORR, they drove around the harbor's marshy

end, passing seventeenth-century houses set along the water. She noted the Brewsters had woven fir boughs and bittersweet around their mailbox. Grace would have to visit them soon and talk about her latest research to Stewart. Even forcibly retired, ORR's former director like to be kept in the loop.

The old houses gave way to a sandy beach on their left. At her directions, Axel turned off to the right and parked in a lot alongside a three-story rambling building that overlooked the harbor. Axel was unhappily eyeing the restaurant, which even in the poor outdoor lighting was a remodeled farm-like house, obviously in need of another coat of paint. "I know you said their food was good, but this doesn't look terribly upscale. Adam took me to a seafood place not too far from here, The Pier. Great French seafood. Couldn't we just get back into my car?" he asked.

As always the water seemed to draw Grace, and she had started to walk to the roadside as he followed. Harbor lights bounced off the low hanging clouds, illuminating boats bobbing at anchor. It might be warming up to snow, and she could see the lights from the Oyster River Research peninsula across from them. From here she could just make out the opening to the Sound. Grace couldn't see it but knew his seaplane was moored closer to town, beyond the Neptune. The wind blew from the land out to the water now, and, as Axel stood closer to her Grace could smell his pleasant aftershave, that clean, masculine scent of him, and feel Axel's body heat. He was a magnificent man to just be standing alongside.

"Trust me," she said. "The food here is New England cuisine at its best." Impulsively Grace turned and tucked her arm into his.

He squeezed back. "My lady's whim is my command."

Just his touch seemed to excite her, but was this a professional dinner, or something else? She was never good at reading cues or sending men signals, Grace was so afraid his intentions might not be hers, and that she would embarrass the both of them, so she just blandly babbled, "At the Captain's Mansion your lobster will come from this harbor. The chef's careful about using all the local seafood and produce he can." As they turned back to walk towards the door, she pointed out. "See that smaller, older building in the back, that's now part of the kitchen wing. That was built by an ancestor of my friend Freya's, before the Revolutionary War. Captain Elijah Dell. He left a treasure, that was supposed to be hidden within its walls."

Axel looked down at her quizzically. "That's why we're eating here–to search for a Revolutionary War treasure?"

"No. It's been found." Grace said, as they walked back arm an arm, past his car and towards the entrance, as she reveled in the happiness of just holding his arm, inhaling his musky, intriguing scent. It just so, so perfect she never wanted to move from here.

Eyeing the plain house door and speaking quietly, Axel asked, "You're sure you don't want to get in the car and go to a fancier place?" Those deep eyes were studying hers.

"This is a good place," she insisted. "Just wait until you taste their hush puppies."

He laughed. "I thought hush puppies were a Southern dish?"

She was guiding him toward. "They are, but New Englanders are relentlessly practical: tastes good, cheap to cook, it's served."

Shaking his head, Axel just kept chuckling as he reached out to open the door for her.

Suddenly Grace was painfully smashed against the wood-shingled wall. Her ears rang with an explosion, as Axel's weight tumbled painfully on top of her. She tried to untangle herself, as a second intensely searing explosion hit. Axel flung his arm out, protecting her face. Gravel and chipped wood rained down on them, and a white smoke choked her throat, as Grace found herself unable to breathe.

Chapter 20

"You okay?!"   Axel was pulling himself off her as they were both coughing from swirling smoke the reeked of burning rubber. As they both looked back hot, flames spurted up from the mangled Escalade. He was climbing up but shaken she just lay there for a moment. Heat radiated from the miraging asphalt, as Axel's car was enveloped in a sheet of white flames, searing the cars on either side of it.

A horrible thought crowded Grace's mind as her ears rang from the explosion. "If I had I agreed to go to a fancier restaurant, we would have been driving when your car blew up!"

Axel pulled Grace up beside him. "Yhep, so I guess it is the Captain's Mansion for dinner tonight."

"You still want to eat?!" she asked incredulously, shaken by their near death.

He looked at his flame consumed car. "We aren't driving anywhere else."

People were rushing out of the restaurant. With still clanging in her ears, Grace could hear, but not understand their questions. Feeling trapped, she looked around and saw a tall man, in a light gray sports jacket who was calling her name. "Grace? You okay?"

She knew him–Mac--but he looked different. Not Freya's son. Not in his blue police uniform. Not in a 'Save the Redwoods' t-shirt. He's was looking at Axel, who still was brushing smoking debris off his suit. Grace tried to focus on the words.

"Is that your car?" Mac asked.

"Was. A rental." Axel looked it.

"Could it have been a malfunction?" asked ever-the-cop.

"Nope. It's a new model. Drove just fine, with no warning lights, no smell of burning.   We parked and while

Grace and I were walking around it blew up."

Hearing more now Grace looked at the burning car. "The second explosion must have been the gas tank, but that first one was a bomb?"

Mac turned to Grace questioning, "Did you see any engine lights? Smell anything, or hear strange sounds?"

"No," she said.

"Then you think it was a bomb set by somebody?" continued the cop. "Did you see anybody fooling with the car?"

Grace didn't understand. "Why didn't it go off when we were back at ORR?"

"Car bombs can be set to detonate on a delay or with a timer," Mac answered her grimly. "Either of you wants an ambulance?"

Axel looked at Grace. She shook her head, it hurt, and her brain felt scrambled.

"Then I'll just call police and fire." Mac dialed 911 on his cell phone. Axel was making his own phone call to his office. "My rental preference? Well, I'd prefer a Sherman tank! I'll settle for a full-sized SUV delivered to the Captain's Mansion restaurant, in Oyster River, immediately."

Mac was finished calling in. Even in a sports coat, he stayed the policeman, as he asked Axel, "Know anyone who has a grudge against you?"

Axel shrugged, saying, "Not that would have done this."

With her pen and a small notepad out, Samantha Carson was beside Grace asking, "You okay?"

Grace nodded, wiping a bit of blood off her nose, with the back of her hand.

The reporter continued. "Dr. Farrington, do you know anyone who might want to hurt you?'

She shook her head, then croaked, "They must've

been after Axel." It hurt to talk and Grace realizing how dry her throat was.

Sam wrote her comment down. Grace started to say that was off the record, then just didn't give a damn. Looking at Mac, Grace said, "There have been more unsigned warning letters. Inger got one. Daniel Novinski got one. Axel has gotten one..." She looked at him.

"Three," he provided.

Grace realized that the reporter was busily writing down what he said. "No! Please–don't put that in print. That's was just for the police."

Sam looked first at Mac, then back to her. "I won't mention the warnings, but the car blowing up, probably by a bomb will be public record. Your name and Mr. Jensen's will be on the police blotter, so I'll have to mention that."

Mac said, "Maybe you could leave off Grace's? Or just refer to her as Grace Rose Farrington, most people won't match that up with Dr. Farrington."

God, she and Axel were nearly killed, and everybody was arguing how to keep the publicity pristine. "That's fine," Grace mumbled to Samantha.

Sam now turned to interview the horrified owner of the restaurant. He stood holding a small, unused fire extinguisher, watching three of his patron's cars burn. Several people had come out with him. Apparently parked next to Axel's burning car, a man was yelling, "Who's going to pay for my Bentley?!"

Axel looked at him, shrugged, then turned to Mac. "Grace and I will be dining inside." He turned towards the entrance and reached out to take Grace's arm to guide her inside.

Grace realized that Mac was still standing trying to get her attention. He looked so strange in that suit when he wasn't in his patrolman's blues, he's usually wearing one of his old Marine sweatshirts and jeans, or one of the endless 'save whatever' t-shirts that Freya couldn't sell in her shop. Grace realized she hadn't seen him in a business shirt, sports jacket, and a real knotted tie since his junior college graduation.

And now that Grace looked at it, she realized Samantha was not in her usual pants suit, the reporter had dressed in a filmy, sparkling midnight blue blouse, with a powder-blue chiffon skirt. Now she was on her knees in the parking lot using her cell phone camera to get an exciting angle of Axel's burning car.

Mac was still talking to Grace, what was he saying, she forced herself to concentrate. "...okay? You sure you don't need medical attention? You look a little lost."

Grace shook her head empathically, "No." She should go inside, but her knees felt weak, and Mac kept talking to her in a lowered voice.

What was he saying? "If you wouldn't mind not telling Freya?"

Not telling what? Muddled Grace said, "You don't want me to say that Axel's car blew up?"

"No, about Sam." The big guy looked embarrassed. "You know, Ma. If she knew Samantha and I were out having dinner, she'd insist on feeding Sam herbal concoctions to make stronger grandkids."

Now, Grace understood totally. The dog and cat had stopped fighting long enough to go out on a date together. And Mac would rather his formidable mother didn't wade in. Grace immediately said, "I saw nothing!" Saying that she took Axel's arm and followed him into the Captain's Mansion.

Inside the brass sconced, wood beamed, and french wallpapered restaurant, Grace looked toward the windows on the harbor saying, "Mac asked you about enemies. They've been marching all around with their placards."

"The picketers? No," Axel said shaking his head. "They're trying to save the world in their weird way. Maybe they're not too rational–but I can't see them killing people over wheat genetically engineered to be drought resistant. C'mon."

The maître d' and waiters were out in the parking lot, so Axel just walked to a table set for four by the front window facing the harbor. He was holding out a chair out for her.

"Your car..." she said.

"Was a rental. My assistants will have a replacement here by the time we finish dinner."

"You still want to eat?" Grace asked incredulously.

"Escaping death makes me hungry." He shrugged again pushing her chair in as she sat. "But first I want a good, strong drink to stiffen my rubber knees. Where are our waiters?" Saying that he put a comforting arm around her shoulders, gave her a careless kiss on the forehead, got them two menus from the maitre d 's stand, then sat down opposite her. "Thank God, you're okay. You're sure about that?"

Well, her heart felt like it would pound out of her chest any minute. "I'm fine." To keep that little lie, she looked away from him and out the window at the black harbor. Ghostly smoke from Axel's still burning car now drifted across the water.

Looking at the menu, he asked, "What do you suggest?" The explosion actually seemed to excite the man, did she have a DNA profile on him? "Did I get a DNA sample from you?"

"Not yet." He still studied the menu. "Next time I'm in your laboratory."

Grace dipped into her fanny pack and pulled out one her collection vials and handed it to him. "We could do it tonight. Could you swab inside your cheek for me?"

He looked at her in surprise.

"I'd like to check your profile for risk-taking genes," Grace explained.

Giving her a lopsided smile he took her vial, unsealed

it, and pulled out the wooden stick with its cotton tip as a bald-headed waiter with a full mustache was coming over. Finishing his gene collection Axel looked up at him and smiled, "Scotch. A double. Cheap and raw." He looked at her, "Grace, what would you like?"

"Southern Comfort Old Fashioned." And, to her surprise, she too was hungry, wanting to order immediately. "And I'll have the lobster-pot platter."

"Sounds good," Axel said. "I'll take the lobster-pot too."

The waiter left, and Grace noted that Mac and Sam were returning to the dining room, walking back to a table laid out with half eaten plates. This was a pricey place for a policeman's salary. At first, Grace expected to be questioned more by the both of them, but seeing Sam looking up deeply into Mac's eyes, and his soft look back, Grace realized it would take another bomb to break them out of their mutual revery.

Of course, if he didn't want it, Grace wouldn't mention this to Mac's mother, but as for Freya pushing for grandchildren, would she really be that welcoming of Sam? Of any woman? As a single mother, Freya had totally dedicated her life to her only son. Mac's father was dead long before Grace moved to Oyster River, and Freya made a point of never speaking of him. As far as Grace knew, Mac's maternal grandparents were dead, and despite a long family history in Oyster River, Freya never mentioned any cousins or other family members close by. It had always been just Mac and herself. How would her best friend react to the woman who was taking her only son away?

Axel was following Grace's eyes. "Are those friends of yours? Would you like me to invite them to join us?"

"No...they look like they want to be alone."

"Make a handsome couple." He looked back and studied her for a moment. "You're frowning. Is there a problem?"

The waiter was bringing a basket of hush puppies. Grace had seen him before when she dined here with David, but she couldn't remember his name. Oh, why was she so bad at names? She should answer Axel. "Sam's a reporter for several of the local papers. Mac, well his mother Freya gave him the name of 'Thor.'"

Axel chuckled. "I can understand why he dropped that!"

She remembered softly. "He was a kid when I first moved here. Mac's a real boy scout–he even made Eagle. He's a great guy, who has terrible luck with women. For his high school prom, he worked for months to afford a rental tux, an orchid corsage, a chauffeured limousine, and, at sunrise, a helicopter ride for his girl. She skipped the helicopter, leaving the dance with another guy."

"Great." Axel shook his head, popping another brown ball of fried hush puppy in his mouth.

Grace continued, "When Mac got back from the Marines, his fiancé dropped him the day before the wedding. After two years with Mac, she decided she was a lesbian."

"That's a kick in the balls," Axel agreed.

"For nearly a year Freya was selling off over thirty, white shell centerpiece decorations, that we had glued together for their wedding."

"That's only two not very bright ladies," Axel pointed out.

"Oh, there were others. One eloped with his best friend."

"No luck what-so-ever?"

"His last serious girlfriend, Mac had to arrest for being part of a car theft ring." The waiter had delivered salads with poppy seed dressing and was now handing them plastic bibs with red lobsters on them. Axel asked her questions about her early life until two waiters arrived with huge platters with steamed clams, crabs, potatoes, corn-on-cob, and two large red lobsters.

Grace advised, "Try the lobster meat first with the drawn butter, then with the green sauce." Between eating, they both looked over at the two, young lovers staring deeply into each other eyes. Mac and Sam seemed completely unaware of the world around them.

As Grace buttered her corn-on-the-cob, Axel expertly used his nutcracker to open up the big claws for their succulent meat. He'd had lobster before. The food was--as usual--excellent, but the stink of smoke and burnt rubber detracted from the ambiance. They ate in silence for a time, then forking a steamed clam he said, "Maybe your friend will have better luck this time, she is beautiful."

Grace spoke with a certain bitter cynicism. "She is an ambitious newspaperwoman, always looking for an inside track on a story. Mac's cop. What if she just sees him a source?"

Chapter 21

There were more interruptions, as various police and fire personnel came to Grace's table, asking pretty much the very same questions about Axel's burning car. There was now two teacups and two slices of tart apple pie before Mac and Sam, but Grace noted these were uneaten, as the pair just stared into each other's eyes.

Axel turned back to Grace. "I've seen that look on a woman's face before, Sam gets him alone tonight, she won't be thinking about newspaper scoops, at least until they wake up tomorrow."

Grace found herself blushing, not for any reason. She still thought of Mac as that always hungry, skinny kid she paid to catch horseshoe crabs for her blood gene studies. If she was having trouble with him having Sam for a serious girlfriend, what would Freya feel? "I hope it works out for him. At least I hope they get to know each other before Freya finds out about it."

"Freya, oh, the mother?"

Yes, the very robust, indomitable mother. "Freya loves her son, and I know she wants the best for him, but..."

Axel looked up from his corn on the cob at the couple. "He looks like a big guy with a gun, who can take care of himself. " He then looked back at her, "Grace, I'd like to know more about yourself, have you ever married?"

"No. No time, my research pretty much fills my life."

He looked unsatisfied with that. "A life with just one goal–that is a bit unbalanced."

"I understand you've been married seven times? That must be some sort of a record."

He smiled, "Not really."

"Seven divorces? I think that would sour anyone on an institution."

He pinned her with those emerald green eyes. "They were all experiences, well worth it, at least at the beginning."

"Then you found out who they were?"

"Before I married, I knew who they were–well, with one exception–they all were intelligent, strong-willed women, fascinated by life. Five of my ex-wives achieved doctorates."

"Interesting. In what fields?"

"Noreen, in Anthropology. Beryl, Fayda, and Maggie were Engineering. Maggie is currently working in Dubai on a massive desalination project, I heard from her last night. Now, Anne, she didn't have a degree but was probably the most intelligent of all my wives–a true Renaissance woman. We met when I hired the electronics development company she founded– Anne refused to take a penny from me in the divorce. I spoke with her Monday, for her vacation, she's testing a new ground penetrating radar she'd designed on an archeological dig in Alaska."

"You're divorced and still talking to them all?"

"Of course. With all, well, almost all of them. Alician had a great bod, so for a time, I overlooked the severe problems that came with it. A big mistake. But by the time I married Alician, I was getting a steel-bound prenuptial, which was still extremely generous. When I met her she was a barmaid; the divorce left Alician a multi-millionaire, but she's always got a lawsuit going against me. My lawyers advised me not to take her calls."

"Your other wives?"

"We're still on pretty good terms. The time we spend together, we were all immensely enriched intellectually and intimately by our associations." He was staring directly into her eyes. "At least I'd like to think so."

She had the feeling he was in full pitch mode. "Specifically you got?"

"Great sex. And a chance to study some magnificent minds close up. Grace, intimacy doesn't have to be forever."

She looked questioningly at him.

He amended. "Or, with the right person, maybe it could." In the candlelight, those green eyes now looked more like smokey jade as they kept staring deeply into hers. "Yes, it most definitely could be a sharing of ideas, bodies, life."

"Couldn't you have done that without marrying?"

There was a twinkle in his eyes. "Hot night in a hotel room? I've done that often. But there comes a time in your life when you want a deeper commitment. Something more than just a great physical workout. Yes, I do prefer more than a one night stand, usually, at first, I like a working trip. Time for business, folded in with time to get to know a fascinating woman. To join with another human on the deepest level. That's the best." He was studying her carefully; she was uncomfortable with the serious tone that the conversation had taken, but he continued. "Haven't you ever felt that need yourself?"

Actually, there were times, but she wasn't going to admit that to a man she hardly knew. "I've had close relationships, physical as well as mental, that were..." she thought of David Gardiner and Kurt MacKay, "that **are** important."

"You speak like the mental and physical can be totally separated. Grace, you can't stuff an entire life into little storage cubbies, life's too messy. Too broad."

She wanted to switch the conversation, so they just ate for a while. Then there was something Grace had to find out from him, "You've traveled the world?"

"As much of it as I could."

"You're setting up a biological station in Cuzco. Had you been to Peru before?"

"Yes." He was now studying the dessert menu. "Now what do you recommend for a New England finish?"

"The apple pie with cheddar cheese or the caramel flan. In fact, I'll think I'll have the apple pie." She had to sound casual about this. "When did you first go to Peru?"

He stopped and seemed to think about it. "I first set foot in Peru during my sailing days, in my twenties. In lieu of college, I'd gone to travel around the world, so I stopped for a time at quite a number of ports including Lima, Peru."

Axel went with the apple pie giving their order to the waiter as Grace tried to ask innocently, "You had the money to travel when you were so young?"

"No. Didn't start getting real money until my thirties back in Vermont. Not impressed with the herbal teas I could buy, I started my own company for healthy, but tasty tea mixes. Started that in an apartment over a garage I was renting, while I was working at Burger King. Soon I pushed my tea blends to high-end coffee shops and on the Internet. On weekends I was also crewing yachts, and I managed to talk this vice president into putting my teas in his company's coffee shops, which were expanding daily. Needed a full factory for production after that. From that tea business, I bought a small heritage seed company and later combined that with a pharmaceutical company working on farm animal diseases. Again I got lucky, and from that, I built what has become Humanity's Harvest."

"That's amazing," Grace said, knowing a lot more than merely good 'luck' must have been involved. "What did you study in college?"

"Never got there, no money for it. My family ran a dairy farm in Vermont. I didn't want to milk cows and shovel manure the rest of my life, so at seventeen I took off to bum my way around the world. Always wanted to sail, so I hung around Boston loading tramp steamers until I got a chance to crew some guy's yacht. You get a reliable reputation and a Captain's license, and you can get paid to move rich guy's boats to where ever. I'd deliver a ship to some foreign port, then I'd find some sort of job, and work until I'd get together a stake to travel to the next country."

"That sounds like a lot a fun."

"Sleeping in cold youth hostels? Backpacking across the Andes? Cleaning fish twelve hours a day? It's okay when you're a kid, but that's why now when I'm the rich guy, and I can afford a luxurious safari, I really appreciate it."

"But you didn't you go back to college? Just talking with you, I know you're extremely knowledgeable about more than just business?"

"On any topic that interests me, I read a lot. Hire tutors if I want to learn more—you'd be surprised how little you have to pay a doctorate or even a Nobel prize winner."

No, Grace wasn't surprised at all. "So you're basically self-educated?"

"As you are," he said as the waiter set their pie plates down.

"I have a doctorate..." she started to object.

"But, if my reading about you is correct, the majority of your work has always gone beyond current theory. Sometimes directly against it?"

"Yes," she had to admit that was true.

Again his intense eyes seemed to create an aura of intimacy between them as he said softly, "The most I've learned in my life was from being in bed with an attractive, super intelligent woman. With no barriers, total connection, you learn everything about a person."

Grace found herself warming, wanting to reach out and touch him—grab him. Was he really offering something, or was his sexy manner just second nature? She broke eye contact and looked at her plate. "That's interesting," she said stupidly and very primly.

He went on as if she hadn't looked away. "You know Grace, the one continent in the world I never visited was Antarctica. I'm planning to remedy that. It's summer there now, with temperatures warming up to 49 F, so I've chartered a retired icebreaker that's been refitted as a passenger yacht.

Pretty basic, but I will be taking a small party of friends on a cruise for three weeks. I'd like you to join us."

"You want me along to analyze the DNA of anything you find in the ice?" she asked seriously.

Laughing at that he said, "No, I was thinking more in terms of you analyzing me." Axel was bending closer to her, "And me analyzing you. You know, all work can stagnate your mind, impede progress to your goals. I'm offering either a private cabin for yourself or half the bed in the master suite with me?"

This was an unexpected offer that she couldn't quite answer.

So he continued, "Sometimes just taking a break–abet an intense one–might actually advance your research."

She was reaching the bottom of her Old Fashioned. The amber sweetness was good, but she was beginning to feel a daring confidence, that probably was rooted in the Southern Comfort liquor. Not such a good idea to negotiate now.

The waiter indicated her glass. "Refill?"

Grace wasn't much of a drinker, and just sitting with this arousing man was intoxicating enough. "No, thank you," she told the waiter. Finally, the wild moment was gone, and Grace could turn back to Axel, saying firmly, "I've pretty well set my life's course by myself."

He leaned back, taking her measure. "You know Grace, in some ways, we are quite alike. You take risks with your research, I've done that with my life. For my thirtieth birthday, I took a solo sail around the world."

That was impressive. "The horns?"

"The Cape of Good Hope? Yes, the wave troughs were low, only four feet high. Had to do it once–never do it again! Nearly died, but the leap was worth it! Maybe you should think about taking a leap in your life?"

She wanted to change a topic that had become too emotional, too hot. Too close for comfort. "I was wondering something about Ekkeko?" Axel raised an eyebrow, but he seemed to well understand the conversation had become uncomfortably intense for her as she continued, "He seems too ambitious to be a glorified office boy?"

Axel lip's compressed. "I hired him to be groomed to take over the South American operations."

"But?"

"He's certainly bright–intellectually," Axel said, holding his drink up for the waiter to see he needed a refill.

"But not emotionally?" she pursued.

"No, Ekkeko's got to lose some of that resentment, get out of that privileged victim worldview, and learn to get along with people. He's trying. In fact, he's got this idea for an outdoor bar-be-que with my people, your scientists, and our picketer friends."

"In December in New England?" That sounded like a terrible idea to Grace.

"Advanced forecasting says we get low thirties, high forties. And, yes, a bar-be-que in New England in December is not your average suggestion, but Ekkeko thinks that the novelty of it being outdoors will cool emotions and bring people together."

Grace just raised her own eyebrow.

Axel smiled lopsidedly, "The way things are going, anything's worth a try." His phone rang. "Jensen." He listened. "Yes. No. No compact! I don't care about the color, I want a full sized SUV delivered to Oyster River. Tomorrow?! That is **not** acceptable!" He listened a bit and obviously annoyed, he shut the phone off. "They're trying to get me a motel room and us a cab, but it seems around here the taxies stop running rather early."

She looked over at an empty table, Mac and Sam had left, so Grace turned back to Axel. "Call them back, a cab is not necessary, I can call over to ORR, and somebody will drive us back." She started dialing Bobby. "When we're at the peninsula, you can borrow my car, or..." Grace held her breath, then plunged in, "Or if you don't want to drive back tonight, you could stay at my condo?"

He looked at her, obviously trying to determine just what she was offering. "How would the logistics of that work out?"

Grace took her last sip of her sweet Dutch courage, then continued. "How tall are you?"

"6' 4".

"Well, then you could sleep perpendicularly on my pull out couch in the living room by yourself, or you could share my queen-sized bed." So now it was all up to him.

His intimate smile broadened. "Yes, your condo. It's not a night for either of us to sleep alone."

Chapter 22

Bobby Jamison picked them up at the restaurant. He had to maneuver past the fire engine parked there, as the burnt Escalade carcass still streamed white smoke. Seeing him, Axel looked as if he expected a fight, probably because of Bobby's angry words over his flirting with Sara, but Axel didn't understand that Bobby's temper blusters were like a summer squall on the Sound: It comes up fast and furious; blasts violent and wild-waved; then blows over to be quickly forgotten.

After protectively determining Grace was all right, Bobby walked over to look at the sizzling hulk of black, burnt metal that was once Axel's rental car. He studied it. "Rear window frame and the back roof are gone. Looks like the back blew off before the fire?"

"Yhep," acknowledge Axel. "We were facing away from it, but it sure sounded like a bomb, then a secondary explosion as the exposed gas tank caught."

Bobby looked at him critically. "Hey, man, somebody tried to stab you in the back with a scuba spear, they're writing you anonymous threatening letters, and they just blew up your car–your public relations leave much to be desired!"

Axel just chuckled bitterly.

Joining them Grace asked, "How could whoever it was have gotten to your car?"

Axel just shrugged. "Well, I was parked at ORR and didn't bother locking it while I was in your apartment. Or until I flew the seaplane in, that car's been sitting alone in the parking lot by the Neptune's marine tender."

When they drove back and parked by Grace's condo, Axel walked Grace to the lobby, as Bobby followed. Helpfully he said to Axel, "Hey, you want to borrow my car? Grace's only runs on alternate days."

"I'm okay, " Axel said, as they all stood awkwardly in

the foyer.

Surprised, Bobby looked from Axel to Grace, who was also just standing there feeling embarrassed, and suddenly he got it. Sticking his hands in his pockets, Bobby gave Grace an arch look and started walking to the back of the building. "Well, now I'm going to my apartment, here on the first floor. Hope you guys have a good night where ever you go."

With her old-fashioned upbringing wearing off, Grace started up the stairs thinking she hadn't cleaned up her bedroom that well, there were dishes in the sink, and that she'd gotten them both into a silly, bumbling situation.

Only it wasn't.

She let him shower first. Straightening up the bedroom, Grace started on the dishes in the kitchen sink when she heard a muffled voice. Hearing him calling for something, Grace went into the bedroom and opened the bathroom door to a cloud of steam and her lavender soap smell.

"Shampoo?" he asked. She pulled it out from under the counter, eyes politely downcast as she handed it to him behind the blue dolphin shower curtain. A long, wet, muscular arm came out, and she found herself being coaxed into the shower, with him laughingly undressing her under the stream of warm water.

It got even better that night in her queen-sized bed. Yes. She could see how this remarkable man had managed to marry seven times!

* * *

The next day as Grace singed Axel's bacon and eggs, she figured to have an awkward moment ahead. Before Kurt took his boat out this morning, he was to be knocking at her door for breakfast so they could discuss their lobster study report. How would she explain Axel to Kurt? Or Kurt to Axel? Yes, Kurt would be coming, especially if he heard somebody had tried to blow her and Axel up last night. How did she get herself into messes like this?

But Kurt didn't show, and Axel ate the overcooked eggs looking at her before he talked her back into bed. Last night Axel had changed the delivery of his new SUV to her condo building. Her apartment bell had rung later, and someone passed him a set of keys, but Axel hung around to walk Grace to her laboratory. She truly enjoyed this magnificent man's company before he kissed her goodbye.

Then her work absorbed her. She gave Axel's sample for Inger to start processing and started on the readouts from the majority of samples taken at the Natural History Museum in New Haven. Mostly confirming what she expected, non-DNA samples, common seed genes, insect contamination, residues of what looked like beer in offering pots, or nothing much at all. In other words for Axel's generous support of her specimen trip up to New Haven, she had virtually nothing to show. Well, getting a negative told you something, mainly that you had to look elsewhere. In a depressed mood, she started to write her Humanity's Harvest report.

Her recommendations, was it worth another trip? Before his murder, Helmut had been sifting through storage for other promising samples. Had he found anything? Had Helmut been replaced? On behalf of Humanity's Harvest, she would have to speak to the new curator when he was hired. Could she get permission to send Bobby up there to shift through further samples? That would cut into his teaching and other work. Maybe Nick? No, that project definitely needed a self-starter. Someone who would keep at it. Inger? She would do a fine job, but it could take days, maybe weeks, and Inger was needed in the lab. Grace kept a list of promising graduate students, would one of them be interested in the job? She would mention that in her report to Humanity's Harvest–but she'd also have to say, that in her opinion the effort probably wouldn't be worth the results.

With that completed, there was something that she personally was interested in, she now had the results from the mummy's arm. Not too surprising, none of the samples had been complete, but having overlap from different samples allowed her to fill in some missing material. Still not a complete picture, but enough to allow her to start looking for the genes she was tentatively associating with leadership characteristics. And she found them. Intelligence. Aggression. Dominance. If she was reading the position of her alleles right, that mummified arm came from a man genetically programmed to have extremely high levels of testosterone. An obvious Alpha.

The printout was incomplete, would more show an even stronger pattern? Perhaps another sampling? Dare she ask the next curator of New Haven Museum? Better get together as comprehensive a report on the mummy's arm as she could. He was male. Eye, hair, and skin color dark. Short stature. And if she made a match on the World Genome project, Grace maybe could fill in a little more history of this man who might have been an Incan noble, maybe an Inca himself.

That night, after work Kurt did show up to walk her home. He waited patiently, for another half an hour for her to finish off a conference call from Woods Hole. Then he stood by as she locked up, casually commenting, "I was headed over this morning, but Bobby ambushed me in the lobby, and he said you got lucky last night?"

She hated the fact her cheeks were heating but was able to answer quite neutrally. "Yes, I wasn't blown up by that car bomb, that certainly was lucky."

"And Axel stayed the night at your place. He get 'lucky' too?" Kurt leered.

"Don't we have an arrangement that covers this?" she evaded. "Don't ask, don't tell?"

"Whal, as much as I love participating, sometimes I

jes like to listen a bit getting warm."

She glared at him. "I'm going home now."

Kurt laughed richly, as they headed out of the lab foyer. Outside, Grace pulled her car coat closer around her throat. Had to get her long winter coat out of the storage cubical in the condo's basement. The harbor water looked like black glass reflecting the ghostly moon, she didn't even hear a wave lapping against the docks as they walked together in the darkness.

"Smell it?" asked Kurt.

Grace breathed air that was cold but just smelled fresh. "Smell what?"

"No urine stink in the bushes. No tent campfire smoke. No unwashed bodies. Our tent city is gone, and good riddance."

Yes, the picketers were gone, but their murderer wasn't. "The car bomb makes it definite. The murder victim wasn't meant to be Helmut, it was supposed to be Axel."

"Aaup. Never could think of a reason why anyone around here would kill a low-level museum curator from New Haven."

Grace thought about that. "But for this last attempt, Josh Jeffers has an alibi. He was in jail when that bomb was probably placed."

"Nope. Your friend the lawyer, Daniel Novinski, got him out that afternoon."

She hadn't expected that. "Then Josh could have done it?"

"Could of–but didn't. Not a backstabbing killing with a scuba gun, not a delayed bomb in the rental car. It's not crazy and public enough for Josh."

"But others? Astrid? She seemed to hold Axel personally responsible for poisoning humanity."

"Helmut's murder doesn't seem like a woman's crime. Just totting a scuba gun around, waiting to get behind somebody. A heavy piece of equipment out of the water, and if someone else stopped ya, how do yer explain hauling a spear gun about on land?"

"Yes, it is kind of an awkward thing to plan," she said thoughtfully.

"Grace, as I've told you before–most murders don't spend much time planning."

"By Ockham's razor..."

Kurt finished her sentence. "What? William Ockham's belief that '*Among competing hypotheses, the one with the fewest assumptions should be selected*'?"

After a long close association, she easily finished his words. "Going by that it's probably someone in Oyster River. Probably with a motive against Axel, because they keep going at it even after Helmut was killed."

"Got me on one of yer spreadsheets? Have me down for possibly killing Axel cause he skipped me, and handed a grant to Huang? Or because he's been eyeing you like a pile of fresh tuna?"

It was good he couldn't see her blush in the dark. How the hell did he know she had a murder spreadsheet? She never showed it to anyone, and the sheet was passworded. Could he have hacked her computer? That would be like Kurt, but, more likely, he just knew her ways of working out problems.

They got up to her condo, and Grace unlocked the door to let them both in. "Want me to zap you a frozen dinner? Or should we order a pizza?"

He was inside, but not taking off his leather jacket off. "Not staying. Jes wanted to see ya safely home. That bomb would've killed the both of you. Maybe it wasn't meant for him?"

She ignored a possible threat to her and just focused on his plans. "You have a date tonight?"

Kurt raised a quizative eyebrow. "Didn't you just

remind me we have an arrangement?"

That was fair. "Yes. We do. Sorry," she said.

He didn't move from the door. "Last night, saw your lights go off in your condo from my boat..." His voice lowered, as if he struggled with some emotion he would never admit. "Too cold fer eaten on yer balcony, but I'm guessing he stayed fer breakfast?"

"Yes, he did," she admitted.

"That's a long time, Grace."

She could have refused to respond, but she owed Kurt. "We seemed to have a lot to talk about."

"Axel coming back to talk more?" Kurt asked, his face still unreadable.

"He's invited me on a vacation to Antarctica. No DNA, just a trip with a few friends..." Kurt raised an eyebrow, so she put it to him. "You want to change the rules of our relationship?"

"Nope." He looked tired. "We can't. People like us, we have our driving passion–it's our life's work, anything else on the side is enjoyable, but will never be the main event."

Grace nodded. He knew her as well as he knew himself, and as he turned to go on what she presumed was a night out she said, "Remember. Use protection."

"Did you last night?" He pushed himself away from the door, kissed her lightly on the cheek and left.

Chapter 23

The long-range forecasts said that Humanity's Harvest's December outdoor bar-be-que would be dry and at--for New England--a balmy forty degrees. Yet the night before, it snowed three inches and the pale white disk of sun seldom peeked out of the low, silver clouds that blanketed the whole harbor as the temperatures kept plummeting.

Grace expected their 'come together' bar-be-que would be moved inside the Roost; she hadn't reckoned with Axel and Ekkeko's inventiveness. Several room-sized white canvas wedding tents had been set up on the snow-covered lawn. Walking inside the nearest tent, Grace found oriental rugs had been laid on the snow, on top of the long tables were draped with white linen brocade, and set with red styrofoam plates and plastic bowls. The tables were piled high with bakery bagels, English muffins, and rounds of hunky french bread rolls. Alongside that stood two forty-two quart stock pots over propane heaters, where a white ski jacketed woman cheerfully ladled out steaming soup. At the woman's urging, Grace took a bowl. It was French onion, and she had to admit it did warm you. She smelled clam chowder from the next pot.

Outside an ice block bar, serving drinks in clear plastic cups. Away from the tents, six foot long, portable bar-be-que grills had been set up--cooking hotdogs, Korean meat sticks, pork ribs, and quarter chickens. There was one whole tent just for the vegetarian dishes of chickpea casseroles, baked beans, veggie burgers, and aspics from fancy jello molds.

She looked about. It was a fairyland setting, with marvelous food and drink, but as a get together, the party was a colossal flop. Axel's people stayed by the bar, the ORR staff clustered east of the bar-be-ques, and Astrid, Daniel, and her protestors were west of the vegetarian tent. It rather looked like the separating layers of alcohol and water that Grace used to tease mitochondria chromosomes out of their cytoplasm.

It didn't help that Axel's people kept glancing over at the activists, and protectively huddling around him. Either they liked the man a lot, or they wanted to protect their jobs. Looking over and seeing her, Axel smiled and waved. Lord, just having that man glance her way gave a Grace a tingly feeling. Soon that feeling increased, as he was coming over, with two oversized styrofoam cups in his hands, "That last tent has the deserts: cupcakes, cookies and flaming, cherry jubilees." He handed her a steaming cup that smelled of wine, cardamom, cloves, and cinnamon–glögg.

Holding the warm cup, she looked about the snowy lawn. "This is amazing. Truly you've created an ice kingdom."

"With you as its Queen, my lady." He half bowed gallantly. She knew her cheeks were red from the wind, and drinking the strong spiced wine left her feeling a little giddy, but it was fun. He was shifting into business mode. "Grace, I wanted to talk to you about that collection group I'm starting in Peru..."

"Mr. Jensen." A young woman in a green ski jacket had come over holding a cell phone out to him. "I have Madrid. It's late over there."

Axel looked harried, as he handed his drink to his employee to hold, while he took the phone. "Excuse me, Grace, this may take awhile." They walked off, the snow crunching under their boots as Axel spoke rapid Spanish into the phone.

Grace sipped more of the steaming drink he'd given her. Strong glögg, spiced red wine. Freya should have been here, she would've loved this. Bobby was trying to push the twins' carriage on the snow crust, and Sara had the hand of a pink snowsuited Ginjer, as they walked from tent to tent.

Seeing the Brewsters, Grace waved, but they didn't see her. Eighty-year-old Stewart and Joyce, walking about, always interested in how ORR was progressing. Gail wasn't here. Tied to her desk in Admin probably. Maybe Grace could take her place at the reception desk for a while, so Gail could look around and get a plate of food.

Starting to do just that, Grace walked past the smoking chicken bar-be-que but was intercepted by Astrid. Today the picketer wore an old quilted coat, with her stringy brown and gray hair long. With her mouth as seriously grim as usual, Grace was relieved to see that lawyer-- Daniel whatever--was following at a distance.

Astrid started in a harsh voice, "Dr. Farrington, you're continuing with genetic engineering, knowing what it is doing to our planet?"

"Increasing rice stocks? Feeding the growing population. Making affordable insulin?" responded Grace firmly.

Astrid made a face that said 'oh you fool' as she continued briskly, "Japan has rightly outlawed generically engineered rice! But what about those North American farmers losing Japanese contracts because their rice crops tested as contaminated from genetically engineered crops in the nearby fields?"

"That's unfortunate," Grace admitted, "and should be actionable in court."

"It's worse than unfortunate! For millenniums, family farmers have been saving a portion of their crops for next year's seed. But conglomerates like Humanity's Harvest want to control all the sales of seed stocks! They've patented the genes engineered in their plants. How the hell can anyone be allowed to patent a life form?!" Astrid glared at her.

"That's a legislative concern–not a scientific one," Grace replied evenly.

Astrid was just building up her steam of outrage. "In

1998 in Canada, Monsanto sued Percy Schmeiser because natural insect pollenation left his canola fields tainted with their genetically engineered genes. They've hauled Percy in court, demanding that he pay their royalty fees for stealing their patented genes! Is that fair?"   demanded Astrid.

When Grace couldn't immediately think of an answer, the disgusted activist turned and walked away.

Grace looked at the lawyer. "That is wrong."

Daniel shrugged. "I agree with you. And the courts have too, to some extent. In the Schmeiser case, they did uphold the patent, but didn't award damages to Monsanto, so that case was pretty much a loss for them."

"Were the farmers who lost their Japanese contracts sales reimbursed?" asked Grace.

"I don't know. But I wouldn't guess so, probably because they couldn't afford to fight a long, drawn-out battle against a well funded, corporate legal staff."

"That's not fair," admitted Grace again.

He shook his head. "The laws regarding G. E. are still just evolving. Before things are settled, some people are going to get hurt." Daniel took a drink of coffee from a steaming Styrofoam cup and looked around. "I gotta admit this is kinda fun."

Actually, for Grace, the bar-be-que had now lost its snow kingdom luster, and just left her stamping cold feet, but there was more she wanted to say. "Your friends view G.E. technology as some sort of nefarious plot by global conglomerates. How do you really feel?"

Daniel thought about that for a moment, seeming to pick his words carefully when he finally spoke.   "I've followed genetic research for quite some time. Actually, when it was originally sold to the public as a way to end world hunger, I thought it might be a great idea."

"But you've changed that opinion?"

"As I learn more, my thinking on the matter has

evolved. That although in theory, G.E. could be miraculous cornucopia delivering endless benefits..."

"Wouldn't that be terrible?" Grace interrupted in a slightly sarcastic tone.

He continued, "I don't feel--I **know**--that G.E. is a bad idea in the real world."

"If the big corporations are making money selling poison to their customers isn't that kind of defeatist in the long run?"

"Well, when like Humanity's Harvest, you have invested thirty to forty million in a pesticide-resistant wheat, you may be very reluctant to even consider the disadvantaged side effects and suppress any publication of such."

Grace felt a need to defend the process. "That pesticide resistance allows farmers more flexibility in spraying pesticides—being able to use larger single doses only as needed, allows the use of less pesticide spraying overall."

"Which also allows the pests to develop immunity, a predictable cycle causing increasing spraying."

Grace nodded. "Developed immunity is always a problem, requiring ongoing research."

"Dr. Farrington, have you followed the canola problem in Canada?"

That did stop her. "Yes, I actually have. To decrease the expense and dangerous use of pesticides in food crops several companies genetically engineered canola plants with genes that made them resistant to herbicides, to make controlling crop-eating pests easier."

"Those crops were grown in open fields, and with the assistance of common insect pollinators they were fertilizing non G.E. crops, sometimes as far as sixteen miles away."

"Yes." Grace agreed. "In open fields, you have wind, water, insect and animal disbursement."

"So you agree, G.E. crops are the gifts that keeps on

giving?" he finished triumphantly.

"I know in Alberta since these canola crops are self-generating and are resistant to herbicides, they have become some sort of super weed."

"Who would have thought that?" Daniel said. "Well, actually a beekeeper in my book, warned them exactly what was going to happen."

Grace understood and somewhat sympathized with his point, but she also had to explain,"Throughout the history of science there have been horrible setbacks and unintended side effects. Even with its tragic fetus deforming effects, the drug thalidomide is currently being used to alleviate the suffering of AIDS and Hansen's disease patients. Yes, the manufacturers put out warnings on the bottle that says these pills may not be taken or even touched by fertile women, but yes, we can all predict what will happen."

Daniel's intense blue eyes stared straight at her. "Dr. Farrington, what is your personal opinion of genetic engineering?"

"I don't do opinions, I do studies. I was particularly interested in those wild canola weeds because some were found, with not only one gene for herbicide-resistance, but two. Those wild herbicide-resistant genes originated from the genetic engineering by two different companies, with two different genetic solutions."

He looked at her, seeming to pale on his clean-shaven cheeks. "These were not deliberately crossed?"

"No, it appears the plants and their insect pollinators managed it all by themselves."

"Than can I quote you, that Dr. Grace Farrington considers testing of genetically engineered crops in open fields to be too dangerous...?"

"No, you may not quote me, because I'm not going to say that." She stopped to order her thoughts, then finished with, "This world seems to have two factions: those that carefully plan evaluate every possible misstep and therefore don't take many chances; and then there are those who even if they see risk, they feel the possible rewards out weigh the dangers. Every important change in this world was probably instigated by the latter group."

Daniel kept hammering. "Could I quote you as saying that more governmental requirements are needed? No open field testing... No bacterial vectors..."

"No quotes!" Saying that she walked away from him. Yes. The Jack Frost Bite Me Bar-be-que was fun, but Grace had enough of socializing. With the snow crust crunching under her boots, she decided to pick up some journals from her lab, then take them over to read while she relieved Gail, so the secretary could get some of the winter feasting fun.

Her lab was dark and locked with Inger and Nick still at the bar-be-que. She unlocked it and stepped inside, and as the lights flashed on, she saw a white envelope on the floor before her. It must have been slipped under the door. It could be anything. Just a request from a student, or a note from Gail, but Grace found herself afraid to pick up the stupid envelope. This was ridiculous. She started to reach down. Then stopped, walked over to her desk, and took out two latex gloves.

Snapped them on she walked determinedly back to the offending envelope.

Grace picked up. Used her glove finger to rip open a loose corner. A single folded white sheet inside. She opened it up. **Farrington, you all were warned to stop playing God with your Genetic Engineering! Now you must all die!**

Before she turned that letter over to police, she did a thorough wipe down for any possible DNA. Still, she didn't expect any to show up, knowing from her previous attempts their anonymous intimidator had been very careful. At her desk, Grace reviewed her Murder spreadsheet again. No new ideas, so she gathered up her journals, walked over to Admin, and released Gail for some Bar-be-que time.

In the evening after closing her lab, Grace was still mulled over a problem on the penetrance of red eyes in rabbits, as she started walking out on the peninsula. She passed her condo and kept walking, wanting time to think. She passed the student dorms, the guest speaker's apartment above the boathouse, more labs, then she saw Kurt's beat up truck parked outside the elegant, eighteen-hundreds greenhouses. She'd better find out how Huang's tanks were coming. At the slightly open door two green hoses snaked out, but the boat pumps weren't spurting water out into muddy puddles anymore.

Inside there was the overwhelming smell of dampness, and there were still wet areas darkening the gray concrete flooring, but she didn't see any deep standing water. Kurt was over in the corner, laying on the floor, tightening one of the pipelines above his head under a long, open trough tank. Grace walked passed filling tanks, and as she got closer, Kurt looked up. "Looks bad and Adam's gonna have a complaint against the plumbing contractors, but Huang's started incubating his algae in the first three troughs."

"What has he got going?" Grace asked.

"Chlorophyta, Rhodophyta, and Phaeophyta." Kurt looked down the rows. "Green, red, and brown, at least he'll have colorful tanks, but what good is it going to do?"

"He's trying to grow and modify all three as proof of his hypothesis of an inexpensive, abundant, taste controllable food source."

Kurt thought about that. "Huang's trying to catch a moonbeam's shine on a wave with a shotgun," he commented laconically.

She looked up at the ceiling fans. "Feels a bit cold in here for growing?"

"Jes turned the radiator lines back on. Had them off to work, that was one of the lines that were leaking. And as soon as the clouds go away, we'll get some sunlight warming this place, and Huang can turn down the pricy heat."

"Next July?" Grace commented tartly.

"Whal, you're getting snow incoming here, but I'll be headed out for the sunny Gulf stream." He looked at her, going from joking to deadly serious. "Sure you're gonna be okay?"

Those dark eyes that knew her so well. Forget a murderer being loose, she always felt low around the holidays. No matter how much she loved her life, how much trouble she had gone to pursue a solitary career, around Christmas being unmarried, without much family left, always got her feeling a little down. "Are there any women aboard that science ship?"

"Two, I understand. Both real good lookers." By the sardonic smile, he knew exactly why she was asking.

"That'll be good for you," Grace said, not bothering to hide her downcast manner.

Kurt laughed. "Not really. I understand they're a couple."

Somehow that made his leaving a little bit easier. "Do you think these tanks will work for Huang?"

Kurt looked down five long lines of meter high tanks. "He's got some seed stock in. Algae grows fast–should have naked eye visible blooms by tomorrow. The growing part should work, but as for his hypothesis and technical ability, I have me doubts." He looked the length of the greenhouse tanks. "Wonder if'n Huang will thank me."

She gave Kurt a 'don't hold your breath look,' as she inspected a metal line he had wrapped with white plumber's tape. Feeling the joint lightly with her fingers–dry. Well, it looked like hell, but the tanks were filling, and the floor was drying. "I don't care what Huang says, I give you the Farrington Good Guy of the Year award," Grace said linking her arm in his as they walked up the line.

And she noted a cloudy, grey-green tintage in the first row of tanks. Looked like Huang's first generation was already blooming. As Kurt reached down and tossed another of his wrenches into his tool bag, Grace felt a draft from the front door opening.

"Looks like another visitor," said Kurt, reaching back into the bag for his heaviest wrench.

Grace looked up to see Ekkeko coming in. Axel's assistant never seemed to crack a smile. She walked over to him saying, "Looks like Humanity's Harvest projects are underway."

"Is that the way it looks to you?" said Ekkeko primly.

"Yes," Grace returned, while Kurt put his wrench back and closed up his tool bag.

Ekkeko only glanced at the tanks. "Axel's not here, and the police have been questioning us."

By 'us' he must mean himself and the other Humanity's Harvest personnel in Oyster River for the bar-be-que. "About what?" asked Grace.

"The death of that worthless museum curator." Ekkeko made Helmut's murder sound like a terrible inconvenience.

"Dr. Roberts?" Grace found Axel assistant's attitude just lousy. "Helmut has–had-- a wife, and a baby on the way, it's doubly sad for his family..."

"Perhaps a judgment on him." Ekkeko's eyes were cold, unforgiving.

That surprised Grace. "Because he was killed? Whatever did he do to be judged?"

"There was a curse placed on those treasures Professor Bingham stole from Peru. Dr. Roberts was part of that theft."

That stopped Grace. "A 'crime' committed a hundred years ago? Before Helmut was even born? What if those relics had stayed in place? Any of the gold ones might've been melted down, the wood left unpreserved would've rotted, ceramics would probably have been sold to tourists for souvenirs, and all of it would have been lost to scientists and historians."

"It is unfortunate the man died, " Ekkeko's tone didn't sound all that grieved. "But it was not a North American's decision that sacred remains could be removed! The curse will follow whoever touches that which is sacred to my people."

"Well," Grace smiled sweetly. "If you'll excuse me, I have to go culture DNA from a forbidden mummy's arm, but I'm not going to worry about the curse–I have tampons."

Trying not to laugh out loud, Kurt kind of choked on that one. Leaving Ekkeko still in the greenhouse, they walked outside. Out in the snow, Grace wondered exactly when Ekkeko had left that reception the night Helmut was killed? And how much more had Ekkeko drunk after she left? And, finally, how seriously did Axel's vengeful assistant take that 'curse' business?

Chapter 24

On Thursday morning, she checked her e-mail. There were several papers she had promised journal editors she would check over.   The first was on DRD7r, some interesting theories–but she was unhappy with the sweeping generalizations made when the research did was too limited to back up far-reaching conclusions. She started typing her critique.

"Grace?"

Lost in the elegant intricacies of DRD7r, Grace only surfaced after the second, patience call. "Grace?"

She looked up from her screen. Freya was standing there. Was it evening? Grace looked at the time and date at the corner of her computer screen. 2:30 PM. Freya should be in her store—selling tarot cards. "What's wrong? "

"You were nearly blown up!" said a horrified Freya.

She hadn't called Freya to tell her, Grace should've, but she didn't want to upset her friend. "Yes, but it wasn't meant for me."

"Like that would matter if you were splattered all over the parking lot?" Freya looked scared. "They tried to kill you with a car bomb?! That's your idea of something to forget about?"

"They were after Axel," Grace said soothingly, seldom had she seen Freya so upset. "They're against G.E."

"It wasn't Astrid and the protestors–they're pro-life!" protested Freya. " They would never try to blow anybody up!"

"Josh Jeffers is with them."

Freya sighed.   "He's out again.   Astrid's lawyer, what's his name? Daniel Novinski. He got Josh out on bail again, just before Axel's car was blown up. Mac's really unhappy about that."

"Do you think Josh Jeffers could have killed Helmut thinking he was Axel?"

"No," Freya said sighing. "Taking a punch at Axel, maybe even sinking his seaplane, that's what a nut case like Josh would do. Not hide in the bushes, waiting for Axel to leave the reception. Following behind and shooting a spear gun into his back. Not planting a bomb in Axel's car," finished Freya in a weary fashion. "Mac says it's not Josh's modus operandi."

Labeling things in Latin doesn't necessarily make them true. "Kurt thinks Josh had the mechanical know how to create a bomb, and the connections to get explosives..."

Freya shook her head emphatically. "I just don't feel he did it. Trying psychometry, I rested my hand on the metal door of his truck when he was parked at the picketers' camp. I didn't get any recent, violent vibrations, and I'm sure I would have if Josh had killed the museum curator."

While Grace did admit her friend's special intuitions had come up with some remarkable things, she didn't have that much faith in Freya's absolving of their resident nut case. "Well, I don't think any of the Oyster River Research staff or students would have a reason for killing a man they barely knew."

"Maybe it was a corporate enemy of Axel's? One that we don't know?"

"Wouldn't he have been recognized by Axel or any of his staff at Huang's reception?" mused Grace.

"Well, it wasn't a friend that put a bomb in his car!" Freya countered.

A masked, suited and gloved Inger carried an eight-inch by twelve-inch blue tray with ninety-six wells protected by its clear plastic cover over to Grace's desk. Grace noted it was nearly full of numbered vials, as Inger said, "Nick left this tray. I've checked. They're all been processed. Do you want them disposed of? Or retained in cold storage?"

Grace looked down at tray. "They are?'

Inger took the plastic cover off, pulling out vials.

"LG00001 through LG00081. Your series being tested for 'Leadership Genes'."

Grace typed the numbers to pull up her master list, noting they were part of the samples she had mostly taken from Humanity's Harvest executives. When Grace looked up, she noted that with a fixed stare Freya was walking toward the tray. Not looking at either of them, Freya started to reach out her left hand with her fingers held just above the tray on Grace's desk.

"Please–don't touch..." Started Inger, but before she could finish warning Freya not to contaminate the samples, Grace waved a staying hand. "They've already been processed."

As they both watched, Freya, who now seemed totally unaware of their presence, passed her hand lengthwise across the tray. Then she swung it back, cross-wise as if she was doing some sort of sacred benediction.

Again Freya made another cross, but this time over a smaller area. She seemed to be centered at the top of the tray. Finishing she curled up three of her fingers into her palm, leaving the thumb and index free, hovering over the tray. Freya stopped. Waited. Then moved her index finger slightly forward. Centered. Then dropped it down, as she hovered over one of eighty-one vials.

Freya spoke in a dreamy voice. "Grace, can I hold this one?"

Inger was shaking her head 'no.' "She doesn't have gloves!"

It violated standard procedure, but Grace intervened, curious to see what Freya was interested in. "They've already been processed, and I'm discarding them. Yes, Freya, you can pick it up with your bare fingers."

Not even seeming to hear them, Freya lifted the 0.2 ML pointed end glass vial. It appeared no different than any of the others, only distinguishable by the printed code number label stuck to its side, which Freya didn't even seem to look at.

"Interesting," she said, gently cushioning the vial between her palms. Folding her hands as if in prayer Freya closed her eyes.

Grace and Inger watched her curiously.

Finally, in a strangely distant voice, Freya spoke, "A born leader–beneficial to his own, but ruthless to all others. He expects, no demands to be worshiped! He resents any disrespect, but conceals it, as he awaits his time. He's ruled by unbounded pride. Always planning. Always jockeying for power. Such a one will accept no outer control, nor feel remorse for whatever he does."

Suddenly she withdrew her second hand so that she could stare into the vial in her hand. "He's not evil, he just lives by his own rules, and really doesn't care about anyone he does not consider his own." She returned the vial to its position, then Freya seemed to deliberately shake off her weird mood, as she asked, "Was that a tray with the Incan mummy's arm you told me about?"

"No," responded Inger.

"Strange," said Freya. "I felt royalty in his breeding." Now she seemed to be back with them again. "Grace, if you're interested in South American mummies, they have one up at the Museum in Bridgeport. I've seen it."

"They do?" That surprised Grace.

"Not on display. I've been in the storage area, and I've seen this guy in a crossed leg, yoga position, squatting in a glass case. Rose said he was from South America."

Inger was dismissive. "Bridgeport? That circus museum? It's all fake stuff!"

"Oh, no," Freya responded. "Yes, the Great Showman started his career by sewing a mummified monkey's torso into a fish's tail–that became the Fiji mermaid–but he was a real impresario. He was one of the first to keep a beluga whale on display for the public. Or try to, but the whale died.   While the Showman was alive he actively hunted down the rarest displays, the most intriguing oddities he could find. When the New Haven Natural History Museum got Professor Bingham's Peruvian collection, the public's interest in Peru soared. Bridgeport had to have its own South American mummy too."

"But," Inger pointed out, "The major revelations in Peru, like Manchu Picchu, weren't brought before the public until the 1920's.   Didn't the Great Showman die in the 1890's?"

Freya nodded her agreement.   "Yes, but he left a legacy in his will for his hometown of Bridgeport, a fantastic museum for the people."

Grace looked at her. "If there is a mummy in storage, would they give me access to take samples?"

Her friend smiled triumphantly, "They will—if you're with me! I've surveyed and appraised their entire mineral collection as their gem consultant!"

"That probably took a lot of your time, you charged them for that?" asked Grace sharply.

Freya flushed a bit. "No, they don't have money in the budget for that. But I got a free year's family pass to the museum, and my name as 'Gem consultant' in their brochure–that's free publicity. They won't make a buy without my expertise."

Grace realized that having someone inside would help. "Freya, could you arrange a collection visit for me? As soon as possible?"

Her friend looked a little surprised, but she used Grace's phone to call and came back with. "It's settled. A museum visit for both us on Thursday."

That made Grace feel if she was imposing. "You can't come on a workday?"

Freya dismissed the problem airily. "That's Mac's day

off, he can mind my store. Dealing with the Rose will take some finessing, so you need me with you."

Okay, Grace nodded and said, "I'll pick you up, and treat you to a fancy lunch afterward. Where do you want to go?"

Her friend's eyes shined with happy anticipation as Freya said, "Jimmy's. It's on the water in New Haven, and they have great fried clams."

It would be more time wasted, but Grace agreed, "That sounds like fun." After Freya left, Grace looked over to Inger. "That vial Freya picked up, check the control number, I want the name attached to it."

Inger looked down at the tray of eighty-one tiny vials. "I don't know which one it was."

Closing her eyes to concentrate, Grace envisioned Freya's hand hovering over the tray, reaching down then lifting out a vial. Using that vision Grace mentally counted. "It was in the eleventh row down and fifth from the left."

Inger pulled on a clean latex glove, reached out and picked up the vial, so she could read off the number, "LG00043."

Using Inger's computer, Grace reached down and doing a rapid one finger type, she put in the password code, then pulled up the master control sheet. Almost all of the LG series had been taken from Humanity's Harvest employees.

Picking up one of those vials at random, Freya had spoken of a born leader, beneficial to his own, but ruthless to all others. Prideful. Always planning. An individual who would accept no external authority, nor feel any remorse for what he had done. For Grace that seemed to be an excellent definition of Humanity's Harvest C.E.O., Axel Jensen. Could Freya had intuited his sample?

She typed in Axel Jensen. His name came up, connected with LG00079. So LG00043 wasn't him. Axel's sample may have been near LG00043 in the tray. "Inger–check those samples, see if LG00079 is in that tray." Freya had often told Grace E.S.P. was a fuzzy sort of vision. Perhaps Axel's sample was just near the one Freya picked?

Inger had written down the number Grace wished, then she methodically started at the upper right of the tray, slightly lifting each vial in the first row, just enough to see the control number. Not finding Axel's, she started on the second row down. Finally, she reached one that was the tenth row down, third across. "This is LG00079, Axel Jensen."

It was close. Oh, hell, it was a small tray, of course, it would be close. But scientifically, what Freya picked bore no real, attributable relation to the vial holding Axel's chromosomes. Still, who did she pick? Just someone random? Grace had known Freya too long to just disregard her strangely prophetic intuitions. Well, if LG00043 wasn't connected to Axel, who was it? Grace switched to the number column and scrolled down the list to LG00043. Then she checked across--the name associated with LG00043 was one she knew. Last name Vascelo, first name Ekkeko.

Ekkeko Vascelo? Axel's Peruvian assistant. The angry eyed young man. He was obviously climbing the higher rungs of the corporate ladder, but Grace found him a little too obviously contemptuous of others, a little too immature to be the world harnessing leader Freya's trance-like, the dreamy voice had described.

Still, Grace had learned over the years that Freya's special intuitions usually turned out to be strangely correct. Unfortunately, they weren't much help if you couldn't understand them at the time, and they only made sense when you looked in retrospect. But they had been uncannily right in the past. Nor could they be explained away by any of the laws of the physical universe that Grace understood. "Keep this tray in cold storage. I may want to take a more detailed look later."

Chapter 25

Thursday for that trip up to Bridgeport, Grace pulled up her station wagon in front of Freya's house. Dressed theatrically in a maroon velvet cape, Freya was already at the curb, carrying two, large shopping bags. Of course, her old car's door locks were failing, so Grace had to reach over the passenger seat to open the door for Freya.

"Grace, the next time you get money, instead of buying more expensive toys for your lab, you need to replace this car!" said Freya sternly as she slipped inside.

"Where's your van parked?" Grace asked pretending innocence.

Freya colored. "In the repair shop...again."

Mac's blue, 1500 Ram crew cab pickup was pulling out of Freya's driveway. "Mac's on duty today?" Grace asked. "I thought he was watching your shop?"

"No," Freya sounded a trifle put out, as she struggled with her seat belt. "He made a point of not saying where he's going. I thought he could watch the shop for me since it's his day off, but he had a previous commitment. Of course, Mr. Bigshot wouldn't tell me what it was."

"Going to the range to practice?" Grace struggled to do a tight turn on a road that ended in the harbor.

"Not without his guns." Freya stopped and looked at the vanishing truck. "He's been doing that a lot lately. Just going out. Not saying where."

Grace could guess where he was going and with who, but she tried to put Freya off the scent with a little humor. "Maybe he's hanging around with a bad crowd, think the high sheriff's selling cocaine?"

Freya sour glare indicated she didn't appreciate the joke.

Grace stopped at a light before Main street. "Did you have to close Haunts of Wôden?"

"No. Lilith's been holding her study group there, so she'll watch the store today." As Grace pulled out on to the main road, Freya asked, "Can we just stop in the parking lot alongside the library for a few minutes?"

"Sure." Another delay, but Freya was giving up her whole working day. Grace pulled down the side road along the Library and parked. Hauling out her shopping bags, Freya got out. Grace followed the taller woman as their shoes crunched on the ice crust behind the one story, cottage shaped library. Under the snow was a grass lawn, that led to a short strip of beach on the Harbor. There was a flock of about six Canadian geese trying to dig up grass in the snow. Seeing Freya reach into her bag and start ripping up bread slices, they headed over. Down by the river that fed into Harbor, Grace could see three or four wild black ducks swimming. Freya pulled out another loaf and handed it to Grace to distribute. "They sell second-day bread for almost nothing. No reason to let it go to waste."

Well, there was a reason. Grace could see it. A yellow painted, steel sign, lettered boldly 'FEEDING WILDLIFE PROHIBITED.' "You're not supposed to feed them, that sign there says."

"What?" Freya threw some to the black ducks that were flying over to them.

"That sign. Looks official," Grace pursued.

"Oh, that's because of Selma! Busybody. She's been trying to ban rice from being thrown at weddings."

"Why?" asked Grace ripping up more bread slices and tossing them. It was the only way they were going to get out of here.

Freya was explaining more, "Selma claims that the reconstituted dried rice will expand in the bird's stomach, killing the bird. There's never been a single case of that! In the wild, birds eat dried rice all the time."

Little snowbirds were landing beyond the geese.

Freya threw them some more bread. A flock of seagulls was swooping over them, one dropping down to catch a crust of bread in mid-air. Where were all these birds coming from? Grace felt like she was cringing in the phone booth in Hitchcock's '*The Birds.*' "But she got an ordinance passed?"

"At every town meeting, Selma kept badgered the town council–finally they passed the 'don't feed' ordinance just to shut her up. That and they weren't too happy with all the droppings the Canadian Geese leave."

"So if she wants to protect birds, why is Selma so against feeding them?"

"She's a bit of fanatic. Selma gets a notion in her head, then she decides we all have to live according to her beliefs. Remember that long hot spell last August? There's no air conditioning in the Town Hall, so Selma insisted the Town Council turn off all the overhead lights to keep the heat down."

Grace looked at her. "But those lights are fluorescents–they don't give off heat?"

Freya nodded. "But to shut her up, the Council turned them off."

"Great."

"Selma's positive that over-processed bread flour is bad. She'll forbid everybody from eating white bread when she can get that law passed! But right now, she wants to forbid the birds from eating it." Freya dug into the second shopping bag and pulled out another loaf and ripped off the plastic wrapping. "But we've had a freeze for several days. These birds need a little bit of easy fat to ride out the winter."

Grace could see that. "Hope I never meet Selma."

"Oh, you have. Selma's been out demonstrating, with Astrid and the C.U.R.S. crew, over at your research center. The short, stout woman with frosted blonde hair." With a flutter of wings, several green-necked mallards were flying in, headed for them. The geese hissed their displeasure at the competition.

And two big, black web-footed swans were waddling up out of the harbor and towards them. In the water, snowy white swans appeared majestic, beautiful as they serenely glide along, but Grace knew from personal experience up close swans were big, nasty-tempered birds, with mean, hard-biting beaks.

Freya looked up. "Here. Take another bag. Just break it up and toss."

To get out of there, Grace grabbed a bag and started to throw more bread, as far away from themselves as she could.

Iridescent feathered pigeons were flying in. Birds must have a bread alert equivalent of Twitter. Grace was throwing out bread, as the swans waddled closer. "Your friend, Astrid, seems to be as much of a fanatic as Selma."

Freya hesitated, then admitted, "Both of them hold strong beliefs. Both of them are willing to walk the distance to save the rest of humanity, whether we want it or not. But Astrid is a bit more of a clear thinker than Selma. You should listen to Astrid. If she's against genetic engineering, she'll have a strong set of facts behind her arguments!"

"But both don't want to stop with just reasoning with people, they want to force compliance!"

Sadly Freya nodded. "Astrid says that G.E. crops spread by themselves?"

"Like most crops, unless they've been engineered to be sterile, they will pollinate and reproduce naturally."

A worried eyed Freya asked, "Grace, is genetic engineering a good thing? Or not?"

That wasn't a question she could easily answer or wanted to answer. "The issues are complex. The possible tremendous payoffs in nutrition, cheaper pharmaceuticals, and even increased longevity have to be balanced against considerable chances of uncontrollable, adverse effects. What you want is a science that progress, but that is implemented with careful thought and safeguards. Redundant safeguards."

Bags empty as they headed for her car, Freya still looked worried. "Somebody tried to kill Axel Jensen. He's a billionaire. They've always got enemies! Maybe he even deserves it, but I don't want you to be blown up because you are standing next to him!"

Grace wasn't too keen on that either.

Chapter 26

With Freya's directions, Grace took I-95 North again, but they weren't going as far as New Haven. Instead, they turned off at another harbor city on the Atlantic, Bridgeport, Connecticut, 'City of Parks'. By population the largest City in Connecticut, with its Victorian gingerbread houses and closed stores. The city was once famed for manufacturing, but Bridgeport's milling machine shops had given way to universities and junior colleges; where once they'd produced polished brass plates and locks, Bridgeport now turned out legions of shiny new students.

Grace had to interrupt Freya's constant flow of conversation to get directions across the one-way streets. They took the ramp off before I-95 soared several stories over the downtown. Passing some run down houses, Grace drove past the blocks of courthouses, finally turning down towards the Port Jefferson ferry that crossed the Sound to Long Island.

Rising on their left, in the middle of old department stores and small soul food restaurants, was a red and yellow brick folly, with a wide central, onion-domed tower. It had a multiple level, red tile roof, and more Victorian curves, pointing towards its smaller domed towers. A carved frieze of the Great Showman and his achievements ran around the biggest dome in the front. Apparently, he wanted to be remembered for more than his circuses, and his two-story granite shaft in Bridgeport's Egyptian gated cemetery, so his will had provided for a magnificent 'Museum for the City of Bridgeport.'

They parked across the road. With Grace leaving her huge collection case in the back of her station wagon until they found something worth sampling. Ever theatrical Freya had worn her maroon velvet cape over her lavender rainbow muumuu, with multiple necklace strings of small, unpolished stones of amethyst and amber. With Grace's mannish black car coat and her conservative pinstriped pants suit, they made an odd pair.   At the desk, Freya grandly announced their arrival. The docent on the ticket desk gave them staff badges to wear and put in a call for the museum's director.

While they waited for the curator, Grace browsed a bit in the 'manufactured in Bridgeport' section: 1850's foot warmers, rifles, typewriters, glass case after case of items once made in this town. Pictures of the docks with square riggers unloading their cargos and heavily loaded wagon teams pulling it away. Yes, Grace had to admit things don't always change for the better.

Where Freya was tall and bosomy, the curator, Rose Van Sise was short and thin, with frosted blonde hair, neatly coiled up in a French twist. Now she was extremely excited, "Freya, there's a large, ruby gemstone from Burma. We're hoping to get a sponsor to pay for it." She looked hopefully at Freya, as Rose typed into the ticket desk computer. "Here's a photo of it on the Internet."

All business, Freya walked behind the desk and studied the screen for a long time before pronouncing as she pointed, "This photo's poor, but you can see the inclusions. That's why it is priced so low for its weight. And that price is way too high. If you want me to look, I think I can find you something larger, clearer, and cheaper."

Rose apparently accepted Freya as the ultimate authority, so they started on a tour of the museum, with Freya doing a high-pressure sell of Grace to Rose. "She's so modest, but with you guys touting local industry, Dr. Grace Farrington's portrait should be on display here, as a Connecticut marvel with her long list of discoveries in the field of genetics!"

Grace winced inwardly as she stood a bit away in a huge room, devoted to a scale model of an entire traveling circus. Hundreds of roustabouts, clowns, horses, elephants, caged tigers and circus acts were carved in wood and painted, then set under a huge, cut away canvas tent. As Grace looked, Freya kept ladling it on. "She's just back from collecting her MacAlpin Guru award, and could probably get you microscopic pictures of chromosomes and genes for you to blow up and display."

A not too impressed Rose looked at Grace saying politely. "Perhaps sometime, a picture and a bio in our rotating display gallery."

Freya kept on, "Grace received a grant from Axel Jensen, of Humanity's Harvest, to do some DNA sampling of Professor Bingham's Incan collection."

"At the Natural History Museum in New Haven?" Rose asked, sounding slightly more interested.

Grace just nodded. They were climbing a wide, marble staircase in the central, circular entrance tower, that lead to the next floor, with its Victorian parlor recreation and it's open, glass covered Egyptian mummy case.

Rose proudly pointed out, "She was an Egyptian priestess."

Grace looked down at the mummy wrapped in yellowed linen bandages, and wondered why every male mummy was a prince, every female a priestess?

Seeing her face, Rose kind of laughed it off. "Well, we don't really know who she is. That mummy case was from another burial, but from the careful preparation and preservation of the mummy, we can deduce she was of the upper classes."

Freya homed in. "I was telling Grace that you had a South American mummy here."

The look on Rose's face was not promising. She obviously wasn't thrilled that Freya was spilling the museum's private information, but she did turn to Grace, asking. "You're interested in South American mummies?"

"Their chromosomes," Grace said. "I'm currently

culturing what I think is a pre-Columbian Incan noble's DNA."

Freya gushed on, "Grace can tell wonders with her chromosomes and genes!   Eye color, hair color, where the person's ancestors came from."

"Amazing," said Rose, still exhibiting only polite interest.   "Could you determine where this mummy came from?"

Grace hesitated. "It might be possible. If the DNA hasn't totally degraded, and if we can find a match with existing identified DNA in a geographical database, say in the Human Genome Project."

As she walked on, Rose murmured, "That might be interesting–someday. But right now, I'm sorry, but I've got to get back to work."

That put a polite end to a worthless trip.

"First!" Freya put up her hand dramatically, then commanded, "Grace pose over there with Rose, in front of Colonel Short's carriage." Colonel Short and his wife stood under three foot tall and used to make a grand entrance in the Showman's circus, riding in a custom built landau pulled by two white ponies.   Freya clicked the photo with her cell phone. "I'll send it to you.   You can put it in the museum's bulletin. The renowned Dr. Grace Farrington visiting your museum."

Again Grace felt herself flushing with embarrassment. She didn't appreciate Freya's attempts to draw this out. Tour competed, they headed downstairs, with Grace bitterly thinking of a wasted trip and half a day's work lost for the both of them. But when they reached the bottom of the stairs, Freya stopped and seemed to sway a little. "Grace..." she called out weakly. Grace reached out to her friend, but Freya had already grabbed the wide marble railing to steady herself.

"Are you okay?" A frightened Grace asked.

Freya said hesitatingly, "I'm feeling a little woozy. I should've eaten before we left."

Concerned, Rose hurried back to their side. "What's the matter?"

"Nothing." Freya let go of the railing, trying to steady herself, saying weakly, "I just have to take a pill–could I get a glass of water?"

"Of course," said Rose, instantly solicitous. "Why don't you both come sit in my office? It's just over there. Can you make it?"

They did, with Freya leaning heavily on Grace's arm. The curator's office was airy, painted a light yellow and almost devoid of objects; strange for someone whose whole professional life focused on collecting things. The only furnishings in the room were three chairs, a clean table top, with a flat computer screen and keyboard. Then on the walls, some circus posters with dancing horses and roaring tigers. "Freya, would you like coffee?" Rose asked as she settled Freya down in one of the chairs before the desk.

What Grace wanted was an end to this worthless time waster, but behind Rose's back, Freya signaled her to sit, while weakly saying to Rose, "Do you still have some of that marvelous orange-spice black tea?" asked Freya.

"Of course," Rose responded. "Dr. Farrington, would you like some?"

After a telling glare from Freya, Grace nodded. When Rose left, Grace whispered, "We're done here."

Freya shook her head. "Not yet. Just be patient!"

Rose returned with three cups of hot water, tea bags, and a box of cookies. Freya swallowed some kind of pill that looks suspiciously to Grace like an aspirin. They all drank their tea black and stayed silent as they ate almond cookies. Then, sounding stronger, Freya started telling Rose stories of her last New York City's buying trip. Mentioning an auction of antique Nigerian wind instruments, that were beautifully and imaginatively carved as African animals.

"I wish we could afford that," sighed Rose. Despite saying she had to get back to work, the curator seemed perfectly content to just sit in her office and drink tea with her old friend. Grace wondered when they were ever going to get out of there?

"Tell Grace how the museum got its original exhibits," Freya urged Rose, taking another cookie.

"Oh, well, the will left us a lot of the Great Showman's things." Rose started reciting what must have been a regular script, "And when the museum was in its early years, the curators commissioned collectors around the world to search for rare and interesting artifacts."

"You have that stuffed Jaguar and condor from South America," Freya reminded.

Rose nodded and took another sip of her tea. "One of the persons authorized was a Senor Jose Cartagena, who regularly combed throughout Central and South America. He provided the museum with blow guns, shrunken heads, botanical specimens, and the original Empress Carlotta Emerald. That emerald was really a treasure, but unfortunately, it was sold off years ago—it entirely paid for the Museum's clay tile roof, but we kept the setting and replaced it with a fake."

Freya persisted. "Tell Grace how you obtained the South American mummy?"

Rose just gave in. "That was the period Professor Bingham was collecting Incan treasures in Peru. It created great interest in the public for South American artifacts. When they opened that Incan wing in New Haven, all the newspapers covered it. The politicians and prominent society people came out to mingle with the premier actors and actresses of the times. A shame the way they're going after that University's museum collection today. Wanting it returned, after a century..."

Freya took another crescent-shaped cookie, then neatly herded Rose back on to the story. "You don't really want that South American mummy in the glass case anyway--maybe if you told the authorities in South America that you have it, they would take it back?"

"We don't know where in South America it came from. The paperwork shows six crates were shipped from Panama, but the mummy's tunic isn't of Panamanian weave or decorative pattern." Rose still seemed to be considering returning the mummy, but shook her head, "It would be very bad precedence. We give back the mummy, then Egypt would want their priestess back, and Ukraine would want their wax-resist eggs..."

Grace asked, " Did your collector get any botanical samples? Plant material, or vessels with food residue?"

Rose only said, "Perhaps. I never really looked."

"Let's stay with the mummy," Freya suggested. "Could Grace see your storage area?"

Even Rose had sense enough to know that an unstoppable object like Freya Dell had to be bowed to. And that was how they wound up, with Grace's car five blocks away, in an old rife manufacturing plant, a long, narrow brownstone block building, with its tall windows all bordered up.

Lighting inside the two-story high stone building came from bare bulbs, hanging down from the high ceiling. Every step they took raised more dust and Grace felt the building was colder inside than it was outside. Which actually would help preserve the DNA. Finally Rose stopped before a patchwork quilt covered box, about four-foot high and three-foot square.

"This is Flat Nose." Rose pulled the cloth off, and Grace looked into the eyes of a bluish skinned man. Well, the 'eyes' were round blackened metal disks, and his nose was squashed, and he appeared to be garbed in a yellowed, wool tunic with a key like design at the edge. It was disconcerting to see him just sitting cross-legged before her. His nose appeared flattened, whether in life or afterward, and his indented arms showed evidence of once having worn bracelets high up, but they were long gone. And Grace noted from the deep indent marks circling his forehead, that he probably regularly had worn some sort of a crown or cornet, but now his majesty's woven tunic seemed to have been badly chewed by moths or mice.

Rose looked at him with distaste. "The public prefers their mummies prone and wrapped in linen bandages. These guys seem to stare at you, it's uncomfortable for most patrons."

Freya has been listening. "These guys? Plural? "

"Oh, yes. Three royal kings." Rose indicated stacks of other wooden crates nearby. "Well, that's what Senor Cartagena wrote in his paperwork, but in those days, collectors routinely exaggerated the importance of the finds they were trying to sell to the museum."

Freya was peering into Flat Nose's dirt-streaked case. "He seems to still have a gold earring?"

"Possibly." Rose wasn't too interested. "He and his friends are more trouble than they're worth."

Grace looked up from the case. "Why don't you get rid of them?"

Rose shook her head. "You wouldn't believe the problems with human remains! A few years ago, somebody dug up an old story about an Indian named 'Albert Afraid of Hawk', who died in 1900 of food poisoning, while he was touring with Buffalo Bill's Wild West show. Well, someone at some newspaper got the story. Dug up some supposed Sioux relatives of Albert's, back in South Dakota.

"Then they had to get legal permission to find the unmarked grave and open it. They decided to raise funds to bring Albert's family out to Connecticut, to disinter him, with full native American religious ceremony. Someone had to raise funds to pay for the casket's transport back to South Dakota. The newspapers even interviewed a self-proclaimed relative who claimed *'the family was relieved to know what happened to Albert.'* Give me a break! At that point, the dearly departed Albert had been dead for over 112 years!"

"It can be a mess," Freya admitted.

"Oh, lord, yes. Remember, they probably didn't do much in the way of death certificates in South America back in the 1900's. If we were to bury the mummies now, we'd have to get permission from the City. Then pay for three grave plots. And with them sitting up like that, they would have to be buried in custom boxes, that would require special, deeper holes. The expenses for the museum would be terrible! I'm spending most of my time begging donors just to put on a simple children's puppet show for Christmas."

"What if you returned the mummies to where they came from in South America?" Freya asked.

"Human remains? We need special legal authorization to just move them within Connecticut. To get them to an international airport would require hiring lawyers to get permissions from the United States government, then permission from whatever country we were shipping them back to. And as I explained we're not even sure where these mummies originated."

That was the chance that Freya had been waiting for. "Grace could tell you that! If you allowed her to just take a small sample, she can read their DNA and tell you where they came from."

"Could you do that?" Rose asked Grace.

Grace explained carefully, "Whether DNA can be extracted or not depends on how well the mummy was originally preserved, and whether it's been able to stay dry and to avoid excessive heat. Then, if we do get any DNA, we would need origin DNA to compare with. The Human

Genome project is doing a tremendous job with tracing mass movements of populations strains. If the Project has something on record that matches your kings, we should be able to come up with a probable area of origin."

They both held their breaths, waiting for Rose to make up her mind.

Finally, she did. "Alright. Let's get this case open."

That required screwdrivers that Grace carried in her collection case, which they had to retrieve from her station wagon. While they were doing that, Rose phoned for her maintenance man to bring over a hammer and a crowbar, to help open the crates. He, and a miraculously recovered Freya man-handled two more crates from the bottom of the stacks with Panama stamps, that Rose believed might be the other two kings.

It was long, dirty work before three ancient mummified figures sat cross-legged before Grace on packing cloths spread over the warehouse floor. The one in the glass case seemed in the best condition, but all three had survived thousands of miles and many centuries remarkably well. With Rose's supervision, they decided on inconspicuous insertion sites for Grace's coring rod. She was going for the densest area of likely material, hip bones.

With Rose talking to the maintenance guy, Grace suited up, with mask and gloves, and said in a low voice to Freya. "If we had ex-ray capacities I might be able to locate the stomachs and get a sample of their last meals?"

Her friend gave a slight shake to her head, and returned in a low voice, "We've pushed enough. Get the bone samples today. See if you can tell Rose anything interesting about the mummies, then maybe we can come back next time for any other stuff."

Grace was quite pleased with her samples, but Freya was uncharacteristically silent when they left the Museum. She turned down the promised lunch with, "I'd rather not, I'm not hungry." Then as they started the hour drive back home, her friend said nothing in response to Grace's comments. In fact, her friend literally said nothing until Grace pulled into the small parking lot opposite the string of whaling ship period houses that were now the upscale shops of Oyster River Harbor. Even after Grace had parked, Freya didn't talk but also didn't get out of Grace's Subaru.

Finally, Grace broke the silence. "Thank you for helping me get those mummy samples."

Freya sat looking out the passenger's window, seeing a thousand miles away. When she spoke, it was slow and lifeless. "I didn't do you any favor."

Finally, without saying another word, Freya took her seat belt off and was climbed out of the station wagon. Grace should be getting back to her lab, but she also got out of the car and walked around. "Freya, what's the matter? Are you really feeling sick? "

Not looking at her, Freya spoke slowly, "Grace, there was a curse placed on those mummies. I can sense it."

"What, one hundred years ago?"

"A curse on all foreign invaders. A curse on whoever touches them. Possesses them. A curse for taking away what did not belong to them."

"Is that why Senor Cartagena and Professor Bingham are dead? I hear Bingham lived into the 1950's–dying when he was over eighty years old! Must not have been too strong a curse."

"If you checked into their lives, I'm sure they would have had setbacks. Failures. Accidents that should've have happened."

"Freya! That sadness happens to everybody–with or without an ancient Peruvian curse being put on them. Besides, why do you care? Everyone involved in that transaction has been dead for over fifty years!"

"No, Grace. You're not dead. Not yet. And you've

touched those cursed mummies!"

Chapter 27

The next day, Grace looked up from the computer screen on her lab desk.   Bobby was standing there, and his body language radiated a problem. "Is this about my lecture this afternoon?" she asked.

"Yhep."

This would be her first lecture for this latest class. God, Grace always got stomach cramps before getting up before a group of eager students, waiting for her to neatly and effortlessly drop her entire life's knowledge of genetic research into their skulls in a hundred and fifteen minutes. Now Bobby was looking like they had a bigger problem. "What is it?"

"Adam gave permission for Axel Jensen to monitor your class today."

That would add some pressure.   Grace opened the drawer of her desk and pulled out some Imodium pills. Damn–why hadn't she got her haircut? Her black curls were down her neck, and she didn't have any lipstick in the lab.

"That's not the problem," Bobby continued. "Daniel Novinski has also signed up for that class."

"Who is Daniel...oh–that lawyer...?"

"For C.U.R.S." Bobby confirmed.

Grace threw her pen down. "Just what I need, trying to teach a class, with an anti-genetic engineering lawyer arguing with the C.E.O. of a major   G.E. promoting conglomerate."

"Yeah, that's what I told Gail."

"Since Daniel hasn't paid for that class..."

"Actually, he filled out paperwork and left a check to pay for an entire semester, just so he could attend this lecture. And, unfortunately, Gail accepted it. "

"Did ORR cash it?"

"Not yet."

"But usually all the slots in my classes are already filled with early registration—correct?"

"Yes, but it's Adam's position that we should try to pacify the demonstrators if possible. It's only a two-hour lecture?"

Grace sighed and washed one Imodium pill down with her lukewarm tea. "They can come. But I want you to personally make it clear to the both of them, they're only watchers! Only monitoring the lecture. I do not want them stating their political positions or arguing in front of my students!"

"Actually, they've both agreed to that already. The person you'll have to worry about will be Justin Feldstein."

"A student? Why?"

"He's a bright guy in genetics—but with the emotional maturity quotient of minus one. He'll be raising his hand and calling out endless questions, trying to focus the class's attention solely on himself."

"Just what I need," Grace said, feeling contractions as she swallowed another Imodium pill with her now cold tea.

* * *

Lecture Room 1B was structured like a bowl, with the lecturer on the bottom floor and spectators' stadium seating raising up all around her. The room dated from the 1920's, but with David's lawyer, Mark Silverstein, on the Board of Directors, he had insisted ORR pay for a decent, up-to-date sound system. Still, years of public speaking professionally had given Grace a good, carrying voice. Today she needed it, with about thirty students shuffling in their seats with their books, pens, and papers.

For her lecture, Grace put on a white coat and stood holding her lectern. Bad speech procedure—but it comforted her. After her first lectures debacle with the overturned pitcher of ice water, and her second, with no water and a dry, continual cough, Bobby routinely set out a capped bottle of water within her reach. To hold off getting started, Grace was twisting the cap open, and taking a delaying drink.

Axel and Daniel were sitting in the back, at the top row, quietly talking to each other. No bloodshed yet. Most of the group before her where post-graduates students. All knew who she was; most of them had come to Oyster River just to study under her. All expected her dog and pony show would be worth the ticket price.

As she looked over those faces, Grace remembered Eric Larsen's genius. He used to sit down in the center, right among the students. Toss off a few statements, then ask the students what they thought about the subject. Making them feel like they were already accomplished scientists, juggling their own concepts and theories. And all the while his comments would be gently guiding them to the truth.

Well, the topic Bobby picked and her slides were aimed at epigenetics. However the lecture quickly degenerated into a question and answer on genetic engineering. Not that either Axel or Daniel said anything. They just sat quietly in the back and watched, as Grace, not for the first time, wished she had Eric Larsen's masterful handling of the more problematic elements of any lecture group.

She started off well. Bobby introduced her, and Grace switched on her first PowerPoint slide on the big screen, pointing out that epigenetics concerned the change in an allele expression or phenotype, but not a change in the genetics itself. A change in phenotype, not genotype, that was not the result of inactive genes being activated, but just read differently. She explained epigenetic change is a regular and natural occurrence, but it can also be influenced by several factors including age, the environment, lifestyle, and disease states. She further explained the most interesting changes to her resulted from an outside influence on the living organism past embryonic development.

A young woman raised her hand and asked, "Dr. Farrington would you consider Epigenetics a coming field for study?"

Grace paused, as she always did, to think before answering a question. "Although what influences the expression of a gene has always been a question since the beginning of the study of genetics, its stress today is an acknowledgment of epigenetics importance as an explanation of expression that we don't as yet fully understand." She paused, then added a personal note. "If I were just entering into the study of genetics today, I think this is where I would be concentrating most of my efforts."

That raised hand, of a stocky male, sitting front and center. She acknowledged him. "Grace, I'm Justin Feldstein." To supposedly speak to her, Justin turned his back to her to face the rest of the students, loudly stating, "I would think you would have answered Genetic Engineering!"

From then on, with Bobby closing his eyes in pain, Grace was presiding over a lively debate on the importance of G.E. She tried to get control back and immediately stopped acknowledging Justin's raised hand, but he just shouted out a rebuttal to every other student that she did allow to speak. It wasn't going well.

Finally, Justin was yelling out "But Grace–Grace! Genetic engineering! That's where it is! That is the only field of study worth doing!"

That last seemed just one disrespect too many for Axel Jensen. From the highest, last row in the back, his commanding voice rolled out. "Mr. Feldstein! It's not 'Grace'–it's **Dr.** Farrington!" Although he didn't really shout, his voice had a resounding edge of steel to it that even seemed to wilt Justin a bit.

Then Daniel Novinski loudly joined in. "Yes. **Dr.** Farrington's advancements in science have earned our highest regard a great number of times–she should be given her full title out of respect."

Frankly, Grace didn't care what anybody called her, she just wanted to get her lecture back on track for the students who were genuinely here to learn.

Justin Feldstein looked a little abashed, but he loudly came back, "**Excuse, me, Dr. Farrington!** But surely with.." he said it an exaggerated, almost mocking tone, "your genius, you understand the primacy of Genetic Engineering to the field. I am sure that..."

Overcoming a childhood of being raised to be polite, Grace cut him off in mid-sentence. "Genetic Engineering, Epigenetics, the complicated, conflicting tangle of gene expression are all integrated facets of the all-encompassing, fascinating secret of how our alleles translate purely chemical reactions into functioning organs and repeatable, inheritable physical behaviors." "But genetic engineering..." Justin started again.

"Has its problems–such as uncontrolled spread! But that's not the topic of this lecture..."

Without raising his hand, Justin spoke out. "There are ways around that! What about the genetically engineered suicide seeds? Plants that will grow for a generation, but whose seeds will be sterile? That's your answer to that whole objection!" He finished triumphantly. "**Dr.** Farrington, I'm surprised **you** wouldn't have thought of that?"

Grace shook her head. "In the nature of chromosome replication, nothing is one hundred percent predictable. Even with suicide seeds, we can assume that a percentage–abit a small one–will be viable and able to transfer their genetic package to the next generation. And if this is a crop engineered to produce say a pharmaceutical, like the flax plant that produces blood protein you may have a serious problem. If this flax is grown in an open field, then you can bet that those altered chromosomes will pollinate distant crops with disastrous results.   And, as we have often sadly discovered in the past, from English Sparrows to the Chestnut Blight, from Zebra Mussels to Killer Bees, once an aggressive, invasive species are released in the environment we are never going to marshal the enormous resources necessary to fully cram that genie back into the bottle."

Multiple hands were raised, but Justin just started loudly talking, "But the answer is simple! Plant your flax crop where there are no other flax plants to cross-pollinate with! Matter solved!" He finished triumphantly, looking around for everyone's approbation.

Grace didn't want to get into this topic, without laying the proper foundation, but, "One of the problems with transgenic plants is the very real possibility of an uncontrolled gene transfer to an unintended species–say from flax to wild grasses. Those grasses might pass down that inserted allele and support the transfer of that gene to either a distant flax or a flax plant in another growing season. Or even more worrisome, that wild grass might pass your inserted gene to some unforeseeable plant, with a totally unpredictable result. "

More meat for bulldog Justin to bite into, "That can be controlled!..."

But as she was answering his comment, Grace had glanced to Bobby, then followed his signaling eyes to the clock high on the wall. Only another twenty-minutes of lecture time and she'd only gotten to the fourth PowerPoint slide–damn it! No. She was not going to force this class to revisit this grade school topic again! **"Okay. That's it!** Ladies and gentlemen..."

"But.." Justin started.

"No more questions! No more comments!" She finished too firmly; waiting for absolute silence. That line-backer-looking guy sitting next to Justin was glaring at him, so he finally shut up.

In control again Grace continued. "We are running out of time–but we will finish this PowerPoint demo today! After class is dismissed, for anyone who wishes to stay, I will take a limited number of questions, but I will not be getting into theoretical or politics of genetic engineering. If you have further concerns that have not been met, arrange a private session with my co-lecturer, Mr. Robert Jamison here, who is fully capable of discussing the whole topic."

Justin, fortunately, did not hang around after the run-over class ended.   There were about twelve people who stayed.   Grace signed several of her books, while she answered some not very penetrating questions. As the others left, both Axel and Daniel talked quietly together over by the door, while they waited patiently for her attention. When Grace joined them, she heard Daniel finishing up, "But you're disregarding the tremendous dangers, for advantages that may only be illusional! That's not good business!"

Axel looked away from him, to her with that winning smile of his. "Very good lecture. Even with that disrespectful jerk down front."

Daniel also agreed. "Yes. It was very interesting---I could understand it all. From those questions afterward, your students really seem to get it."

There was something Grace wanted to know. "How are you guys coming with your differences?"

The two, tall men looked at each other, seeming to be sizing the other up as if they were going into physical battle, but with a slight smile, Axel said, "There are some platforms we might be able to agree on."

"Yes." Daniel nodded. "Axel here agrees that with genetic engineering, safety has to be paramount. I think my International Food Web Center Foundation can go along with that. I'm going to put his comments in my next bulletin."

"So it's just a matter of setting up reasonable, workable parameters, that point the way for progress?" asked

Grace.

"Well, the devil seems to be in the details." Daniel lookedat Axel, his face changing from 'in control' to an almost grim nervous twitch. "By the way, I've joined your exclusive club."

Axel asked, "Club?"

"Yes. Got an anonymous threatening letter," he said it with an almost twisted kind of pride.

Grace looked to him. "Did you give it to the police?"

He thought about that. "Not yet."

"But you are?" Grace prodded.

Daniel hesitated. "Might be a conflict of interest. Don't know who wrote it–but it might be from a client of mine."

"What did it say?" Axel asked.

Daniel reached into his suit jacket and pulled out a stamped envelope, which he started to hand to Axel.

"Should that be handled without gloves? Wait a second." Grace opened her fannie pack and pulled out two latex gloves, from the stash she always carried. She pulled them on, then took the envelope from Daniel.

It looked just like the others. Standard business envelope with self-stick label, cheap typing paper, all printing probably done by a computer with the same thirty dollar, untraceable printer. Even the warning was pretty much the same: **'By giving in you're hurting the Earth! Stop, or you will die too!'**

"What does this mean? 'Giving in'?" Grace asked Daniel.

"Well, I've been speaking out at the C.U.R.S. strategy meetings. Suggesting that those, like Axel, pushing genetic engineering might not totally be the spawn of Satan. That we could draw up, say a sample contract, carefully delineating reasonable safeguards, that will allow experimentation with its possible benefits, but still protect the fragile environment, we must live in."

Yes, Grace could see Daniel Novinski, as the Supreme Court justice he dreamed of being. See him quietly deliberating a judgment based on balancing the rule of law, public desires, and the practical necessaries of providing for the medical and nutritional needs of an ever-expanding world population.

A pained Axel looked at him. "So because you dare to try to mediate a peaceful solution someone wants to take your life?"

At this moment, they all seemed united, herself, Axel and Daniel. Yet, despite their conciliatory positions, standing there looking at them, Grace was left with the horrible feeling that this was an issue that one of them would never be allowed to live to agree upon.

Chapter 28

By the next week, Grace knew none of the material taken from the second Bridgeport mummy's pelvis was replicating. Damn. She really wanted to see that read out. Grace picked up the phone. "Freya? It's Grace."

"You okay?" came back the anxious reply.

"Fine, but when we were at the Bridgeport museum, you told the curator, Rhoda...."

"Rose," Freya corrected.

"Rose. That you would be bringing up some mineral samples to show her?"

"Someday."

"When?"

"And this is important you, why?" Freya asked suspiciously.

Kurt was always saying Grace was like an aircraft carrier plowing ahead when she went after something she really wanted. "The samples from the second mummy, the one we called 'Stomach Scar' failed to replicate."

"Oh, bless the Goddess, that means you want to take more samples, right?"

"Think it would be possible?" she asked Freya hesitantly.

"Grace, two weeks ago you didn't even know there was one mummy, not less three in storage in Bridgeport, right?"

"Yes.

"And now you have working samples for the other two mummies–but you're not satisfied?"

"Yes."

"Grace, why do you care?" asked Freya absolutely not understanding.

"Well, by their treatment these mummies apparently were of very high status in their society."

"Presumably."

"Nobles. Leaders. I'm studying alleles..." she had to change her word choice, when not talking to scientific types, "genes for leadership qualities.   I think that I'll find something in the first and third mummies, something that I am going to want to confirm in the second mummy. I'd like to send Nick up there to collect another set of samples."

"Your assistant? No, not a good idea."

"But..."

"Rose wasn't too happy the first time. Especially that I told you what was in the museum's storage. She might feel we are using her."

Why was Freya opposing this so? "But if you took some mineral samples up, and I just happened to come along with you. We could feel her out, right?"

"Then you're going to make another trip up, with your collection equipment? That'll be more time off from your work..."

"I thought maybe I could just happen to have my sample case in the car?"

Freya was silent, then asked, "Grace, is this worth both of us losing another day's work?'

Grace knew her friend was testing the importance of the matter. "To me, it's worth it."

Sighing Freya said, "And once you've decided to do something, it'll take an act of the Goddess to stop you–no–slow you down. Okay. Thursday. Bring up one of those textbooks you've written, signed to her."

"You think the curator would be interested in genetic research?"

"No, but I think a fancy, fat book, that looks very scholarly, and that's dedicated to 'my very good friend'..."

"Rhoda.."

"Rose!" she corrected. "Don't you make it out until I write out something for you to copy," said an exasperated

Freya.

"Okay, and I pick up special cookies and tea from the Cheese Shop to bring up."

"And flowers for our funerals," Freya continued in an unhappy voice.

"What?"

"I know you don't understand or believe this–but I told you, Grace, those mummies are cursed! Anyone around them will take on that curse!"

* * *

Curse or no curse, the trip up to Bridgeport went well. Coming out to look at Freya's mineral samples, Rose smiled widely to see her. "Dr. Farrington, since you were here I've had a chance to study some of your work. Freya was right–the museum should consider you a modern industry! And the others, scientists who have worked at Oyster River Research: Dr. Larsen, Dr. Huang..."

"Please call me Grace. Eric Larsen was a marvelous person. You know, if you were interested in doing a display on him I could check with his family. I'm sure they'd do a temporary loan of his Nobel award material and his books and photographs.   And there's Dr. Stewart Brewster, a true pioneer in the cellular field."

"I've read about him," said an impressed sounding Rose.

"He's still alive. He might consent to come up for a reception."

Rose nodded. "Something to think about. How did our mummy samples turn out?"

This was Grace's chance. "Number one mummy and number three are culturing, but the samples I took from the second mummy failed."

"Oh, that's a shame. But you've got two."   Rose seemed to be hurrying. "I've got a Birthday party of children coming in, and I have to set up the room..."

"Perhaps we could try again? Take another series of samples. If you'd allow it?" Rushing her words Grace sounded desperate to her own ears. "I just happen to have my collection case in Freya's van."

Rose looked at Freya. Seemed about to say no explaining, "Our maintenance man is off today..."

Freya brushed away the problem. "Grace and I can move the crates ourselves. All we need is the key to open up the storage building."

Before leaving they helped Rose set up the party room with crayons and coloring mats, so soon, they were at the long, block building, with Rose opening the door and showing Freya how to rearm the security system after they'd finished. "I've got to do a tour for the party children," she said sounding harried. "Sure you can do this by yourselves?"

"We'll be fine." Freya airily told her.

But without that maintenance man's strength, it was a lot harder to pull out the Peruvian crates from the bottom of their stacks. And of course, on their first try, they pulled out and uncrated, 'Missing Finger' by mistake, so had to nail him up and start again. When 'Stomach Scar' was opened, it took the two of them struggling to lift the heavy mummy out of the crate.

Like his brothers, Stomach Scar was mummified sitting upright, his legs crossed. He still retains his dried hair, which had gone reddish over the ages. Grace looked at it, as a possible source of DNA, but decided it didn't look promising. The skin was dark-bluish gray. Remains of a garment had slipped down to his hips. In life, he'd apparently had a long, whitened scar running diagonally across his stomach. A battle injury? Must have been when he was a lot younger, because it had healed and scar had begun to smooth before his death.

As Grace pulled on her latex gloves and surgical mask, she studied the face that looked more like a puppet than human. This one too seemed to have an indent running around his forehead from having worn some sort of rigid headgear. A crown? Holes in the earlobes–once he wore earrings. Looked like they were torn out. And some seeds –maize kernels? Sprinkled in his lap? Offerings from the funeral? Or later, by supplicants begging their noble ancestor's favor?

Grace managed to get some seeds in a collection vial. Traces of what looked like gold foil flakes were on his chest. Not as good mummification as 'Flat Nose' but like 'Flat Nose,' 'Stomach Scar' seemed to be an older man. Fifties? Sixties? Hard to tell in his crumbling state.

Now, where would she take her cores from? The pelvis hadn't worked out too well. The mouth seemed to have structure, with probably a full set of teeth under there...but the lips were pinched closed. Glued? Sewn? If she tried to access the teeth by coring, she'd do too much obvious damage to the face.

Skull? No. Try the long bones of the leg–maybe access from underneath the body? "Freya, help me lift him–I want to go from underneath." He was heavier than Grace expected. They had to lower him gently, then Grace moved the stained, rotting cloth, to find an opening to enter into the thigh. The first insertion, she missed bone. Using the same entry hole, she tried a different angle and was gratified to hit something solid, that resisted her coring rod.

She looked over to Freya, who had set her huge calico quilted handbag on the dirty board floor and opened it as she was laying out various items. "What is that?" Grace asked.

"Oil of peppermint." She shook a bulbed glass vial, "Pollen." Freya pulled out a weedy branch, about twenty-four centimeters long.

"That is?"

"Sage," Freya replied absorbed in what she was laying out.

"What are you doing?"

"Setting up for a purification ceremony."

"Wiccan?" Grace asked.

"More Navajo–very, very loosely based. It will show our respect. Align the spirits of the dead with peace, and bring back harmony...I hope. "

"Do you think the curator would be okay with that?"

"Rose's not going to object–if we don't tell her." Freya was setting a long-handled, school teacher's brass bell on the concrete, along with some small white rocks.

Grace wasn't too happy with this. "Do you need to do that now? What if Rose comes back? She'll think we're crazy."

"Be thankful. Usually, I'd be doing this skyclad."

Yhep.   A forty-year-old, six-foot-one-inch tall Scandinavian woman, performing a Navajo purification ritual naked would be a bit much.

Near the three mummy cases, Freya was walking widdershins about a chalked circle, lightly tossing a golden powder down on the floorboards.

"What is that?" Grace sneezed.

"Corn pollen."

"Where do you get that stuff?"

"E-bay," Freya answered.

Bent on her knees, her back hurting from the angle, Grace sat back, "What is all that going to do?"

"I'm trying to neutralize your mummy's curse."

Grace looked up from setting out her coring tools. Sometimes she wished she could neutralize her helpful friends. "What if Rose sees the pollen or chalk?"

"In all this dust?" Freya took out a pointed chalk stick from endless her bag and drew a five-pointed star in the dust. Then she set a thick, white candle in the center, which she lit, after dripping a few drops of fragrant peppermint oil on the wick. At least their cursed mummies might smell better.

While Freya softly prayed, Grace tried to find the

insertion hole she used the first time to go in for another try at the hip bone. Getting into it, Freya was chanting a little louder. Grace twisted in her rod and hit something hard, finally withdrawing another sample. Did she dare take another? Yes.

Finally finishing Grace put her tools and samples away, stiffly standing up. Freya was still chanting and sprinkling the pollen. Grace found herself folding her hands down before her and bowing her head in respect for someone's deeply held religious beliefs.

Then as Freya packed up her bag, Grace used a collection brush to sweep the dust back to its natural state. It took them both pulling hard to get 'Stomach Scar' upright and nailed back into his crate, then back into his place with the other boxes stacked on top.

Grace was anxious to get going, but Freya still lingered. Running her hand under the worn quilt that covered 'Flat Nose's' glass display case.

"What's the matter?"

"The anger—it's still here."

"Didn't your ceremony cleanse everything?"

Freya spoke tiredly, as she turned away from the case. "No. No, the Shaman who originally placed the curse was very powerful. Very hating. Through time and distance, his anger still lingers here."

After they carefully locked up and returned the bags to the car, Freya suggested that it would be politic to just drop in and say goodbye to Rose. They found her in the museum's birthday party room, picking up broken crayons after a visiting fifth-grade class.

"Did you get the samples you needed?" Rose asked in a friendly fashion.

"I hope so," said Grace. "As soon as I can work up the three profiles, I'll be getting back to you."

"That'd be good. We would really love to know

where those mummies actually did come from." The curator commented politely.

"Have you found any more paperwork, from the man who originally collected the mummies?" Freya asked.

"Senor Cartagena? No. Unfortunately not," said Rose. "I've told you all the documentation that I could find."

"He just took his money and ran," Freya flippantly commented.

"Oh, no," Rose said. "The finder's fee was never paid. The museum sent him a check, but the Panamanian Police returned the check to us–uncashed. Apparently right after Senor Cartagena shipped the mummies, he suddenly became ill."

"Ill?"

"Yes. He died unexpectedly. Poor man, he was only forty-two."

Freya looked hard to Grace.

Chapter 29

Driving Kurt up to the New Haven airport with a sleet storm predicted was something she nearly assigned to Nick. Grace hated driving in icy conditions, but she wanted to be there to see Kurt off. So she helped pack his suitcases, drove him up, and there came that painful moment of parting. Knowing it would be months before she'd see him again, she kissed him hard. But Kurt was so 'up' about his ocean current study. Talking about it. Bragging. Planning. He didn't even look back as he strode off into the terminal. For a brief moment, Grace wanted to run after him–drop everything–take the trip on the science ship as his assistant and spend Christmas with him.

Ridiculous, she had work to do.

As she drove back, sloppy wet snow splashed on the windshield, and the radio announced they were closing the airport. God, she hoped Kurt's plane got off before they closed, well, he wasn't calling her to come back to pick him up. Getting off I-95 she found herself driving past roads with lighted frames fashioned like holiday candles and stars hung off lampposts, there were Christmas tree lots, and signboards with happy, loving families united around their roaring fireplaces. Nothing she really needed to see at this moment.

Even without their tent city, the picketers were still marching, but across the road from ORR. They now circled at the entrance of the fish hatchery, as the wet snow sleeted down on them. Grace stopped in the Admin building to sign more papers, and Gail was decorating a small, live tree in the lobby with the Brewster's old glass ornaments. Smiling to see her, Gail looked up and asked, "Kurt get off in time?"

"Just made it. I see the demonstrators are back marching across the street. Don't they have shopping to do, lives to live?"

"Tomorrow I was thinking about bringing out a Dunkin Donuts jug of hot coffee and a box of donut holes to them," said the ever kindhearted Gail. "Well, it's almost Christmas." Actually, it made Grace feel better to chip in twenty dollars for that. Doing something Christmasy broke a little of her sadness at seeing Kurt go. Leaving Gail, Grace set out for her lab, chilled by a world that was cold and gray, with dark low hanging clouds. The snow, like confectioner's sugar, was beginning to dust the grass, and the dark gray harbor water. Funny, how the holidays always made her a little melancholy.

Not that she'd had a story tale childhood to miss, but there were times, all of them about the table at Grandmother's Christmas dinner that Grace wished she could just revisit one more time. Even the hours spent freezing as they always had, as they checked every Christmas tree in the lot to find the perfect one that Grandma would finally accept.

A flash of faces from her childhood, gone forever. Towns changed. Things like that made something like the MacAlpin award seem more like evidence of an empty, lonely life. Last Christmas, Kurt and she had snuggled through a snowstorm on his boat, with mistletoe hung from every overhead. This year, she'd be alone in her apartment, hiding and not answering the phone, trying to turn down well-meaning invitations for the 'old maid.' Hell, she'd better take two Midols and get back to work.

When she walked into her lab, there was only one person there. Ekkeko standing behind her desk, obviously reading the papers on it.

"May I help you?" Grace asked a trifle frostily. Where the hell was Inger and Nick? Probably working in the Cleanroom.

Ekkeko didn't even register embarrassment at being caught. "Axel Jensen sent me to make his apologies. He had expected to be coming in this weekend. Unfortunately, he had to fly down to Lima."

"He'd hadn't mentioned he'd be traveling?" Well, that meant she wouldn't be inviting him to Freya's Winter solstice fest. Trying not to sound disappointed Grace said, "Hopefully it'll be nicer weather down in Peru then we're having here."

"The fools in Cuzco are demonstrating against Humanity's Harvest's potato experiments."

"Genetically engineered?"

"No. Peru has a ban on genetically engineered food until ten years pass. Of course, Jensen feels that a Yankee can always dictate to the natives," finished Ekkeko angrily.

"Your government is against feeding their own people?" asked Grace, not quite believing it.

"The government would eagerly follow, but the Parque del la Papa have fought back."

"The what?"

"Communities of farmers that demonstrate," he said with pride. "Actually we Peruvians do not need outsiders coming to us, telling us how to live."

"So you'll be giving up penicillin, plastic, and air conditioning?" Grace asked tartly.

"We are not against technical advances–just those who would force their way on others, perfectly capable of finding their own way."

"If you don't approve of Axel Jensen's practices why are you working for him?"

He stopped and seemed to reevaluate his stance, and said, "The samples from the museum up in New Haven that you were paid to study?"

"Some of the seed samples are still in the replication stage. However, I have sent Humanity's Harvest a preliminary report."

"I've studied it. Unless I see something in your next report that warrants further study, I don't really think your continuing work would be advantageous to Humanity's Harvest."

He was firing her? That was certainly okay with Grace. "As I said, I will be sending out the final report when it's completed to my satisfaction."

Those black eyes studied her. "I've already advised Jensen, that I feel we should also sever any further monies for Huang's algae fantasies."

Grace noted, Ekkeko never referred to Axel as 'Jensen' in his presence. She stated mildly, "I have nothing to do with Huang's projects." Nor less interest.

Ekkeko was just standing there. "Jensen will be flying in when he returns from Peru, next Thursday at eleven. He wishes you to know that."

"That'll be nice," she said smiling at him coldly. "Now if you'll excuse me, it sounds like I have to immediately start searching for another sponsor to sustain myself and my employees in our worthless quests."

Ekekko seemed to have completely missed the dripping sarcasm in her voice, but he looked surprised. And he looked rather put out as if he wanted her to argue with him, or try to justify Oyster River as a research facility, or perhaps beg for her reinstatement with Humanity's Harvest. None of which she intended to do. Grace looked back at her desk.

"Oh, of course," Ekkeko's tone changed, "If you could find the Sustenance of the Gods...I and Jensen might consider continuing your contract."

"Food of the Gods?" The special food source fed to the Inca that Axel mentioned the old documents referred to. "A form of maize, which might never have existed. Or might have existed, and now may be extinct. Either way, I am currently studying other matters. Again, if you'll excuse me."

Finally taking the hint and looking a bit put out, Mr. Ekkeko Vascelo left her laboratory. Leaving Grace to again wonder how there can be such a divide between the genes for intelligence and those for basic maturity. Shaking her head, she went back to her work.

Sometime later a voice broke into her reverie. "Remember, Grace, you've got Freya's dinner tonight." It was after five now, and Inger was staying on her own time to set up a little three foot high artificial Christmas Tree in the lab. She must have paid for it herself. Grace would have to give her money for that. And Inger had strung some of the Christmas Cards that had been sent to Grace over laboratory door frames. Oh, God. What date was it? It was already December eighteenth.

Grace hadn't bought any presents. Hadn't sent out cards even. Well, her Aunt would expect something from her coming late as usual. But she'd have to get presents to wrap up for Bobby's kids. And Sara. And she'd need to write a bonus check for Bobby, Inger, and Nick, maybe something for Gail–did she have the money to cover it? She'd have to check. Ask Inger? Grace had her paying the bills. And Grace must buy something for Freya and Mac since she'd surely be at their house on Christmas day.

More time away from work. But, she had friends now and had to behave responsibly or her friendships would wither and die. Grace started a *'Christmas'* spreadsheet, what she had to do and who she was buying for, with what budget. The first 'To Do' pull up her checking account and find out what she had to spend, then ask Sara what the kids are into–Ginjer must have outgrown Thomas the Train by now. Maybe the twins would want Thomas stuff? A bottle of Chivas Regal for Kurt, when he got back. And...what about Axel? What do you get a billionaire? She had a feeling if she asked him what he'd like, Axel would say a lot less lavender in her shower shampoo.

After work Grace drove into the small village of Oyster River. She could go to the mall and the bigger stores, but this was the traditional place to start her Christmas shopping. She parked in the public lot and walked across to the street of elegant, expensive little shops. Those shops preserved from an old whaling town that managed to maintain the character of its white, clapboard buildings through its years of poverty.

The trees planted at the edge of the sidewalk still had some yellow leaves hanging. But although yesterday's snow was cleared from the sidewalks, it clung to the dirt and roofs, giving a Santa's workshop feel to the village decorated with its trimmings of fir roping. In the Gull's Eye art gallery, on the wide chestnut board flooring between the paintings hung on beige display partitions, Elise had set up seven-foot-tall wire 'trees'. These were decorated with an assortment of ornaments from clothespin dolls to garnet encrusted solid silver snowflakes.

Grace walked about seeing singing cloisonne nightingales, wooden camels, and a Santa with a rife, sitting in camouflage on a hunting stand. Finally, she picked boxes of hand blown clear, bubbled glass ornaments that looked like they had clouds of white opaline snow on top of them. They glistened iridescently in the light like soap bubbles, and Grace thought they would give a tree a look of a winter wonderland. Grace bought a set for Freya, Sara, Inger, and Gail. Thought about it and got two more sets for the Wilshusens and the Brewsters.

At the liquor store, she took care of presents for the males, Kurt, Bobby, Nick, and Adam. Then she headed for the Cheese Shop. The two show windows had cute, mouse-faced Annalee dolls dressed up as Mrs. Claus, Santa, Reindeer, and Elves, in a Santa's workshop full of new, gourmet kitchen tools.

Inside the Cheese Shop smelled of freshly baked croissants. The narrow aisles between jars of imported jam and pickled herring were crowded with last minute shoppers.

Grace got some raspberry-shaped hard candy for herself, and some marzipan fruit, and an apricot pie for tonight's dinner at Freya's. While Grace waited on line, she dug the sampler crackers in the cheese spread tasters. That white cheddar dip spread was great. She added that to her basket.

She never got around to sending out Christmas Cards, but maybe she should change that. At the register, Grace saw a weathered barrel with boxed Christmas cards on sale–she picked one up. A white house and brown barn that reminded her of her grandmother's farm in Vermont. She'd send out a few.

Everything needed to be wrapped before she could give them. She needed wrapping paper. Grace just left her presents in the car, then walked over to Freya's house on that old road too narrow to park on. Carrying some wine, cheddar dip, and the apricot pie she just let herself in. Freya was back to leaving the door unlocked, and now Grace was locking hers. There was irony in there someplace. She walked through the heavy brocaded, Victorian furnished parlor where Freya did private psychic readings for clients.

Grace pushing through the heavy purple velvet curtains across the double doorway, to the lighter, airy, Swedish modern dining room table that was covered with mistletoe balls. Freya was gluing up more for the store. Must be selling well. Pushing open a wooden door to her right, Grace walked into that warm, sausage smelling kitchen. This was in the older colonial section of the house, with gray wood cabinets and a worn, yellow linoleum floor. There was a stone hearth, but Freya cooked on a commercial, steel stove salvaged from a restaurant that floundered. In his police uniform, Mac was already sitting at the table eating.

"I'm sorry I'm running late," said Grace handed Freya a bottle of Brotherhood's holiday spiced wine as a house gift. They were eating on that small four chair table in the kitchen tucked near a window that overlooked the open wood porch and the harbor beyond. Grace walked over to the big pot on the stove and filled a soup plate with slippery spaghetti, as Freya was pouring sangria into a tall, blue glass for her. "That's okay. Mac had to start eating, he's got to be back on duty soon."

Her tall son hurriedly sat shoveling in a plate of spaghetti, covered with Freya's homemade sweet sausage sauce. "I don't have to shoot anyone, all I have to do is breathe on them."   He aggressively huffed a strong garlic smell.

Two baskets were piled high with mozzarella garlic bread that smelled so good. For the first time today, other than seeing those cells replicate, Grace felt happy. As she sat down before a big, free-form wood-burl bowl of crisp green salad, Freya said, "Try the dressing—it's a new recipe I'm developing for Haunts of Wôden's. May try to sell it to the Cheese Shop too."

Grace tried it.   "Poppyseed, buttermilk,...anise? Unusual. I like it."

Most meals Freya made her own fresh oil, herb and wine vinegar dressings. She designed and had special paper packets printed up to sell her herb mixes at her new age store. "My yule party will be on the Saturday of the 22nd this year–Grace, you've got to come!"

Looking up at his stern mother's marching orders, Mac shot a secret smile to Grace.

"I'll try,"   Grace promised

"Not like last year! You said you'd come..."

"Well, I got on a conference call with Japan. I couldn't get off."

"Don't Japanese scientists have holidays?"

"I think they're Shinto, and they don't celebrate Christmas, but the problem was a troublesome mutation in their rice wine brewery yeasts. When your brewery is turning out thousands of gallons of mucky vinegar, it's not something you can skip working on for a weekend or so."

Freya was just continuing on as if Grace hadn't spoken. "And you have to stay through the jumping of the log and the blessing of the pine boughs! This year you must get your Nobel!" Freya set her own goblet on the table and then moved back to the stove. "The living pine brings good luck."

Without thinking, Grace said, "You don't really believe that."

Freya looked liked her best friend had slapped her. "I believe in that...as much as you believe in the 'big bang' theory."

Grace should have stopped talking here, but instead said, "I'm not an astronomer, so I haven't studied the big bang theory, and I have no opinion on it what so ever."

"That's disingenuous!" Freya hotly interrupted. "Don't you ever wonder who created that DNA you are always studying? You believe in DNA don't you?"

Why was Freya so uncharacteristically combatant tonight? "I believe it exists because I can photograph it. Study it. Predict it–somewhat."

"Then you know everything about it?" Freya still spoke angrily.

"Far from it. I expect to spend the rest of my life studying what it is, and I really don't have time to waste fantasizing about why it is."

Freya appeared hurt, and Grace felt it had nothing to do with DNA or the Goddess, as Grace's friend continued, "I do believe in a life force. I do believe in prayer. I do believe in giving thanks for the blessings bestowed in the past year. And I guess you don't!"

Oh, Grace had stepped her foot into to it this time. "I'm sorry..."

Moving in to divert attention from Grace's

clumsiness, Mac pointed out, "Got a police bulletin. Two women were spotted committing a 5-023 in the Library Park. Two Caucasians. A tall blonde perpetrator, acting in concert with a shorter, curly, black-haired accomplice." With a coy smile, he dipped his garlic bread in Freya's thick sauce.

Oh, boy. "What is a 5-023?" Grace asked trying to sound disinterested.

Mac stared sternly at her. "Breaking town regulations by feeding endangered wildlife!"

Now back by the stove, getting her own plate of sauce, Freya commented, "The wild ducks wouldn't be endangered if someone would feed them when the ice forms."

Grace found herself coloring with stupid embarrassment. "Why do they have a silly law like that?"

"Doesn't matter," said Mac sternly. "We officers must enforce the laws–whether they're silly or not. The town felt not feeding the ducks was so important, they used to taxpayer money to have a sign put up." Mac managed an authoritative glare at both women.

Freya looked archly at her son. "And yet there are those who would still commit that heinous crime?"

"Somebody better stop doing it." He switched his tone to almost pleading, "I'm going to have to run you in, Ma. It looks bad!."

Freya only punched towards her son's shoulder, but Mac with long experience expertly ducked aside. Then his mother went on the offensive. "I've heard a certain policeman has been seen around town dating a red-haired reporter?"

Mac colored, and shot a look at Grace, who tried to look clueless, which she was.

"Don't look at Grace! My good friend didn't even bother to tell me!" Freya glared first at her, then she hammered back at her son, "Why haven't you brought her home to dinner? To meet your mother?"

Back looking like a teenager, Mac shrugged, "Ma, you've been railing against Samantha Carson ever since she did that profile piece on Grace."

"She implied Grace was some anti-feminist, recluse!" Freya said angrily.

Grace looked up from her wine. "Please leave me out of this!"

They were totally ignoring her, as Mac shot back, "You were ripping Sam when she did that expose on cheating fortune tellers."

"She mentioned my store!"

"Only as a place to buy tarot cards! She didn't say some of those scam artists had their business cards pinned to your neighborhood info board, which Sam could have!"

Freya glared at him. "If she is good enough to date, then you should bring her home?"

Mac went for the big one. "To stay overnight in my apartment downstairs?"

"No!" Freya colored. "I'd just like to meet her. Maybe one of our regular dinner nights with Grace?"

Her mouth full of garlic bread, Grace groaned inwardly.

Mac just shook his head. "Not a great idea, Ma. When you, Grace, and Sam start going at each other, I won't know which one to shoot first." Saying that he grabbed the last of the garlic bread, and headed out. "Those ORR picketers are getting me a lot of overtime and a new tournament rife."

He left fast, but Freya stared after him in a concerned manner.

Grace didn't want to interfere, but said, "He's a grown man."

"I don't care if dates anybody, but why does it have to be that meddling, little bitch!"

"That's certainly being non-judgmental," Grace

commented. They should leave the topic, but Grace hated seeing her old friend in such obvious pain. Trying to pour a little oil on the troubled waters, Grace looked to Freya saying weakly, "Maybe Sam's not all that bad?"

"She isn't? Was she fair when she did that hatchet profile on you years ago? You might have lost the Nobel that year because of it!"

"That is ridiculous! Firstly, you don't 'lose the Nobel' because you don't run for it. And secondly, that profile was partially my own fault, because I refused to take time to give her an interview. And Sam has apologized. She said her editor had put in most of that 'anti-other women's accomplishments' stuff."

Freya looked back down at her dinner. She hadn't been eating, just pushing the spaghetti around her plate.

Grace waited, then said. "I know you love Mac, and you've pretty much built your whole life around your son."

"So?" Those proud blue eyes glared at her.

"It must be hard to see him with a young woman," Grace stumbled.

"What are you saying? That I'm in love with my son? That's not true! I date, I've had lovers."

"But never in this house."

"That's a rule I've had since he was a kid. And that's a rule we both agreed to when he set up the apartment in the basement."

"Maybe it's time to rethink some of those rules..." Grace tried.

"But Mac makes the worse choices! They break his heart! Like idiot Laura! Then Alician, his great finance."

"He was lucky Alician didn't marry him."

In obvious pain, Freya said, "Mac is always trying to find the weak one. Protect her. Nurture her."

Like Freya had done with Grace all those years ago. Find the bruised and beaten by life and quietly set about to heal them. "I think that's a Dell family trait, and a good one."

Freya said nothing.

Grace continued, "I don't know too much about Samantha Carson, only that as a reporter, she works hard. That if you tell her it's off the record, she respects that. Sam seems to be an attractive, healthy girl. Seeing her look into Mac's eyes, I think they both deserve to be left alone to let something either grow or die by itself."

"But he's been hurt so many times," fretted Freya.

"I'm more worried about you. You've made him the emotional focus of your life for so many years, you've never spoken about Mac's father?"

Freya abruptly rose, picking up dishes to take into the kitchen. "So that's it? I'm a bitch of a mother who uses her own son as a husband substitute? I'm jealous of any girl that goes after my boy? Is that what you think of me?!"

"Of course not!" Grace was just trying to make peace.

In an agonized voice Freya demanded, "Don't you see what she's after?"

"A handsome young hunk."

"Oh, you think so? What if this 'girl reporter' just wants a cop's inside view of a murder investigation? What if like Alician, she's just using him?"

Grace reluctantly agreed that despite Sam's obvious infatuation with Mac she may already be using him as a source. Grace could well understand someone's primary loyalty to their work, but... "I don't know, Mac really likes her. Can't you just give her a chance?"

"Grace, I think our dinner is finished for tonight." Not waiting for an answer, Freya turned her back and left the room. Alone Grace started clearing the table, hoping Freya would cool off and come back, but the evening was over. And as Grace gathered up her friend's dishes, she wondered if their friendship was also finished?

Chapter 30

Early the next morning Inger had placed a small selection of the lab's Christmas cards that she thought would interest Grace on her desk.   There was one in the center, a photo of ice-capped peaks.   The Andes.   Grace slowly opened it, reading, *'We could be sharing this,'* signed in bold pen by Axel Jensen.   She started to throw it away, then reconsidered and placed it against her computer screen stand.

Nick was working on the New Haven mummy arm samples today. Hopefully, they'd also be getting a look at the Bridgeport cursed mummies. Inger felt the maize, seed, and potato samples from New Haven should be completed by January fourteenth so Grace could send her last report into Humanity's Harvest. And the quarterly lobster mold project report–that was a problem. Grace really wanted Kurt's input on the current deviation of results, she could have Mac contact him on his HAM radio, but Grace had no intention of shouting Affiliated's proprietary information over a high-frequency shipboard radio. Should she wait until he got back?

Grace was studying the results on her screen when a man's big hand reached down and picked up her Christmas card. With a little jump of her heart, she looked up. Tall, sandy hair, with a black leather briefcase, but not Axel. It was Daniel Novinski.

He studied the card. "Andes?" He squinted a bit more, "Or Sierra Leone in Africa?"

"Andes. South America," Grace said.

"Always wanted to see them."

"Didn't you when you were in the merchant marine?"

He still studied the card, then said carelessly, "Only saw them from a ship. Maybe someday."

"It's always good to have a goal." She thought about her own wish list. "Someday I'm going to see Easter Island."

"For DNA?"

"Nope, just because I want to. Are your picketers staying with us for Christmas?"

"Again, they're not my demonstrators," clarified Daniel.

"I'm sorry, Curs' picketers."

Daniel didn't look happy. "Actually, Astrid and I have agreed that we have different paths to follow, so after dealing with some loose ends, I'll be leaving Oyster River, looking for my next cause."

"Then you're no longer Josh Jeffers' lawyer?" asked Grace.

He looked pained. "That's one of those loose ends I haven't finished with yet. I just got him out on bail." Daniel sounded concerned. "Five hundred thousand! He's got some reputation with the court."

"Could his brother Greg raise ten percent of that?" said a surprised Grace.

Daniel hesitated. "No, actually, the money came out of my Foundation."

"I thought lawyers weren't supposed to get involved with their clients?"

He laughed a touch bitterly. "That's the theory, but I'm sure he's innocent of Helmut's murder, and I feel sorry for him. But Jeffers is out now, and he is still a nut! He blames Humanity's Harvest and especially Axel for his being in jail."

"Do you think he was one of those guys discussing how to detonate a bomb?"

Daniel had to think about that. "Hell, I don't know, but I know he hates Axel. Fortunately, I hear Axel has left the country, so will be out of my client's reach."

"Not really. He will be coming back to Oyster River."

Daniel really looked worried. "Do you know that for sure?"

"I think Ekkeko said he'd be in my lab next Thursday around noon."

Now Daniel's face hardened in an unreadable lawyer's mask. "Well, I'll try to put a leash on my client, but that's going to be hard because I'm a lawyer, so he hates me too. Look, actually that's what I came for, could you pass it on to Axel that Jeffers is out and unhappy?"

"I will. And to control your client, you might try talking with Josh's brother, Greg." There was something else she had to know. "Have you gotten any more of those threatening letters?"

"No. You?"

"Not since what I already told you," she said.

He smiled widely, saying characteristically optimistically, "Then we're going in a positive direction, aren't we?"

* * *

By noon Inger interrupted her to remind Grace she was to meet Freya for lunch. Were they still talking? Since Freya still hadn't called her to cancel, they might be back as best friends again, but when Grace headed down the steps to the Haunts of Wôden, voices raised inside the store made her realize a storm was brewing.

Hearing the little bell on the door tinkle when she walked in Freya and Mac abruptly stopped shouting, and they both looked embarrassed. Freya was behind her central counter, and in uniform, Mac stood in front of it. Between them was a newspaper looking like *The Sound Times*. "Grace, did you see this?" Freya hotly demanded. "It says you're getting more threatening letters. You never told me that!" There was a lot of hurt and betrayal in Freya's voice, but Grace suspected that her part in this was minimal, and the Viking fury was directed at her equally stubborn son.

"I told you the first day there was a childish letter..." started Grace.

"It says here you got more than one," Freya finished icily.

Grace looked to Mac. "You told Sam that? That was confidential police information."

He looked embarrassed. "No."

Freya glared from one to the other. "No, my loyal son didn't tell me my best friend was being threatened. I had to read it in the newspaper!"

Stiffly Grace walked over and picked the paper off the counter. Headlined *ORR Staff Threatened!* The story was bylined by Samantha Carson. A fast reader, Grace scanned it, finding everything the police knew was in this story. Sick, she looked to Mac. "You told this to Sam?"

"No!" he said sounding defensive.

Freya slammed her hand on the counter. "But now we know why Miz Tight jeans was dating him, don't we?"

Mac was still on the defense. "No, I never talked with her about the case. Somebody might lose their job over this," he finished bitterly.

A furious Freya yelled, "Probably you—even off duty you keep your police notebook in your jeans pocket, so now we know why she was so eager to get your pants off!"

An equally angry Mac lashed back, "Believe me when I'm with her with my pants off she isn't busy writing!"

"You're proud of that?" Freya snapped at her son.

"Aaup!" he said.

"Well, then you can get out of my store! Get out of my house! Go move in with your Miz Benedict Arnold! See if I care!"

"Fine, Ma, maybe I will!" saying that he turned and left slamming the glass door after him, setting the bell bouncing.

Grace had been following him with her eyes when she heard what sounded like a sob from Freya. She looked back to her friend, but Freya's eyes were stony as she said, "Your friend Sam betrayed you too!"

"I don't know if it's betrayal–it's her job," started Grace.

The face Freya turned on her showed deep hurt. "Grace, you never learn, jobs don't mean more than humans!"

"We're going to lunch..." Grace reminded her.

Freya shook her head. "Not today."

Grace started again, "About moving, you know your son didn't mean it, you should..."

Near tears, Freya turned her back to Grace saying, "Just go, please!"

When Grace left the store, she saw Mac standing on the sidewalk, one store down. He looked drained as he was just getting off his phone. "Mac, can we talk?"

"I'm really talked out now!" He said, not the norm for the usually calm kid. Even as he towered above here, she would always think of him as a Freya's gangly, corn silk haired son.

"You're not moving in with Sam are you?"

He looked at her disbelieving, "We dated a few times–that's all. I may move out of Ma's, maybe I should, but Freya needs my rent money."

"That story in the paper..."

"Yes, it's a bylined by Sam," he reluctantly admitted.

"Those threatening letters–they weren't supposed to be leaked! She promised."

"Sam promised not to write what she overheard from you or me. She didn't do that," he said staunchly.

"Then where did she pick it up from?"

His face turned stormy. "From someone inside the police department–who should've known better."

"But not you?"

"Nope."

"Do you know who told her?"

"Aaup. He's got big mouth."

"Ben!" Grace said without thinking.

"Aaup."

"But your Captain isn't going to know that. He'll know you've been dating Sam, he'll think it was you!"

"He does, and he chewed me out–which is better than having him think Ben blabbed again."

"You could be fired! You'll never get promoted."

"Nope. The information about the letters was going to be coming out soon. The detectives want to try to flush out whoever is responsible, it just came out a little earlier than they had planned."

"Mac..."

"Grace, don't worry." He must have seen the concern on her face. "I didn't get a formal reprimand, it's not going in my file. If the Captain thinks it's me it'll be okay, he likes a good showing in the Intercounty shooting competitions. We've won the last four years because of me. What he, and I, and Ben are worried about is you and the people out there at Oyster River Research."

Chapter 31

Getting back to her Lab Grace pulled up her two murder spreadsheets. First, she started with *Who Murdered Helmut*. Her assumptions weren't working, so it was time she went back to the beginning and took a different tack. When she was stuck, Grace often tried to invert the hypothesis. What if Axel wasn't the intended victim, instead it was Helmut? But her problem was who would have wanted to kill Helmut? His wife? His boss? Unknown robber–again she dismissed all those, but Grace was visualizing another possible pattern, one that really disturbed her. What if it was Axel who had killed Helmut?

Helmut was excited to meet Axel, but what if he already had? Maybe Axel could have been Dutch, the man responsible for his brother's death? Helmut could have lied about not knowing Axel, coming to the reception wanting to blackmail him? She knew Axel was a lifelong ambitious man, who started with nothing, then raised money to build his companies from the herbal tea business to a pharmaceutical conglomerate.

Did Axel sell drugs? Working with Axel's DNA, she had determined he had a set of risk-taking genes. With a man so good a planning, organizing, and merchandising could he have run a drug ring?   Was Axel afraid that Helmut could expose him? But the night of the reception, Axel had made a point of taking Helmut under his wing and introducing the man about. Axel would've never have done that if he thought Helmut could recognize and expose him as a drug smuggler, would he?

If Axel was Dutch why hadn't Helmut immediately recognized him? Helmut hadn't seen 'Dutch' in years, more wrinkles, more weight, and a goatee? Maybe Helmut didn't recognize him, but Axel recognized Helmut? With the way Helmut felt about his brother's death–no, he wouldn't have blackmailed his brother's killer, he would have exposed Axel immediately. This was getting ridiculous! Yes, Axel was Caucasian, tall, light-haired, but then so was Nick, Daniel, and at least five other men at that Reception. Corporate positions seemed to favor tall, blond males.

On Helmut's murder sheet she typed in a row for Axel, but adding up and subtracting the other columns she came out with a weak 15 percent. And there was a definite problem with the motive, she didn't really know what 'Dutch' looked like. She pictured him fair like Helmut, but he could have been short, fat, and black haired? She should have questioned Inez. Further she typed that into her 'To Do' column.

Never the less, Grace couldn't believe that a man as empathetic and generous as Axel Jensen would set Hindrick up to die, then be so cold-blooded as to hunt Helmut down and shoot him in the back with a spear gun. Not the Axel she knew, or did she only believe that because she was beginning to have strong romantic feelings for the man?

* * *

Grace had Inger printout four copies of the readouts for the New Haven museum samples, and Nick punch them into little booklets. She could just mail them, but that seemed so cold. Especially since her original visit up to New Haven had led indirectly to Inez being a widow–a pregnant widow.

Inger called and made an appointment for Grace to see Inez at the museum.

Grace wanted to talk with Helmut Robert's window, but also dreaded it. She found Inez, with stacks of packing boxes in Helmut's crowded office. Her face looked a little bloated–probably from crying, and the baby bump was really beginning to show, but she greeted Grace with clear, strong eyes. "The University has been very kind. They've given me months...but now I feel it's time to get this over with."

"I'm so sorry. It was my fault..." Grace started.

"What was your fault?" she genuinely looked puzzled.

"That I invited Helmut, then I had a headache, and left the reception early leaving him alone."

Inez looked startled. "You blame yourself? Oh, that is so foolish! I was the one pushing for his visit to Oyster River. And I only did that, because I knew Hellie wanted to go so badly." Her eyes brightened. "You don't know how excited and proud he was meeting someone as famous as you! He told everyone–even people just coming to the museum-- that he met the great Dr. Grace Farrington and he had been assisting her."

Grace wanted Inez to know, "He did so well that night. He met Adam Greenfield the President of ORR, and several of the Board of Directors. And I introduced him to Axel Jensen. Axel told Helmut that he had heard favorably of his work up here at the museum."

Inez eyes brightened with happiness for her husband, then hardened again. "It's not your fault Hellie died. It is not mine, because I pushed him to go. It is the fault of the person who killed him!"

"Have the police told you if they have a suspect?"

"I don't think they're doing anything," she said dejectedly.

"No! The police are working on it," Grace insisted. "I know one of the policemen on the case. A murder in his and his Captain's town is being treated as a personal affront to the police department." Inez just smiled sadly, and Grace continued, "Do you know anyone who might have wanted to hurt your husband?"

"No. Hellie was a good, sweet man." She stopped, unable to go on.

Grace asked again, "No one that was jealous of him? No old boyfriend of yours?"

"No. Hellie was my first and only. Anyway, the detectives seem to think the killer was after another man?"

"That's a possibility. Helmut resembled Axel Jensen, the C.E.O. of Humanity's Harvest. They both were tall, with longish, blond hair and were wearing light colored jackets that night. Axel has business enemies, but none that he thinks would want to kill him in Oyster River."

Inez bit her lip. "Hellie was killed because he wore the wrong jacket? Well, I guess that's better then him being killed for the pennies in his pockets." She walked to the wall above his desk with its family pictures. Some were already in the box. Reached up Inez took down the photo of Helmut's eagle scout brother. "My Hellie was always on borrowed time."

"What?"

"He told you about the drug deal his brother was killed in. It was worse then he had said. Their 'amigo'--Dutch–set it up with some corrupt policia. He wanted both Helmut and Hendrick killed."

"Why?"

"No sharing profits. No witnesses. No problems. My uncle said Dutch had arranged things so, that Dutch was 'sin alma.'"

"Sin alma?" asked Grace.

"It's Spanish. It doesn't translate too well..." She thought about it. "It means a man of no soul. No conscious. No guilt. No feelings for anyone but himself."

"What did Dutch look like?"

Inez shrugged. "A white man. Hair like dried grass, like my husband's. Older. Taller than Hellie, but shorter than Hendrick."

A man very much like Axel Jensen Grace thought. "Do you have any photographs of Dutch?"

"No, he always ducked when I had my camera. He said his *'mug was too ugly.'*"

"Are you really sure there isn't just one photograph? Maybe with him in the background?"

Inez thought about that for a long time and then slowly said, "There was one picture. We were eating outside, on my uncle's patio. Fernando took a picture of Helmut and myself. Hendrick and Dutch were also at the table."

"Can you get that picture from your uncle?"

"Why?" Inez looked confused. "When Hellie and I first met, that was fifteen years ago. Dutch would be entirely different looking today."

"Some features and facial relationships don't change with age. Ear angles. Distance between eyes. There are special facial recognition software, and I do some work for the police so I might be able to utilize one of their programs." She didn't say so to Inez, but Grace had to know that her Axel Jensen wasn't Inez's Dutch.

Inez looked at her boxes. "I think I have a copy of the photo—at my apartment, in a box of family pictures. If I find it, I could scan it and e-mail it to you—if it is important?"

"It is. Very important!"

There was an awkward silence. Then Grace asked, "What will you do now?"

"I am close to finishing my doctorate. The University will let me keep the assistant's job here until I finish, but I can not live on just an assistant's salary afterward. They already hire someone to replace Helmut as curator. I can stay on in our apartment on campus until I graduate, and there will be some insurance money." She touched her growing belly lightly. "It is a boy. Helmut wanted him named after his brother Hendrick—not after himself--but I will call the baby Henry. It is more American, and it is also Peruvian. Our son will be born an American, and then I think I will go back to Peru—we will be with my family." She took down the photo of herself and Helmut when they were just kids themselves. Looked at it sadly, then placed it carefully in her box, then Inez forced a smile for Grace. "Your DNA studies? The University wishes to know how they came out?"

Grace pulled out the booklets and handed her one. "I'd like to resample the seed labeled Maize 963 if I could. It seems to be an older variety, but didn't culture well." Grace flipped pages of her copy. "These are the vessel residues. Pretty much what we suspected. Maize, yeast. Probably beer.

"There were two partial samples, that didn't seem to fit in with patterns already on file. I'm going to check with Humanity's Harvest to find out if they want me to continue studying them."

"The mummy's arm?" asked Inez.

That was interesting. Flipping to the end of the booklet Grace found the pages. "The best sample was HH01013. I did get an almost complete profile of human DNA. Male. I'm still breaking it down. I did find two genetic markers that are usually associated with aggression and dominance, lending more support of the supposition that the person who owned that arm was a leader, a noble. The sample has already matched for South America and the Andes region with the Genome project, with some connection to the highlands of Peru. Do you think your superiors would pay for a radiocarbon dating test of the arm?"

"I will ask."

"I'll let the museum know if I get anything more."

Returning to her lab late afternoon, Grace found Nick and Inger were excited, with Nick telling her, "We finally processed the results from the second Bridgeport mummy. You wanted to wait to look at them until we had all three profiles."

Grace sat down before her computer screen. No matter how many times she'd looked at new data, it always excited her. First up NH00003. She checked a print out of the control sheets to verify. Yes, NH00003 was Flat Nose. As expected, NH00003 was male. Eye color–brown, black hair. She looked to Inger. "Check the list of 'leadership' genes that I've been proposing against NH00003."

Inger nodded and got to work on her computer.

She studied Flat Nose's data profile again. "Inger, with NH00003 we're also going to test for the Reckless gene."

Inger noted that in her work log. "What about NH00008? And NH00011?"

"Yes, I want Missing Finger and Stomach Scar done too. And I want to test all of the best samples for NH00003, NH00008, and NH00011 for Warrior Gene."

"You think they'll have it?" asked Inger.

"If they were Incan nobles, or warrior kings or related to the high Inca? Yes, I think it's possible they might show that."

Grace started scanning Flat Nose's profile again. "Nick, did you check with Genome Project on possible origins?"

From across the room, he answered promptly, "We've got a possible tie-in on all three of the Bridgeport mummies to South America, Andes Mountains. They even match ancient samples found in Cuzco."

"Good. We'll have something positive to report to Rose in Bridgeport."

Grace closed Flat Nose's profile and pulled up Missing Finger's, a line, very much like a jagged mountainous landscape painted across her screen. Almost all chromosomes had specific genes that were copied multiple times. This happened from accidental duplications over hundreds of thousands of years. Those exact mistakes combinations would be passed intact to the person's descendants, until the next mutation. Counting and comparing those multiple copies were how paternal and maternal relationships were determined. Sometimes copies were only three, sometimes three thousand, or even twenty thousand. "Dark eyes. Dark hair. Stomach Scar or Missing Finger had a lot genetically in common with Flat Nose. Well, they came from an isolated mountain population." But Grace was realizing that what she was seeing went beyond remarkably close.

She wiped the screen clear and pulled up Stomach Scar. His pattern stood out–with an instant familiarity. In her mind, Grace could overlay the three perfectly. "Inger, put up three profiles on the wall screen with the Y centered. Make NH00003's line red, NH00008's blue, and NH 0001's profile in green."

Soon all three lit up the screen, with their Y male chromosomes overlaying perfectly.

"Flat nose, Missing Finger, and Stomach Scar?" Inger asked. "We got something!"

Grace looked up at the main screen on the wall as Inger was smiling at her, eager to confirm her own discovery by asking, "Pappa, Grandpa, and Grandson?"

Studying those lines intersecting and overlaying each other, scrolling across the main screen Grace noticed something else. "From the female line, it looks like they may have been mating brother and sister. Consanguineous, which is consistent with what we know of Incan Royalty."

"Was that only done with the Inca himself?" Nick asked.

"I don't know, it might have been all nobles," Grace said.

"But if these men were mummified and displayed to be venerated by the populace, they could have been successive ruling Incas?" suggested Inger.

"Possibly." Grace agreed. "We may have a bloodline of successive men who sat on the royal Incan throne." But as Grace looked at those profiles, she had another Farrington Fusion. "Nick, have you got a preliminary on LD00113, the mummy's arm from New Haven?"

Inger's eyes grew wide. "You think?" She started typing on her computer. It took several long, long minutes, and then Inger was saying, "Do you want it on the main screen as an overlay?"

"Yes, make it royal purple." Grace studied the big screen on the wall, craggy mountain ridges scrolling across her screen. Not a perfect match–but close. Probably two or three generations apart, with a different female line, more distant cousins than brothers, but the paternal Y DNA was the same. "Four matches. Four related males, possibly of noble heritage. Possibly Incan rulers." That was amazing, but something was bothering her. That pattern, with its sharp highs, deep lows, and the unusually short Y. She had seen one like it before. Recently. Where?

Grace's mind pulled up a picture of Freya reaching into that tray of vials. Selecting one. Speaking of its strength, dominance, and ruthlessness. What was in that tray? Samples from the LG, her leadership study. Grace rapidly pulled up screen after screen of profiles as she looked for a special one.

Then, with trembling fingers, Grace pulled it up on her laptop screen. LD00043 rolled before her. Silently Grace looked through it knowing what she would find. Oh, generations of maternal DNA had changed totally, but not the paternal Y chromosomes–passed from royal conqueror father to royal reigning son.

She didn't even need to check the control sheet to know his name. "It looks like we've got the fifth sample in that line."

"A fifth?!" squealed an excited Inger. "From where?"

"Pull up LD00043, make it a brown line and overlay it on the main screen. As Inger typed in her instructions, Grace studied the version on her own screen, "Inger, we'll do a closer study on hair, eye, and skin color, but I expect he'll come out a short, dark-haired man, with brown, almost black eyes."

Her assistant was staring at the main screen with its

five overlaid profiles in awe. "His Y matches the other four?" Inger blinked, staring with disbelieving her eyes. "Where did that sample come from?" She checked the number. "Oh, my God! It's one of the Leadership Gene studies. Almost all of them came from Humanity Harvest employees–all of them were live subjects. We've matched a live man with four that are museum mummies now?"

"Looks like it," confirmed Grace.

Now Inger looked upset, saying plaintively. " Grace, I processed him and all the others. I look at every sample we've taken, but I never saw a connection. How did you?"

Grace tapped in the password, opening the database that matched LD00043's number to its origin. Not that she needed to. "The number comes from a Humanity's Harvest's executive." And Grace figured she knew which one, even before it popped up on her screen. Number LD00043 was Ekkeko Vascelo.

"You've got it? He's one of the Humanity Harvest executives?" Inger sounded like she still couldn't believe it.

"Yes."

"Have I met him?"

"Ekkeko Vascelo. Short. Dark. Very superior attitude."

"Yes. Yes!" Inger almost shouted remembering. "Axel's assistant. Monday he was in here demanding to know where you were as if you should be here just because he wanted it."

Grace studied the overlay of Ekkeko's male Y chromosome over the profile for Flat Nose, Missing Finger, Stomach Scar and Unknown Arm. All a perfect match.

Nick gave a low whistle, and Inger looked back at the screen in pure disbelief. "He can't possibly know there is a chance that he's a living descendant of an Inca ruler? Of several rulers?"

"Probably not," said Grace.

"Grace, are you going to tell him?" Inger asked.

She had to think about that. What did Grace really know? The DNA was clear. A clear male descendant relationship between all five men. As to the fact, the first four were royal nobles, that was mere supposition from their histories, jewelry, and advanced mummification. Were they actually of royal blood in life, and later mummies that were worshiped by their people as direct connections to the Sun God–she really didn't know. And there was no way to ever prove it either way, at least with the current level of technology, and the limited DNA databases available to her.

And to the fact that one or more of them might actually have served as the Royal Inca himself--as a God-King--that was stretching her evidence to the limit. Only the fact that the Incan Royal family was close-knit, and that the DNA showed at least two of these samples resulted from the interbreeding of brother-sister or father–daughter, also a royal prerogative.

One other thing, not as verifiable as her vials and DNA, but something she'd come to believe in: Freya's reaching into that anonymous tray of vials; lifting one out and giving a spontaneous reading of that individual's character. Her friend described a born leader, with a ruthless drive for power that would accept no outer control, nor feel remorse for anything he does. With whatever unknown power that she possessed, Freya had alerted on Ekkeko's vial.

Ever wishing to test and verify a result, Grace wondered if she brought the samples of the museum mummies mixed in with other vials to Freya, what would her friend's reaction be? From a scientific viewpoint, it would be an interesting experiment. Although Grace knew of no acceptable scientific basis for Freya's 'second sight' powers, she had seen it in action before. But should Grace try it with their strained relationship now? Especially with Freya's intuition of an Incan curse placed on anyone who dared touch those mummies?

And there was another problem, as Inger had pointed out, what--if anything--should Grace tell Ekkeko? Did she have a right to instantly change the man's beliefs about himself and his family heritage? Being descended from an Incan noble she thought would be positive, but what if it wasn't? Grace looked to Inger."I don't know what I'm going to tell him if anything. I'm going to have to think about this further."

Chapter 32

It was a morning three days later when Inger came over to Grace's desk. "You've got an e-mail, with an attachment from an Inez Roberts that you requested?"

Grace looked up from her screen. "Which folder?"

Soon she was opening a file and staring at a faded color photo. Not too good. A distant shot. Four people at a table, obviously unaware of being photographed, because none of them were looking at the camera. Inez's e-mail indicated that from left to right it was Helmut, herself, Hendrick and Dutch.

A youthful Helmut stared with open love at Inez, who looked back with equal joy at him.   At the end of the table, Dutch seemed to have a slight, cruel smile on his face, as if he had some secret joke that the rest couldn't know. It was the third person that held Grace's attention. Hendrick, Helmut's protective, older brother, was staring at Dutch as if in distrust. Or was Grace overlaying her own emotions on a smudgy photo? The faces were so frustratingly small. "Inger, do we have any photo enhancement software?"

"Photoshop. I use it for reports."

"Know how to enlarge a face?"

"Which one?" Inger asked as she came back over to Grace's desk. Her assistant quickly copied the attachment into the publishing program.   Opening the photo in Photoshop, she placed a circle around the 'Dutch' figure. Hitting keys, Inger enlarged that circle, which became grainier as it filled the screen. "Poor original, not enough pixels."

"It's all we're going to get," said Grace.

Inger adjusted the contrast, and the face came up stronger, but now just the photo's forehead was filling the screen.

"Bring it back to where I can see the full face."

Inger scaled it back.

Now, Grace could see a man in three-quarter profile. Long, wavy blond hair, tied back in a ponytail. High, intelligent forehead. Were the eyes light green or dark brown? Not possible to tell with this poor quality photo. Skin white. Even teeth. Strong chin. Clean shaven. Hard to compare a chin line now that Axel wore a goatee.

Of course, it was several years and maybe thirty pounds difference, but Dutch could be Axel Jensen. Or he might not. "We've done some special DNA work for the State Police lab. That guy in charge, what was his name?"

"Paul Jackson?"

"That's probably it. Can you get in touch with him and ask if his facial recognition software could compare two photos for me?"

"This one and what other?" Inger asked.

Grace walked over to one of the desks by the front doors. Ekkeko had passed out copies of Humanity's Harvest's annual report to each of the labs. She opened one up, and as Grace expected, there was a brilliant, full-color headshot of its charismatic founder and C.E.O.

She brought it back to her assistant, and Inger looked to the report and asked in shock, "Compare Dutch to see if he's Axel Jensen?"

"Somebody taking my name in vain?" said the devil himself, as he walked into Grace's lab. In spite of herself, Grace found her heart beating a little faster when Axel came over to her. Grace closed the Annual Report and slipped it to Inger, who quickly picked it up and walked away from them.

"Your hair looks softer cut that way," he said quietly. "You know, I could be around on the twenty-fifth if you needed an escort for Christmas?"

She had been thinking of that. "My friend Freya is Wiccan. They celebrate Samhain-- which is the Winter Solstice--on the 22nd with a big party, you might like it.

That's next Tuesday."

"And Christmas is on the 25th," Axel said. "Maybe I could get a motel room around here and stay for both?"

The ball was in her court, Grace took a deep breath and proposed, "Why a motel, when my apartment available?"

That satyr smile again. "Sounds good. I've got some business today, but I'll fly back before Tuesday."

His very voice warmed Grace to her toes, and she tried to find a neutral topic. "How did Peru work out?"

"What?"

"You were meeting with officials there because the activists were giving your company trouble? Ekkeko said you flew down to straighten out some problem."

He sighed. "No big deal–just a lot of smiling and shaking hands. Outside the U.S. business can't be conducted over the Internet, you have to go there directly and press the flesh."

If he was wanted for a drug deal, even if it was fifteen years ago, would Axel be so confident going to Peru? "What are you setting up actually?" Grace asked.

"A mobile specimen collection group, that should eventually be surveying all of South America, but we're starting with the Peruvian highlands.   They'll be taking samples of flora and fauna for up to six months, and if it's warranted, then move on to the desert, then maybe the Amazon or Antarctica?"

He must realize the hopeless ambition of his program, Still Grace said, "One tree in the Amazon can hold enough specimens to keep a DNA researcher going for decades."

Axel smiled ironically. "Yes. What I'm proposing is not the 'World Genome' project. It's more a triage rescue mission. A fast snapshot to see what is there, to see if immediate further research is warranted. This isn't going to be secret, if we find something it'll go on the Internet, maybe to spur on another company or researcher."

"But you're looking for the golden food source of the Incas?' Grace said.

He shook his head. "Or whatever else I can find. Just trying to collect as much basic DNA as we can, before it's wiped out by climate change or civilization spread."

"That would be wonderful," Grace admitted.

"I'd like to hire you to head the project. You can get out of this lab and see something of this world, and I promise you will be well compensated."

It was a wonderful project, but she had her own work. "I can't."

Axel didn't take no for an answer. "How about just a month of your time? Time to see what's needed, set up the protocols, interview possible personnel, specify needed equipment. Basically get it running."

Grace smiled. "You couldn't afford me."

Seeing an opening, the devil homed in. "No? Actually, I brought something interesting with me." Axel lifted up an unremarkable, black leather briefcase. Inside were stacks of magazines, no, colorful equipment catalogs. With a flourish, he opened one on the desk before her. It was amazing. She found herself reverently turned page after page. This was a comprehensive listing, that would never be sent to a lone researcher–this would only be sent to someone would command the resources of a worldwide conglomerate, or a first world country.

She was looking at the latest in mass DNA sequencing equipment. Instruments with optic and imaging capacities beyond anything she'd ever dreamed she'd own. As Grace mentally totted up an impossible wish list, she felt she was facing the Prince of Darkness, and he was offering her the treasures of the world.

"Can't afford you?" Those fathoms deep sea green eyes stared into hers. "Try me."

This man, who was willing to spend any amount of his

own wealth to save the world's precious genetic heritage, could not be the killer of Helmut Roberts, or of Helmut's brother years before. Yet something nagged at her mind, a 'knowing' that wouldn't quite fuse into a coherent theory, so Grace pushed it away. Lord, this man could have no idea of just how he was turning her on physically, clouding her mind by just standing near where she could smell the maleness of his aftershave. She asked tentatively, "Will you be in Peru too, directing this project?"

As if he had just won the lottery Axel sat on the edge of her desk, and he smiled confidently. "Oh, yes, and I'd be willing to throw my body into the pot of your inducements. That'll be just before my first official vacation in years to Antarctica. Hopefully, you will be embarking with me." He waited. She started to say no, but he held up a hand, "Let me dream a little."

As Freya kept telling her, sometimes you had to realize that if the facts weren't there, you had to go with your intuitions. Obviously smelling victory, he added, "How about a three or four weeks setting up my collection unit, and then a week or two aboard my yacht, headed for Antarctica? Less than two months out of your life–you can spare that?"

She found herself almost mesmerized, asking, "Will we pass Easter Island?"

That stopped him. "It wasn't planned, but we could." He leaned back and thought about it. "We'll be embarking at Callao, Peru. Easter Island is off of Chile, it's a bit out of the way, but, hell, I've been in that area before but have never walked on it! Yes, Easter Island will most definitely be part of our trip!"

"How long would I be away from ORR?"

"That's negotiable isn't?" The devil smiled broadly.

What was the old joke? *You've agreed to do it for money–that shows me what you are –now we're just negotiating the terms.* Well, she could be brought. "I'm going to be looking at your catalogs, and I am interested in helping set up the Peruvian project, it sounds like a great idea. I could allow two weeks to that if this deal covers hefty consulting fees, and some special travel arrangements?'

"For you–first class all the way."

"Actually, I'm thinking of taking three others with us," said Grace in a meditative tone.

"Inger? Bobby? Freya?" he asked.

"You wouldn't know these three, and they are going to have some unusual requirements..."

"No problem," announced Axel.

"It may be very costly," Grace warned.

"If you need them to assist you, they're coming."

"Well, actually if we could get everybody to agree, these three would be classified more as a grand public relations demonstration, a gesture that will require extensive legal work, some of it International."

He didn't seem to be put off by that. "The head of Humanity's Harvest legal department will call you this afternoon."

And first Grace would need to talk to Rose, but right now she told him, "I want to be fair up front, I do have to say no to the pleasure trip..."

Again that teasing satyr's smile. "Will I still be allowed to try and change your mind?'

She thought about it. "Agreed. Let's pick out your weeks." She was pulling up her calendar, as another thought hit her. "And where is Ekkeko? I'd have to talk to him."

"Only by phone." Axel was pulling up his calendar on his phone. "Ekkeko's already on his way to Peru to start setting up." He looked down at her, she actually felt a pull of regret that they weren't up in her bedroom right now. Seeing the way that tailored shirt fit his broad chest, Grace almost wanted to just chuck it all, take his seaplane up into the clouds with him today...but that was not practical.

Axel was still talking, "Is there anything you want me to tell Ekkeko?"

Grace hesitated. Did she pass on private DNA pedigree analysis through a third person? No. That would be unethical. "If this trip happens, I can speak to Ekkeko directly."

He smiled with triumph. "We both can. If you go, I'll be there with you, maybe we'll get to spend some personal time together if that's what you want?"

Actually, Grace would like that a lot. "I'm having lunch with Freya today. Did you want to join us?"

He smiled wistfully at her. "Wish I could. After this, I've got walk over to talk with Huang about his algae."

She cut him off, "Ekkeko said you were ending the project?"

"My assistant sometimes thinks he is running things. I see what progress is being made, I understand Huang's tanks are working?"

"They are."

"If so, I'll give him some more time. And then when I'm done with Huang, I've got to drive over, park this rental car at the Neptune, and have their tender boat take me out to my seaplane before one o'clock. I've got to fly to LaGuardia airport, pick up Delta for a Denver connection to San Francisco." He looked deeply into her eyes again. "I'll be back for Freya's Samhain. Since it is Wiccan will we be skyclad?"

Grace found herself blushing. "No."

"Do I need to buy tickets?" he asked.

"I'll bring wine and cheese to cover our contribution," she said.

"But we'll have to shower first at your place, and I have some special plans for Christmas. Then I'm planning on seeing you in Peru, and I'm betting we'll be bundling together in my yacht off of Antarctica."

As she stood up, Grace thought for a moment they were going to kiss, then Inger, the spoilsport, came up from behind. "Grace, if you're going to meet Freya on time, you'll have to leave now."

Used to interruptions Axel only said, "Grace, I'll walk with you to your car."

When they came out, Grace was surprised to see another tall, blond man in a business suit and black briefcase, Daniel Novinski, standing by Axel's black Cadillac Escalade. Was he waiting to talk with Axel?"

"Nice car," Daniel started.

"It's a rental," Axel returned pleasantly.

"Mine gets better mileage," Daniel said proudly, indicating the bright red Prius parked alongside. "Fifty-eight mpg highway."

"Your demonstrators are gone?" asked Axel viewing the now empty grassy bank.

"Not 'my' demonstrators," Daniel answered. "But yes."

Grace was glad to hear that. "You guys have made peace?"

The lawyer only half smiled. "Mr. Jensen and I have found some reasonable ground for compromise. If his crops are to be genetically engineered, Axel's company will not grow them in open fields--at least until their safety is established by an independent laboratory. And an ongoing study, that will be financed by the G.E. industry and specifically Humanity's Harvest will be set up to monitor the long-term effects of genetically engineered food."

"With the result that Daniel is dropping his lawsuits against my company," Axel added. "Allowing Humanity's Harvest to continue with genetic engineering to enhance and increase the world's food supply."

"Astrid and her Curs people have agreed to this?" Grace asked.

Daniel shook his head regretfully. "Not really. Astrid doesn't accept anything but total capitulation. She and her more extreme people have never learned that to live successfully in this world, you sometimes have to accept compromises. Others in her group are more realistic, and have moved on to picket the circus up in the Bridgeport's arena–for enslaving their elephants."

Grace said, "A good compromise. Spoken like a Supreme Court Justice-to-be."

Daniel flushed a little, embarrassed or pleased?

His car wasn't locked, so Axel just opened the door and placed his briefcase on the passenger seat. "Before I drive over to the tender boat, I've got to talk with Huang, but I've got to be in the air by one." A last quick, intimate smile to Grace and Axel finished with, "My people will be calling to make your travel and legal arrangements."

She nodded, as Axel took long, strides away from her. Finally, Grace forced herself to look away from him and turned to found Daniel still watching her.

The lawyer asked, "He's flying out today?"

"He's taking his seaplane to LaGuardia."

"I'm really relieved about that," said Daniel, following as she walked to her Subaru Forester.

"Why?" asked Grace.

He hesitated and looked back to the empty grass by the dock, now only littered with discarded pamphlets and soda cans. "I spoke with Josh Jeffers again–he's ranting about Axel, claiming Jensen was the reason he was put in jail."

"That isn't true."

"Yes. I know it. You know it." Daniel smiled ruefully. "But like a lot of my clients, Josh is not known for his grounding in the reality of the situation."

She decided to put him on the spot. "Then you think he killed Helmut Roberts?"

"Actually, no." He thought about it. "You know, believe it or not, there are some males and females with the C.U.R.S. movement that may have even less contact with reality then Josh."

"Then you think the killer was going for Axel, not Helmut?"

"Yes. I think Alex knows that. That may be why he's kind of hurrying out of town."

As Daniel looked at Grace, he seemed a bit relieved. "When Axel's gone, and our friends are marching somewhere else, I think it's going to be a lot safer around here for you. Grace, want to have that lunch with me now?"

"Sorry, I've got another appointment, and I'm already late. Some other time."

Before Oyster River, she turned off the main road and parked in the asphalt lot that ran around both sides of the brown boarded Neptune. The old restaurant and marina on the edge of the water was one story, with a seasonally closed 'clam shack' window and picnic tables on the right side. It had a gas pump for the boats on the left and a ramp that ran down to the docks below. In the summer it would be filled with tourists boats for lunch, but now the docks were only tied up with the red tender boat, a police boat, and some brave souls' bright yellow Kayaks.

Restlessly Grace walked to the pilings that held up the pier. She stood looking out at the green water, with ORR's peninsula across the harbor. To her right Grace could see Axel's white and red striped seaplane, moored to a yellow buoy out in the harbor. The wind blew towards her, as she inhaling that clean, salty air of high tide. That plane would soon take Axel away from her. But they would be together for Christmas and then in Peru and maybe Antarctica–still, she was just starting her leadership gene investigation, she shouldn't spare the time now. She never could spare the time from her work.

And although she was really going to miss that man's blunt sexual magnetism, she was glad to see Axel leaving. Knowing he'd safe from some nut. Mac Dell's truck pulled into the parking lot with Freya at the wheel, so Grace walked over and asked, "Your van still at the shop?"

"Yes," said a resigned Freya.

At Neptune's entrance stood the namesake seven foot tall, bearded, wooden figure holding a triton. The place never looked terribly upscale, but smelled great, with wood smoke and clams. Grace wished she'd brought Axel here while he had been in Oyster River....maybe next week for Christmas. Maybe after Peru, if he still stayed around. Maybe if she did the unthinkable and took time off from her work to go to Antarctica with him...well maybe, he might be coming back to Oyster River quite regularly. Humanity's Harvest headquarters were in New York City, not that far from her.

Inside the restaurant was decorated as an under-the-sea grotto, with even brown 'stalactites' hanging from the ceiling. The waitress settled them at a window table, automatically bringing over a red napkin-covered basket of biscuits and unsweetened iced tea. They ordered without even looking at the menu as Grace commented, "We both showed up on time. A record."

Freya looked up from the cheddar biscuits, out on the windows overlooking the Harbor. Now Joe was casting off the long, wooden tender boat with Axel standing at the cabin. Seeing him going, again Grace felt a sense of loss, why couldn't she have just said yes to that Antarctica trip?

Commenting on the absurdity of the sight Freya said, "A George-Washington-Crossing-the-Delaware with his black leather briefcase held firmly by his side."

Grace laughed at the incongruity of it all. "Did you see the Macy's Thanksgiving parade? The business suited men, marching in precision drill as the briefcase brigade? All with their identical black leather cases held high in unison?"

Then suddenly, in a Farrington Fusion of fact and supposition, Grace understood it all. Understood what had happened years ago in Peru, what happened the night Helmut died, and the horror of what was happening now--if she couldn't stop it!

Chapter 33

"We've got to stop them!" Grace yelled jumping up.

"Stop who?" said a startled Freya looked up from squeezing the lemon slice in her iced tea.

"That tender boat. C'mon!"

As the waitress and several patrons stared, Grace grabbed her fanny pack and ran out of the restaurant, pulling her jacket back on. Ever faithful, Freya followed, yelling to the waitress, "Georgia, don't clear! We'll be back!"

Her Subaru was outside, Grace started to run towards it and then realized, that with Axel on the water, a car wasn't going to do them a bit of good. She froze. Looked about the parking lot.   Cars. Picnic tables. Entrance to the dock. Grace started running toward it.

Freya was following yelling, "Grace. Grace!"

Grace stopped at the top of the ramp. In the summer there would have been the red Neptune rental rowing boats, canoes, and some motor boats, but they'd been dry-docked ashore for the winter. With the tender gone, there were only two yellow kayaks tied up and the town Police boat. The Oyster River Police Zodiac was a high cabined, blue and white launch for patrolling the harbor. Was Ben there? "**BEN?!**" Grace called out. Nobody answered her shout.

Grace turned to Freya, "The tender driver..."

"Joe Turner."

"Do you have his cell phone number?"

"Does he had a cell phone?" Freya asked.

"How do they reach his boat? The Neptune–how do they reach him? If they want to give him orders?"

Freya squinted over the water, with its dancing sunlight spots. "He's got a radio. Probably not turned on. He never does–uses up the batteries..."

Grace was dialing Axel's cellphone. It rang–then the robotic voice mail kicked in.   Did Axel do texts?

The tender was halfway to Axel's seaplane. Grace looked helplessly around. Then she ran down the ramp towards one of the bobbing, yellow kayaks. "Freya tell the restaurant that I'm just borrowing somebodies boat–I'll return it!"

"Grace!" Freya was following her down. "You'll never catch a diesel by paddling a kayak!"

Helpless, Grace stood there on the bobbing dock–knowing her friend was right.

Freya was scrambling down the wooden ramp. "The police boat–start casting it off!" Lifting her long rainbow skirt, Freya was already scrambling on to the white, and blue low decked launch with its high cabin. It dipped slightly with her weight.

Grace ran to the first cleat, and threw the rope loop off, yelling up to Freya. "You have the key?"

"Nope. But I know where it's hidden!"

Grace ran to bowline. Freeing it, she jumped on board as Freya was inserting the key. She turned it. A short puff of smoke. Freya tried again. Nothing–then a loud growl as two, powerful engines caught. Freya had to raise her voice to be heard over the engines. "What are we doing?"

"Stopping Axel from getting on his plane!" Grace directed as Freya reversed, backing them away from the dock. Grace finished pulling in the wet lines as Freya cleared the dock and swung the patrol boat out into the harbor.

But as they pulled out, even Grace could see they hadn't a chance of catching up to the tender, with its long head start. Still, all Grace's life she had always been driven to keep trying, no matter how long the odds against her. "GO FASTER !" She yelled to Freya above the engines.

Freya just gave her a doubtful look but pushed the throttle forward, and the powerful Mercury engines plowed through waves. They were center harbor, as the tender boat reached Axel's moored plane. Joe slowed the tender to a slow putt, and he seemed to be leisurely circled the plane.

Freya yelled over the engines, "Why are they doing that?"

"Preflight check! Can you do sirens?"

Freya desperately glanced around at the rat's nest of computer cables, knobs, dials, radio mikes, and cords. Grace flipped a switch, and the FM radio blared *Wichita Lineman*. Freya turned a knob, and the red and white rotating lights flashed on. No siren!

Grace yelled over the engines, "Don't try! You might cut the engines!"

Freya was looking ahead, trying to angle into waves, instead of hitting them head-on.

But they were still way out of hearing distance, as Joe navigated the tender alongside the plane's floats near the pilot's door. Intent on his flight, Axel wasn't paying them any attention. Grace could see the old rubber tires tied on the tender's side, rubbing up against the plane's pontoons, as Axel looped a rope around a strut to hold the vessels together. He was getting into position to make the jump from tender to plane's floats.

Even with only a mild breeze, small waves were making it difficult for the tender to stay lined up alongside the seaplane. The police boat was closing fast, but the tenders' stern was facing them. The two men were looking away, concentrating on the bopping seaplane.

As Grace could make out, Joe had taken the briefcase, giving Axel two hands free to climb on board. Axel made a leap, then balanced on the platoon with one hand on a strut, as he pulled open the pilot's side door. Then he stretched out and reached back for his briefcase. Joe handed Axel his case, which Axel lifted up inside the plane. After letting the loop of rope drop back to the tender, Axel hauled himself aboard as Joe released the plane from its anchoring buoy.

With a hand salute, Joe revved his engines and was

pulling off. He quickly swung around and was motoring back towards the Neptune. As soon as the tender was in the clear, the seaplanes two powerful propellers started to rotate on either side.

In the old wooden tender boat, Joe neared them, as Freya motored on, with warning lights revolving wildly. Joe waved to what he probably expected was Ben, then looked puzzled as two women powered past him, leaving the big, wooden tender to roll in their wake. Freya turned the wheel slightly, aiming toward the rear of the seaplane. Its propellers were turning, building up momentum as it cut a wide, whitewash of its own.

Freya shouted over the engines and wind, "We won't catch him! He's got to far a head start. Try too contact him on the radio!"

Grace grabbed the handset and flipped levers. She caught static and some fisherman telling his buddy *'blues were running at the point.'*

"What's an airplane's radio band?" Grace started going through bands–catching static and more boaters' crosstalk.

Freya just shrugged, cutting the launch to the side, as Grace pushing down on the handset.

The plane ahead of them and was starting to pick up speed, with white foam waves spreading out in a widening 'v' behind it.

"We can't catch him?" Grace shouted in despair.

Shaking her head, Freya said, "Too far ahead!." Then the sea woman glanced fast ashore, at the post office flag streaming downwind of them, and yelled to Grace. "The wind's behind him. He can't take off. He'll have to turn around and power into it."

"Cut in front of him!" Grace yelled.

Freya looked doubtfully at her, but ever faithful, her best friend maneuvered hard to port, "HOLD   ON!

Backwash!"

The glorified rubber boat hit the planes waves and bounced upward. Grace started to fall to the side. She dropped the useless radio handset, as Freya painfully grabbed her arm. With Freya's left hand she held Grace anchored, while the Viking Maiden herself gripped the steering wheel.

"Why are we trying to stop him?" Freya asked, her voice bouncing with the boat.

"Helmut–the curator who was killed, was involved in something in Peru with a friend called Dutch. Smuggling drugs. He dragged his brother, Hendrick into it. When Dutch wanted to end the deal, he tried to kill both Helmut and Hendrick! Helmut's brother died. The museum curator was bitter...he wanted revenge."

"But isn't Helmut the one who got killed?" asked a confused Freya.

Ahead Grace could see the seaplane bumping troughs of waves, almost bouncing into the sky. "Because his old South American business buddy killed him to keep the old whole drug scam secret!"

"Axel Jensen's a murderer?! Why are we trying to catch a murderer?! Call the police—have them meet his plane somewhere when he lands. Dial 911!"

"No!" Grace's voice was growing hoarse. "Just try to stop him!"

"Where's Axel going?"

"LaGuardia airport on Long Island."

Ahead Grace could see Axel swinging the seaplane in a long U-turn, to pull into the wind that was blowing behind them. He'd probably hadn't even seen them yet. And when he did, he just sees a crazy police boat skittering recklessly across the harbor.

"Block him from taking off!" Grace tried to yank at the wheel–but Freya had the advantage of height and weight. Still, Grace's loyal friend turned the boat into a direct collision course with the seaplane.

"We have to get in front of him!" Grace demanded.

"He might crash and drown!" Freya warned.

"We have to chance it!"

"Grace–those airplane engines are a lot more powerful than this boat! He'll cut us up like a salami slicer."

"We have to stop him!"

Axel had swung the seaplane completely around. The Beech was now facing them, revving its formidable engines up to a roaring full throttle as it started its race for enough speed to take off. Still, Grace's loyal friend aimed towards the seaplane, now skipping over waves, picking up speed. Freya looked over her shoulder and shouted. "Those storage lockers–get us life vests!" With Freya steering toward the plane, Grace pulled out neon orange life vests–of course, there would n't be much left to find in this near freezing water after they'd been cut up by the sea plane's dual spinning propellers.

Handing Freya a life vest to pull on, Grace grabbed the wheel, trying to aim the Zodiac directly in the pathway of the racing plane.

Freya was shouting above all four engines, "Grace! Boats and planes aren't cars! We've got no brakes! We stay in that plane's path, we're going to kill him and ourselves!"

Axel must have seen the police boat. God–Grace looked desperately--how do you turn the sirens on this thing? She pushed a button and found her voice echoing with the loudspeaker. "We've got to stop him! Axel! Stop!"

To avoid a collision, Axel was steering the seaplane to starboard. He was going to pass them on the left at an angle. Holding on the wheel with one hand, Grace waved wildly with the other arm. She wanted to turn them more toward him, but Freya was taking back the wheel tight with both hands–her eyes fixated on the clear blur of those twin, oncoming blades.

"Shit!" Freya yelled above the screaming engines. "His wake may overturn us!"

Unable to overcome Freya's strength, Grace let go of the wheel and used both hands to wave wildly above her head.

Axel's seaplane was starting to lift, bouncing off the top of waves. They were directly in its path. Over the Kodiak's engines, she could hear the seaplanes more powerful engines screaming.

Then–those engines cut! The plane bounced down in the water, the tail raising up. Grace thought it was going to overturn, but Axel managed to keep control as it bounced up and down again. Rocking wildly. Still rotating, the plane's propellers slowed from a clear transparent whirl to black blurs then separate spinning blades as Axel fought to retain control. He was steering the plane away from them.

Grace could see him through the windshield of the plane.

Freya elbowed Grace aside, taking full control of the wheel and turned hard to port aiming the bow into the waves of wash from his plane. Coming up on the pilot's side, as Axel's plane slowed to stop.

Freya pulled back on the throttle, and the patrol's engines thunder lessened. Rocking from two foot back-washing waves of both plane and boat, Freya still expertly slowed and cut power, swinging around to face the plane's nose, then pulling alongside.

"Grace–there's boat hook on that rack," Freya ordered.

Scrambling down, Grace pulled used the hook on a strut to pull the police boat closer to the plane. Leaving the engine idling, Freya hurried to grab another hook and pull them in.

At this point, Grace realized that they'd just stopped and nearly wrecked an expensive seaplane in a stolen police boat. For what? Some guesses on her part.

Using the boat hooks, Grace pulled at the Beech's struts as Freya edged closer to the seaplane. A furious looking Axel opened the door. "What the hell?!" Seeing them, he swung out. Clutching the handholds, he managed to land on a bobbing pontoon. Taking a moment to stabilize on the rocking perch, he glanced angrily down, as his weight causing a dip, and a cold wave rolled over the bottom of his leg, soaking his pants and shoes. "Grace?"

Grace opened her mouth and didn't know where to start.

Still holding on with one hand, Axel slammed the plane's door shut to keep the sea spray out. Then balancing in the pontoon, he held on for a moment to synchronize with the sea's rhythm, then letting go, he hopped from the bopping plane on to the police boat.

"Why did you do that?" Shaken, he climbed up looking from Freya to Grace. "How did you guys get a police boat?"

Grace started, "You were in Peru?"

"I've told you that," he said sounding confused.

"With drugs? Maybe ten or fifteen years ago?"

He looked at her totally stunned, then looked to Freya for maybe a sane person to speak with.

The impassive Viking maiden just looked back at him, saying, "Trust me, it's easier to just answer her!"

"Using drugs?" he asked.

"No—well maybe using, but mainly smuggling and selling?" Grace said.

Axel seemed to think about that a moment and said, "I never smuggled or sold drugs in Peru. Scout's honor."

Grace turned to Freya. "Get us away from the plane!"

Axel protested. "It's unlocked! My briefcase is still in there..."

"Freya!" Grace commanded.

Freya obediently pushed the throttle forward, shouting

over the engines. "Now that we've kidnaped Axel–are we going to run for it? Or do we cut Mac and Ben in on the ransom?"

But Grace had turned back to Axel. "The museum curator, Helmut Roberts, he had a brother named Hendrick. Did you ever know either of them until the night of the reception at Oyster River?"

"I didn't know of Helmut until the reception. Was his brother there too? Hey! My seaplane is not moored–it's floating free!"

The Oyster River patrol boat was pulling away from the drifting seaplane, and Grace could hear loud sirens in the distance.

Freya looking over her shoulder, "Oh, shit! Ben must've gotten a Coast Guard boat after us." She looked at Axel. "Can you try to answer her before we're arrested for stealing the town's only patrol boat?"

Grace was focused on one thing. "Axel, that briefcase you were using–it's not special or expensive is it?"

"Someone from my New York office dropped it off this morning with papers to be signed. It's a cheapy from Staples, I guess. It's a standard, black leather briefcase."

The Coast Guard's sirens were drawing closer.

Grace felt she'd made a total fool of herself, but she continued. "You leave your car unlocked?"

"Yeah. Around here. But, Grace, I've got to take off. I'll miss my connecting flight on Long Island."

Before she could answer the ripping exposition knocked her against the steering wheel. Freya fell beside her. Axel on top of them. The patrol boat started to tip–then righted, as a second, louder explosion consumed Axel's seaplane exploded with a blinding-bright white ball of fire. Even yards from it, Grace felt her skin burning with radiated heat. Freya struggled up and opened the throttle pulling them further away from the flaming debris raining down in the green harbor, which sizzled as hot metal hit freezing seawater.

A shocked, still Axel sat up on the decking. "Well–maybe it wasn't such a great day for flying after all."

Freya looked at Grace. "So if this guy is the victim–who's the killer?"

"We're going to have a hell of a time proving it. But if Inez can testify and maybe get paperwork from South American, I'd say the killer was the third young guy who wanted to make money for his college education. Who someday dreamed of being a Supreme Court justice, but was terrified that Helmut would ruin everything he'd built. Daniel Novinski. He killed Helmut because he was afraid the curator would recognize him as 'Dutch,' the drug smuggler that was responsible for his brother Hendrick's death." As Grace continued the seaplane was listing, the left wing dipping into the hissing water. "Daniel had a black leather briefcase with him when we met him at your car. You left yours in the car, with the door unlocked and I drove off. You went into Huang's lab, and I think he switched briefcases in your car, planting the bomb."

"But how did Daniel know I'd be there...?"

Grace felt herself flushing. "My fault. He said he was worried that Josh Jeffers would attack you, so I told him when you'd be in Oyster River. You told him when you were flying out. Knowing that, he could set the bomb to go off when you'd be in the air."

"Astrid's lawyer is a murderer?" a shocked Freya asked.

Obviously favoring his left knee, Axel rose. "If he had something going with the curator, that's a reason for him to kill the Helmut–but why kill me?"

Grace had also figured that out. "To shift the focus of the investigation from someone trying to kill a museum curator, to some wacko activist trying to kill the C.E.O. of a genetic engineering conglomerate. Like Josh Jeffers, who Daniel had solicitously raised the bail for out his own foundation's funds so that your murder could be pinned on him."

"I was being murdered as an afterthought? Great," Axel said bitterly, as he looked at the burning, still sinking wreckage, whose spreading black rainbow oil slick was smoothing the water around it. "Lady, this is the second time I missed dying because of you." He put a long arm around Grace's shoulders, pulling her toward him. "I got to keep you close for luck!"

Epilogue

Landing late, a sleepy Grace hadn't seen much of her hotel room in Cuzco. It had been a busy two months, Daniel Novinski hadn't confessed–but some of his explosives purchases had been traced. The police identification software had come up with a match with his bone structure to Inez's photograph of 'Dutch.' And, more importantly, trace DNA from the spear in Helmut back had been matched to Daniel. Finally, a C.U.R.S. activist admitted that she wrote the first threatening letters, then confessing it all to her lawyer, then Daniel just apparently took over from her with the following letters. Finally, some digging verified his large, unexplained cash deposits around the Peruvian drug smuggling period, so Daniel Novinski was being bound over for trial.   Working out the 'stealing the police' boat charges took a lot more explaining. Thank god for close-knit town politics and police fraternal 'understandings.'

Two weeks later, Grace was ordering a new, advanced sequencer, so two months later she found herself on a plane to South America. The sequencer was payment for just setting up Axel's D.N.A. collection unit. Not for--as much as she regretted it--for staying to share his master suite on his Antarctica expedition.

The first day in Cuzco she had woken up blurry-eyed, with severe jet lag; well, more probably with higher attitude wobblies. Grace reached into her cosmetic bag for the prescription Doug had filled back home. There was a complimentary, sealed bottle of water on her end table alongside a paper covered glass.

This hotel had some modern hostelry touches like plush beige towels and fancy lime soap, even solar heating, and a flat screen t-v. But the ancient room was all thick walled colonial style. Her room had high yellow plastered ceilings, with dark peeled log beams. Grace dressed in a work shirt and pants then finished hanging up her single formal dress to get the packing wrinkles out.   The rest of the bag consisted of casual outfits and climbing clothes that she would need for the sampling expeditions with Axel. It would mean this room would be a base, and from here, they would be camping with a more primitive lifestyle. Grace glanced at her watch, in half an hour she had to meet Axel and Ekkeko.

On knees that felt a little rubbery, she walked down stone stairs, down to a yellow tiled lobby. Even if it was summer in South America, with two-story high arched ceilings, it was cool here. Maybe she should have worn something heavier than her jacket.

Axel was there, seeing Grace, he said something in Spanish to the yellow-ruffled skirted maid. She smiled and hurried away. Grace expected him to be dressed in his usual safari type outfit, but he was wearing a midnight blue, custom fitted business suit. She had to admit he had the body to wear it well. He was signing papers for another assistant, while Ekkeko stood restlessly beside him.   Axel looked up and smiled lopsidedly, "Grace, I know I promised a wake-up meal..."

"But you've got another engagement?" she finished.

He truly looked apologetic. "In an hour, the local officials have scheduled a ceremony for the return of the three kings. I'll be representing Humanity's Harvest up on the dias–since you were instrumental in returning those mummies, I am sure they would like to honor you. Will you join us?"

"I'd rather not, thank you," said Grace, rather too firmly.

The maid returned, carefully carrying a tray with three cups and a white china pot with orange flowers on its side. Axel smiled approvingly at her, then after pouring the teapot, he took one on the bone china cups, with its delicate saucer and offered it to Grace. "Try this. Cocoa leaf tea."

Grace shook her head, her stomach felt queasy. "Not right now."

"It'll help you feel better," he still held out the cup.

Knowing he was right, Grace took it, balancing the fragile saucer. Cocoa leaf came from the plant that gives cocaine, but it was perfectly legal to drink here. Taking a short sip, Grace found it warm, not burningly hot. Grace took a deeper sip. She'd never really liked the watery coco leaf tea before, even though it did help adjusting to the thinner air; but this was a full-bodied drink, with a sugary vanilla taste and an accent of cinnamon. The spices made the drink palatable, even quite pleasant. She drank the cup slowly. When the maid offered up the pot, Grace nodded for another cup.

Axel flashed her a warm smile. "That's fine. I'll be getting together with you right after the ceremony–we **will** have some time together on this trip. We'd have more if you would reconsider my offer of Antarctica?

"You've still got an extra cabin?"

"I'm holding open a private cabin if that's what you want." He said lowering his voice confidentially, "But I'm still offering to share the master suite with you. It's got a great two person rain shower."

She found herself blushing. He laughed and continued, "I want to have dinner with you tonight? And after the ceremony, we can both do some sightseeing."

"That would be fine," Grace said, wondering if that internal glow she was feeling did show.

He flashed her one of his warm, delighted smiles, that promised of intimacy to come, and again she could understand how, without even trying, this man could have married seven times. "This place is more traditional, but we could move to a more modern hotel?" he asked.

"No." She looked around the cool lobby, with its

huge green leaved plants and gilded framed classical paintings. "I rather like this. Any recommendations on a restaurant for breakfast?"

Axel looked down at the papers he still held, read them quickly, and as he was signing he said, "Are you up to leaving the hotel?"

"Yes. I'd like to look around a bit," she said.

"You may need a guide."

"That isn't necessary."

"Well, it's market day. I feel a lot better if you would take Ekkeko with you until you acclimated." He looked up at her with those deep shamrock green eyes. "Humor me?"

She looked to Ekkeko. "That really would be an imposition."

Ekkeko immediately offered, "It would be my honor to guide you about the city of my birth."

Axel pointed out. "On market day it's always a bit crowded here, with the locals coming for food and the tourist snapping pictures everywhere, and now the formal ceremony for returning the mummies in the main square?"

"They're going to be displayed outdoors?" Grace asked.

He shrugged. "Before the cathedral. It's traditional. The museum people are definitely unhappy about possible damage, but the politicians and local tourist board types won out. Our three kings will be enthroned in the marketplace, as they once were six hundred years ago for some sort of returning dedication ritual." He looked down at more papers from another assistant. "Per your scheduling, we'll be going into the backcountry for your sampling at the end of the week. I'm told they have some interesting specimens waiting for us."

With a rather dismissive glance at the hovering maid, Ekkeko pointed out to Grace, "There's a small restaurant near here called Dava. It has authentic vegan and Andean cuisine–I think you'll like them for your first meal here."

Grace nodded and followed the slight man out the arched hotel entrance, down stone steps, to a cobblestone street. The thin-aired, mountain sun's brightness hurt her eyes. She had slathered on suntan lotion, but as Grace also raised a hand up to shield her eyes, she figured maybe she should pick up some sunglasses. They were in an old, actually ancient part of the city, where now blue-jeaned farmers mixed with camera-toting tourists and woman in brightly dressed Indian garb selling produce from baskets.

With a sour look, Ekkeko pointed to several woman in long, multi-tinted orange flounced dresses. "Dancers for the fiesta circus."

She noted his dismissive tone. "You don't approve of catering to the tourist trade?"

"They are descendants of a proud, conquering people. They should not grovel to a tourista who carries some Sols in his pocket."

From the side, a dark-eyed senorita smiled coyly at him. Ekkeko ignored her, continuing bitterly, "Tonight she'll go home and change into silver lame jeans to go out nightclubbing. Now she dresses like a prancing pony in some Spanish circus."

"Probably dressing and dancing for the tourists can be a paying job," Grace said. "Maybe even an enjoyable one. In my country, people wear Civil War uniforms for re-enactments, and they do it just for fun. If they are paid, it's minimal and doesn't come close to covering their expenses, but they willing dress up to represent and connect with a heritage they are very proud of."

Ekkeko steered Grace to a one-story, stuccoed building, with low stonework on the bottom of the walls. They went through an open, wood framed door and inside it was dark and cool, smelling of frying vegetables. Ekkeko translated the menu, and their waiter brought samples of the produce to the table and some complimentary roasted corn.

Ekkeko suggested that Grace request 'mild spice' when ordering.

"I like spicy food," she protested.

"Try it my way first, you can always add chili peppers later."

She ordered the tamales Ekkeko suggested. As they waited for it to be cooked, Grace tried to start off casually, "You don't seem to like the Yankees in your country. How do you feel about working for a gold ribbon one, like Axel?"

He hesitated. Of course, Ekkeko could lie–that would be the discreet thing to do when questioned about your employer, but Grace felt he wouldn't, and he didn't. "Working with Jensen is teaching me what I need to know. With what I learn from him, someday I will use when I run my own conglomerate."

"Based in Cuzco?"

"Or South Korea–or where ever it is advantageous for my purposes."

"Uh huh." Grace had been trying to decide whether to bring up a subject that she felt she should. "You know I did genetic profiles on the three mummies we have returned from the Bridgeport Museum."

"I am very surprised you got any material to examine–how can you be sure you weren't just developing contamination from the Yankee raiders?" Ekkeko coolly questioned.

"From one entry hole, I took multiple internal samples–one I think I have was contaminated by insects, but even the poor showing of the second mummy yielded up interesting Y chromosomal DNA, that's existence was confirmed by the other two. All three exhibited male genetic markers that were related."

"That means?"

"A family relationship. Y chromosomes are passed

from father to son." The waiter was carrying over plates that smelled delicious, an appetizer apparently. "Interestingly, I also had one other sample that I had taken from the museum up in New Haven. An arm, once housed in the Catholic Church as a 'saint's relic,' was credited by legend to be from an actual Inca who once ruled over Cuzco."

"Once he ruled an Empire—now he's viewed in a glass case by tourists with cameras." Ekkeko did not sound amused.

Yet Grace felt she had to continue. "The arm's DNA matches the same male family line as our three mummies."

"Couldn't many others in an Andean population have the same mutations?"

"I'd say those close configurations would be in individuals in about one in a million samples."

"Then you feel that those four mummified bodies were of the same line, maybe generations of nobles, perhaps each once having been enthroned as a reigning Inca?"

"What I feel is not provable, but I believe very possible," said Grace. "As I studied them, I realized that recently I had seen another, similar genetic profile."

He looked up, steeled eyes glaring at her.

"It was your profile, Ekkeko. You share a Y chromosome with four possible sons of the Sun. I can't prove it–but I feel you are a direct male descendant from a line of men who may have once ruled the largest pre-Columbian, South American Empire. An Empire that stretched from what is now Columbia to Chili."

Ekkeko said nothing. Just calmly stared back at her, with his usual haute manner.

"You don't look surprised?" Grace said.

He looked away, out to the tourists in the street. When he finally spoke, it was in a cool, distant voice. "There are stories passed down through my family. That once we were of the nobility. God-kings, who ruled absolutely. Once we owned everything from mountaintop to mountaintop, and once we were worshiped as Gods." He seemed to come back into her world painfully. "Then, they lost it all–to five hundred, gold-maddened barbarians."

"Not just five hundred Spaniards. I've heard that some of the Incas subjected tribes willingly joined forces with the Conquistadores to fight against--what they considered-- were their oppressors."

An ironic smile twisted his thin lips. "So they joined with the Spanish, creating new oppressors so that they could suffer even more. That is the wisdom of my people," he spoke with a touch of contempt.

The smiling waiter now carried over two platters. Grace got a seafood tamale: shrimp, scallops, and chunks of some pickled fish in a white cream sauce served over cubed potatoes. Until she bit into that pungent mix Grace hadn't realized how hungry she really was.   And Ekkeko was right, 'mild' spice was more than strong enough for her.

Ekkeko politely joined her but didn't seem to be interested in his thin, white crepe-style wrapped meal. As she finally finished, he asked, "Where shall we go? Do you want to buy souvenirs? Study the vegetables the mountain people bring to market?"

Grace thought about it. "I've changed my mind, I'd like to see that marketplace ceremony."

"It will be crowded...we must hurry." As he looked at his watch, as he took out paper money to pay for their dinner.

Grace reached for her bag. "Half of that is mine."

"Jensen appointed me your personal guide, so all of this can go on my expense account."

A taxi would have helped, but the streets were literally filled with people and llamas, chickens in crates, dogs, and Japanese tourists taking pictures of it all. Ekkeko seemed to know a few shortcuts the tourists didn't. Down what looked to be a private alley, then another, and soon they came out to a wide square, set before an imposing, old, square-cut stone church

In the center, a wooden dais, with chairs for the dignities, had been raised and beside it, a higher wooden platform had been set up. The taller wooden platform had three knee-high, cutwork embroidered, wine-purple velvet throws over some sort of benches.

At the edges of the square was a farmer's market. With Ekkeko following, Grace walked along that, smelling onions and caged rabbits. She took a closer look at baskets of vegetables being bartered for. Looking for something she didn't recognize–searching for that golden maize or potato. Not finding it.

The pressing thongs of people spread out. A lot of tourists, but the majority of the crowd seemed to be locals, and not only ones dressed in bright costumes for tourists. The crowds were getting thicker. A patiently following Ekkeko spoke to her in a low tone. "It is wise to keep your handbag in front of you. There are always those looking for easy pickings."

Grace shifted her fanny pack up front, but she couldn't believe any of the excited people here would be a danger. Finally, the sound of bells and the murmuring of the crowd lowered to nothing. All over the square, people seemed to be moving aside, creating a wide, open processional pathway.

As she stopped to watch, a young man in a church robe entered the square, swinging an intricately carved metal incense burner. Spreading its bluish-white smoke he circling the crowd. What did they call it? A thurible Grace remembered–that's what they called the swinging incense burners in the Catholic church.

When he passed, the boy swings the blue smoke near her. It didn't have the sweet, nutty smell of myrrh. No, this was a cinnamon, vanilla, balsamic smell. The thurible was from the ancient Catholic church, but the incense mixture was from a far, far older time. Back to the Indios of South America. The Empire of Incas. The Sun God's children.

She heard high, haunting notes. Young men following him were blowing into wooden pipes. Some in the crowd sang. A parade seemed to be coming past them headed toward the Cathedral. Young girls in flounced skirts of green, yellow and blue danced before her.

Over the heads of the crowd, Grace saw Axel and several other men marching to the lower dias and climbing up to stand respectfully by chairs. On that platform, she saw what were obviously local dignitaries, some in feathered regalia capes and some in business suits. Axel and the higher officials then sat down on the lower dais.

A slightly built, grey-haired man was announcing something in Spanish. Grace couldn't make it out, but the crowd was respectfully silent. Finally, she saw two lines of four strong men carrying a platform, with a cross-legged figure sitting on top. She expected an elaborately garbed saint figure. Instead, she recognized the dark, bluish skin of one of the Bridgeport Museum's Mummies. The one, the curator, had called "flat nose."

Instead of his former moth-eaten, yellowed wool tunic, the flat nosed mummy was now adorned in a fabric tunic of light cinnamon color.

"They've dressed him in a new llama wool tunic," Grace commented.

Ekkeko shook his head. "The tunics are of woven of vicuña. The rarer vicuñas can only be sheared every three years.   That is why it is so expensive. The wool is softer. Finer. Only vicuña is fully worthy to adorn a royal personage, returning to his home...to look over his people. To protect his own."

Reaching the higher platform, the bearers stopped and waited. From the highest platform, two other short, muscular looking men reached down and reverently lifted the dried body up to be enthroned on his velvet covered bench.

Behind the first, came the bearers with two more mummies on platforms. These two were also lifted up and enthroned. As they passed her, Grace realized the Sun God's descendants were now returning to a square that they once reigned over hundreds of years ago.

The speaker continued in Spanish with the crowd cheered wildly. Grace just found herself looking at the first mummy. Seemingly aloof from his crowd before him, the blue-skinned, disk eyed mummy looked beyond the populace as if expecting them to come to worship at his feet.

Below the God-Kings on their benches stood three white-cassocked priests, now the central, dark-skinned one gave a benediction to the crowd. He turned but did not bow before the honored ancestors. The crowd was silent.

Grace turned herself and watched the God King's descendant watching it all. Ekkeko said nothing, but the slight man stood straighter–taller. For Grace, the reunification was complete.

Turning back she stood there watching Axel on that stage, in time he looked down at her, with a smile that made her feel, at least for him, she was the only person in the square.   Grace smiled back.   There was more to life than DNA, and she'd be finding that out. When he got off the stage, Dr. Grace Farrington would tell Axel, that she was going to be sharing that Antarctica trip with him.   But not alone in a singles cabin, if she went, she'd share the master's suite with him.

The End

**For more books by Lynn or to contact the author,
please go to lynnmarron.com**

OTHER GRACE FARRINGTON OYSTER RIVER RESEARCH DNA MYSTERIES:

ORR: THE NOBEL PRIZE MURDER

Turned down for this year's Nobel Prize, fortyish genetics pioneer Grace Farrington finds out the new head of Research of Oyster River is the man who stole her research! When Dr. Marshall is murdered on ORR's house boat, Grace finds herself chief suspect and is further implicated when following an1800's witch's Curse of Three, two more people die in Oyster River Harbor. While finding herself romantically involved with a billionaire patron and a red-necked colleague, Grace must use her scientific reasoning and her eclectic group of friends (scientists, cops, psychics and some other slightly eccentric New Englanders) to solve the murders before she's arrested or killed herself.

ORR: FATAL DNA

Grace Farrington is considered a genius in her field, so it is not a surprise that when doing some special DNA sleuthing she discovers a convoluted motive for murder as she attempts to desecrate a body in a funeral home. Her life suffers further complications when her new age friend Freya involves her in a seance that triggers a desperate search for a lost Revolutionary War ransom. Of course, no one has found the treasure in over two hundred years, but they didn't have Grace's skill at reading the secrets of Colonial DNA. Distracting entanglements are the three men on her romantic horizon: rough-edged fellow scientist Kurt MacKay; old moneyed David Gardiner; and a new billionaire, the handsome Jack Stuart, who arrives in the New England town of Oyster River Harbor with an intense interest in both her research and her body. Grace is determined to keep her mind on mitochondria, even as Kurt is attacked by a local fisherman. But when her sometime lover is accused of murder, Grace has to act, only to find out too late that the next targeted victim is herself!

MYSTERY WITH A TOUCH OF WITCHCRAFT AND ROMANCE:

THE SEAPORT PSYCHICS MURDER

When their Old Craft worshiping mother dies of stab wounds on Beltane, her young triplets are separated for seventeen years. Raised without knowledge of their witchcraft heritage, Holly Corey returns to the Connecticut seaport of her birth. Reunited with her two brothers, her only goal is turning 'Witch House' into a viable Bed and Breakfast to keep the three of them together; that is until she meets Sgt. Travinski, the handsome policeman, who is determinedly pursuing both Holly (for love) and her brother Frost (for murder).

MURDER AT THE ALTAR

In the second of the Mystic triplets mysteries, brother Noel is accused of poisoning a fellow Beluga trainer at the Aquarium. When Holly Corey starts investigating she visits her Old Craft mentors, Sarah and Abby Hoyt. Unfortunately, against their advice, Holly accepts two new long-term guests at the Corey Bed and Breakfast: Lilith (once a member of her father's coven) and Lilith's younger warlock architect (and sometimes lover) Gregory St Clair.

Lilith is pressing to buy the Old Mill that the triplets' mother ritually suicided in, while Gregory is trying to seduce Holly up onto the high altar at Grace La Fleur's Church of Nature's

Bounty. Afraid of the Wiccan ritual, but needed to know more, Holly drags Sgt. Paul Travinsky up to the beginnings of the naked Yule celebrations that wind up being raided by his fellow cops. While the Sergeant is being told to stay away from Ms. Corey or give up his job, Holly finds herself in danger of losing her life--or her soul--to the combined efforts of the Rasputin like Gregory, and the powerful, mind-controlling Lilith.

PARANORMAL ADVENTURE

ADAM'S UNORTHODOX, UNNATURAL LEGAL PRACTICE

Inheriting his Great Uncle Quentin's unconventional law firm in Missouri Adam Martin finds himself defending the rights of a succubus, zombies, a semi-senile seer, mermaids, a dryad, and gorgons. Soon he is writing contracts for werewolves, consulting with ghosts, and protecting unfairly accused fire starters. While this is going on, he is trying to stand up to his six foot tall *'Cherokee'* law secretary, and deal with his staid, disapproving family of conservative lawyers led by the formidable 'hang them high' Judge Jeremiah Martin. Yet while struggling to save his clients and his law practice, Adam still has time to romance some very intriguing and unusual females.

FANTASY ADVENTURE

CENTAURESSES OF THE SILVER DRAGON

Jace a centaur of Clydesdale proportions, leader of 'The Regiment,' a band of sword and shield mercenaries. Having won all their battles on the field, they are betrayed by a treacherous prince and outlawed. In unchartered lands, Jace desperately searches for a patron to keep his band together. He finds that mainstay with the lovely Silver sisters, tall shes with long legs, pale gray hide with black stockings and cream dabbled hindquarters. To Jace alone, the ravishing Silver Star promises endless wealth if his Regiment clears her clan's mines from a ravaging dragon.

But there are problems: Jace is sure his alluring patroness is lying, as he does not believe in dragons; Some of his warriors are rebelling against his leadership, and he is desperately trying to conceal a leg wound that is worsening. His brutal choice: abandon the Regiment and the Lady Star or face a challenge to his leadership that will only end in death!